Dear Reader,

I'm thrilled to share my new saga, *A Mother's Heartbreak*, with you. I have taken a step a little further back in time with this novel, to the late 18th century, an era which fascinated me as I discovered more about it in my research.

    A Mother's Heartbreak is set at the grand estate of Bramley Court – a house which has seen its share of scandal, tragedy and secrets, and it features two strong women at the heart of the story. Abi and Imogen are each dealing with loss in their own ways, and one of the things I most love about this story is their friendship. I hope I have kept you guessing again as to the mystery at the heart of the book, and I very much hope you enjoy this story.

    I do love to hear from you, my lovely readers, so please do visit me at my website www.jenniefelton.co.uk, on Facebook www.facebook.com/JennieFeltonAuthor or follow me on Twitter @Jennie_Felton for my latest news!

Love,
Jennie x

Praise for Jennie Felton's captivating sagas:

'Believable characters, a vivid sense of time and place, thoroughly enjoyable' Rosie Goodwin

'Fans of Katie Flynn will love this' *Peterborough Evening Telegraph*

'Enthralling . . . Jennie Felton . . . writes her stories straight from the heart . . . evokes time and place with compelling authenticity, and conjures up a feisty heroine and a cast of engaging characters' *Lancashire Evening Post*

'Sweeps us back to a time of struggle and hardship in a story packed with high emotion, dramatic landscapes and the harsh realities of living and working in a mining community' *Blackpool Gazette*

'Has everything a family saga should have – happiness, extreme sadness, love, death, births, etc. but above all it was a real page turner . . . Thank you, Jennie, for writing such a wonderful book' *Boon's Bookcase*

'If you like the style of Catherine Cookson, Josephine Cox or Katie Flynn then you'll enjoy this' *Books With Wine And Chocolate*

'A great read with a cast of believable characters' *The People's Friend*

By Jennie Felton

The Families of Fairley Terrace Sagas
All The Dark Secrets
The Birthday Surprise (short story featured in the anthology
A Mother's Joy)
The Miner's Daughter
The Girl Below Stairs
The Widow's Promise
The Sister's Secret

Standalone
The Stolen Child
A Mother's Sacrifice
The Smuggler's Girl
A Mother's Heartbreak

A Mother's Heartbreak

JENNIE FELTON

HEADLINE

The right of Jennie Felton to be identified as the Author of
the Work has been asserted by her in accordance with the
Copyright, Designs and Patents Act 1988.

First published in 2022 by
HEADLINE PUBLISHING GROUP

First published in paperback in 2023 by
HEADLINE PUBLISHING GROUP

1

Cataloguing in Publication Data is available from the British Library

ISBN 978 1 4722 7497 7

Typeset in Calisto by Avon DataSet Ltd, Alcester, Warwickshire

Printed and bound in Great Britain by Clays Ltd, Elcograf S.p.A.

Headline's policy is to use papers that are natural, renewable and recyclable
products and made from wood grown in well-managed forests and other
controlled sources. The logging and manufacturing processes are expected
to conform to the environmental regulations of the country of origin.

HEADLINE PUBLISHING GROUP
An Hachette UK Company
Carmelite House
50 Victoria Embankment
London EC4Y 0DZ

www.headline.co.uk
www.hachette.co.uk

For my grandson Daniel David Tanner Carr
With love and best wishes for your A-level exams and
a future that works out just as you hope.

Acknowledgements

My thanks, as always, go to Kate Byrne, my wonderful editor, and the team at Headline who take care of everything necessary to get my books on to store shelves and beyond, including Sophie Keefe, Alara Delfosse, Rebecca Bader, Isobel Smith, Rhys Callaghan and Sophie Ellis.

Grateful thanks too to Rebecca Ritchie, my lovely agent at A. M. Heath, who is always there when I need her as well as working hard on my behalf. Not forgetting her helpful assistant Harmony Leung, and also Gosia Jezierska.

Thank you to Anne Mackle of *Books with Wine and Chocolate*, for her continued support and lovely reviews.

And last but not least to all my readers. Thank you so much. I hope you continue to enjoy my books and keep in touch with me.

Prologue

Summer 1788

'Where is he? Where is my baby?'

The young woman's voice was shrill with panic as she ran frantically from room to room of the grand house.

'Missus, come and sit down, do. Please! You'll do yerself a mischief!'

The elderly maid took hold of the young woman's arm, steering her into the drawing room. But Imogen Hastings was too distraught to be restrained for more than a minute.

'Where can he be?'

She ran to the window. Outside, early afternoon sun lit the manicured lawns, turning them emerald green beneath the cloudless azure sky. Her husband, Hugh, still wearing his business coat, was striding across the grass, his anxiety apparent in every urgent step, while Freddie, his eight-year-old son, trailed miserably behind Bella, the nursemaid who had been minding Robbie. Rex Doel the gardener, his boy and the stable lad had spread out to search beneath shrubs and behind the summer house, while the housekeeper, Mrs Mears, stood at the balustrade beside the front entrance to the house looking for all the world like a great black crow in the severe uniform that was her habitual attire. But of the small fair-haired boy who was the cause of his mama's distress there was no sign.

As Imogen watched, they widened their search, heading for the wooded slopes that dipped away into the valley beyond, and she lost sight of them as they descended. She turned away from the window, wringing a fold of her skirt between her hands, tears running unchecked down her cheeks.

'Oh Mary, what could Bella have been thinking? She knows not to let Robbie out of her sight!'

The maid only shook her head helplessly. She had a pretty good idea of what had occurred. She had seen Bella talking – or flirting, most like – with Jem, the stable lad, over by the summer house. They'd gone inside for a quick kiss and a cuddle was her guess, and Robbie had wandered off unnoticed. A terrible way Bella had been in when she'd come running in to raise the alarm, and if that wasn't a guilty conscience, Mary didn't know what was.

'He'll be all right, missus, just you see,' was all she said, though truth to tell, she was almost as worried about Robbie as Imogen was. He was only three years old, and a delicate child, and the grounds of Bramley Court were vast, as befitted the residence of a wealthy coal-owner. Beyond the thick wooded area, pitted with ditches and foxholes, there was a lake, and a shaft from an old mine excavation, which, although it was fenced off, might prove irresistible to a little boy, who would be able to wriggle beneath the rusty old wire easily enough. Mary shivered at the thought. If anything happened to that child, it would break her mistress's heart. Imogen idolised him, and Mary knew that the terrible time she'd had giving birth to him meant that she would never be able to have another baby. She loved Freddie dearly, but he was Sir Hugh's late wife's son, not hers, and when all was said and done, it could never be quite the same.

With an effort, Mary pulled herself together, hiding her anxiety. 'Well, if you won't sit down, at least let's get you a cup of tea – or summat stronger. A nip of brandy is what you could do with. 'Twould do you the world of good.'

'Oh, I couldn't! Hugh wouldn't like it,' Imogen protested, but when the maid pressed the glass into her hand, she sipped at it, coughed, then took another sip, and some of the colour returned to her cheeks.

'See? I was right, wasn't I?' Mary said with satisfaction. 'Now will 'ee come and sit down?'

'I think perhaps I should . . .' Imogen was reluctant to admit that the unfamiliar alcohol was making her feel dizzy, but she sank into one of the brocaded chairs.

A few minutes later, a commotion in the hallway made her jump to her feet once more. Footsteps. Hugh's voice, recognisable, yet somehow quite unlike his usual commanding tones. The sound of a woman sobbing.

Imogen started for the door, the brandy glass, forgotten, still in her hand.

'Missus, no . . .' Mary tried to intercept her mistress, but Imogen pushed past her, then halted abruptly in the doorway, her whole body paralysed with shock and horror, unable to tear her eyes from what she was seeing.

Hugh, his face stony yet ravaged, holding Robbie in his arms. A Robbie who did not move, nor cry. A Robbie with pond slime matting his fair hair, and clothing that dripped water on to the Italian tiled floor.

'He was in the lake,' Hugh said. His voice was flat, devoid of any emotion. 'We found him in the lake.'

Imogen gasped and ran to her little son. 'Do something,

3

Hugh! You must do something for him!'

Hugh stood unmoving, his lifeless child in his arms. 'It's too late, Imogen. He's gone.'

'No! No!' she screamed, clutching at Hugh's arm, her fingers encountering the small cold, wet leg that draped over it. 'No! Not Robbie! Oh no, no, no!'

Her own legs were giving way beneath her; only Mary, reaching for her, saved her from falling. The darkness came and swallowed her up. Imogen's life as she knew it had died with her son.

Chapter One

Eighteen months later

As the carriage bowled along the narrow tree-lined lane Abigail Newman clutched the edge of her seat with one hand while holding on firmly to her reticule with the other. She'd never travelled at such a speed in her life before. But the clip-clop of the horse's hooves was reassuringly steady and the brougham was a good deal more comfortable than the pony and trap she was used to – and a good deal less bumpy.

Her stomach had tied itself in knots nevertheless, and not only because of the strangeness of riding in such a grand contraption. Abigail was on her way to begin a new life as governess to a little boy who, according to his father when he had interviewed her, could be something of a handful.

At the time Abi had assured him she had plenty of experience of dealing with little rascals. Ever since she was old enough, she had assisted with the dame school that her mother, Maisie, ran in a room in the vicarage, and she had been confident that she would thus be equal to her new duties. Now, however, she realised that in the dame school, her mother had never been far away. A glance or a sharp word from her and the naughtiest of children was quickly put in his place; it was almost always a 'him', for the few girls who were pupils were invariably well behaved. But at Bramley Court, home of Sir Hugh Hastings and his family, she would be in sole charge. There would be no one to back her up when it came to discipline; she would have to sink or swim alone. And Abi couldn't help wondering if she had overestimated her own abilities in her eagerness to escape her claustrophobic life as a vicar's daughter in a small Somerset town.

Yet wasn't it what she had always dreamed of? she asked herself. The chance to be independent, to make her own way in the world, instead of being stuck at home and in very real danger of becoming an old maid? Her only real relationship had ended in a disaster that had changed her life forever and haunted her still. Though there had been would-be suitors over the years since, there were none that Abi would have considered marrying for even a moment, despite her mother's best efforts to persuade her to make a match of it with Jasper Fairweather, the squire's son. He had made no secret of his infatuation, gazing at her with moony eyes whenever they met, and had even tried to kiss her in the church porch after Midnight Mass one Christmas Eve. Since Maisie was usually critical of any young man who looked in her direction, Abi couldn't help thinking that her enthusiasm in Jasper's case was because she fancied the idea of being related by marriage to gentry.

As a rule, Abi went out of her way to please her rather domineering mother, partly from a sense of duty and partly from gratitude for the way Maisie had stood by her in the darkest time of her life. But this was a bridge too far, and she had told her mother in no uncertain terms that she could not even consider such a thing. Aunt Sukie, Maisie's sister, and never one to mince her words, had been even more outspoken. 'He's nothing but a dandy, with not a shred of substance,' she had declared. 'Truth to tell, I'm not sure he's all there. There's too much inbreeding in that family.'

As for the others who had shown an interest in Abi, they were even less suitable. Clarence Coles, the churchwarden, who was twice her age and a widower, would follow her into the vestry when she was changing the water in the big vases that adorned the altar, throwing away the faded flowers and arranging fresh ones. He stood so close beside her that she was trapped between him and the sink, his breath almost as foul as the dirty flower water, his clammy hands hovering, so that Abi's skin crawled.

Then there was Sebastian James, younger and single, but vastly overweight as well as off-puttingly full of himself, with a booming voice that was admittedly an asset to the church choir, but horribly overpowering at all other times.

No, Abi had wanted none of them, and doubted she would ever meet anyone she could fancy, let alone trust or marry. But neither could she bear the idea of remaining in the vicarage, still doing her mother's bidding, until she had nothing but a lonely old age to look forward to. She had ached for her independence, and to see something of the world. But whenever she tried to talk about it, Maisie was quick to object.

'You don't know when you're well off,' she would say. 'You wouldn't be as comfortable anywhere else as you are here.'

Then, whining, pleading: 'I don't want you to go, Abigail. It would worry me to death. Say you'll forget such a silly notion for your mother's sake.' In the end, Abigail had always capitulated.

But then their lives had been rudely torn apart. Abi's father, Obediah, had suffered a stroke and died. One day he had been his normal self, visiting parishioners, working on his sermon for the following Sunday; the next Maisie had found him lying senseless on the kitchen floor, still clad in his nightshirt. The doctor was summoned, but it seemed there was nothing to be done. 'Only time will tell,' he had said morosely. 'Either he will show signs of recovery, or . . . In a few days we shall have the answer, one way or the other.'

There had been no miraculous recovery. Five days later, without ever regaining consciousness, Obediah had breathed his last.

Maisie was distraught, constantly torturing herself with tearful outbursts. 'Look at his dear cloak hanging there. To think he'll never wear it again.' And: 'Only two places to set at table. It's more than I can bear.'

It was Abi who had to make all the funeral arrangements; Abi who followed the coffin into church and out to the grave in the shadow of the church tower – Maisie had taken to her bed, saying she couldn't bring herself to watch her beloved husband lowered into the cold, wet ground.

For a whole week it had rained ceaselessly, and in the event Abi had been glad that her mother was not there to see the muddy water that had collected in the grave, or the way the bearers' feet slithered on the wet grass and the sodden bands around the coffin almost slipped through their hands, so that it landed in the grave with a splash. She couldn't get it out of her own head; for Maisie it would have been the stuff of nightmares. She would in all likelihood have created a dreadful scene, and Abi had whispered a prayer of thanks that at least they had been spared that.

The days that followed were dark ones. Still the rain fell from heavy clouds, so that the whole world seemed lost in a grey mist, and things only became worse when, barely two weeks after the funeral, the bishop visited.

After he had offered his sympathies, the main reason he was here became apparent – he had come to break the news that Abi had been expecting but not mentioned to her mother for fear of upsetting her even more. With Obediah dead, a new vicar was being appointed, and he would expect to move into the vicarage. It would mean that Maisie and Abigail would lose their home, and with it the room they used for the dame school. It had been closed since Obediah's death, but now it seemed unlikely to ever open again. Maisie, however, was not ready to accept that, and it was when Sukie, her sister, visited that Abi had the first inkling that her mother had plans of her own.

'You'll just have to move in with me until you sort yourselves out,' Aunt Sukie had said, practical and pragmatic as ever, and predictably Maisie had protested vehemently.

'But this is my home! I can't leave my home!'

'You'll have no choice, my dearie,' Sukie said tartly. 'I know we don't always see eye to eye, but at least you'll have a roof over your heads.'

A secretive look that Abi knew well crossed her mother's face. 'We'll see about that.' She didn't elaborate, and it was only after Sukie had left that she shared with Abi what she had in mind.

'The curate at St Nicholas has been appointed to fill your father's shoes,' she began. 'Now as you know, he's a single man, and has been living with his sister, a spinster lady who he plans to bring with him to keep house for him. I explained to the bishop that we have nowhere to go as yet, and suggested that the new vicar should move in with us for the time being. I'm still waiting on a decision, but if it is favourable, as I expect, then it's a perfect opportunity for you. If you play your cards right – get him to wed you – all our problems will be solved. We can remain in the house, reopen the school, and all will be as it was. Except, of course, that we have lost your dear father,' she added, her eyes filling with the inevitable tears.

Abi was horrified by the suggestion. 'You can't mean for me to marry a man I've never met – even supposing that he should want me! From what you say, he's a dyed-in-the-wool bachelor—'

'And you are a very handsome young woman' Maisie interrupted her. 'Do you think I haven't seen the way men look at you? Now if you had wed the squire's son, we'd have nothing to worry about, but you wouldn't hear of it, and now time is fast running out for you. Besides, you're a good girl, Abigail. You won't see me lose my home, I know you will not.' She fixed Abi with a pitiful look. 'Say at least that you will consider it. For the sake of your poor mother's health and happiness.'

'Oh Mother . . .' Abi could feel the strings of obligation tightening around her again. How could she refuse to even give the new vicar a chance when her mother had just lost her husband, and was threatened with the loss of her home and the school she loved?

'Do this and I'll never ask anything of you again,' Maisie begged.

Except that it wasn't a plea, it was as good as an order, and Abi felt a stab of resentment. For now, though, she nodded, anxious not to upset her mother.

'We'll see,' she said noncommittally.

How her mother managed to get her way about almost anything, Abi didn't know. Sometimes she wondered if Maisie had dark powers most unfitting for a vicar's wife. Against all Abi's expectations, agreement was reached with the bishop and the new vicar. For the time being, his sister would remain in her own home and Maisie would take care of his meals and his laundry. He was offered, and seemed satisfied with, the second largest bedroom – Abi's – while she was forced to move to the smallest one. Since he was allowing Maisie to remain in the master bedroom and reopen her dame school, she didn't see how she could refuse.

The new vicar's name was Malcolm Rayner. He was softly spoken, tall and lean, with a narrow face and an aquiline nose, atop of which perched rimless eyeglasses. But for all his unimposing appearance, there was a warmth about him that boded well for his relationship with his parishioners, and the suggestion of a core of iron beneath his skinny frame. Though she had been ready to find fault with him in every possible way, Abi found herself liking him a great deal. But there was not the slightest hint of romantic attraction. She could imagine they could become good friends, but never more than that.

Malcolm soon seemed very much at home without ever taking for granted the meals that were placed in front of him or the clean laundry that appeared as if by magic in a tidy pile on his bed. Besides her pleasure at being able to reopen the dame school, Maisie was relishing her restored status as first lady of the parish, and Abi wished she could enjoy her burgeoning friendship with Malcolm without being constantly badgered by her mother to make an effort to trap him into marriage.

One evening, before she left for a meeting of the church wives, of which she was president, Maisie made some particularly pointed remarks and, putting on her hat, smiled knowingly.

'I'm off then, so you two can have some time alone together. It will be at least nine before the Raine sisters finish washing the teacups and I can lock up. Those two are the slowest workers I've ever encountered.'

With that, she departed, and as the front door closed behind her, Malcolm turned to Abi, his eyes glinting with amusement behind the thick lenses of his eyeglasses.

'Am I right in thinking your mother is trying to do a spot of matchmaking?'

Abi flushed scarlet. 'I'm afraid so.' There was little point in denying it. 'But please don't think I have anything to do with it. I like you, yes, but . . .'

'I dare say every mother is anxious to see her daughter happily wed,' he said easily.

'It's more than that,' Abi confessed. 'She is dreadfully upset at the thought of having to leave her home, and hit on the idea that if you and I . . .' she blushed again, 'if you and I, well, were together, she'd have no need to.'

'I see. She's a dark horse, your mother.' To Abi's relief, he didn't seem to have taken offence. 'Perhaps, then, I should set her mind at rest. I'm comfortable here, and well looked after, and provided you have no objection, I'd like the arrangement to continue indefinitely.'

Abi frowned, puzzled. 'But I thought your sister . . . ?'

Malcolm pulled a wry face. 'My sister, I think, is glad to see the back of me. She's been betrothed for the past twenty years, yet never wed, and I believe I am to blame for that. We lost our mother when I was just nine years old, and our father when I was fifteen. Hetty was the only family I had left, and she looked after me as if I was her child, rather than her brother. She always said the long engagement was because she had no desire to take things further, and I accepted her word for that. But since I moved in here, she and her fiancé are talking of setting a date. There's nothing now to stand in their way. So you see, things have worked out very nicely – just as long as I don't blot my copybook,' he added with a twinkle.

'But why didn't you say so?' Abi asked.

'I didn't want to presume.'

'And you're not offended by my mother's . . . matchmaking?'

'Not in the least. I'm flattered that she might think me a suitable husband for her precious – and very beautiful – daughter.'

Abi felt a twinge of alarm. Surely he wasn't going to suggest going along with her mother's plan? He'd never shown the slightest inclination that he might have feelings for her, but suppose he did? What then?

As he reached across the table towards her, her stomach contracted. But as if he'd read her mind, he merely patted her hand reassuringly and grinned that wicked smile she'd seen on more than one occasion.

'I have no designs on you, Abi. Don't misunderstand me, I have grown very fond of you, but not in that way. I shall never take a wife.'

Abi was confused. Unlike Catholic priests, there was no reason a Church of England minister should remain celibate, and she couldn't understand why Malcolm should be so sure that he would not one day fall in love and wish to marry.

His eyes held hers. 'Don't think badly of me.' He sounded almost apologetic.

'Oh, I don't! I couldn't . . .'

'I hope not. I value you so as a friend.'

'And I you.' She hesitated, a vague suspicion dawning. It was clear that Malcolm didn't want to say more about his reasons for remaining single, and she was embarrassed by the thought that had entered her mind. 'I suppose we all have our secrets,' she added awkwardly.

Malcolm relaxed visibly. 'So what is yours?' he asked, raising a quizzical eyebrow.

The question caught Abi off guard. Oh, she had her secrets,

but she would guard them even more closely than Malcolm guarded his. Safer by far to admit to her dreams.

'Sometimes I feel like a caged bird, and I long to fly free,' she said. 'To see something of the world beyond East Denby. To make my own decisions and choices instead of Mother making them for me. And to build a life that is truly my own. Do you think that is wrong of me? But I have no idea how I could ever achieve it. How to even begin. I can't talk to Mother about it – she would only do her best to place obstacles in my way. And I know no one who could advise me.'

For long moments Malcolm sat deep in thought. Then he said, 'With your teaching experience, I'd imagine a post as governess would suit you. And I happen to know of a family looking for just such a person to home-educate their son, a boy of nine.'

'Really?' Abi's face was alight with interest. 'Who are these people?'

'You may know that coal is mined in Somerset some ten miles south of here? Sir Hugh Hastings, the boy's father, is the major shareholder in two profitable pits, as well as owning the land on which they stand. His estate is vast – he even owns the nearby village. He is a good friend of mine, and if he has not already filled the position, I would be happy to recommend you to him.'

Abi was almost speechless. 'You mean . . . ?'

'I could get word to him – if you so wish.'

'Oh – yes! Please!' This was beyond her wildest dreams, but she mustn't build up her hopes. The position might already be filled, or this grand gentleman – Sir Hugh – might not find her suitable.

'Leave it to me.' Malcolm patted her hand again. 'But perhaps it would be better to say nothing to your mother until I receive a reply to my suggestion.'

Abi quickly agreed. There was no point in upsetting Maisie when nothing might come of this. But little quivers of excitement were running through her veins. Oh please! Let this be my chance! she prayed silently.

In less than a week, Malcolm had word from Sir Hugh that he would travel to East Denby and interview the young lady Malcolm had recommended, and Abi could no longer delay telling her mother. Predictably, Maisie was horrified, raising every possible objection and even resorting to tears, but when she saw that Abi would not be moved, she adopted the black displeasure and stony silence of a mother sadly wronged. She took none of her ill-humour out on Malcolm, however. He was, after all, the reason she was able to remain at the vicarage. Much as it pained her, she couldn't afford to bite the hand that fed her.

Sir Hugh arrived on a great bay gelding. Though he employed a coachman and owned no fewer than three carriages, he liked to ride whenever possible, and had headed cross-country from Bramley, much of which was his own land.

Malcolm was there to greet him, and Maisie, though stiff and unsmiling, nevertheless bobbed a curtsey and invited him into the parlour, where Abi was waiting nervously. She and Malcolm then retired, leaving Abi alone with the grand gentleman.

Sir Hugh was an imposing figure, tall, broad-shouldered and handsome, though there were threads of silver in his dark hair, which was parted on one side and fell in a loose wave over his ear, and also in his moustache. He was perhaps in his late thirties, Abigail judged, and though he looked serious, possibly even a little stern, she could see a warmth in his hazel eyes that suggested he was capable of kindness.

'So, you are interested in becoming governess to my son,' he began without preamble. 'Unfortunately, because of his unacceptable behaviour, he has been asked to leave his school, and I have decided it would be best if he be educated at home.' He gave Abigail a rather doubtful look, his eyes narrowing. 'I trust you have sufficient experience to tutor Frederick in the essential subjects at least.'

'I believe I do,' Abigail assured him.

'At present, the most important thing is whether you are able to control the boy and encourage him to take more interest in learning,' Sir Hugh continued. 'Do you think you would be able to cope with his antics? You are very young.'

Abigail lifted her chin and met his gaze squarely. 'I am five and twenty years old. And I assure you we have our fair share of young rascals at my mother's dame school, where I have been helping her with the teaching ever since I left school myself.'

'Hmm.' A corner of Sir Hugh's mouth curved up in what was almost a smile at Abigail's spirited response before he became serious again. 'And you won't be tempted to return to your position here? I don't want to have to begin looking for a replacement governess in a few weeks or months.'

'I wouldn't let you down, sir,' Abigail promised. 'I've long wished to see something of the world outside our small town, and this would be a wonderful opportunity for me.'

'Bramley Court is somewhat isolated,' Sir Hugh informed her. 'As you would be living under our roof, it's doubtful you would see much more of the world than you do at present.'

'A very different world, though, sir. And a challenge I would dearly love to take up.'

He thought for a long moment, and Abi held her breath. Then he nodded.

'Very well. I'm prepared to offer you the position. How soon can you begin?'

* * *

When Abigail left the vicarage in the grand carriage Sir Hugh had sent for her, Maisie was in floods of reproachful tears, but Malcolm had taken her hand in his.

'This was meant to be, Abi,' he said. 'But remember, if ever you need a friend, I am here for you. Don't hesitate. And,' he added, glancing at the weeping Maisie, 'don't worry, I will take good care of your dear mother.'

'Thank you. For everything.' Excitement and anticipation had bubbled in Abi's veins. But now, as the carriage drew ever closer to Bramley Court, the nervousness in her gut sent out tendrils that clutched and tightened. Would Frederick Hastings prove too much for her to handle? Would his mother be antagonistic towards her? Would she be treated as a servant, or as one of the family? And if the latter was the case, how would she adapt to their grand ways after the simple life she was used to?

The carriage turned off the lane and into a broad drive that wound between manicured lawns, and Abigail sat forward on the edge of her seat so as to get a better view of the imposing house they were approaching. It was built of a pale stone that glowed almost yellowish in the early spring sunlight, and the main door looked to be approached by two or three steps flanked by balustrades all in the same stone as the house itself.

This was it, then. No turning back now. She swallowed her nervousness and prepared to begin her new life.

Chapter Two

'They be comin' up the drive, sir!'

The elderly footman who had been tasked with watching for the return of the carriage tapped at the door of Sir Hugh's study and opened it cautiously.

Sir Hugh straightened up from the ledger he had been working on, though truth to tell, his mind had been wandering. Since he'd offered Miss Newman the post, he'd found himself questioning his decision, wondering if it was the right one or whether he had simply been swayed because he had found her very personable. She was, when all was said and done, relatively young – as well as undeniably pretty – and Frederick was proving to be a real handful. But her spirited response when he had questioned her age and experience had shown him that she was not to be underestimated, and he hoped she would draw on that steel when dealing with the boy.

'Thank you, Briggs.' He closed the ledger. 'Summon Lady Hastings, if you will, and Frederick too. And be sure Mrs Mears attends to Miss Newman's luggage when it has been taken to her room.'

'Yessir.' Briggs, the footman, attempted a bow, but bent as he already was, it was no more than a bob. In Sir Hugh's opinion, it was high time the man retired, but he'd been in service here for fifty years and more, and Mr Handley, the butler, who had been with the family himself for almost thirty years, had been vocal in his efforts to persuade Sir Hugh to keep him on.

'It would be the death of him if you dismissed him. And you wouldn't want that, would you, sir? He might not be of much use, but he's no trouble either. And your father would turn in his grave if he thought you'd sent him packing.'

'You are right, Handley. The place wouldn't be the same without him,' Sir Hugh had agreed reluctantly. He didn't want to upset the butler; for all his long service, he was as ruthlessly efficient as he had ever been, and training a replacement would be a long and tedious business.

'Make haste then, Briggs!' he urged the old man as he hovered, then retreated, not with the speed his employer might have wished, but with a dogged determination to put one foot in front of the other.

Sir Hugh rose, and was just exiting the study himself when a loud whoop startled him, and to his annoyance he saw his son come sliding down the highly polished banister and land with a bump against the newel post at the foot of the stairs.

'Frederick! You have been told time and time again! You will not slide down the banisters. Have I not made myself clear?'

'Sorry, Pa.' But he didn't look sorry. His pudgy face was flushed with pride at having managed both flights of stairs from his room without falling off.

'Get down from there this instant!' Sir Hugh said sharply. 'What sort of impression will behaviour like this make on your new governess?'

Freddie hoisted one plump leg over the banister and slid to the ground, landing heavily. Sir Hugh was of the opinion that he needed to lose some weight, but Imogen maintained it was down to the stodgy food he'd eaten at boarding school – fatty breakfasts, dumplings and suet puddings, not to mention the treats from his tuck box – and he would soon lose his 'puppy fat', as she called it, now that he was at home.

Sir Hugh was constantly surprised by the way she stood up for the boy. It wasn't as if she was his mother – Marigold, Sir Hugh's first wife, had died in childbirth along with her baby when Freddie was four years old. What was more, the boy seemed resentful of his stepmother, failing to treat her with the respect she was due. Yet still she looked for the best in him. And since the tragic loss of Robbie, her own beloved child, she had become even more protective of her stepson.

'Go out to greet your new governess, and try to behave yourself for once,' Sir Hugh ordered now. Adding: 'And where the devil is Imogen?'

Briggs appeared on the little landing at the top of the first flight of stairs. For all his other frailties, his hearing was still good, and he must have caught Sir Hugh's last words.

'She says she's not comin', sir.'

'What do you mean, she's not coming?' Sir Hugh demanded.

Clutching the banister, the old footman took a few cautious steps down towards his employer. 'It's not her business, is what she said. And would you kindly explain to the governess that she is indisposed.'

Sir Hugh shook his head in frustration, took Freddie by the shoulder and propelled him to the front door. The carriage had already drawn up; the coachman had alighted and was now helping down the young lady who was to be Freddie's governess.

Sir Hugh forced a smile and stepped forward to greet her.

'Come on, milady. Buck up now, do. It's only right you welcome the new governess.'

Mrs Mears, the housekeeper, was a formidable figure, hatchet-faced, tall and strongly built, with iron-grey hair swept back into a severe bun and keys jangling on a ring from the belt around her waist. When she had overheard Briggs tell Sir Hugh that Lady Hastings was refusing to join the welcoming party, she had gone in search of her, bristling with disapproval. She had little patience with anyone who was unable to control their emotions and move on. Sir Hugh had managed it. Lady Hastings should at least make an effort to do the same.

As she had expected, she had found her ladyship in her sitting room, slumped in her chair, head bowed to her chest, and kneading a crumpled handkerchief between her hands.

'Listen to me now,' she continued in a hectoring tone. 'If you don't present yourself, and quickly, Sir Hugh is going to be most displeased with you. Is that what you want?'

'Freddie is his son, not mine.' Imogen plucked at a fold in her skirt. 'A governess was his idea. It's for him to welcome her.'

Mrs Mears drew herself up to her full height. 'That is hardly the right attitude to take with regard to Frederick's education. You are his stepmother, and it is your duty. You'd be there like a shot, I don't doubt, if it were—' She broke off, realising perhaps that this time she had gone too far, and Imogen raised her head sharply, her eyes blazing with unshed tears.

'Robbie? That's what you were going to say, wasn't it? But my Robbie is dead, Mrs Mears, and now I am going to lose Freddie too, no doubt, to this new woman. I don't feel like welcoming her. I will meet her when I feel ready to do so. You can tell my husband that.'

Mrs Mears raised her eyebrows, surprised by the uncharacteristic outburst. Since Robbie's death, Lady Hastings had become a shadow of her former self. It was only when Sir Hugh was angry with Frederick, as he often was – understandably, in Mrs Mears's opinion – that some of her old spirit resurfaced as she flew to his defence.

'Very well, I will relay the message to his lordship,' the housekeeper said coldly, and left the room, her keys jangling on her belt.

No doubt milady would dissolve into floods of tears the minute the door closed after her. But Mrs Mears could summon not an ounce of pity for the woman who had taken the place of the first Lady Hastings, her former mistress, whom she had cared for from the time she was a child. Marigold. Her lovely Marigold.

'This is Miss Newman, your governess. Miss Newman – my son, Frederick.'

Sir Hugh placed an arm around the boy's shoulders, urging him forward to shake hands, but his son broke free, scowling.

'Freddie,' he said emphatically. 'I hate being called Frederick.'

Abigail smiled and held out her own hand, hiding her misgivings at this unpromising beginning.

'Freddie, then,' she said. 'And my name is Abigail, but I much prefer being called Abi.'

'I hardly think a given name is an appropriate way for a boy to address his governess.' Sir Hugh's tone was firm, but not unkind. 'You will call this lady Miss Newman, Frederick.'

Freddie pulled a face but took Abi's hand nevertheless, shaking it solemnly. 'Pleased to meet you, Miss Newman.'

'That's better.' Sir Hugh nodded approvingly and Abi was aware that he could not see the mutinous look on his son's face. She wished she dared wink at the boy, but with Sir Hugh facing her, she couldn't risk that. Hopefully she would have the opportunity to bond with him before too long.

'Would you care for some tea?' Sir Hugh asked.

Abi hesitated, unsure whether it would be impolite to refuse, though she really wanted to find her feet before having to manage a teacup and the cakes and biscuits that would be sure to accompany it. She was still feeling nervous, and the fear of spilling tea in the saucer if her hand shook or trying to reply to a question when her mouth was full made her even more apprehensive.

'Perhaps you would prefer to freshen up first,' Sir Hugh suggested, as if he had understood her anxiety.

'Thank you. Yes, I would,' Abi replied gratefully.

'Very well. Mrs Mears will show you to your room.' He tugged on a bell pull, and almost instantly a wizened, bent old man appeared. Had he been listening at the door? Abi wondered.

'Yes, sir?' The man's voice was a dry croak.

'Summon Mrs Mears if you please, Briggs.'

'Yes, sir.' The old man disappeared, bobbing a half-bow.

'Past his best, I'm afraid,' Sir Hugh apologised. 'But one cannot dismiss such a faithful old retainer.'

Once again Abi was at a loss to know how to respond, but she was thinking that Sir Hugh must have a kind heart in spite of his somewhat formal manner.

She was saved from answering by the arrival of a woman she assumed must be Mrs Mears, and who was, to say the least of it, a daunting figure.

'I'm sorry, sir, but I have been unable to talk any sense into Lady Hastings.' The woman's voice matched her appearance – cold and brisk.

Sir Hugh sighed heavily, then, realising that some sort of explanation was required, turned to Abi.

'I must apologise for my wife, Miss Newman. She is of a somewhat delicate constitution.'

'I'm sorry to hear that,' Abi said, thinking this was probably not unusual amongst ladies of the upper class, who had no need to soldier on as working-class women had to. A fit of the vapours, she'd heard it called.

'There are reasons for her frailty,' Sir Hugh continued, as if reading Abi's mind again. 'You will learn them very soon, but this is perhaps not the best time, when you are anxious to freshen up from your journey.'

A choking sound from Freddie made Abigail turn towards him, and she was shocked to see he was stifling a giggle.

'Frederick!' Sir Hugh's tone was a warning that couldn't be ignored. The boy thrust his hands into his pockets and straightened his face into a parody of innocence.

Sir Hugh turned to the housekeeper. 'Mrs Mears, this is Miss Newman. Will you kindly show her to her room? And Frederick, you may leave too. Look in on your mother and ask if there is anything she needs.'

Freddie muttered something under his breath and earned another searing glare from his father. But it was Mrs Mears who spoke up.

'He doesn't like it when you call her his mother,' she said tightly. 'Lady Marigold was his mother, and always will be.' With that, she turned abruptly to Abi. 'Come this way, Miss Newman.'

Abi followed her up a single flight of stairs and into a passage hung with portraits, daunted by the housekeeper's appearance and manner, and startled by the way she had dared to speak to Sir Hugh. What she had revealed explained, of course, why Lady Hastings had not played any part in her appointment as governess – something she had wondered about – though for all she knew, that might be the way the gentry did things. But it posed more questions than answers. Who was Marigold? Had

Sir Hugh been married before, or was Freddie an illegitimate child? And why had Sir Hugh chosen not to explain Lady Hastings' indisposition?

'Your room.' The housekeeper opened a door and stood aside for Abi to enter.

It was much larger than Abi had expected, and filled with light that streamed in through the long casement windows, beyond which she could see a small wrought-iron balcony. The furniture all matched, constructed of a warm dark-brown wood that Abi thought might be chestnut, and decorated with intricate carvings, and there was what looked to be a stand for either a bonnet or a wig in a corner. On the bed, on top of a richly embroidered quilt, lay Abi's travelling bag, open, with some of her clothing stacked in piles beside it.

'I haven't yet had time to finish putting your things away,' Mrs Mears said stiffly, 'but if you prefer, I will return later, when you have rejoined Sir Hugh and Master Frederick.'

'Oh, there's no need for you to do that.' Abi was horrified at the thought of this unpleasant woman handling her most personal garments and, most likely, sniffing at their inferior quality. There were private items too – likenesses of her mother and father, her journal, and her prayer book and Bible.

Mrs Mears's lips tightened, but she did not argue. 'As you wish. There's water in the jug, soap in the dish, and a clean towel on the rail of the washstand. Oh, and don't think of venturing onto the balcony. It's not safe. None of them are.' Then, without another word, she turned and left the room.

Determined not to be intimidated, Abi picked up the piles of underwear that lay on the bed and placed them in a drawer, then slipped her nightgown under the pillow. As she did so, she felt a crawling sensation on the back of her hand and swiftly withdrew it to see a huge spider scrabbling up towards her wrist. She gasped; she wasn't afraid of spiders, but it was a shock to find one beneath her pillow.

Freddie, she thought. That was the reason for his seemingly inexplicable giggle when his father had suggested she go to her room. He must have put it there anticipating it would crawl onto her face in the middle of the night and give her a fright. He wouldn't have expected her to find it so soon.

She cupped the spider in the palm of her hand, carried it to the window and freed it onto the windowsill. It scurried away, and she closed the window again and finished her unpacking. But she was beginning to wonder just what she had let herself in for. An aristocratic employer who had failed to warn her of the state of his wife's health, a surly housekeeper who was secure enough in her position to disrespect her master, and a charge who was not only rude but also liked to play cruel tricks. Sir Hugh had been honest about Frederick's behaviour, it was true, but now she had met him for herself, her doubts about controlling him had intensified.

Had she had made a terrible mistake? Was she going to regret taking up this position? The last thing she wanted was to return to East Denby with her tail between her legs and admit to failure. No, she decided, the situation would have to become impossible before she could even think of doing that.

Calmer now that she had resolved that she must at least give herself the chance to accept things as they were here, she slipped out of her gown and hung it in the spacious wardrobe. Then she went to the washstand, poured some water – cold – into the matching basin and began to wash off the dust of travel.

Abi was still in her chemise and drying herself when she heard the click of the door opening. She spun around, alarmed, covering herself with the wholly inadequate hand towel, to see a wraith-like figure in the doorway. Golden ringlets hung limply around a face so pale that the dabs of rouge high on her cheeks stood out in sharp relief like the painted face of a china doll, and the woman's eyes were red and puffy. No – not a woman, a lady; the fashionable high-waisted gown made of what could only be the finest silk bore witness to that. With a sense of shock, Abi realised this must be Imogen Hastings.

'Milady?' she ventured.

The wraith took a few steps into the room, the silken gown swaying gracefully about her slight figure.

'And you must be Freddie's new governess.' Lady Hastings' hands worked at the lace-edged handkerchief clutched between them. 'I must apologise for not greeting you earlier. I was . . . upset.' She faltered, and dropped her chin so that the ringlets brushed the ivory skin at her breastbone.

'Please – don't apologise,' Abi said swiftly. 'You are unwell, I understand.'

In the light of her ladyship's appearance, she thought she was understating the case. Was Lady Hastings seriously ill? Dying, perhaps, of consumption, or some other ailment? If she had only a short time left, it might explain why Sir Hugh had been so quick to offer Abi the post of governess, so as to establish some continuity in his son's life. And it could also be the reason he had been unwilling to discuss her absence from the welcoming party so soon.

It was possible, of course, that Lady Hastings might be equally reluctant to talk about her condition, Abi thought. Deciding it was best to pretend there was nothing out of the ordinary here, she dropped a curtsey and summoned a smile.

'My name is Abigail Newman, but I expect you know that already,' she said. 'Freddie – Frederick – is to call me Miss Newman, but I'd really like it if you would call me Abi.

"Miss Newman" makes me feel so old!'

She hoped she had not overstepped the bounds of propriety, but she could think of no better way of easing the awkwardness of the meeting, and to her relief, Lady Hastings did not appear in any way offended.

'I will do so, of course, if that is what you would like. And I would be happy if you would call me Imogen.' Her lips twitched with the faint suggestion of a smile. 'I, too, feel old when I am referred to as Lady Hastings.'

A warm glow flushed Abi's cheeks. At last, in this strange household, she had found a kindred spirit, even if she was wasting away from some terrible illness. But at the same time, she was aware that such familiarity might not be acceptable to Lady Hastings' husband.

'Won't Sir Hugh think me disrespectful?' she asked doubtfully.

The sadness returned to Lady Hastings' eyes. Abi's observation had struck home.

'Maybe. Hugh can be stuffy, it's true. But . . . perhaps when we are alone?' Another half-smile. 'Which I hope we will be sometimes.'

'I hope so too,' Abi returned. 'And perhaps you would like to sit in on some of Freddie's lessons?'

Imogen's smile was faltering again, and, feeling cross with herself, Abi remembered that her ladyship was not Freddie's mother, but a stepmother. Then, to her surprise, Imogen took a step towards her, reaching out to grasp her hands.

'Be kind to him, please,' she begged earnestly. 'His father has no patience with his pranks, and I know he can be a scamp. But he's only a little boy. Little boys are so precious, and they grow up so quickly . . . if they are the fortunate ones . . .'

'I will be kind to him, of course,' Abi said, puzzled by the suggestion that she might be anything else. 'I might have to discipline him sometimes, but it won't be harsh. That's not my way.'

'And you'll keep any misdemeanours from his father?' Imogen pleaded.

'If I can,' Abi promised, and was shocked to see tears welling in the other woman's eyes.

'I am so glad you are here,' Imogen whispered. 'Freddie needs someone like you. And so do I. My life has been very lonely since . . .' She broke off abruptly, wrenching her hand from Abi's and dabbing at her eyes with the sodden handkerchief. 'I'm sorry. I can't talk more now. I need to be alone.'

Without another word, she turned and fled. Had she been about to confide the reason for her wretched appearance and her concern for Freddie? Abi wondered. As things were, she was none the wiser, but more convinced than ever that something was seriously wrong here.

Concerned and puzzled, she reached for her gown and got herself dressed.

Chapter Three

Imogen fled along the corridor to her own suite, and through her sitting and bedroom into the room that had once been Robbie's. She sank to the floor beside his bed, weeping. Here, in his room, it was almost as if he were still alive, hiding somewhere, and would pop out at any moment with a cheeky 'Boo, Mama!'

Since the tragedy of his death a year and a half ago, nothing had been changed – Imogen would not allow it. His little bed was still made up, with a stuffed toy – a monkey – resting against the pillow and his nightshirt spread out over the back of a child-sized wicker chair as if ready for him to put on when it was bedtime, while the music box that had helped him to fall asleep sat on the nightstand beside his bed. Some of his favourite toys still lay on the floor where he had left them. Building bricks, a wooden pull-along duck, a jack-in-the-box and a wind-up carriage that could career around the room before crashing into the furniture or simply running out of steam. Imogen would not have a single thing disturbed.

Sir Hugh considered it unhealthy, but tactfully refrained from saying so, but Mrs Mears, who could be unspeakably cruel, was more outspoken. 'He's gone,' she had said tersely. 'He won't be coming back. You know that – you saw him dead and buried.'

Imogen had closed her eyes and clapped her hand over her

mouth. She wasn't going to explain to this woman, who seemed to resent her so, that while the room waited for Robbie, it was almost as if he was still with her. That she felt his presence close by. And that recently, in the dead of night, she had thought she'd heard him calling to her. 'Mama! Mama!' Mrs Mears would say she had been asleep and dreaming, and perhaps she was right, but that wasn't what Imogen wanted to hear, or to believe.

Oh, if only she could hold him in her arms again, tight against her chest! Feel his little body, soft yet at the same time firm and wholesome. Bury her face in his downy hair. Breathe in the sweet milky smell of his skin. She couldn't – as yet. The whispers of 'Mama' had to be enough for now. But Imogen couldn't let go of the irrational hope that one day he would return to her.

Oh, she knew what the evil woman thought of her. She'd overheard her talking to Hugh – perhaps she had been meant to hear. She wouldn't put it past her.

'She's lost her mind,' the housekeeper had said. 'She'll finish up in the asylum, mark my words. It's the only place for her.'

Thankfully, Hugh had defended her. 'It's early days,' he had said. 'She is still in mourning. God knows, I was close to madness myself when I lost Marigold. It will pass. Given time.'

Mrs Mears had snorted derisively. 'If you say so, sir. I wouldn't be so sure myself.'

That had been some months ago, and now Imogen was aware that Hugh was losing patience with her. But she couldn't help herself. Consumed by her grief, she spent much of her time in Robbie's room, torturing herself with her memories, burying her face in the clothes that still bore the scent of him. And since she had begun to think she heard him calling to her in the night, she would lie awake, listening, until exhaustion overcame her.

Now, the effort she had made to summon the courage to go and speak to the new governess had drained her scant reserves. She buried her face in the covers of Robbie's bed and wept. Then, as she grew calmer, fragments of the brief meeting floated into her mind. She thought that Miss Newman – Abi – was a good person. She had kind eyes and a soft voice, and Imogen had known instinctively that she would be sympathetic to her grief if – when – she learned about Robbie's death.

How close she had come to telling the governess everything! The need to unburden herself to someone who would not judge her had been almost overwhelming. Yet when it came to the point, she hadn't been able to do it. Perhaps one day, when they knew each other better, they might become friends. The thought was a small spark of hope in the darkness that imprisoned her. She was, as she had said, so lonely. If there had only been someone with whom she could share her grief, unburden herself, maybe she could have begun to come to terms with the terrible thing that had happened. But there was no one. Mrs Mears was cold and cruel – Imogen suspected she resented her for taking the place of Marigold, whom she seemed to have placed on a pedestal. The ladies she met socially were not her friends but Hugh's, and to Imogen they seemed superficial and self-absorbed, full of their own importance and engaging in games of one-upmanship. As for Hugh himself, things hadn't been really right between them since Robbie's death.

Once, in the early days of their relationship, he had been generous with his time as well as his money; nowadays it seemed he was always too busy for her. His mines were his passion, she'd always known that, but recently he was more obsessed with them than ever, and although he employed an agent, he seemed set on overseeing everything himself. Perhaps it was his way of dealing with the loss of Robbie, she thought. If only they could have shared their grief, things could be so different. But Hugh seemed not to want that. He had distanced himself from her, and if ever she tried to talk about their lost son, he was quick to put a stop to the conversation and escape, as soon as he could, to his study.

'Going over and over it will do no good,' he would say shortly. 'You must try to put it out of your mind.'

Put it out of her mind! As if she had lost a bauble, rather than her only child! Didn't Hugh care that Robbie, his son too, was dead? Surely he must? In the first dreadful dark days, they *had* grieved together. Though devastated himself, Hugh had been her rock, the only constant in a life torn apart. But then he had begun to change. While she propped likenesses of Robbie on sideboards, mantel shelves and cabinets, Hugh seemed irritated by them; when she refused to have a single thing moved in Robbie's room, he had been impatient, even surly. It was morbid, he had said. She couldn't understand how he could say such things. It was as if he wanted to erase all trace of their son, while she was desperate to hold him close. She'd seen him weep, for the first and last time, when he had carried Robbie's limp and dripping body into the house on that terrible day, but since then . . . Even at the burial he had remained dry-eyed and stoic. Gentlemen were supposed to hide their emotions, she knew, but this . . . If he had loved and needed Robbie as she did, surely the cracks would show sometimes. No, he couldn't be as devastated as she was, and believing that alienated her from the one person she should have been able to share her grief with, the one person who might bring her some release, if not comfort.

But of course he still had Freddie. Though the boy's behaviour might sometimes make him angry, Freddie was his son. Unlike her, he had not lost everything. And if he was hard on him sometimes – which in her opinion he was – it was only because he was determined to keep him on the straight and narrow and raise him to be the perfect honourable gentleman, kind, hard-working and worthy of respect. Imogen would have preferred Hugh to take a gentler approach, but she understood his reasons for the harsh punishments he doled out, even if Freddie did not.

Sometimes she wasn't sure if Hugh appreciated that Freddie had lost his little brother, just as they had lost a son, and might also be blaming himself for what had happened. Though the nursemaid should have been watching them both, at five years older than Robbie, Freddie was expected to keep an eye on the little boy, and they had been in the garden together on the afternoon Robbie had wandered off and tumbled into the lake. She suspected he was racked with guilt at not taking better care of his little brother. In her opinion, much of his bad behaviour now was his way of expressing emotions beyond his understanding, and her heart ached for him.

This was why she had begged Abi to treat him kindly, and keep any bad behaviour from his father, and she sensed now that the young woman would do her best for him.

The tiny spark of hope flared again, that Abi might become a friend who understood her pain where Hugh did not. Sometimes she wished she had never met Hugh, let alone married him. But then she would never have had Robbie, and though the loss of her son was unendurable, she could not wish that he had never been.

How had it come to this? she wondered.

Oh, she had known Marigold had been the great love of his life – he'd confessed as much when he had asked her to marry him. And though she had been dismayed and, to be truthful, hurt, she had been able to understand. Hadn't Jeremy, an army captain who had died at Yorktown, Virginia, fighting in the War of Independence under Lieutenant General Cornwallis, been hers? When she had lost him, she had thought she would never love again, but when Hugh had come into her life, she had learned she was wrong.

With Hugh she had rediscovered feelings she had never expected to experience again. Warmth and desire and dizzy excitement that made her pulses race, tugged forgotten cords and sent shivers through her. Lust and longing. Hope for the future. Even if it might have been less than she would have wished for, she had gladly accepted his offer. As they built a life together, Marigold would become a precious memory, she told herself, still held in his heart, but no longer a shadow between them.

The first years of their marriage had been happy ones. Yes, she had met with Mrs Mears's dark disapproval, and yes, Freddie hadn't tried to hide his resentment that she had taken his mother's place. But Hugh was unfailingly supportive of her, as well as kind, generous and attentive, and Imogen had felt sure she would eventually win them round. In any case, Freddie was soon to go to a good public school as a boarder, and as Imogen settled into her new role, Mrs Mears's attitude troubled her less. She was, after all, only the housekeeper, and if her attitude became unbearable, surely Hugh would intervene.

She had been overjoyed when she found herself in the family way, and Hugh had been as delighted as she was, though Freddie's behaviour had deteriorated. A new baby as well as a new mother was unsettling him, she had thought, and was determined to ensure that he did not feel usurped in any way.

Robbie's birth had been a long and difficult one – two whole days Imogen laboured before at last her son drew his first breath – and when it was over, the doctor had warned that she would never have another child. But in that moment, it hadn't seemed important. Robbie was here. He had survived the trauma of his protracted arrival and so had she. She had the son she had longed for, and given Hugh a second child. Her life and her happiness were complete.

Tears pricked her eyes now as she remembered that tiny person, wholly dependent on her. The downy head, slightly pointed from the long hours in the birth canal, ears flattened, nestling against her breast. The perfect fingers, with their little pink nails, clutching her thumb. The periwinkle-blue eyes gazing up at her from behind long dark lashes. The tiny feet kicking out strongly when his binder was removed.

Robbie. Robbie. Oh Robbie . . .

The small boy taking his first steps. Uttering his first word: 'Mama'. Just as she now heard it in the night. His first birthday. His second, and third. Trotting beside her down to the lake to feed the ducks . . .

The lake. Oh dear God, the lake. Imogen's heart seemed to stop beating.

The lake. No . . . no . . . no!

The limp body dripping water onto the hall floor as he was carried in in his weeping father's arms . . .

It was then that the dream truly had ended. Robbie was gone, and things would never again be the same between her and Hugh. And as the gulf deepened, Imogen found herself thinking more and more of what he had said when he had asked her to marry him. Though she had put her doubts behind her, now they resurfaced, adding to the weight around her heart. The memory of those words was etched in her mind; they haunted her.

She'd never replace Marigold, never could. She was second best and always would be. And worse, Hugh hadn't loved

Robbie as he loved Freddie, because Freddie was Marigold's child.

Imogen slipped lower and lower into the slough of despond. Torn from her rock, she was drowning, just as Robbie had drowned. Her only wish now was to be reunited with him.

Chapter Four

When Abi made her way downstairs again Sir Hugh was nowhere to be seen. Instead, it was Mrs Mears who appeared in the hallway, as forbidding a figure as before.

'Sir Hugh is in his study, and would not want to be disturbed. His working day has already been disrupted,' she said, her tone short and accusatory. 'If you would care to go into the drawing room, I will find Freddie and you and he can begin to become acquainted. I assume you will wish to begin lessons tomorrow?'

'Certainly,' Abi replied briskly. What else would she do all day?

Mrs Mears nodded abruptly and started up the stairs. Freddie must be playing in his bedroom, Abi assumed.

She went into the drawing room, taking in the lavish furniture and fittings that she had been too nervous to notice earlier. A grand piano occupied one corner, and the brocaded chairs and a love seat were gathered around a small circular table. A gilt-framed portrait – presumably one of Sir Hugh's ancestors – hung over the mantelpiece, and watercolour paintings of rural scenes adorned the walls. Rather than sitting down, Abi crossed to the window, looking out onto the manicured lawns between which the carriage had travelled.

As she heard the click of the door being opened, she swung round to see her charge entering the room.

'Freddie! That's what you would prefer to be called, isn't it? How nice to see you again.'

Freddie was scowling and kicking the toe of his boot into the oriental rug that covered much of the varnished board floor. 'Miss.'

Abi forced a smile. 'Yes, that will do nicely. You don't have to address me by my full name. Shall we sit down? It would be good if we could get to know one another before we begin formal lessons.'

Freddie pulled a face, as if he wasn't much looking forward to lessons, but gestured towards one of the brocaded chairs, indicating where she should sit before taking a seat opposite her. Whatever his faults, his manners, when he chose, were those of a gentleman.

'This must be very strange for you, Freddie,' she began. 'You are more used to being taught along with a number of other boys, and by a man, I presume. Well, I have to admit it is strange for me too. I am used to teaching a class of maybe a dozen children, both boys and girls. But I hope we can both soon adjust and enjoy our lessons. Tell me – what are your favourite subjects? What are you good at, what do you struggle with, and what are you bored by?'

For the first time, Freddie seemed to engage. 'I like mathematics and the sciences, but that is because I'm good at them, I expect. History and geography – well, they are not too bad, I suppose, but I hate English.'

Abi's heart sank. Arithmetic and nature study were well within her scope, but Sir Hugh hadn't mentioned science when he had interviewed her, and it hadn't occurred to her that it might be required.

'I'd have thought English would come naturally to you,' she said.

'Oh, the grammar is easy enough, and I like making up plays,' Freddie said dismissively. 'But we had to learn poems and speeches from Shakespeare. I couldn't be bothered with that girly stuff. Can you imagine having to stand up in front of the class and pretend to be a woman? "The quality of mercy is not strained . . ."' he recited in an affected tone, which, given that his voice had yet to break, was uncannily as William Shakespeare must have intended.

Abi smiled. 'I understand.' But actually all her qualms were returning. This was far beyond anything she'd been required to teach in the dame school, where the only things that had to be committed to memory were the times tables, the Lord's Prayer and the Creed.

As if sensing her discomfort, Freddie smiled slyly. '"Once more unto the breach, dear friends, once more; Or close the wall up with our English dead!"' This time he made his voice lower. For all his disdain for learning speeches, he was a natural-born actor, Abi realised.

'Well?' His normal voice resumed, he challenged her with a direct gaze. 'Can you carry on, miss? Because I can.'

Abi felt a rising sense of panic, but she was saved from answering as Sir Hugh, whom neither of them had realised was there, spoke from the doorway.

'I am pleased you learned something, at least, at that school, Frederick. It cost me a great deal of money.' He sounded almost amused; it made him seem much more approachable, Abi thought, and when he turned his attention to her, his tone remained pleasant. 'I regret you were told I was too busy to spare you some time,' he said. 'That is not, and never will be, the case. I am anxious to keep abreast of Frederick's progress.'

'I'm pleased to hear that,' Abi managed.

'I think, too, it would be good if we were to talk before you meet my wife,' he continued. He turned to his son. 'Frederick, you may leave us. Amuse yourself elsewhere.'

Freddie rose. 'Yes, Papa. Thank you, Miss Newman.' Perfectly polite again, he left the room and closed the door behind him.

'Actually, I have already met Lady Hastings,' Abi confessed as Sir Hugh settled into the chair that Freddie had vacated.

'I see. And what was your impression of her?'

She hesitated, anxious not to say the wrong thing.

'Well?' Sir Hugh pressed her.

'She came to my room to apologise for not being there to greet me when I arrived,' Abi hedged. 'I thought that was very kind of her, as she seemed . . .' Again she hesitated, not wanting to use any of the terms that truly described Imogen's apparent ill-health or her sudden tearful departure.

'Upset?' Sir Hugh prompted her.

'Yes,' she agreed, relieved.

'Precisely.' Sir Hugh leaned into the back of his chair, hands resting on his knees, and his eyes met hers with a directness that for some reason she found unsettling. 'I was reluctant to burden you with the details of Lady Hastings' condition so soon after your arrival, but I think, on second thoughts, that it would be only right for me to explain. The fact of the matter is that my dear wife is suffering grievously, and you should know the reason for it.' He paused.

'She is ill?' Abi ventured

The pause lengthened, and a chill prickled over her skin. She'd been right. Lady Hastings was very sick, perhaps dying. But when Sir Hugh eventually spoke, what he had to say was not in the least what she had expected.

'My wife is not ill per se. Except in as much as her physical health is affected by her mental and emotional state. The sickness, Miss Newman, is an affliction of her nervous system, and that came about because of the dreadful loss we suffered a year and a half ago.'

Once again he paused, and Abi waited, dumbstruck.

'Our son, Robert, died tragically at just three years of age,' he said at last, and Abi realised the loss had hit him hard too. Yet he was holding his emotion in check, as gentlemen were wont to do.

'Oh – I am so sorry!' she managed. 'I had no idea.'

'Imogen has taken his loss very badly,' he went on. 'Frederick is my son by my late wife, Marigold, while Robert – Robbie, as she calls him – was her only child. She doted on him. Worshipped him. His death was, of course, a terrible tragedy for all of us. But I am afraid to say Imogen seems quite unable to come to terms with his loss.'

'Understandably,' Abi murmured. And then, before she could stop herself: 'What happened?'

The moment the words were out, she regretted them. It wasn't for her to ask questions that would force Sir Hugh to recount the details of such a terrible event. But to her relief, he did not seem to take offence.

'He and Frederick were playing outside, on the lawns,' he said, and although his eyes had gone far away, his voice was as firm and measured as always. 'His nursemaid was supposed to be watching him, but she was neglectful of her duties. As for Frederick, he was taking scant notice of his little brother – he was chasing butterflies to add to his collection, no doubt – and did not realise Robert had wandered off. There is a lake in the valley beyond the grounds of the house, where Imogen used to take him to feed the ducks – perhaps Robert thought he would go to see them, or perhaps he simply got lost. He must have missed his footing and tumbled into the water. Whatever, it was there that we found him. Too late, sad to say, to save him. Our little Robert was already dead. He had drowned.'

For the first time his voice faltered, and Abi waited in silence, at a loss to know what to say. Then he recovered himself and continued.

'When I brought him into the house, Imogen was there in the hallway. She saw him, limp in my arms, plant life clinging to his body and legs, stagnant water dripping from him. It has affected her so deeply, Miss Newman, that for the moment recovery seems beyond her. On occasions she can become more rational, though clearly grief-stricken. At other times . . . To be truthful, I fear for her sanity. For her very life.'

Abi's horror was growing as the tragic story unfolded. 'You mean . . . ? Oh, you can't mean, surely . . . ?'

'That she may be driven to desperate measures to escape the hell she occupies, yes,' he confirmed. 'I would ask that you be vigilant, and notify me at once should you notice anything suspicious in her behaviour. Then I can have Mrs Mears watch her even more closely than she already does.'

'Of course!' But it occurred to Abi that if she were in the same state as poor Lady Hastings, the last person she would want in her immediate vicinity was the dour, almost threatening Mrs Mears. Why, she could be mistaken for the Grim Reaper himself!

'Good.' Sir Hugh straightened. 'So you are now in possession of the full facts. I acknowledge that I should have told you at the time I offered you the position of governess, and for that I apologise. I confess I also asked Malcolm not to mention it. For my own selfish reasons I was afraid it might be something of a deterrent to you, and I was most anxious for you to accept the post.'

'It wouldn't have made any difference,' Abi said, and shocked as she was by these revelations, it was no more than the truth. So eager had she been to make her escape into the wide outside world, not even a raving lunatic would have dissuaded her from taking the position, and Imogen was far from that. Simply a poor soul overcome with grief.

'There is one other thing.' Sir Hugh smoothed the legs of his trousers over his knees so that they hung perfectly. 'I am of the opinion that much of Frederick's bad behaviour stems from what happened that day. He blames himself, I believe, and is tormented by guilt that he failed to keep Robert safe. It's nonsense, of course. He was only eight years old himself, and eight-year-old boys cannot be held responsible for what was a terrible accident. If anyone was to blame, it was the wretched nursemaid, who was neglecting her duties. But for all that, Frederick was Robert's big brother, and he is alive while Robert is dead. Perhaps you would bear that in mind, Miss Newman, if he misbehaves.'

'Of course.' But Abi was puzzled that Imogen should have asked her to keep Freddie's misdemeanours from his father if like her he believed the boy's bad behaviour stemmed from his feelings of guilt. There was clearly something of a distance between them.

'You may think me too strict, Miss Newman,' Sir Hugh went on as if he had read her mind. 'I know that Imogen believes I am too hard on him. But rigorous discipline is the cornerstone of raising a boy to grow into a gentleman. It's no more than the treatment my father meted out to me, and it did me no harm. Nevertheless, if you can help Frederick to find some peace of mind, I shall be most grateful. I have tried to tell him he was not to blame, but anything I say with regard to the matter falls on deaf ears. I think it possible, however, that he may listen to you as his governess, and perhaps eventually his friend.'

'I'll do my best,' Abi promised.

'It may be that you will be good for Imogen, too,' he added.

It was the first time he had used his wife's Christian name when speaking to Abi, but he immediately reverted to his usual briskness.

'That will be all, then. But I will see you at dinner.'

'Oh!' Abi almost gasped in surprise.

'You did know you would be dining with the family?' Sir Hugh asked.

'I didn't,' she admitted.

'Ah – I assumed Mrs Mears would have told you.'

'No, she didn't. But thank you, sir.'

As she went back upstairs, Abi was thinking that Mrs Mears's omission was yet another act of spite. But her opinion of Sir Hugh had changed greatly.

Despite all appearances to the contrary, it seemed that beneath his gentlemanly reserve, he was a loving husband and father who was grieving for a lost child, and Abi found herself intrigued by the complexity of the man who was her employer.

On reaching the upper landing, Abi hesitated, wondering if it would ease Imogen's mind to hear that Abi now knew what she herself had been unable to articulate. The door on the opposite side of the passage was ajar, and through it she could see Freddie, on his hands and knees, playing with what looked like a fort and model soldiers. She tapped on the door, and when Freddie looked up, she asked: 'Which is your mama's room, Freddie? I wanted to speak to her.'

'The one at the end of the passage is her sitting room,' he

said. 'That leads into her bedroom, and next to that is what used to be Robbie's room, and then mine, here. They're all linked – you can come through this way if you would care to. She'll be in Robbie's room, I expect. She spends a lot of time there.'

He indicated a closed door to the left of where he was lying on his tummy on the floor.

'That's a kind offer, but I don't think I should simply materialise like that,' Abi said. 'It wouldn't be proper, and I might startle her.'

'As you please,' Freddie said, offhand again, and turned back to his fort, moving a lead soldier from the battlements to the drawbridge.

Abi left him and walked along the passage to the furthest door – Imogen's sitting room, if she had understood Freddie correctly. She knocked on it and waited. When there was no answer, she moved to the bedroom door, but then thought better of it and instead knocked on the door next to Freddie's room. After a moment, she heard movement from within – the creak of bedsprings, a rustle of silk – and the door opened slightly.

'Oh, Miss Newman, it's you!' Imogen sounded surprised, but calmer than she had been when she had fled from Abi's room.

'Abi, please,' Abi reminded her gently. 'I wondered if I could have a few words with you.'

Imogen opened the door more widely. 'Do please come in. I'm afraid I was very rude earlier on, but . . .' Her voice faded away.

As Abi went inside, she was startled and perturbed to see the made-up bed, the nightgown and the toys, and averted her gaze so as not to appear to be staring.

'I just wanted you to know that I understand now why you were so upset,' she said carefully. 'Sir Hugh has told me of the terrible time you have endured, and I wanted to say how sorry I am for your loss.'

Tears welled in Imogen's eyes once more, and Abi reached out and touched her arm lightly.

'I won't keep you now, but if there is anything I can do, please know that I am here for you.'

'There is nothing anyone can do,' Imogen murmured brokenly.

'I can listen if you need a sympathetic ear,' Abi said. 'Believe me, I do know something of what you are going through, though I won't pretend to have suffered a tragedy as great as yours. And anything – *anything* – you might say to me I shall treat in complete confidence.'

She squeezed Imogen's arm again lightly, then turned away and left. She had said what she had come to say, and she didn't want Imogen to feel pressured in any way, didn't want her to feel her grief was being intruded upon.

The one thing she wished she hadn't mentioned was her own heartache, but Imogen's distress had recalled it for her all too clearly. It wasn't the same, of course. The son she had lost had never drawn breath; she'd never held him in her arms, never changed his linen, never seen him take his first steps or heard him speak his first words. Her son, who had not survived his birth. Her son, whom she still mourned though he would have brought such shame and disgrace to her and her family if he had lived. Her illegitimate son, who had never been spoken of again.

Tears pricked her eyes now, but her sympathy was all for Imogen, who had lost a living, breathing child. How much worse must that be!

With an effort, she pushed the memories to the back of her mind as she had learned to do over the years. If she was to dine with the family, she had better look out something suitable to wear.

She opened the closet – so little to choose from! – and selected her Sunday-best gown of sprigged muslin, then shook it out and hung it beside the window, where the sun streamed in and a gentle breeze stirred the hangings. She could think of no better way to ease out the creases of travel. But now she must prepare for the ordeal of dining with gentry.

Chapter Five

Very soon Abi had begun to settle in and feel less daunted by her unfamiliar surroundings, the standing of the family and their way of life. Her initial impression of Mrs Mears had proved correct – she was certainly the most unpleasant woman Abi had ever met. But she was growing fond of Mary, the elderly sweet-natured maid, who was clearly devoted to the family, and Prudie Doel, the wife of Rex Doel the gardener, was a friendly soul who was always ready for a chat when their paths crossed.

As for Freddie, he was still apt to try the boundaries with his silly pranks, but at least there had been no more spiders in her bed. He had been disappointed she hadn't fled in hysterics when she found it, she guessed. He'd probably lain awake grinning in anticipation of her screams before he'd realised spiders didn't scare her. But neither did the other things he'd tried – a giant slug in the basin on her washstand, an early bumble bee shut in her room – and when she didn't react at all, he'd gone back to playing tricks on the servants. She'd heard Cook berating him for hiding her rolling pin, and Mary had pricked her feet on the straw he'd put in the toes of her slippers.

Abi had set a routine with regard to Freddie's lessons, which she began immediately after breakfast. At ten o'clock, she allowed him a break for a glass of milk and an apple. Luncheon was at one sharp, but she released him half an hour before so that he could get some fresh air and hopefully work off some of his energy with a bit of exercise – plump Freddie didn't care for that – as well as wash his hands and tidy himself before the meal began. She resumed lessons promptly at three, and released him for the rest of the day at four thirty. As for the subjects to be studied, she varied them just as they had at the dame school, and if the weather was fine, as it seemed mostly to be so far that spring, she took him outside for what she called 'nature study', teaching him to recognise trees, flowers and birds.

Inevitably, Freddie wanted to take his butterfly net, and though she did not approve of butterflies being kept in captivity, and certainly not pinned to a frame, she allowed him to catch them as long as he promised to release them again before they returned indoors.

To her relief, he caught very few; his bulk slowed him down considerably. But it was the same rule for ladybirds – he always had an old enamelled snuffbox in his pocket – and for caterpillars, which he plucked from the cabbages and put in a glass jar with a muslin cover.

'They are pests!' he informed Abi when it was time to empty the jar. 'Doel, the gardener, says so!'

And Abi returned firmly, 'That's as may be, Freddie, but you shouldn't be cruel to any living creature.'

Freddie huffed in disgust, removed the caterpillar, dropped it on the paved path and stamped on it with the toe of his boot. 'That one won't eat our cabbages,' he declared with satisfaction.

'Oh Freddie . . .' Abi shook her head reprovingly. 'That was not a nice thing to do.' But she decided this once to take no further action. Freddie had been very well behaved so far, and she didn't want to damage the rapport that was beginning to build between them.

Besides, she'd seen her father do the self-same thing, picking the insects off the young vegetables and disposing of them, and he was a man of God. She could hardly blame a little boy too much.

Abi's reservations about dining with the family had proved unfounded. Sir Hugh ensured she was included in the conversation, often asking about Freddie's lessons and the progress he was making, and Abi was able to answer truthfully that he was a very bright boy and seemed to be absorbing whatever she taught him.

When Sir Hugh retired for a cigar and a glass of brandy and Abi and Imogen were alone, the conversation still revolved around Freddie. Imogen was as interested in how he was getting on as his father was, and often popped into the classroom, sitting quietly at the back and smiling when he was able to respond to one of Abi's questions with a quick and correct answer, or when Abi praised him for a piece of good work. But on some evenings she seemed to retreat into herself. Abi thought that talking about her grief might help her, but she didn't think it her place to raise the subject, and on those occasions Imogen would excuse herself as soon as was polite and go to her room. There she would lose herself in her memories, Abi guessed, and her heart bled for this sweet and tormented lady.

One morning a few weeks later, Freddie did not seem at all well when he appeared at the breakfast table. He was snuffly, and if he was slow to use his handkerchief, ribbons of greenish mucus ran down towards his upper lip. He was flushed, yet complained of feeling cold, and whereas he usually wolfed down generous portions of bacon, eggs, kidneys and whatever else was on offer, today he pushed kedgeree around his plate and ate virtually nothing.

'We don't waste good food in this house,' Sir Hugh admonished him.

'I don't want it,' Freddie muttered miserably. 'Please may I leave the table?'

'Not until you have cleared your plate. And sit up straight, or I'll have a board strapped to your back to make you.'

Abi cringed. Freddie was clearly unwell, and Sir Hugh, who seemed to be in a very bad mood this morning, was only making things worse. But to her surprise and relief, Imogen spoke out.

'Do you have to be so harsh, Hugh? He is not himself, are you, Freddie?'

'*Frederick*,' Sir Hugh said with heavy emphasis, 'is quite old enough to speak for himself. Come on, boy, spit it out. What the devil is wrong with you?'

To Abi's dismay, she noticed tears gathering in Freddie's eyes, something she'd never seen him come even close to before. With a start, he scraped back his chair, wiped his nose with the back of his hand and fled from the room.

Furious now, Sir Hugh brought his fist down on the table, so hard that cups jiggled in saucers and cutlery rattled on plates. 'Come back here this instant!'

But Freddie was long gone.

'Hugh.' Imogen laid a restraining hand on her husband's arm. 'Don't. Please. Can't you see he is ill?

'Poppycock! Since we lost Robert, you think the worst of every situation. Do you want to turn the boy into a milksop? Because I certainly do not. It's no more than a common cold.'

Abi could see that Imogen was hurt by his attitude, but to her credit, she wasn't ready to give up. 'There's measles in the town. I heard the maids talking about it. It's rife, they say.'

'And how do you suppose that can have anything to do with

Frederick's sniffles? He hasn't been to town, has he?' Sir Hugh asked.

'No, but have you forgotten? George Buchan came here to play with him on Sunday afternoon. He was sniffly too. I thought at the time it was just as you said – nothing more than a cold, or perhaps hay fever. There's tree pollen at this time of year, isn't there? But since I heard the talk of the measles . . . Could it be that George was infectious and has passed it on to Freddie?'

Sir Hugh shook his head impatiently. 'The Buchans would never have let him near anyone with infection. You know very well how protective Millicent is of her son.'

Edmund Buchan was Sir Hugh's right-hand man in the management of the collieries, and the family often met socially.

'Even so, these things happen,' Imogen persisted. 'Measles is not to be taken lightly, and I think you should ask Dr Mounty to call.'

'I don't want to call Mounty out on a fool's errand. Heaven knows, we've bothered him on enough occasions when he has been unable to find anything wrong. Give it a day, and if he's not better, then I will think about it.'

Imogen subsided, defeated. But when Sir Hugh had finished his tea and left the table, she turned to Abi. 'What is your opinion?'

Abi considered carefully. She didn't want to go against Sir Hugh, but like Imogen, she thought that whatever was wrong with Freddie was more than simply a cold or hay fever, and she knew that measles could be serious, with umpteen possible complications. A boy who had attended the dame school had developed pneumonia, and another had almost died of what the doctor had described as 'brain fever'. The school had had to be closed for almost a month in an attempt to stop the spread of the disease.

'I think we should keep a close eye on him,' she said. 'I had the measles when I was a child, and I don't think you can catch it again, so I'm perfectly willing to sit with him. Have you ever been infected?'

'I don't think so,' Imogen said doubtfully.

'I'm sure you'd remember if you had,' Abi said. 'The rash, the dreadful cough, the high fever – it's not something you'd forget. Unless of course you were very young, but if that were the case, it's unlikely you would have survived.'

'You think I should stay away from Freddie until we know one way or the other?'

'I think it would be wise,' Abi confirmed.

Imogen sighed helplessly. 'Poor Freddie! Oh why did I suggest George Buchan should come for tea?'

She was blaming herself, Abi realised.

'It's not your fault,' she insisted, fearing that this could send Imogen deeper into the depression that plagued her. 'You simply thought that having company would be good for him. Now, I'll go and sit with him. If he deteriorates, I'll let you know at once. And do try not to worry.'

Seated at his desk, Hugh reached for the paperwork that was awaiting his attention, then pushed it away again. Could it be that Frederick really was ill? If so, his reaction had been unkind and unreasonable, and his only excuse was that he had a great deal on his mind and had slept badly. He'd started the day in a foul mood, and his son's whining and Imogen's defence of him had only exacerbated this. But he really shouldn't take out his ill temper on them, and he wished he hadn't done it. Especially in front of Miss Newman. She would think him a bully and a boor. And for some reason, her good opinion of him mattered to him more than he cared to admit.

Well, it was too late now for regrets. The damage was done. But once he'd dealt with any urgent correspondence, he'd go and find out if there really was something wrong with Frederick, or if it was just another instance of his bad behaviour.

With a sigh, he pulled his paperwork towards him once more.

Abi found Freddie huddled beneath the bed covers, only his hair, damp with sweat, visible. She managed to lay her hand on his forehead – as she had thought, it felt as if he had a raging temperature. She tried to ease the covers back, but he clutched at them, shivering violently.

'I'm cold,' he managed through chattering teeth.

'No, Freddie, you're far too hot.' She went to the window, opening it wide, but by the time she got back to the bed, he had already pulled the covers back up to his ears.

'Freddie, please!' she begged. 'We have to cool you down.' But there was no arguing with him.

She hurried downstairs. Of Imogen there was no sign, but she found Sir Hugh in his study, apparently going over the day's menus with Mrs Mears. Abi ignored her, going straight to Sir Hugh.

'Freddie is really ill,' she said directly. 'You must call the doctor right away.'

Sir Hugh frowned, somewhat taken aback by her tone, and before he could reply, Mrs Mears took the initiative.

'What's wrong with him?'

'He has a raging temperature but he's refusing to let me cool him down,' Abi told her. 'I think he has caught the measles from the boy who came to tea with him on Sunday.'

'Have you looked for a rash?' the housekeeper asked.

'As fast as I take the blanket off him, he pulls it back up again,' Abi told her.

'Well, we'll see about that,' Mrs Mears said firmly. 'If you'll excuse me, sir, I'll take a look at him myself.'

With that, she hurried out of the study and up the stairs, Abi following.

In his room, Mrs Mears took one look at Freddie and wasted no time.

'Come on, young man, I want you out from under those covers. *Now!*' She turned to Abi. 'Wet the flannel in the water jug so I can sponge him down. And Frederick, do as I say and let me have that blanket, or I'll have your guts for garters.'

To Abi's relief, though he whimpered pitifully, Freddie did as he was told. She poured some cold water from the jug into the matching basin, dropped the flannel into it and carried it to the bed.

'You see?' Mrs Mears pointed at a rash covering Freddie's neck and chest. 'Measles, without a doubt. Go and tell Sir Hugh the doctor is to be sent for without delay – and that Mrs Mears said so.'

Sir Hugh was still in his study, but he now looked concerned rather than cross, and when Abi relayed the housekeeper's message, he did not argue, but nodded and rose immediately, no doubt feeling guilty for the way he had spoken to Freddie at breakfast.

'I'll go myself if Mrs Mears thinks it necessary,' he said. 'Mounty will treat the case with more urgency if I speak to him personally.'

Abi returned to Freddie's room, where he was protesting feebly as Mrs Mears squeezed cold water from the flannel onto his chest.

'Well?' the housekeeper said shortly.

'Sir Hugh is going to fetch the doctor himself. I looked for

Lady Hastings – I thought she should be told – but I couldn't find her anywhere.'

'Oh, never mind her. She's most likely moping in Robert's room,' Mrs Mears retorted. 'A fat lot of good she would be with her weeping and wailing. Get another flannel, Miss Newman, and you can hold it to his forehead while I attend to his torso.'

Abi complied, grateful for the first time for the housekeeper's authoritative manner. She had complete control of the situation, of Freddie, and Sir Hugh too, and it was a huge relief to Abi, who had felt totally overwhelmed. For all her dislike of Mrs Mears, she couldn't help feeling a grudging respect.

At last Freddie's temperature began to come down, and Mrs Mears sat back on her heels wiping beads of sweat from her own forehead with the sleeve of her black gown.

'Right, my lad, you just lie quiet or you'll be bad again. No more of your nonsense, do you hear me?' Her tone was firm but not unkind, and Abi realised just how fond she was of the boy. She had learned that the housekeeper had cared for his mother from her childhood until her death, and it was clear that she felt responsible for him now. It could well explain her resentment of Imogen, and perhaps even of Abi herself – the two interlopers with whom she was forced to share his care.

Footsteps on the stairs, and the sound of voices, and Abi realised it must be Sir Hugh, back with the doctor. Should she leave? she wondered, but already the two men were blocking the doorway. Mrs Mears was staring, a puzzled expression replacing her usual hawk-like disapproval, and Sir Hugh hastened to explain.

'Dr Mounty is unable to attend himself. This is his new junior partner, Dr Giles Stanley.'

Abi, who had retreated to a corner of the room in order to make herself as inconspicuous as possible, was almost as surprised as Mrs Mears. In her experience, doctors were elderly and ponderous, with whiskers, eyeglasses and formal attire. This man, however, was probably no older than his early thirties. He wore no coat, and his fair hair flopped fashionably over one eye.

He wasted no time in examining Freddie, and when he had finished, he straightened up, sitting back on his heels. 'Well, my lad, it's the measles without a doubt. You're going to feel pretty rotten for a few days, maybe longer, but I'll give you something that should help.' Abi recognised a faint Somerset burr in his voice. So he was a local man, then.

'He'd be a lot worse if I hadn't managed to get his temperature down.' Mrs Mears, who had refused to relinquish her place by the bed, spoke smugly.

Abi thought nothing of it – it was typical of the housekeeper to want to take all the credit. But to her surprise, Sir Hugh spoke up.

'We have Miss Newman to thank for alerting us to the seriousness of the situation,' he said with a nod in her direction. 'And she was of invaluable help to you, Mrs Mears, if I am not much mistaken.'

'She did her bit, certainly,' Mrs Mears agreed grudgingly.

'Miss Newman, I presume?' The young doctor turned towards Abi, and she couldn't help but notice that his eyes were an extraordinarily light blue, the colour, almost, of her mother's favourite moonstone brooch. 'Well done for spotting the signs. Early intervention is very necessary if we are to alleviate or even prevent complications later on.'

Abi felt her cheeks flushing scarlet at the praise – from a doctor, no less, and a very good-looking one at that.

'I couldn't help but be concerned,' she said, suddenly shy.

'And not without cause . . .' Dr Stanley broke off, startled, as the door was thrown open and Imogen came bursting in, pushing past both her husband and the doctor and making straight for the bed.

'Freddie! Oh my poor dear! Mary told me you were much worse and that Dr Mounty had been sent for. Why wasn't I with you? I should have been here for you!' She dropped to her knees, reaching for Freddie's hand.

'Lady Hastings!' Mrs Mears stepped forward and grasped Imogen's arm. 'You shouldn't be near him.' She turned to Sir Hugh. 'Her ladyship has never had the measles – or so we believe. If she should catch it from Freddie, the Lord alone knows how it will end.'

'Is this true, Imogen?' Sir Hugh asked, alarmed.

Abi found her voice, speaking for her ladyship. 'It's what she said, sir.'

'Then you must stay away!' Sir Hugh's tone brooked no opposition.

'I can't do that!' Imogen rose to her feet, facing her husband with defiance. 'He needs me!'

'Don't be foolish, Imogen,' Sir Hugh said impatiently. 'God knows, I've lost one wife. I have no stomach for losing another! Tell her, Stanley!'

The young doctor, who had been repacking his medical bag, looked up. 'You must not put yourself at risk, Lady Hastings,' he agreed.

'I'll take care of this.' Mrs Mears was her usual assertive self. 'Come along with me, milady, and leave Sir Hugh to talk with the doctor in peace. We'll make you a nice cup of warm milk and you'll soon feel better.'

Hypocrite! Abi thought. You'll be back to bullying her the minute you have her to yourself.

'I must apologise for my wife's behaviour,' Sir Hugh said

after Imogen and Mrs Mears had left. 'I am afraid she has not been herself since we lost Robert.'

'Dr Mounty mentioned something of it to me. A tragedy indeed. Have the potions he prescribed not helped at all?' Dr Stanley asked.

'They make her sleep, certainly, but she's often in a fog when she should be awake. And as you have just seen, she can lose total control of herself and her grip on reality. She could think only of her compulsion to get to Frederick. Mrs Mears maintains that all she needs to do is pull herself together, but she seems quite unable to do so.'

'Unfortunately, it's not always quite that simple,' the doctor ventured. 'Grief can play strange tricks with both the mind and the emotions.'

'Some of her behaviour is quite inexplicable, it's true,' Sir Hugh admitted. 'Amongst other things, she claims to hear Robert calling to her in the night, when the boy has been dead for more than a year.'

Abi noticed that Freddie was looking decidedly uncomfortable, and didn't think they should be discussing Imogen's problems in front of him. 'Sir Hugh . . .' she said quietly, and as he glanced in her direction, she nodded meaningfully towards the bed.

To her relief, he understood her. In his concern for his wife, he had thought of nothing else. 'No doubt it's the wind in the creeper outside the window,' he said lightly. 'Unless, of course, it's you, young man, playing one of your tricks. You'd think it funny, no doubt, to pretend to be Robert.' He patted Freddie's shoulder affectionately, but the boy shrugged away, burying himself beneath the covers once more.

Sir Hugh turned to the doctor, who had been listening with undisguised interest. 'I'm afraid my son is something of a scamp and always up to mischief. At least the measles should quieten him down for a while. So – what's to do with him?'

'The fever will continue for several days, and it's best if he remains in bed and the room is kept cool.' Dr Stanley was once more the consummate professional. 'I would also draw the curtains – the light is hurting your eyes, I expect, Frederick. I'm afraid I've nothing that will bring the temperature down, but it's important for him to drink plenty of fresh water. I will leave a linctus that will help if a cough develops, and I would suggest that warm drinks would be helpful too. Most importantly, we want to avoid complications such as pneumonia.'

He extracted a bottle from his medical bag and offered it to Abi. 'I'm sure I can leave this in your capable hands, Miss Newman, to administer if you think it necessary. Be sure to call on us if Freddie's condition gives you cause for concern. Or if Lady Hastings shows any signs that she may have contracted the illness.'

'But she was only with Freddie a few minutes,' Sir Hugh pointed out. 'Surely—'

'The disease is highly contagious. A few minutes could be enough. We'll hope not, of course, but I urge you to be vigilant.'

'Of course. Thank you. And perhaps you would care for some refreshment before you leave?' Sir Hugh added.

'That's kind, but I fear I must be on my way. I have more calls to make.'

Dr Stanley turned to Abi. 'I am sure you will take good care of your charge, Miss Newman. And I think he will be only too happy to see a pretty face at his bedside to cheer him.'

Abi felt the colour rise in her cheeks again, a flush of pleasure at both the praise and the compliment. 'I shall do my very best for him, Doctor,' she promised.

* * *

'I'm sorry you have to rush off, Stanley,' Sir Hugh said as the two men reached the hallway. 'I was hoping to pick your brains concerning my wife's condition. Dr Mounty, I fear, seems to be at a loss as to know what to do about it. Don't misunderstand me – he has been a tower of strength to us over the years. But he's long in the tooth now, and set in his ways, while you, no doubt, are more conversant with up-to-the-minute treatments. Would you be prepared to take over her care?'

'I'm flattered, Sir Hugh, and I'd do so gladly, but I'm afraid Dr Mounty must be your first port of call,' Dr Stanley said after a moment's hesitation. 'I am merely his junior partner, and he wouldn't appreciate me poaching his patients.'

'I understand, of course,' Sir Hugh said swiftly. 'I wouldn't want to upset Mounty, or place you in an awkward position. Nevertheless, I would value your opinion most highly, should the opportunity arise.'

'I would be only too happy to oblige – with Dr Mounty's approval, of course.'

Dr Stanley smiled. He was thinking it was his good fortune that Dr Mounty had been unable to attend Frederick this morning. It had afforded him an opportunity he had been hoping for – a chance to become acquainted with the Hastings family, and hopefully find a solution to a problem of his own.

Chapter Six

'I'll take over here.'

Abi, who was sitting at Freddie's bedside, started as Mrs Mears appeared in the doorway.

'Oh no – it's fine, really. I'm sure you have other things to do.'

'Nothing that won't wait. Frederick is my priority just now.'

Argument would be useless, Abi knew. She would have liked to remain with Freddie – he was after all her reason for being here. But if Mrs Mears was set on being the one to sit beside him, nothing would deter her.

'I understand.' Reluctantly Abi rose from her chair. 'But please do call me if there is anything I can do to help.'

'I doubt there will be,' Mrs Mears said shortly. 'I am more than able to care for Frederick now that his mother is no longer here to do so.'

She had been right then, Abi thought as she left the room. Mrs Mears had transferred her affection and attention from the late Lady Hastings to the son she had left motherless. Well, all credit to her. But did she have to carry her allegiance so far? Why did she feel the need to alienate everyone else who cared for Freddie? Abi knew she had no right to feel affronted; she had only been here for a few short weeks. But Imogen was another matter entirely. It was clear she loved her stepson dearly, and

Abi could only imagine how hurt she must feel at being thrust aside by the housekeeper, especially when she was grieving so deeply for her own son. She hoped with all her heart that she could be a friend to the poor lost soul who seemingly had nothing left but her memories.

After all the frantic goings-on of earlier, the house was quiet, apart from Cook's tuneless humming and the clink of heavy pans coming from the kitchen. There was no one in the parlour, and Abi guessed that Sir Hugh was in his study, working, and Lady Hastings either in her sitting room or in what had been Robbie's room. She stood for a few moments wondering how to pass the time until luncheon, and decided this was as good an opportunity as any to do some exploring. The sun was shining, the fresh air would do her good, and the peace of the countryside would calm her racing thoughts and anxiety – or at least she hoped it would!

As she opened the front door that led out onto the lawns, she was startled to see a carriage pulled up on the driveway and a coachman helping down a lady who, in spite of the warmth of the day, was wearing a green velvet coat over a gown of ecru lawn. Her face was obscured by the ostrich plumes in her hat as she descended the carriage steps, but as she straightened up, Abi saw that she was strikingly beautiful, and about the same age as Imogen. A friend, perhaps, or a sister or cousin? She hoped so. Imogen had confessed to her loneliness and a visitor was just what she needed.

As the lady approached the steps, she fixed Abi with a look that was quizzical and almost suspicious.

'I'm Abigail Newman, Freddie's new governess,' Abi offered. 'But if you are here to visit Lady Hastings I should warn you there is measles in the house, just in case you have never had it yourself.'

The lady tossed her head so that the plumes on her hat shivered and waved. 'Oh, I had it years ago. It was nothing. And it is Sir Hugh I am here to see. Perhaps you would be so good as to announce me. Miss Constance Bingham.'

'Yes, of course.' Somewhat put out by the lady's haughty attitude, Abi went back into the house and headed for Sir Hugh's study, where she tapped on the door and opened it. 'Miss Constance Bingham is here to see you, sir.'

Even before Sir Hugh had a chance to rise from his chair, Miss Bingham had swept past Abi and into the study.

'Hugh.' Her tone now was warm, almost playful, then haughty once more as she half turned towards Abi. 'Close the door, if you please.'

Abi did so, but she was bristling now. She'd come here unsure what her place in the household would be, and had been pleasantly surprised at the way she was regarded. Yet this woman – she didn't feel like calling her a lady – had treated her with the utmost disdain. Who was she? Abi wondered. And what was her business with Sir Hugh? Clearly, from the way they had greeted one another, they were friends, at the very least.

The carriage was still drawn up at the foot of the steps, the coachman leaning nonchalantly against it, and Abi couldn't help giving it a curious glance as she passed, before telling herself it was none of her business and turning her mind to deciding which way she would go to explore the estate.

As she reached the point where the lawns and a short expanse of unmown grass ended, sloping down into the woods, Abi hesitated. She could see no clearly defined path ahead and she thought she could take any number of routes through the trees to reach the valley below. Might she get lost? Surely not. The grounds of the house extended far beyond the wooded slope; any route should take her back. Making up her mind, she began wending her way between the trees. From time to time she had to make a slight detour if she happened upon a fallen branch, the stump of a tree that had been felled or a patch of bramble, but for the most part the descent was relatively easy.

It was very quiet here; just the occasional flutter of a startled bird, and, once, something moving in the undergrowth. Her footsteps were deadened by a thick carpet of last year's fallen leaves, with perhaps an underlay of many years of rotted foliage, and the scent of wild garlic was strong. Several times she paused, enjoying the peace and the satisfying feeling of being close to nature, so different to the atmosphere that prevailed in the house. The tensions there were complicated, she thought, though almost certainly they stemmed from Robbie's tragic death. People grieved in different ways, and when emotions were raw and bloodied, misunderstandings could easily arise that could cause rifts, tensions and even resentment.

As the trees became less dense, the sun filtered through the leaves, shafts of brightness that heightened the woodland colours, and beyond, where the ground flattened out, it sparkled on water. Abi felt a shiver run up her spine. This must be the lake where Robbie had drowned. She felt guilty suddenly, as if she was trespassing where she had no business to be, as if being here was somehow ghoulish. She hadn't realised the path through the woods would lead her to it. Visiting the scene had never crossed her mind, yet it was as if she had been unconsciously drawn here.

For a moment she considered retracing her steps back to the grounds of the house, yet still she went on, through the ferns that were now thick underfoot, as if pulled by a magnet, until she came to the water's edge. Here by the bank it was quite shallow, moving gently over the stones, but further out, even in the sunlight, it looked dark and murky. She shivered, imagining what might have occurred. Perhaps the bottom of the lake shelved sharply. Perhaps Robbie had thought he could paddle in the sparkling water close to the bank and had suddenly found himself out of his depth. A tear rolled down her cheek. She brushed it away with her fingertips, looking across to the far bank, wooded as this one was, and was surprised at the sheer size of the lake. She'd imagined something more like a pond, not this expanse of water with a family of ducks paddling Indian fashion across it.

As she let her gaze roam, following the curve of the bank, something caught her attention and she stiffened suddenly. A flash of pink amongst the shadowy greens and browns. Someone was there, half hidden by the dipping bough of one of the trees. At this distance Abi could not be sure, but her immediate thought was that it could be Imogen. She was almost certain Imogen had been wearing a pink gown earlier, and if she spent most of her time in Robbie's room to be close to him, as Freddie had said, could it be that she also came here, to the lake where he had lost his life?

A sudden sense of foreboding twisted her stomach, and she started along the bank in the direction of the figure, picking her way round clumps of vegetation and negotiating the stony dips and rises while struggling to keep her balance. At least the recent dry weather meant the ground was baked dry. No sooner had the thought crossed her mind than she heard a tinkling sound and came upon a broad patch of mud that had formed at the foot of a small waterfall.

She had two choices – to follow the stream to higher ground where she could cross it, or to plough through the muddy pool. She glanced down ruefully at her shoes – no doubt they'd be ruined – but a sense of urgency was driving her, and she had no idea how big a detour she would have to make before she could find a good place to cross. If it was indeed Imogen standing at the lakeside, she wanted to waste no time in reaching her. With the upset of Freddie's illness coming on top of her already precarious mental stability, there was no knowing what she might do. Without further thought she plunged into the boggy ground, ploughing her way through and almost losing a shoe as the mud sucked it down.

Thankfully the path rose again almost at once and she was able to make better progress. She could see now without the slightest doubt that the figure at the edge of the lake was Imogen – and also that she was actually standing ankle deep in it, her skirts wafting gently with the movement of the water. With no idea how quickly the bank shelved beneath the reeds and water lilies, Abi was afraid to call out for fear that if she startled her, she might lose her footing and plunge in. She moved stealthily towards her, but Imogen seemed quite unaware of her. She stood motionless, staring into the water as if mesmerised.

When she was close enough, Abi waded into the shallows, the stones underfoot digging into the sodden soles of her shoes. 'Milady! Imogen! It's me – Abi!' she said softly, reaching out to catch Imogen's arm and hold on to it firmly. 'Come on now, milady. You can't stay here. Let's go home.'

Imogen turned towards her, but there was a faraway look in her eyes and a dazed expression on her face. 'Miss Newman?'

'Abi. Remember? Come on now.' She tugged on Imogen's arm, urging her towards the bank, and at last, to her enormous relief, they were both back on dry land.

'You shouldn't be down here,' she chided Imogen gently. 'Goodness knows what you might catch in that water, and I don't just mean a cold. There's likely rats and all sorts—'

'But this is where Robbie was!' Imogen interrupted her plaintively. 'He calls to me in the night. "Mama – Mama!" He wants me to come to him.'

Abi tried reason. 'He's not calling from here, milady. If he was all the way down here, you'd never hear him from your room.'

'He does call to me!' Imogen insisted, tears welling in her eyes.

Abi gave up an argument she was clearly not going to win. 'We need to get you back to the house. Can we reach the grounds from here?'

Imogen didn't reply, having seemingly retreated into a trance, but Abi felt sure there must be a way back to the house from this spot. It seemed wholly unlikely that Imogen had come all the way round the edge of the lake, along the route she herself had taken.

'Come on. I'll help you.' She took her by the hand and started up the slope between the trees. To her relief, Imogen followed meekly, and far more sure-footedly than Abi had expected, and when the path they were on came to a dead end, she took the lead. Even in her present state, she seemed to know the way, and Abi suspected that she came here more often than anyone knew.

As they breasted the rise that gave on to the grounds of the house, Abi was dismayed to see that the visitor's horse and carriage still stood on the drive. As she too saw it, Imogen froze, and Abi could tell that Miss Constance Bingham was no friend of hers. But as long as she and Sir Hugh were still in his study, Abi hoped she would be able to get Imogen into the house and upstairs without the two of them meeting.

She ushered Imogen past the horse and carriage and through the front door. Voices were carrying clearly into the hall – Sir

Hugh, and Miss Bingham's affected tones. The study door must be open, Abi realised. Miss Bingham must be on the point of leaving.

'Let's get you into some dry clothes,' she said softly, giving Imogen a gentle push towards the stairs.

Just in time. As Imogen disappeared around the corner, the voices grew clearer and nearer, and Abi glanced down through the banisters and caught a glimpse of green velvet and ostrich plumes. Aware that her shoes were tracking mud across the rugs, she kicked them off and followed Imogen through her sitting room and into her bedroom.

Imogen's shoes were not muddy, but they were sodden, as was the hem of her gown. She appeared to be making for Robbie's room, and Abi caught her hand, led her to her own easy chair and suggested she sit down.

'We need to get those wet shoes off before you catch a chill,' she said, managing to sound far calmer than she felt. 'Can you take them off yourself, or shall I do it for you?'

Imogen's eyes, fastened on the door to Robbie's room, had gone far away again, and when she made no reply, Abi knelt beside her, easing her feet free of the shoes and drying them with a towel from the washstand rail.

'I think you should change your gown too,' she said, crossing to the wardrobe. 'Which one would you like to wear?' Still Imogen made no response.

Abi opened the wardrobe door and gazed in bewilderment at the array of gowns that met her eyes. Not for the first time, she wondered why Imogen did not have a lady's maid. Perhaps it was that she valued her own privacy too highly, or simply that she had grown up managing without one.

She selected a pretty day dress and held it up for Imogen's approval, but it seemed the other woman was still in a world of her own. Only when Abi had helped her out of the pink gown with its soiled hem and into the clean one did she begin to respond. Just a simple 'thank you', but it gave Abi hope that she was beginning to come out of her trance.

'That was a very foolish thing to do, you know,' she chided her softly. 'You really shouldn't go down to the lake alone.'

Imogen's eyes were full of tears again and she reiterated what she had said earlier. 'But he calls to me! I hear him in the night. He calls to me because he wants me – and I want nothing more than to be with him!'

The same alarm she had felt when she had first seen Imogen standing ankle deep in the water flooded through Abi, made sharper now by her final words. Had she been attempting to wade into the lake rather than simply standing dangerously close on the bank? Was she so grief-stricken she wanted to drown herself in the same stretch of water where her beloved son had died? Abi was very afraid that might have been in her mind. She would have to speak to Sir Hugh; he had, after all, asked her to report any signs of Imogen harming herself, and it was possible that this was just one such occasion.

As if she had read Abi's mind, Imogen reached out suddenly and clasped her hand.

'Don't tell Hugh, please. Promise me you won't tell Hugh!' she begged.

Abi hesitated. She didn't want to make a promise she knew she could not keep. If she kept silent and something similar occurred with tragic consequences, she would never forgive herself.

'I think Sir Hugh is working in his study, and he doesn't like to be disturbed,' she hedged. 'Now, shall I have a drink sent up to you? What would you like? Lemonade? Tea?'

'Nothing, thank you.'

'Would you like me to stay with you for a while?'

Imogen shook her head. 'I think I'd rather be alone just now.'

'Very well.' Abi turned away. There was nothing more she could do here. In the doorway, she hesitated, worried still, and was unsurprised to see Imogen heading for Robbie's room. Perhaps there she might find some comfort, she thought.

Her feet were squelching uncomfortably in her wet stockings, and the sodden hem of her gown felt cold against her legs. She'd go to her room to change, and then she would seek out Sir Hugh and tell him of her fears for Imogen's safety.

Sir Hugh stood at the window of his study watching Constance Bingham's carriage drive away, deep in thought and disbelief at what had just passed between them.

He had known Constance for almost all his life, and once, when they were both young, they had enjoyed a dalliance that had ended when he had met Marigold and fallen deeply in love.

Over the years, apart from meeting sometimes at parties, soirées and balls, he had seen little of her, but in more recent times she had begun calling at the house, seeking, it would seem, to re-establish a social connection. At first he had been polite but cool – she had a reputation these days as a loose and wanton woman, and he didn't wish to be associated with her. Then, when she had begun flirting with him and alluding to their old relationship in front of Imogen, he had decided to put a stop to her visits once and for all. When Imogen was out of the room he had told her in no uncertain terms that he would not have her upsetting his wife, and she was not welcome at Bramley Court.

She had departed in high dudgeon, but the visits had stopped, and it was only when he'd paid a visit to Pridcombe House, home of Sir Percival Symonds, lord of the neighbouring manor, to try once more to settle a long-running dispute, that their paths had crossed again.

Hugh had once again failed to come to any agreement with Percy, and was riding away, furious and frustrated, when he had seen her walking with a King Charles spaniel at her heels in the parkland that bordered the drive. He was far too angry to even consider stopping to speak to her. But Constance had other ideas. She stepped on to the drive, raising her hand and smiling, and he had little option but to rein Hector in and greet her.

'Constance! It has been a long while, and to meet you here is quite unexpected.'

'Have you not heard? I am often at Pridcombe these days.' Her tone was arch.

'Really?' Hugh said noncommittally, though in fact he had heard the gossip – and given her reputation, he had been inclined to believe it. She had taken to charming and bestowing her favours on wealthy gentlemen who could keep her in the manner to which she aspired, and Percy, who had been widowed a year or so previously, was known to still have an eye for the ladies.

'For me, the burning question is why *you* are here.' Constance tilted her head with a look that was both teasing and flirtatious. So, she thought she could still wind him round her little finger, Hugh thought, the anger he was trying to control bubbling to the surface.

'I'm in no mood to discuss it, Constance,' he said shortly. 'I suggest you ask your friend Percy. I'm sure he will be only too willing to tell you.'

'Oh Hugh!' She pouted. 'Don't be a boor! I was so pleased to see you.'

'Perhaps. But I'm afraid the feeling is far from mutual.'

With a brief nod in her direction, he clipped his heels into

Hector's flanks and rode on, his thoughts returning to his plans for the further development of his coalfield.

It had always been the coal rather than the estate that had interested Hugh, and since Robbie's tragic death it had become something of an obsession. Expanding his empire to build a worthy inheritance for Freddie had provided a way of dealing with his grief, giving him focus and helping to fill the chasm that had opened up within him. Quite simply, it had been his salvation. But his progress was being impeded by Percival Symonds. His neighbour was stubbornly, and perhaps spitefully, refusing to allow him passage over a parcel of Bramley Court land that Hugh's father, Sir Roderick, had leased out to Percival for extra grazing for his cattle long before coal had been discovered in the valley.

When a coal seam was found on a neighbour's property just three miles south of Bramley Court, Hugh had tried to persuade his father to undertake an exploration on his own land, but without success; Sir Roderick didn't like spending money that might see no return. He had also argued that Symonds' lease should be revoked. He felt sure Symonds would be less cautious, and there was nothing to prevent him from excavating the leased land himself, or even sinking a mine if he so wished – such a thing had been unthought of when the lease was drawn up. But again his father refused to discuss the matter and just as he expected, Sir Percival had jumped on the bandwagon, forming a mining company with five other shareholders and instigating investigations which revealed seams of coal did indeed lie beneath his land. To make matters worse, it was the leased parcel that provided the best and fastest route into the nearby town of Hillsbridge and its network of good roads, and his neighbour had made full use of it. With no problem transporting the mined coal to the cities of Bath, Bristol and Wells, and even east to Frome and into Wiltshire, his Pridcombe mine had flourished, and Hugh could only fume impotently as Symonds grew rich on the proceeds.

It was only when his father had died, six years ago now, that Hugh was able to pursue his ambition, and with the support of three other investors, one of whom was the owner of an iron foundry, he had sunk the first of his coal mines, Bramley, and three years later his second, New Bramley.

There was a fly in the ointment, however. The best route to the transportation hub remained the one used by Symonds, and to reach it meant crossing the leased land. Symonds, however, refused to allow access. Naturally, this infuriated Hugh – it did, after all, belong to Bramley. He looked once more into the possibility of revoking the lease, but when he discovered that it would cost a small fortune in lawyers' and court fees, he accepted he had no option but to transport his coal by way of the more circuitous route through the narrow lanes to the main road.

With Robbie's death and his plans for Freddie's future, however, it had become more important than ever that some agreement was reached over access to the leased land. If he was to sink another mine as he planned, he wanted it to be closer to where, judging by the difference in output, the seams appeared to be richer and less faulted. But that meant that it would have to extend below the disputed land. In addition, a new canal was being built in the valley to transport the mined coal to the local towns and cities and even further afield, and this would really only benefit him if he could use the route Percival did.

He had been determined to find a way to resolve the situation, but when he had called on his neighbour, Percival had refused to discuss it. It was the reason Hugh had been in such a foul mood when Constance had crossed his path – angry, frustrated, and without the first idea as to how he could achieve his objective.

But now, today, she had called on him and surprised him with an offer of help. For old times' sake she was willing to talk to Percy and persuade him to change his mind.

She could do it if she chose, he had no doubt. The old man would be putty in her hands. But Hugh also knew that she would want something in return, and already she had hinted as to what that might be.

He gazed out of his study window, hopeful yet troubled. The access to the leased land was within his grasp. But, where Constance was concerned, he needed to tread carefully. Very carefully.

Chapter Seven

Before going to speak to Sir Hugh, Abi looked in on Freddie. He appeared to be sleeping, but Mrs Mears still kept her vigil at his side.

'How is he?' she asked in a whisper, but the housekeeper merely scowled, held up a warning finger and shooed her away.

'Don't disturb him,' she mouthed.

Abi crept out, feeling duly chastened, and went downstairs, where she tapped on the door of Sir Hugh's study. When there was no reply, she tapped once more, opened the door and went in. To her surprise, her employer was not at his desk as she had expected, but standing at the window, staring out and apparently deep in thought.

'I'm sorry to disturb you, sir, but I must speak to you,' she said.

Instantly Sir Hugh swung round, his alarm evident. 'Is it Freddie?'

'Oh no. He's asleep, and Mrs Mears is with him. I'm sorry if I gave you a fright.'

'I'm not in the habit of taking fright, Miss Newman,' Sir Hugh said drily. 'So what is it you want to talk to me about?'

For a moment Abi hesitated, worried that she might be overstepping the mark. He had asked her to let him know if she noticed anything about Imogen that gave her cause for concern, yes, but this was a different Sir Hugh, in a quite different mood.

'Well?' he prompted her.

She took a steadying breath. 'I'm worried about Lady Hastings. I was out for a walk, getting some fresh air, and I saw her down by the lake where your little son drowned.'

'Imogen goes anywhere she feels close to Robert. As witness the hours she spends alone in what was his room.' Sir Hugh's tone was resigned.

'She wasn't simply *by* the lake,' Abi said as forcefully as she dared. 'She was standing in the shallows, and she seemed to be in a trance, just gazing out at the water. Her shoes were soaked through, and she had gone in far enough to wet the hem of her skirts. I managed to persuade her out, brought her home, and got her into dry things. She begged me not to tell you, but I knew I must. You did say you were afraid she might be a danger to herself, and I honestly don't know what would have happened if I hadn't found her when I did. She said some very peculiar things . . .'

'Such as?' Sir Hugh's eyes had narrowed; she had his full attention now.

'She said he wants her to go to him. And that he is there at the lake. That's why I fear she might have walked right into it to try and find him if I hadn't been there to prevent it.'

'You did the right thing in telling me.' His tone made it clear he was taking this very seriously. 'Now I can consider the best course of action.'

'I'd rather she didn't know I've spoken to you about what happened,' Abi said. 'I think she is coming to trust me, and I don't want to lose that trust.'

'Quite. I think it would be best to approach this with the greatest care. Alerting her might well be more harmful than helpful. Don't worry, I won't mention this conversation to her.'

Abi nodded, satisfied, and turned to leave.

'Abigail . . .'

She stopped, startled, and turned back. It was the first time he had addressed her as anything but Miss Newman. 'Yes, sir?'

'Thank you.' There was something in his tone she'd never heard before, something in the way he was looking at her that made her suddenly self-conscious.

'You know I'll do whatever I can,' she said awkwardly.

'I know.' He paused, and for a long moment she had the distinct impression he was about to say something more. Then, in the blink of an eye, it was gone. 'Thank you,' he said again, but this time it sounded like a dismissal.

Somewhat flustered, Abi climbed the stairs to her room, closed the door and leaned against it. Her heart was hammering against her ribs and there were flutters like trapped butterflies in her stomach. The way Sir Hugh had looked at her. Something unsaid. She'd imagined it, of course she had. He was her employer. A member of the landed gentry. He was grateful to her for being there for Imogen, that was all, and the fact that she could have thought otherwise for even a moment was sheer madness. Stop it! Stop this now! she told herself.

She crossed to the window and opened it, taking deep breaths of fresh air scented with honeysuckle, wishing she could step out onto the balcony. But it wasn't safe, Mrs Mears had said.

At last her cheeks cooled and her breathing steadied, and she decided she would take the opportunity to write to her mother and to Malcolm. She had promised to correspond regularly, but lately it seemed there were just not enough hours in the day.

She fetched pen and writing paper and sat down at the dressing table to begin.

* * *

When afternoon surgery was finished and the last patient had left, Dr Mounty locked the door and he and Dr Stanley retired to his consulting room to enjoy a glass of good Scotch whisky and talk through the cases they had attended to that day. Dr Mounty enjoyed these sessions, enjoyed giving the young doctor the benefit of his long experience, and enjoyed even more his glass of whisky, which no doubt accounted for the high colour in his cheeks and the purple veins in his bulbous nose. Approaching seventy, he was a rotund figure who still sported a Cadogan wig and wheezed when he spoke, which was not a good sign, Dr Stanley thought, though it boded well for his own chances of taking over the practice.

'So how did you find Frederick Hastings?' Dr Mounty enquired now.

'He certainly does have the measles.' Dr Stanley took a judicious sip of his whisky, and went on to elaborate and report on the medication he had prescribed for the boy.

'And Sir Hugh was not offended that I did not attend myself?' Mounty asked.

'Not that I am aware of. He was simply happy to have a physician take a look at the boy,' Stanley replied.

'Good. Then in that case, I think you should continue to treat him.' Dr Mounty poured another finger of whisky into his glass, which was already empty. 'I have been thinking for some time about reducing my list, and I would prefer not to have to make the long ride out to Bramley Court. It does nothing for my gout, which is insufferable just now.'

'If that is your wish.' It was exactly what Giles Stanley had been hoping for. 'You will want to continue to treat Sir Hugh and Lady Hastings yourself, however, I imagine?' he added tactfully.

Dr Mounty harrumphed. 'It's the same long ride, is it not?

What's the point in me having a junior partner if he won't take on the more onerous calls?'

'I'm flattered you should entrust them to my care.' Giles Stanley always buttered up the senior partner when the opportunity arose.

'Better you than Oliver Harvey,' Dr Mounty remarked wryly. 'That scoundrel has been angling for their business for years, and if Sir Hugh should have reason to think I had somehow failed them, he'd worm his way in in an instant.'

Oliver Harvey was also a medical practitioner in the locality, and he and Dr Mounty had long been rivals in the battle for patients' allegiance, especially those who could be relied upon to pay their bills promptly.

Dr Mounty took another pull of his whisky. 'Did you see Lady Hastings today?'

'Briefly.'

'And how did she seem?'

Giles Stanley hesitated, not wanting to report just how unhinged Lady Hastings had appeared or mention the scene she had caused. If the old doctor knew just how ill she really was, he might yet change his mind about treating her himself.

'I saw her for a few moments only,' he said, quite truthfully. 'It would seem she has never had the measles herself, and Sir Hugh is anxious to ensure she has no contact with Frederick while he is infectious.'

'Very wise. Ah well, let us hope she is on the road to recovery. A difficult case, and so sad.'

'Indeed. Is there anything else you wish to discuss, sir?'

'No, that will do for tonight. I am ready to head for home. And you, young whippersnapper, no doubt have plans of your own.' With a knowing smile, Dr Mounty drained his glass and set it down on his desk. 'Goodnight, Stanley.'

'Goodnight, Dr Mounty. I'll clear away the glasses before I leave.'

Dr Mounty chuckled. 'I see there are advantages to having an assistant besides having him take the weight of far-flung patients from my shoulders.'

'I certainly hope that will prove the case.'

As Dr Mounty left, Giles poured himself another whisky and raised his glass in a triumphant toast to himself. Really, things were working out most satisfactorily.

Imogen sat, as she so often did, on the floor beside Robbie's bed, her face buried in his nightshirt, his cuddly monkey in her lap. Her neck ached and her feet, twisted beneath her, felt like pincushions, but she scarcely noticed. She would have been far more comfortable, of course, if she had lain on his bed, but she didn't often do that. It didn't feel right. The bed was his; he was the only one who had ever slept in it. It was here, curled up on the floor beside it, that she had sat night after night to read him a story or sing him to sleep. And it was here that she felt closest to him.

At last she sat up, stretching her neck and straightening her legs. If she didn't move soon, she would stumble on her dead feet when she tried to rise, and if anyone saw, they might think she had been at Hugh's brandy to lift her spirits. She didn't want that; bad enough that they thought she was losing her mind. To be cast as a drunkard as well would be too much.

As she levered herself up, holding on to the edge of the bed, something lying beneath it caught her eye. Puzzled, she reached out for it. As she had thought, it was one of Freddie's toy soldiers. What was it doing here, in Robbie's room? Freddie was very possessive of his soldiers. He'd never allowed Robbie to play with them, and had once had a tantrum when the little boy had taken one from the display he'd laid out in and around his fort. Had Robbie taken it again in a fit of mischief and hidden it here underneath his bed, where it had remained ever since? But she'd never noticed it before, and surely, when the maids swept the room, as she reluctantly allowed them to do from time to time, they would have found it? Unless, of course, they didn't clean under the bed. That wouldn't surprise her.

She looked down at the little soldier in his painted scarlet coat, black knee boots and tricorn hat, turning it over between her fingers. Freddie would be dreadfully upset if he thought he had lost it – he knew and loved every one of the little models – and she was suddenly overcome with tenderness and a gnawing anxiety for him. Suppose he took a turn for the worse? Might the measles claim his life? She couldn't bear the thought of losing him too.

She got to her feet, desperate suddenly to know how he was doing. If he was awake, she'd return the little soldier to him; if not, she'd leave it on his nightstand so he would see it when he woke.

Freddie's temperature had risen again, not as badly as this morning, but enough for Mrs Mears to begin sponging him down once more, and he was having strange fever-induced dreams. He was at the seaside, fishing in a rock pool full of baby crabs, but they kept swimming out of his reach. A whole shoal of little fish suddenly flew up out of the water, circling his head. He didn't like it. He ducked forward to escape them and stumbled into the rock pool. Water splashed over his face and bare chest and his feet scrabbled on slimy seaweed that covered sharp, jagged rocks. And the fish were coming for him again, closing in like a thick cloud of gnats. 'Mama!' he screamed. 'Mama!' But she was too far away to hear him . . .

And then she was there beside him, taking his hand, pulling him out of the water. He sobbed with relief. The dream faded and he sank back on to the warm sand . . .

Mrs Mears turned sharply from the washstand as she heard the rustle of silk and the sound of slippered feet on the bedroom floor.

'Milady!' She banged the jug down so hard on the marble top that it almost cracked, and rushed towards her mistress – too late. Imogen was already on her knees beside the bed, clutching Freddie's small hand. Mrs Mears grasped her beneath her armpits and hauled her unceremoniously to her feet. 'Have you taken leave of your senses?'

'He needs me!' Imogen was struggling wildly to free herself.

'And you need to stay well away!' Mrs Mears began to drag her towards the door. 'Stop being such a fool!'

Under normal circumstances, the slightly built Imogen would have been no match for the housekeeper's solid strength, but just now, she was a woman possessed. It was all Mrs Mears could do to keep hold of her, and with a sudden jerk, she twisted her head and sank her teeth into the housekeeper's restraining hand.

'Aargh!' Mrs Mears gasped through gritted teeth and she instinctively loosened her grip as blood spurted from the wound. 'You mad bitch!'

Quick as a flash, Imogen wriggled free and dashed back to Freddie's side, just as Abi, alerted by the commotion, appeared in the doorway.

'Oh no!'

'She bit me!' Mrs Mears, outraged, was rummaging for a handkerchief to stem the bleeding. 'She's mad! Stark raving mad!'

Abi pushed past the housekeeper and hurried to the bed, where Imogen was once again bending over the sick boy.

'My lady.' Her tone was soft, soothing. 'Please, my love. You mustn't be near Freddie.'

'But he needs me!' The words seemed to be the only ones Imogen could utter, over and over again.

'He needs you fit and well when he recovers.' Abi touched Imogen's arm. 'And let's not disturb him while he's resting – sleep will do him good. If you come with me now, back to your room, you can look in on him later.'

Imogen turned to her with anguished eyes. 'Can I? Really?'

'You can see him from the doorway. But you mustn't come closer than that until he's better. And he will be, I promise.'

She put an arm around Imogen, gently leading her away from the bed and – although Imogen stole one last lingering look over her shoulder – out of the room.

Abi too turned back. 'Don't worry, I'll take care of her,' she informed Mrs Mears, whose only reply was a furious stare.

If the woman had been hostile to her before, Abi knew she had burned her boats and destroyed any chance of a truce. But she really did not care. All that mattered was Imogen – calming her down and keeping her safe.

Sir Hugh was dining alone. After the dreadful upset with Mrs Mears, Imogen was in no fit state to join him, and, unwilling to leave her alone, Abi had asked if their meals could be delivered on a tray to Imogen's sitting room. Sir Hugh had agreed. He was just finishing his egg custard with stewed plums when Mary came tapping on the dining-room door.

'The doctor's here, sir.'

'Mounty?' Sir Hugh asked.

'No, the young one who came this morning. Says he felt it his duty to have a look at Frederick before nightfall.'

'Show him in, then. Don't leave him standing on the doorstep.'

'I did, sir. He's waiting in the hall.' Mary sounded affronted.

Sir Hugh laid down his spoon, wiped his mouth on his napkin and rose from his chair. 'Thank you, Mary.'

To his surprise, however, there was no sign of Dr Stanley in the hallway, and he could only assume he had gone straight up to Freddie's room. Somewhat presumptuous, he thought, but he supposed the doctor was to be admired for his concern for his patient. He made his own way upstairs.

Dr Stanley was indeed already examining Freddie, and Mrs Mears was telling him how the day had gone.

'Not much change, really, Doctor, though he did become a bit delirious this afternoon.'

'I was dreaming. Don't you know the difference?' Freddie interjected, only to be shushed by Mrs Mears.

'Children are to be seen and not heard, Frederick. You know that,' she said sternly.

'I think on this occasion he can be forgiven, can he not?' the doctor said with a smile. 'His temperature seems to be normal now, however, so I think it will not be too long before he will remember his manners.'

'Let us hope so,' said Sir Hugh with a glance at Frederick that for once was not reproving, but almost playful. 'Good of you to come, Stanley. Is Mounty still indisposed?'

The young doctor straightened up. 'He has asked me to take on Frederick's care, since it was I who attended him this morning.'

Sir Hugh nodded, satisfied. 'Good. That is just as I would want it. I think the medication you left for him must have helped. He has been sleeping a good deal, is that not right, Mrs Mears?'

'It is. And through all the commotion too.'

'Commotion?' Dr Stanley repeated, frowning. 'He really needs to be kept quiet.'

'Oh, I know that, Doctor. But there was nothing I could do. Lady Hastings, it was, forcing her way in to see him, just the same as she did this morning. You saw for yourself how she was, quite out of control. It took the both of us – me and Miss Newman – to get her out of the room.'

'Dear, dear. Would you like me to take a look at her?' Dr Stanley offered.

'I don't think that will be necessary. She is somewhat recovered, and Miss Newman is with her.' Sir Hugh nodded towards the bed, effectively closing down the subject. 'So – what is your opinion with regard to Frederick?'

'The illness is progressing much as I would have expected. It will be a few days before he is out of the woods, but at present I don't think there is cause for concern. I'll leave him some more linctus in case the cough worsens.'

'Good.' Sir Hugh nodded his approval. 'Would you care for a noggin of cognac before you leave, Stanley? I was about to have one myself when you arrived.'

'I don't know that I should.' the young doctor demurred.

'I insist.' Sir Hugh ruffled his son's hair. 'Try to get a good night's rest, Frederick, and hopefully you will feel better in the morning.'

'I'm afraid it will be at least a week before he begins to feel well,' Dr Stanley cautioned as they left the room.

'And goes back to being his usual mischievous self,' Sir Hugh said with a rueful smile. 'But for now, let's just enjoy that glass of cognac.'

When the two men were settled in his study with their brandies, Sir Hugh set his glass down on the occasional table at his elbow and sat forward in his wing chair.

'I'm afraid I had an ulterior motive in persuading you to

share a drink with me,' he said apologetically. 'I'd very much like to talk more to you about Imogen. I'll understand, of course, if you do not feel at liberty to do so, since she is Mounty's patient. But I am most concerned by the turn things seem to have taken, and I—'

Dr Stanley raised a hand. 'Forgive my interruption, but you need not worry that discussing Lady Hastings with me is in any way unethical. Dr Mounty is suffering badly with gout, and has asked me to look after the whole family until he is fit to make the journey out here again,' he said, distorting the truth so that Sir Hugh would not take offence at Dr Mounty's decision. 'I hope that is agreeable to you. He would have liked to tell you himself, but . . .'

'Of course. Poor Mounty. Though his gout is, I fear, a classic example of "Physician, heal thyself". But as I am sure you have gathered from what I said this morning, I shall welcome the change. I reiterate – Mounty has served us well over the years, but he is not as young as he once was, and neither is he versed in the more modern treatments that you are no doubt familiar with.'

'I'm flattered you should think so,' Giles Stanley said modestly.

'I am simply looking for the best possible treatment for my wife, who, far from improving, seems to be getting worse. As you have seen for yourself, at times she behaves like a madwoman – she actually bit Mrs Mears when she tried to prevent her going too close to Frederick – and this business of thinking that Robert is calling to her has had some very worrying consequences. This afternoon Miss Newman found her standing in the shallows of the lake where Robert drowned, staring into the water. It seems she believes that the fact that she hears him calling to her means he wants her to join him.'

Dr Stanley frowned. 'That is worrying indeed. You are suggesting she might have tried to drown herself if Miss Newman hadn't found her?'

'Exactly. It's Mrs Mears's opinion that the time is coming when she needs to be locked away for her own safety, but I really do not want to have to resort to that if there is any other way. Is there nothing we can do to rescue her from the dark place she is sinking into? Some new treatment, perhaps, that you know of?'

'I'm sorry, Sir Hugh, but I am afraid in truth I am no more qualified to help than Dr Mounty. It seems to me that what Lady Hastings needs is specialised help.'

'Such as she would receive in an asylum,' Sir Hugh said heavily. 'Perhaps there is something in what Mrs Mears says.'

'If these hallucinations continue, it may come to that,' Dr Stanley conceded. 'In the meantime, I will undertake some research into the subject, and you have my assurance I will do everything in my power to aid her towards recovery.'

'I'm most grateful, Stanley.' Sir Hugh reached for his brandy. 'And for your care and concern for Frederick too.

Dr Stanley drained his glass and rose. 'I only wish I could do more for Lady Hastings. At least when physical illness strikes, there are a number of remedies at my disposal, even if they do not always achieve the desired result. But when the problem is what appears to be a broken heart . . . I'm afraid there are no easy answers.'

'Quite,' Sir Hugh said sadly.

When the young doctor had left, he returned to his study and poured himself another – very large – glass of brandy.

Chapter Eight

With Freddie's illness disrupting the routine she had established, Abi was able to spend more time with Imogen, though she always made sure she left when Imogen showed signs of wanting to be alone. She recognised that the other woman still needed time and space to grieve, to sit in Robbie's room and remember him. But she took care to watch her like a hawk on the rare occasions she left the house to sit or walk in the gardens, anxious that she might find her way down to the lake again. For that reason she had declined Sir Hugh's suggestion that she might take the opportunity to go home and visit her mother for a few days, though the offer had been a tempting one. Since those few awkward moments in his study and the ridiculous thoughts and feelings she'd had afterwards, she felt uncomfortable in his presence, though there had been no recurrence of the episode, and their encounters were just as they had been before.

With each day that passed, Freddie was showing signs of recovery. His cough was still troubling him, but his chest hadn't congested, his temperature had returned to normal and the rash was fading. Mrs Mears had returned to her own room at night rather than sleeping at his side on a chaise that had been brought in especially for the purpose, and since she no longer spent every waking hour with him, Abi had taken to sitting with him for a few hours each day, reading to him.

As he steadily improved, she decided it was time for something different, and remembering he had said he liked making up plays, she searched Sir Hugh's library and found a copy of Christopher Marlowe's *The Tragedy of Queen Dido of Carthage*.

'I'm going to make you do some of the work today,' she said, taking it to his room, and went on to suggest that he should read the parts of Jupiter, Hermes and some of the other male characters, while she read the lines of the females, Venus, Juno and Dido herself.

So engrossed were they in the game, as Freddie thought of it, that neither of them was aware of Dr Stanley standing just outside the half-open door and listening until he came into the room with a cheerful 'Bravo!'

Abi felt the colour rushing into her cheeks; while Freddie almost certainly enjoyed having an audience, there was nothing she wanted less. She hated being the centre of attention, and besides, her dramatic skills were nowhere near as good as his.

As Mrs Mears had been caring for Freddie, Abi hadn't seen Dr Stanley since the day of his first visit, and now she was struck all over again by his youth and his undeniable good looks.

'Doctor! How you startled me!' she managed. 'I hope you haven't been listening to our reading and comparing our efforts to the players you have seen on visits to the theatre.'

'If I have, it can only be a favourable comparison. I am most impressed by Freddie's talents, and by yours too,' he added, his startlingly blue eyes teasing her before turning to Freddie. 'You seem much recovered, my boy. But reading from the printed page is not straining your eyes, I hope? They can be affected by the measles sometimes, and you must be careful not to damage them. They are very precious, your eyes.'

'They are aching a bit, sir,' Freddie replied, and Abi bit her lip, hoping that she had not caused a problem with her well-meaning idea to entertain him.

'Oh Doctor, I had no idea. I'd never have suggested it if I'd known.'

'No harm done, I'm sure,' the doctor assured her. 'Just don't allow him to read for too long, and be sure the light is bright enough for him to be able to see without having to strain. Now, Freddie, since you seem so much better, I think we can allow you to leave your bed and get dressed. In fact, we could take a stroll in the garden. It's a warm, fine day, the fresh air will do you good, and I can better assess what you are capable of. Can you find him some suitable clothes, Miss Newman?'

Abi looked through the drawers and wardrobes. 'What about these?' She held up some garments for the doctor's inspection and he nodded his approval.

'Capital. Now, Frederick, let's have you out of that nightshirt.'

Freddie pulled the covers up over his chest, looking at Abi balefully.

Dr Stanley smiled. 'Would you mind leaving us, Miss Newman, to afford Frederick some privacy.'

'Oh, I'm so sorry, Freddie.' It hadn't occurred to Abi that he wouldn't want her to see him naked. She thought of him as a little boy. But it was a measure of how much better he was if he felt bothered by such things. She left the room and waited outside the door until the two of them emerged.

'We'll leave you in peace for a while, Miss Newman,' the doctor said. 'Don't get up to any mischief, though, while we are gone.' The look he gave her was decidedly flirtatious.

'Of course not, Doctor,' she said briskly. If he thought she was going to respond, he was very much mistaken. He was, she decided, just the sort to take advantage of any young woman given the chance.

Freddie was looking rather wobbly as he walked off along the passageway, but Abi supposed that was only to be expected, since it was the first time he had been on his feet in more than two weeks. But he was in good hands. Dr Stanley wouldn't be doing this unless he was sure his charge would come to no harm. Sir Hugh had said he had a much more modern outlook than Dr Mounty; perhaps this was the way medical practice was progressing.

No matter that he fancied himself as something of a modern-day Romeo, she had every confidence in his abilities as a doctor and his dedication to the welfare of his patients. And really that was all that mattered.

When Abi went downstairs to return the book she had borrowed for Freddie's lesson to the library, she found Mrs Mears in the hallway, leafing through what looked like a bundle of envelopes and small packages before placing them on the silver platter that stood on the hall table. Abi's heart leapt; she was waiting for replies to the letters she had written home.

'Is there anything for me?' she asked eagerly.

Mrs Mears looked up, treating her to a contemptuous stare. 'Why would you think there would be?'

'I'm expecting to hear from my mother,' she said, attempting not to sound as defensive as she felt. She hated that the house-keeper made her feel this way, but she wasn't used to such open hostility.

Mrs Mears sniffed. 'This is the mail that came by coach. I don't suppose your mother can afford to send letters that way.'

Abi lifted her chin, determined not to allow the woman to sneer at her family. 'The mail coach doesn't pass through our village.'

'Well, if she has to rely on the post boys, you'll be lucky if anything arrives before Christmas,' Mrs Mears said with grim satisfaction.

Abi knew she might well be right. Sir Hugh had warned her of the problems of entrusting mail to the post boys on horseback. Not only were they much slower than the mail coach, as the roads they travelled were badly maintained, full of deep ruts and thick mud in wet weather, they were not entirely reliable either. Badly paid as they were, they had been known to steal from the bags they carried, and they were often targeted by highwaymen, who didn't stop to pick the most valuable contents but rode away with the full bags so as to examine them where there was no danger of being apprehended.

Abi turned away, but Mrs Mears was not done with her.

'Why are you not with Frederick?' she demanded imperiously.

'Dr Stanley has taken him for a walk in the gardens, and when I have returned this book to the library, I am going to sit with Lady Hastings for a while,' Abi returned as coolly as she could manage. And this time when she turned to leave, the housekeeper did not stop her.

Abi was in her room, preparing a lesson for when Freddie was fit to resume formal tuition, when she heard voices in the corridor. It sounded as if he and Dr Stanley were returning from their walk. She packed away her books and made for his room, but to her dismay, she could hear that Mrs Mears was with them, presumably having followed them upstairs.

'It's too soon,' she was saying, her tone making her disapproval clear. 'The boy needs to regain his strength before going gallivanting. We don't want him to be ill again.'

Abi hesitated. She didn't relish the prospect of another encounter with the housekeeper so soon. But neither did she want to slink away. She had as much right as Mrs Mears to take an interest in Freddie's welfare – more, perhaps, since she was his governess.

'I think I am the best judge of what is of benefit to Frederick,' she heard Dr Stanley reply. 'You enjoyed being out in the fresh air, didn't you, lad?'

As Abi entered the room, Mrs Mears was still holding forth. 'Enjoyment is all very well, but if he suffers a setback, I shall hold you entirely responsible, Doctor.'

Dr Stanley ignored her, turning instead to Abi. 'Miss Newman! Mrs Mears doubts the wisdom of Freddie taking a walk. But as I'm sure you can see, the roses are returning to his cheeks already.'

'They certainly are,' Abi said, risking the housekeeper's wrath.

'It's as well he rests now,' Dr Stanley continued, still speaking to her, 'but perhaps you could ensure he has a short constitutional each day as long as the good weather holds. In fact, if I am out this way, I might well come and join you.'

He was doing it again. Flirting outrageously. But Abi had to admit it was actually quite flattering, as well as something of a welcome diversion.

'That would be nice, wouldn't it, Freddie?' she said disingenuously.

'Yes! I'd like that!' Freddie agreed eagerly.

'Are you not going to call to see him tomorrow? Ensure that your rash decision to take him outside has not caused him harm?' Mrs Mears asked icily.

'I don't think that will be necessary. Now, Frederick, I suggest you sit out in your chair instead of remaining in bed. You need to be up and about so that you regain your strength and are able to do all the things we talked about, do you not?'

He patted Freddie on the head and the two shared a conspiratorial glance.

'What's all this?' Mrs Mears asked suspiciously.

Dr Stanley smiled. 'Frederick and I have interests in common, don't we, young man?'

'And what would they be?' The housekeeper's tone was sour and sarcastic.

'Freddie leans towards the sciences, as you will know, Miss Newman. You may well be qualified in those subjects, of course, but it occurred to me that I could perhaps be of some use in that regard.'

'That would be a great help,' Abi said quickly, before Mrs Mears could object. 'I'm able to teach him to identify most trees and wild flowers, but that's about my limit, I'm afraid. I don't even know the names of all the butterflies he catches – though I do ensure he releases them again,' she added.

'So you would be happy for me to spend some time with him?' Dr Stanley asked, and when Abi nodded, he turned to the housekeeper. 'You see, Mrs Mears? I do have my uses. Who knows, between us, Miss Newman and I may yet make a doctor of him. While exercise in the fresh air can only sharpen his brain as well as benefiting his health.'

'Well, I hope you know what you are doing,' the housekeeper said shortly. 'Dr Mounty would never allow—'

'But he has handed over Frederick's care to me,' Dr Stanley said smoothly. 'And now I must be on my way. I have other patients to call on.'

Abi couldn't help but feel rather smug at the way the doctor had put the evil housekeeper so firmly in her place. And although she had had misgivings of her own about the wisdom of taking Freddie into the gardens when he had barely set foot to the floor for more than two weeks, she had to admit he did look far brighter.

That was more than could be said for Mrs Mears, whose

expression was thunderous, though it wasn't long before she recovered herself.

'You must at least lie down on the bed and rest for a while, Frederick,' she said authoritatively.

She'd never change, Abi thought. But at least she did seem to genuinely care for the boy's welfare. And one thing was in no doubt – when he was back to his old self, Freddie would be well able to stand up for himself.

A small smile lifting the corners of her mouth, she headed for Imogen's rooms. She couldn't wait to tell her that Freddie had actually been well enough to take a walk. Such good news would surely help her on the road to recovery herself.

Sir Hugh was not in the best of tempers as he worked his way through a mound of paperwork. What did he employ an estates manager for if not to look after the houses in the village? It was his job to arrange for any necessary repairs and maintenance, and it was tiresome of him to expect Sir Hugh to check every invoice – for a new door lock, or emptying a cesspit – and also, in Sir Hugh's opinion, quite unnecessary. As long as the tenants paid their rent and caused no trouble, it wasn't for him to worry about. He had quite enough on his plate with Imogen's problems and his coal mines. And now, added to that, Constance's involvement.

In his present mood, the knock at the study door came as an almost welcome interruption. 'Come!' he called.

'Good day, sir.' It was Dr Stanley. 'I thought you would like to know that Frederick is much improved and was well enough to take a turn around the grounds today. I hope you have no objection to that?'

'Why would I? The sooner he is able to take some exercise the better, in my opinion.'

Dr Stanley nodded. 'My sentiments exactly. Your house-keeper, however, was less amenable to the idea. In fact, she objected most strongly and is warning of dire consequences. I am not at all convinced that she is the best person to be in charge of Frederick's convalescence.'

'She has old-fashioned ideas,' Sir Hugh said. 'You must forgive her for that. But her intentions are good, and she is only doing what she thinks best for Frederick. She is very fond of the boy.'

'Perhaps, and certainly she nursed him well through the worst of it. Nevertheless, I am of the opinion that Miss Newman would be a far more suitable companion for him now. In fact, I have asked her if she will accompany him on a short con-stitutional each day and she has agreed. Subject to your approval, of course.'

'Oh yes, yes. Whatever you think best. We are entirely in your hands, Stanley.'

'Thank you, sir. I will call as often as I am able to ensure that he is progressing as I would hope, and I have promised to share some of my knowledge of the sciences with him. They appear to interest him, and he certainly shows an aptitude for them. Do I have your blessing on that score also?'

'That is very decent of you, Stanley. I'm glad to hear the boy has interests other than getting into mischief. Miss Newman is an excellent teacher, but as far as I am aware, science is not considered a suitable subject for a young lady to be versed in.'

'Indeed.' Dr Stanley hesitated for a moment, then went on. 'And how is Lady Hastings faring? Has she had any more hallucinations?'

'Not to my knowledge. In fact, she has seemed rather better this last week or so, though she still spends most of the time in her rooms.'

'I see. That sounds hopeful. But would you like me to take a look at her since I am here?'

'Not now, Stanley. I'm rather busy, and I think it would be best if I was present when you spoke to her.' Sir Hugh was anxious to get rid of the doctor and finish looking through the paperwork his estates manager had left him.

'As you wish. But you know if you need me at any time . . .'

'I do. Thank you. Now, can you see yourself out?'

'Indeed. Don't trouble any of your servants.'

It sounded as if Mrs Mears's nose had been well and truly put out of joint by Dr Stanley, Sir Hugh thought when he was alone again. Well, good for him. He wasn't afraid to stand his ground, whereas Dr Mounty would very likely have sided with the overbearing woman.

Sir Hugh had no great liking for his housekeeper. Though she was certainly efficient and kept the household running smoothly, he sometimes wished that he had not promised Marigold, on her deathbed, to keep her on. 'It's for me to see that she always has a roof over her head, and is cared for as she cared for me when I was a child,' Marigold had said. Now Mrs Mears was a cross he had to bear, but he would never renege on his promise. Even so, he couldn't help wishing she was more like an older version of Abigail.

A sudden rather unwelcome thought occurred to him. Dr Stanley was always full of praise for Abigail. Had he taken a fancy to her? It would hardly be surprising if something developed between them – they were both very attractive young people. But for some reason Sir Hugh found the very idea of a romance developing between them an unwelcome one.

Oh for heaven's sake! he chided himself. You don't want to lose a good governess, that is all. And that is a pretty selfish way of looking at things.

With a sigh, he dragged his thoughts back to the paperwork that awaited his attention. The sooner it was out of the way, the sooner he could give some thought to the problem of Percival Symonds, and the complications of his own making regarding Constance.

Chapter Nine

Good as her word, Abi accompanied Freddie on his daily walk around the gardens, though on the days when Dr Stanley called to visit, she excused herself, knowing Freddie enjoyed spending time alone with the doctor. On the third occasion, however, he was having none of it.

'Are you avoiding me, Miss Newman?' he asked.

'Of course not! It's just that I thought you were busy teaching Freddie the sciences on your walks,' she said quickly. 'In any case, I have things to do.'

'You know what they say about all work and no play?' he challenged her. 'And,' he added, his ice-blue eyes twinkling wickedly, 'as a poor doctor who mostly sees no one but the old and sick, it would be a great treat to have the company of someone as young and pretty as you. Humour me today at least. I promise to be on my very best behaviour.'

'Oh . . . very well.' Flattered, though rather embarrassed by the compliment, Abi had to admit to herself it would be quite pleasant to be in the company of someone closer to her own age. And really, where was the harm? She didn't think he would try to take liberties, but if he did, she would put him firmly in his place.

'Good!' He steered Freddie towards the door. 'Come along, young man, let's get out into the sunshine.'

'Can we go somewhere different today?' Freddie asked as they left the house. 'I know you favour the lawns and the woods, but I'd like to show you the walled garden. It's one of my favourite places. And yours, isn't it, Miss Newman?'

'It's lovely, yes.' Freddie had taken her there more than once on their daily walks. Even this early in the summer it was a suntrap, and there was already blossom on the fruit trees – miniature apple, pear and plum, and even a peach.

'And where is this walled garden?'

'Hidden away,' Freddie said mysteriously. He started towards the path that led around the house. Abi and Dr Stanley followed as he led the way through the kitchen garden, between neat rows of cabbages and kale. The beans and peas had already been planted, and wigwams of canes erected for them to climb up when they began to grow.

The garden was reached through an archway in the stone wall; as they passed through, the air became fragrant with the scent of blossom.

'How splendid!' The doctor was clearly impressed as the garden opened up before them: a circular path surrounding a central patch of earth containing soft fruit bushes – gooseberry and blackcurrant – and a strawberry bed. The miniature fruit trees were trained against the walls, and on three sides camomile-covered benches took up some of the space between them.

Freddie made for one of the benches and plopped down on it, releasing its fragrant scent, then jumped up again.

'I'm going to look for caterpillars. That's what you wanted, wasn't it, sir?' he said with a cheeky grin at Dr Stanley.

'Freddie!' Abi exclaimed, mortified. But he was already off, leaving the garden at a fast trot.

'Shall we sit down then?' Dr Stanley indicated the camomile bench.

Abi remained standing. 'Did you plan this?'

'No, I swear. It's just more of Frederick's mischief.'

'It's hardly proper for us to be alone, is it?' Abi protested.

'Oh, come on, Miss Newman. We are here now, and this is a very beautiful spot. Do sit down, and we can get to know one another better.'

Abi hesitated, then conceded defeat. 'Oh, very well. But only for a short while. I don't suppose Freddie will be gone for very long, and if he is, I shall go and look for him.'

She smoothed down her skirts, brushed a few clusters of apple blossom from the seat and sat down. Stanley sat too, a little too close for comfort.

'Do you mind, Doctor?' She indicated the far end of the bench.

He laughed, but obliged, moving further away. 'You have a hard heart, Miss Newman. But do please call me Giles. I'm not on duty now.'

'Very well.' Abi smoothed her skirts. 'But if I am to call you Giles, I think you should stop calling me Miss Newman. My name is Abigail, but it's most often shortened to Abi.'

'I see.' He grinned wickedly. 'The thing is, I think Miss Newman suits you. It's the perfect moniker for a governess. Sir Hugh insists on it, so Frederick tells me.'

'You've been talking about me with Freddie?' Abi asked, surprised.

'I've asked him what he knows about you,' Dr Stanley admitted. 'I'm curious as to where you hail from, and what brought you here. But Frederick seems to know very little beyond that his father engaged you when he was expelled from his boarding school. And he likes you, it seems,' he added with a smile. 'That is certainly a feather in your cap.'

'I try to make his lessons interesting,' Abi said.

'I gathered as much. But would it be impertinent of me to ask if you would enlighten me as to how you came to be a governess?'

'It's really not very interesting,' Abi said.

'Nevertheless . . . satisfy my curiosity.'

'My father was a vicar,' Abi began, and went on to tell him of the dame school that had been threatened with closure following her father's death, and how Malcolm had saved it.

'Are you and he sweethearts?' Giles asked.

'Oh no, nothing like that! We are just friends,' she said swiftly.

'So do you have a sweetheart?'

Her heart ached suddenly for the sweetheart she had once had. But there was no way she was going to speak about him, or the tragic events that had torn apart her life, destroyed her dreams and left indelible scars on her heart.

'That's quite enough about me,' she said firmly. 'It's your turn now. Where is your home? Do you have family? And how did you become a doctor?'

'By following in my father's footsteps.' Giles brushed away an apple blossom that had landed on his knee. 'I was fortunate enough to gain a place to study at the faculty of medicine in Edinburgh – it's widely regarded as the crème de la crème. Following that, I joined my father's practice for a while, but I had been schooled in the latest treatments and techniques, while my father is somewhat old-fashioned. I chose to branch out on my own, which is how I came to take up the position as Dr Mounty's junior partner. He is every bit as old-fashioned as my father, but he is nearing retirement, while my father will continue to practise for the next twenty years at least. When Mounty hangs up his stethoscope, I shall take his place and run the practice as I like.'

'I see.' Abi was impressed by his ambition, though it somehow seemed at odds with the casual charm he radiated. 'How did your father react to you leaving?' she asked. 'My own position is somewhat similar, and I have to confess my mother was – and probably still is – very upset.'

'In truth, I think he was glad to see me gone,' Giles admitted. He paused for a moment, then asked: 'How is Lady Hastings faring? Sir Hugh tells me she is much improved, but as her husband, I would expect him to be reluctant to admit just how ill she is.'

'Since Freddie passed the danger point in his illness, she does seem better,' Abigail told him.

'No more episodes of hallucinations?'

She hesitated. Only this morning, Imogen had told her that she had heard Robbie calling to her again in the night, but for some reason Abi was reluctant to share this with Giles. She was saved by the sudden appearance of Prudie Doel, the gardener's wife, propelling Freddie in front of her.

'This young man be clearly better,' she declared, her tone conveying annoyance. 'Up to 'is old tricks, 'e is. I caught 'im puttin' slugs in my clean washing. I'm goin' t' 'ave t' do it all again, thanks to him.'

'Oh Freddie!' Abi groaned. 'I am so sorry, Mrs Doel.'

'I should think so too! Nasty slimy things . . . what 'e needs is a firm 'and. 'E'd be over my knee if 'e were mine, I can tell 'ee.'

'I'll make sure it doesn't happen again,' Abi promised, though she wasn't sure how she could do any such thing. 'Freddie, apologise to Mrs Doel, and think yourself lucky it's not you who has to do the laundry all over again.'

'Sorry, Mrs Doel,' Freddie muttered, but he didn't look very sorry, and Abi thought she caught a smirk on Giles's face, which annoyed her intensely. Really there was nothing funny about Freddie's pranks.

At that moment, the clock in the bell tower chimed the hour – midday – giving her the excuse to bring this encounter to an end. 'We really should go in,' she said. 'Luncheon will be served soon.'

'Just make sure 'e washes his 'ands well, seein' as 'ow 'e's bin messin' wi' them filthy things.' Prudie couldn't resist a parting shot as she stalked away, understandably still furious.

'So how are you going to punish him, Miss Newman?' Giles asked, sounding amused.

'I think a stern warning will suffice this time, given how ill he has been,' Abi said. 'But don't think you can get away with this sort of thing, Freddie. Next time there will be consequences.'

'Yes, Miss Newman. Thank you.'

Giles, as she was now supposed to call him, treated her to one of his wicked smiles. 'You have a kind heart as well as a pretty face, Miss Newman,'

She ignored him. 'Come along, Freddie. Mrs Doel is quite right. You need to wash thoroughly before luncheon.'

With that, she led the way back to the house.

As she tidied herself for the midday meal, Abi's mind returned to Giles's question as to whether she had a sweetheart. If he'd been angling because he was interested in striking up a relationship with her himself, he was going to be disappointed. Her heart still belonged to Connor. Her memories of him were still too vivid. The love they had shared, the precious times together, their hopes and dreams. All shattered. Stolen away. Yet still as perfect as they had ever been, unsullied by time or the harsh realities of life.

Now, as she brushed her hair at the dressing-table mirror, it seemed to her that the face looking back at her was that of her sixteen-year-old self. The naïve young girl, giddy with first love.

Unaware of what lay ahead. Before she could stop them, the memories came rushing in.

The secret meetings with Connor. The walks in sunlit lanes and shady woods, her hand in his. His smile, which lifted her heart. The wonderful flood of warmth when she was in his embrace. The kisses that set her on fire. The day when they had been so desperate for one another that nothing would do but to be as close as a man and a woman could be.

It was a hot summer's afternoon. Connor – a farmer's son – was out on his father's land mending fences to ensure the herd of heifers did not escape when they were moved from the field near the farm, where they had munched through all the grass. He had told Abi where he would be that day, and when her mother had closed the door after the last of the dame school pupils, Abi had said she was going to take a walk, and had gone in search of Connor.

She found him in the meadow that sloped steeply down to the river. He had just finished fixing the last of the weak spots in the boundary fences on three sides; the fourth was left open so that the heifers and Reuben the bull could go down to the river to drink and cool off if the weather became too hot.

The top part of the meadow was visible from the farmhouse and yard, which meant they risked being seen together if they remained there, but further down it was hidden by a fold in the hill, and so they walked down to the water's edge. A few weeks on and the herd would have turned the riverbanks and the lowest reaches of the meadow into a quagmire, but for now the grass was deep and lush. Out of sight of the farm, they could scarcely wait to be in each other's arms, and sank down in the greenery, their weight creating a cool, sweet-smelling nest. The memory of it was so clear that Abi could almost believe she was there again, sunlight dappling through the leaves. She could taste Connor's mouth on hers, feel his hands on her breasts, her stomach, her thighs, and the rising tide of desire that was sweeping her away, allowing her to forget everything but their closeness, and the need to be closer still. Nothing else in the world mattered.

For a while, when it was over, they lay in one another's arms, lost in wonder. Then Connor pushed himself away and sat up. 'I'm sorry, Abi. I am so sorry.'

'No!' She sat up too, straightening her skirts. 'There's nothing to be sorry for. I wanted it too.'

'But we shouldn't have. *I* shouldn't have. Let's hope we get away with it.'

'No one saw us,' she said, then, as she saw his anxious expression, light dawned. 'Oh, you mean . . . ? Surely not! It was only the once!'

'Once can be enough. But don't worry, Abi, I'll take care of you whatever.'

She squeezed his hand, though the thought of what her mother and father's reaction would be made her sick with dread. 'I know you will, Connor.'

It wasn't to be. A week later, Connor was dead, crushed to death by Reuben, his father's bull.

Abi was devastated, too shocked to believe it at first. He couldn't be dead, her love, her soulmate. He was too young to die! It was all a bad dream – it had to be – and soon she'd wake and everything would be as it had been.

But there was no escaping reality for long. Her father was to officiate at the funeral, and through him Abi knew every detail of the arrangements. But when she said she would like to attend, Maisie wouldn't hear of it. 'The family won't want a whole lot of gawpers,' she said harshly, and her father patted her hand and said more kindly, 'Best not, Abigail.'

Did they suspect? she wondered. But it didn't matter now. Nothing mattered but that Connor was dead. She couldn't bear that she would never see him again, walk in the fields and lanes hand in hand, feel his arms round her and his lips on hers, never share the future she had dreamed of. Her whole world had fallen apart, and the void that was left was unbearable.

But worse was to come. Still heartbroken and in a state of shock, Abi paid no heed to the nausea that plagued her – it was hardly surprising given that she cried herself to sleep each night, then woke at three or four in the morning and lay awake until dawn. After a couple of months, she did realise that her courses hadn't come, but put it down to being unable to eat properly and guessed that grief had upset the whole of her system. It was only when she noticed the changes to her breasts, the darkening of her nipples and the tenderness, that she felt the first ripples of anxiety. But she dismissed them. It had only been the once, and her first time. She couldn't be with child. Even when her waist began to thicken, she refused to believe it, pushing it to the back of her mind. It was just too dreadful to contemplate. Connor had said he would look after her if the worst happened, but Connor wasn't here. She would have to face the wrath of her parents and the shame of being a fallen woman all alone, and the thought of it terrified her.

It was Aunt Sukie who first suspected that she was pregnant. She took Abi aside and questioned her. To begin with, Abi denied it fiercely, but when her aunt persisted, she broke down and confessed the truth.

'Dear me, what a kettle of fish!' Sukie exclaimed, then quickly became her usual pragmatic self. 'Well, first your parents will have to be told, and then we can set about deciding what is to be done.'

'I can't tell them!' Abi wept. 'It'll be the death of them!'

'I doubt that,' Aunt Sukie said briskly. 'They'll be shocked and upset, of course, but you can't keep this to yourself any longer. Do you want me to tell them?'

'No!' Abi knew it wouldn't be right for them to hear it from anyone but her.

'Would you like me to be with you then?'

She swallowed hard and nodded. 'Would you?'

'Of course.'

Even with Aunt Sukie there to support her, the confession and her parents' reaction was every bit as dreadful as Abi had known it would be. Maisie was in hysterics – fortunately Sukie had brought smelling salts with her – and though Obediah said little at first, he appeared to have aged ten years in as many minutes.

'Oh Abigail – that it should come to this,' he said at last. 'I know you are not the first young woman to let herself down, but I never expected it of you. Who is this man you have been meeting without our knowledge? Will he be willing to shoulder his responsibilities and make an honest woman of you?'

Choked by fresh tears, Abi was unable to reply, and Sukie answered for her, explaining the tragedy that had occurred.

'Oh, the shame of it!' Maisie wailed. 'Your father a vicar, and you no better than a common slut! No one must know. It would be the ruination of us. Could she come to stay with you, Sukie, until . . .' She broke off, pressing her handkerchief to her mouth.

'Willingly, but I don't think that is a good idea,' Sukie said. 'If she was seen, gossip would spread like wildfire and doubtless reach East Denby before you could say Jack Robinson. It's my opinion it would be best for you to be honest about what has happened. It would be a nine day wonder and then be forgotten.'

'And what would happen to my school? Who would send their children to a house of ill-repute?' Maisie was becoming hysterical again. 'No, there has to be some other way.'

'I'm afraid I don't know anyone who can get rid of the baby,' Sukie said, deliberately blunt, and this, of course, provoked a horrified reaction from Obediah.

'Don't even speak of such a thing, Sukie. No, the best course of action is for Abigail to go into hiding here before her condition becomes obvious. We will explain her absence by saying she is away visiting.'

'And who will deliver the baby?' Sukie asked sceptically. 'The local doctor or midwife? Do you imagine all that could be kept quiet?'

'I have a cousin who used to attend deliveries in her village. She would be discreet.'

'And afterwards? What will happen to the child?'

'I shall make enquiries and arrange for it to go to a good home.'

Throughout all this Abi had remained silent, ashamed that she was the cause of such trouble. But now she could remain silent no longer. 'No!' she burst out, surprising herself. 'No! I can't be parted from my baby!'

Three pairs of eyes turned to her. 'What?' Maisie cried. 'Don't be foolish! You can't keep it! Your life will be ruined, as will ours.'

Abi simply shook her head, spreading her hands protectively over the slight swell of her belly, overwhelmed by a sudden fierce rush of love. She'd felt little harbingers of it before, when the baby had stirred deep inside her, but she had refused to acknowledge them, foolishly trying to pretend that this was not happening to her. Now those same feelings gathered into a flood tide that could no longer be ignored.

The baby she was carrying was Connor's, the only part of him left to her. She would protect it with her life, and she would never give it up to strangers.

'We'll see about that!' Maisie said in her most schoolmarmish tone, but Sukie put an arm round Abi and smiled at her encouragingly.

'Don't worry, my love. Nothing has to be decided now. We can talk it all over nearer to your time.'

'I won't change my mind,' Abi whispered softly but determinedly. And little knew that fate would rob her of any choice.

Tears filled her eyes now as she remembered. The torture of the weeks spent in hiding. Her father barely able to look at her, her mother speaking to her only when necessary, and then in clipped, censorious tones. Her determination to keep her baby and the trauma of not knowing how she was going to manage it. The loneliness. The physical discomfort. And then the fateful day, a month before her due date, when she caught her foot in a ruck in the carpet and tumbled head first down the stairs.

She had been rendered senseless by the fall, but there was no question of the doctor being called. Her parents were steadfast in their determination: no one must see her in her present condition. As she regained full consciousness, Abi was aware that the pain she was experiencing was not only in her head and neck; a nagging ache in the small of her back grew steadily worse until it became clear that her labour had begun. Obediah's cousin, Millicent, was sent for, but by the time she arrived from her home ten miles away, Abi, in agony, and still muzzy from her fall, was vainly attempting to push her baby into the world.

She was only vaguely aware of Millicent rolling up her sleeves and calling for hot water and clean towels, and many hours later, exhausted from her efforts and racked with pain, she had the strangest sensation of standing outside herself as her baby was finally freed and slithered out of her body.

'Is it a boy?' she managed weakly. Somehow, she had been sure from the beginning that it was.

Millicent, fussing over the infant, who was completely enveloped in one of Maisie's towels, didn't reply, and Abi felt a frisson of anxiety that he wasn't crying.

'Is he . . . ?'

'Everything is as it should be,' Millicent assured her. 'Just you rest now.'

Tired out, completely spent, Abi did as she was told. Her eyes closed and she drifted into a deep and dreamless sleep.

It was only when she awoke hours later that her mother told her. Flatly, her voice devoid of emotion. Abi's baby *was* a boy, but he had not survived his long and difficult birth. Had not even taken a first breath. But it was for the best.

'No!' Abi had wept. 'No, no!'

For her mother, a stillbirth brought an end to the nightmare. To Abi, it was the end of the world, a loss from which she had known even then she would never recover.

Nine years ago now, and it seemed like yesterday. Hurt just as much as it ever had . . .

The sound of the gong being struck to announce that luncheon was ready drew Abi out of her reverie. She wiped the tears from her cheeks, finished tidying her hair and went downstairs for the midday meal. But the ache of loss went with her.

Chapter Ten

One morning a few days later, Abi was surprised to find the ground floor a hive of activity. The servants bustled in and out of rooms laden with stacks of dust sheets, overseen by a hatchet-faced Mrs Mears. Peeping into the drawing room as she passed, she saw that the sheets were being draped over the furniture, and guessed what was going on.

'Are the chimneys being swept today?' she asked Imogen as she entered the breakfast room.

'Yes, and I do so hate it!' Imogen admitted. 'The sooty smell is horrible, and that's not the worst of it. It upsets me dreadfully that those children are forced to climb up inside, poor little souls.'

'It has to be done.' Sir Hugh was loading his plate with kidneys and bacon from the chargers on the sideboard. 'If it is not, the soot could catch alight. It's believed that was the cause of the Great Fire of London.'

'Perhaps. But those little mites . . . Last spring that horrible man lit a fire in the grate to make his apprentice climb faster. I hope you are not using the same sweep this year. I just cannot bear the thought of it.'

'I couldn't say.' Sir Hugh carried his loaded plate to the breakfast table and took his seat. 'Mrs Mears made the

114

arrangements. But if it upsets you so, Imogen, you don't have to witness it. It's a fine day; I suggest you take a walk, get some fresh air.'

Imogen bowed her head, conceding defeat, but it was all Abi could do not to echo her sentiments. She knew, of course, that master sweeps used climbing boys – and sometimes girls – but the practice hadn't reached her home village. Unlike this grand house, most of the cottages and terraced houses were two-storeyed and low-ceilinged, so that they – and the vicarage – could be serviced by a local man who toured the streets with his brushes in a handcart calling out 'Sweep! O! Sweep!' to advertise his presence. Now the full horror of the wretched existence of these poor children made her blood run cold.

'Why don't we take Freddie for a nature ramble?' she suggested. 'So many wild flowers are in bloom now that weren't before he was ill. We could walk along the drive to the road – the fields will still be wet with dew.'

'I should like that,' Imogen said gratefully. 'Then I need not see the poor lamb at all. And by the time we return, it will all be over.'

To Abi's dismay, as they made their way along the lane, two figures appeared walking towards them: a stocky man wearing a battered top hat, and a thin urchin boy struggling with a bundle of brushes and scrapers almost as big as he was. The chimney sweep and his boy. With thick hedges on either side of the lane, there was no way they would be able to avoid passing them. Imogen's pace slowed. Abi glanced at her and saw that she was biting her lip, her face screwed into an expression of distress. She took hold of her arm and instructed Freddie to take his mother's other hand.

'Why?' Freddie asked scornfully.

'Just do it.'

Unused to his governess using such a sharp tone, he did as he was told, though he gave her a puzzled look.

As they came closer, the sweep roughly pushed his apprentice in front of him so as to pass the trio, who were taking up most of the lane, and Abi nodded to him. 'Good morning.'

The man touched the brim of his hat and walked on, but Freddie, fascinated, turned to look after them. 'Why is that boy wearing ragged clothes?' he asked loudly.

'Shh! They'll hear you!' Abi cautioned.

'But why?'

To Abi's surprise, it was Imogen who answered him. 'You must not blame him, Freddie. Not every child is as fortunate as you. And if he did have a good waistcoat, shirt and trousers, they would soon be spoiled when he climbs up our chimneys.'

'He's going to climb up our chimneys?' Freddie's eyes were round, as if he had never heard of such a thing before. Abi realised that of recent years he would have been away at school when the annual spring-clean took place, and when he was small, he had probably been kept in the nursery, out of the way of all the soot and dust. 'Can I go back and watch?'

'No, you cannot,' Imogen said firmly. 'Miss Newman is going to give you a lesson in nature study.'

Abi was pleased that Imogen had recovered herself so quickly, and hoped it was a sign that she was on the mend. She looked around for something to point out to Freddie, and spotted a rabbit sitting in the middle of the lane up ahead.

'Look, Freddie! He'll make a run for it when he sees us!'

Just as she spoke, the rabbit bounded towards the hedgerow, disappearing with a flash of his white scut.

'Oh, I wish I could have caught him!' Freddie exclaimed in frustration, the sweep and climbing boy forgotten.

'I'm afraid you can't begin a collection of rabbits, as you did with butterflies,' Imogen said, and she and Abi exchanged knowing smiles. Trust Freddie!

The walk had been a pleasant one, long enough, Abi thought, to allow the sweep to have finished his work and left with his unfortunate apprentice. But as the house came into view, she was surprised to see both a pony and trap and a horse-drawn wagon pulled up on the drive at the front steps. The pony and trap she recognised as Dr Mounty's; the wagon she had never seen before. A burly man in working clothes was emerging from the house. He threw a tool bag into the wagon and climbed into the driving seat.

Imogen clutched at Abi's arm, anxious suddenly, and bemused. 'What is happening?'

'Don't worry. I'll find out.' Abi headed for the wagon, calling to the driver to wait.

The man picked up the reins, glowering at her. 'I 'aven't got all day, yer know.' His coat, Abi noticed, was thick with plaster dust and what looked like soot.

'Lady Hastings would like to know why you are here,' she said, a feeling of foreboding gnawing at her stomach.

'Had to knock down a bleedin' wall. Climbing boy got stuck in the chimney.'

Abi's blood ran cold. 'Oh no! Is he—'

'Couldn't say,' the man interrupted her impatiently. 'He's out, that's all I can tell yer.' With that, he flicked the reins and the horse lumbered off.

This was going to upset Imogen dreadfully, Abi knew. Goodness, she felt sick herself. She turned to see Freddie standing close behind her. He must have heard everything. But before she could stop him, he was dashing towards his mother, eager to be the bearer of the news.

'Mama! What do you think? The sweep's boy got stuck in the chimney!' he cried excitedly.

Imogen turned pale, her eyes huge and horrified. 'Tell me it's not true!'

'I think it must be,' Abi said gently. 'Freddie, take your mother into the garden, and I'll go and find out how he is.'

'I want to see!' Freddie objected.

'You'll do as I say and take care of your mother.'

'No, I have to know the worst.' Imogen's voice was shaking but determined. 'I'm coming with you, Abi.'

Full of trepidation, they set off towards the house, Freddie running ahead of them as fast as his plump legs would carry him. At the door, however, he hesitated, waiting for Abi and his mother, as if he had suddenly realised the seriousness of the situation and was apprehensive of what he might see.

Imogen took his hand, and with Abi leading the way, they went into the house.

In the hall, where everything was covered in a thin layer of dust, Mary, Handley and old Briggs, all clearly shocked, stood at the foot of the staircase, looking up. They turned as the little party entered, and Briggs ducked his head and touched his forehead as was his custom.

'Milady . . .'

'Oh, such goings on you wouldn't believe!' Mary burst out. ''Tis terrible! I wouldn't go up there if I was you.'

'I have to, Mary. This is my home.' Imogen spoke quietly but firmly.

'You don't have to, Imogen.' Abi didn't usually address Lady Hastings by her Christian name in front of the servants, but now she spoke without thinking. 'Let me go. It will only upset you if something dreadful has occurred.'

But there was no dissuading Imogen, though she did allow

Abi to go first. Mary attempted to stop Freddie following them, but he ignored her and, with excitement getting the better of his nervousness, pushed ahead of Abi and dashed along the corridor towards the sound of voices. Moments later, Abi heard him scream shrilly. Though her heart was pounding in her chest, she hurried up the last few steps, leaving Imogen to follow at her own pace.

The commotion was coming from Freddie's room, and when Abi reached it, the scene that met her eyes was one of utter chaos.

A heap of hastily gouged-out stones lay beside a gaping hole in the wall where the fireplace had been, but to her relief, she saw that the climbing boy was sitting up on a blanket that had been laid on the floor, with another draped around his thin shoulders. Dr Mounty was kneeling beside him, tending to his torn and bleeding hands and arms as he coughed and gasped for breath. Mrs Mears, her face set in a grim expression, towered over the little tableau, while the chimney sweep, arms folded defiantly across his chest, looked on. But it was Freddie who was the centre of attention now – a Freddie who kicked and struggled as Sir Hugh attempted to restrain him.

'My room!' he yelled furiously. 'Just look at my room! My fort! My soldiers! What's happened to my soldiers?'

'Frederick!' Mrs Mears fixed him with an angry gaze. 'Stop that at once!'

Almost instantly, Freddie stopped struggling, though his cheeks, red as ripe strawberries, still bulged with fury. He was more frightened of the housekeeper than he was of his father, Abi realised. Or had more respect for her, at least.

'That's better,' Sir Hugh said sternly, releasing his arms. 'Your fort and soldiers aren't damaged – we moved them out of the way. Now, are you going to behave yourself, or do I have to take a slipper to your backside?'

Freddie hung his head, but not before Abi had seen the tears glistening in his eyes.

'But where am I going to sleep?' he muttered piteously.

'We'll not worry about that now,' Sir Hugh said shortly. 'You should be ashamed of yourself. Now go downstairs, sit quietly, and think yourself lucky it was not you who was stuck in the chimney.'

'But Papa—'

'No arguing. Off you go.'

Chastened, Freddie slunk away, and once again everyone's attention turned to the climbing boy, who was still coughing hard.

'Oh, can you not do something for him?' Imogen had entered the room unnoticed by her husband; now she spoke, her voice tremulous but full of desperate pleading.

Sir Hugh swung round. 'Imogen! You shouldn't be here either. It's only fortunate you were out for the worst of it. We thought the boy was lost, but thank God he has survived and is responding well. Is that not right, Mounty?'

Dr Mounty looked up from his patient. 'He's alive, certainly, thanks to the builder being able to tear down the wall to get to him. But his airways are clogged with soot and dust. He'll struggle until he can clear them, I fear. And it's possible the damage may be lasting.'

'Huh! We'll see about that!' The chimney sweep pushed himself away from the wall, grabbed the boy by his shirt collar and hauled him to his feet. 'Ye'll be fit fer work t'morrow, my lad, or ye'll have no supper for a week.'

Dr Mounty began to protest, but it was Imogen – an Imogen Abi had never seen before – who rushed to the boy's defence.

'No! I won't have it! This poor child is not to be put up a chimney ever again!'

The sweep turned on her belligerently. 'An' 'ow else is 'e goin' to earn 'is keep? 'Twasn't my fault 'e got stuck up that chimberley. 'Tis too narrow be far.'

'Then why did you make him climb it?' Sir Hugh demanded.

''Twas you wanned it cleaned,' the sweep said truculently.

'Not at the expense of this poor boy's life.' Now that the worst of the danger was over, Sir Hugh was becoming furiously angry. 'You thought only of how much more you could charge for an extra chimney. Well, I may tell you – you need not expect to be paid at all. And before you complain, let me tell you that you are fortunate indeed that I shall make no demand for recompense for the damage to my wall, which will have to be rebuilt.'

''Twasn't me as sent fer that bloke to knock it in,' the sweep argued, but more quietly. He would never get the better of the gentry, he knew, and might very well end up worse off. 'An' as fer 'im . . .' he glowered at the boy, who was still coughing intermittently and trying to clear his throat, ''e's gettin' too big ter be any use t' me anyways. 'E can go back to the orphanage where 'e belongs.'

With that, he let go of the boy, who sank to the ground once more, and pushed past Abi and Imogen. His boots could be heard clattering along the passage and down the stairs.

'I don't wanna go back ter that place!' the boy spluttered, tears gathering in his inflamed eyes.

'And nor will you!' Imogen declared. 'We can find him work, can we not, Hugh? In the stables, perhaps, or the grounds?'

'Possibly. We'll talk about it later. He'll certainly have to remain here until he's recovered from his ordeal.' Sir Hugh turned to the doctor. 'What should we be doing with him?'

'A hot bath, keep his wounds clean and dressed, and most importantly, get some good food into him. As I said, his airways will have to clear themselves.' Dr Mounty straightened up with some difficulty, repacking his medical bag. 'He'll live to fight another day, but only if he's sent up no more chimneys.'

Sir Hugh gave the elderly man a hand to help him to his feet. 'Rest assured, we will do what we can for him. Perhaps Dr Stanley could call tomorrow to ascertain how he is faring.'

'I'll make sure of it.' The doctor paused. 'I sincerely hope you were not offended by my asking Stanley to take over the care of your family. I am not as young as I used to be, and I find the long journey here troublesome.'

'Of course I am not offended, Mounty. Young Stanley explained the problems you have, and I quite understand. But I must tell you how grateful I am for your ministrations over the years,' he added tactfully.

'It has been an honour.' Dr Mounty turned to Imogen. 'Now, perhaps I should take a look at Lady Hastings. All this must have shocked her badly.'

'There's no need, really!' Imogen protested, but Abi could see her hands were trembling.

'I think it would be a good thing,' she said gently.

Sir Hugh stepped in. 'Allow the doctor to take a look at you, Imogen. Better safe than sorry.'

'Shall we go to your room, milady?' Dr Mounty started unsteadily for the door, clearly exhausted by his exertions. No wonder he was ready to turn over the family's care to his young partner, Abi thought.

'Will you attend to the boy, Mrs Mears?' Sir Hugh asked when they had left. 'I would imagine some of Frederick's older clothes will fit him, and when he is clean and tidy, find him something to eat.'

Mrs Mears pulled the blanket from the boy's shoulders, revealing a strawberry birthmark just below his hairline and a mottled scar covering almost all of his lower arm. Abi was horrified. It looked to her as if he had been burned at some time, and the thought that it might have been caused by his cruel master's mistreatment made her shudder.

'I'll take him to the scullery. Come on, lad, pull yourself together.' Mrs Mears was her usual impatient self, and Abi cringed, guessing how roughly she would treat the poor little climbing boy.

'And I'll find Freddie,' she suggested. Though he had behaved very badly, she had some sympathy with him. It must have been a shock for him to find his room in such a state, and she knew how jealously he protected his fort and his soldiers, which were now scattered all over the floor.

In the event, there was no need for her to go in search of him. He appeared in the doorway, somewhat shamefaced, clearly having been listening outside in the passageway.

'Well, Frederick, and are you prepared to behave like a gentleman now instead of a heathen savage?' Sir Hugh demanded.

'Yes, sir. I am sorry. And please, may I look for my soldiers?'

'Are they really all you are concerned about?' His tone was still stern, but Abi thought she detected a note of what might have been amusement. 'A boy of your own age half dead, a gaping hole in the wall, doctor's bills to be paid and luncheon delayed so that I will either have to miss it or be late for an appointment this afternoon, and you can think of nothing but a few tin soldiers.'

His eyes met Abi's over Freddie's head, and she felt it again – that connection between them. 'Boys!' he said, raising an eyebrow.

Then he returned his attention to Freddie and the moment had passed. 'Find some clothes you no longer wear and take them down to Mrs Mears, who is in the scullery attending to the poor little chap, and then you can look for your missing soldiers.'

With that, he turned abruptly and left the room.

Abi's heart was pounding against her ribs, making her feel quite breathless. What in the world was happening to her? She hadn't felt this way since . . .

'Let's find some clothes for the boy as your father asked, Freddie,' she said, but her voice was unsteady, and though the butterflies were settling, to her intense discomfort the shadow of them remained.

By mid afternoon, some semblance of normality had returned to the house, though Imogen had been badly upset again when Sir Hugh had insisted Freddie would have to sleep in Robbie's room – it was too dangerous for him in a bedroom with a gaping hole in the wall. Sir Hugh had snatched a hurried lunch and left for his appointment, whatever that might be, and though neither Imogen nor Abi had much appetite, Freddie had tucked into a huge portion of beef and kidney pudding, followed by apple pie and custard – proof that he had recovered well from the measles and unfortunately was likely to regain all the weight he had lost when he was ill. Abi couldn't help being anxious about Imogen, though. The shock of what had happened had clearly taken its toll, and the fierce way she had stood up to the chimney sweep and insisted his boy was to stay at Bramley Court had shredded her nerves. As she picked at a meagre serving of pie, Abi complimented her on her determination to rescue the lad from his wretched existence, and something of the same fire tightened her features and shone in her eyes for a few minutes.

'Poor children like him have no one to care for their wellbeing,' she said fiercely. 'Ruthless and greedy men take them out of the orphanage and treat them as slaves. They are paid only a pittance, or maybe nothing at all but their board and lodging, and that will be no more than a filthy cot to sleep in and a hunk of bread and jam to eat. It's pure wickedness – I wish I could save all of them. But at least that is one little boy who will not have to jeopardise his health – his very life! – climbing chimneys.'

'But where will he live?' Abi asked. She couldn't imagine that he would become a part of the household.

'Oh, Hugh will arrange something,' The fire had gone out of Imogen as swiftly as it had sparked. She had done what she needed to do, and now she seemed exhausted.

'I think you should go to your room and rest,' Abi told her. 'All this will have done you no good at all.'

'I expect you are right.' She smiled weakly. 'You usually are, Abi.'

Before long, the peace was shattered once more as Rex Doel, the gardener, and the lad who assisted him arrived with brushes and shovels to clear up the mess, moving the loose bricks from the middle of Freddie's room and piling them in a corner, and sweeping up the soot and plaster. Freddie kept a watchful eye on them to be sure they didn't damage his fort.

There was no point in trying to do any lessons today, Abi decided. She had at last received letters from home – short and sweet from Maisie, who was too busy with her dame school to write much, and long and gossipy from Malcolm. She really should reply, but she could think of nothing but the dramatic events of the day, and she couldn't face going over all that just yet. A book might take her mind off things, she thought, and went to the library to look for one. But she couldn't concentrate on that either, and she was staring into space, the book open in her lap, when she heard voices in the passage outside.

'So, he's off to see one of his lady friends, I suppose,' said Mrs Mears, sharply disapproving as ever. 'And while he's tickling his fancy, it's left to me to make arrangements for that boy to stay with Rex and Prudie and decide what's to be done about Frederick's sleeping arrangements. If he'd treated Lady Marigold this way, you can be sure I wouldn't have stood for it.'

'Oh, surely he wouldn't . . .' Mary sounded perplexed. 'Not a gentleman like him! Why, if it's true, his father would be turnin' in 'is grave.'

Mrs Mears snorted. 'Gentlemen can be the worst, as you should know, Mary. You've worked for them long enough. But mark my words, if Imogen is put in the asylum – which is where she should be – he'll have another woman here before you've had time to change the sheets on the bed. That Constance Bingham, I wouldn't be surprised, and if not her, another one, just as bad . . .'

Their voices faded as they moved away along the passageway. Shocked, Abi snapped her book shut. She'd forgotten all about Miss Constance Bingham. Now it came flooding back. The imperious command to close the door. The muted conversation in the hall as she'd been hustling Imogen up the stairs. Sir Hugh's preoccupation when she'd gone to tell him what had happened at the lake. But surely there was an innocent explanation for Miss Bingham's visit? Abi couldn't believe Sir Hugh would carry on an affair under his wife's very nose, and at a time when she was so in need of his love and support.

Yet hadn't Imogen confided that things were no longer as they had once been between them, and that now her husband seemed to have no time for her? And it was easy to see that Sir Hugh – good-looking, well-to-do and charismatic – would have no trouble in attracting a lady friend if he so chose. Indeed, he had made Abi's own heart flutter when she'd fancied something unsaid had passed between them.

She frowned and bit her lip, then firmly pushed the unwelcome thoughts away. What Mrs Mears had said was just another example of her spite, and hopefully Mary wouldn't believe a word of it. She got up, returned her book to its place on the shelves, and left the library for a walk in the gardens, where she hoped the fresh air would clear the bad taste that the housekeeper's words had left in her mouth.

Chapter Eleven

Although she had taken the sleeping draught Dr Mounty had left her, Imogen was restless, tormented by bad dreams that brought her to full wakefulness. But there was no escape from the horror of the day's events. Even though she had not witnessed the worst of it, visions of the poor little climbing boy stuck in the chimney plagued her as she tossed and turned. In her mind's eye she saw his scrabbling feet and bleeding hands as he tried in vain to gain purchase in the narrow flue, felt his panic, heard his frantic cries and his rasping struggles for breath as soot and dust clogged his mouth, his throat, his lungs.

Unable to bear it any longer, she pushed aside the covers and went to the window that looked out over the grounds to the west side of the house. She was still muzzy from the sleeping draught, and the moonlight seemed to be playing tricks with light and shadow as the trees and flowering bushes swayed in the breeze that had risen. Across the lawns she could just glimpse the gardener's cottage. The climbing boy, whose name it seemed was Jimmy, had been lodged with the Doels, though when he was employed here permanently, as Hugh had promised, he would move into one of the attic rooms that provided the servants' quarters. A light was burning in one of the upstairs windows of the cottage, and it worried Imogen. Had the boy

128

taken a turn for the worse? She gripped the windowsill, gazing into the flickering moonlight until her head began to swim and she had to fumble her way back to sit down on the bed.

It was then that she heard it: the soft child's voice calling to her in a whisper: 'Mama!'

'Robbie!' Breath caught in her throat and she pushed herself upright. 'Oh Robbie, you're here! Come to me, my darling!'

No answer. Nothing but silence. But the shadows cast by the moon through the wind-blown branches of the trees danced and swayed over the varnished boards of her bedroom floor, and she could almost believe Robbie was there, playing one of his favourite games, when he would hide and she would pretend she could not find him.

'Oh Robbie, you are so naughty! But I see you!' she called softly in the same teasing tone she had used back then. 'Come out, you little imp.'

As she waited, her skin prickling with anticipation, she heard something else, a sound she recognised though she could scarcely believe her ears. Had she drifted back to sleep and was dreaming it? She pinched herself to be sure it was not so. But she felt the nip of her fingernails through the fine lawn sleeve of her nightgown, and still she could hear it. The whirr and rattle of Robbie's wind-up toy running across the bare boards in his room.

Her breath came out on a long, soft sigh and she pressed her hands to her mouth as a feeling of awe and wonder suffused her. Though she had almost convinced herself it really was Robbie who called to her in the night, at the same time a small voice of reason had whispered it could not be. But now she was in no doubt.

Trembling with joy and excitement, she crossed to the connecting door, which was slightly ajar – she never closed it properly. Just as she reached it, she heard a thud as the toy collided with a piece of furniture, whirred frantically and fell silent. She pushed the door wide and stepped into the room, which was illuminated, just as hers was, by moonlight. She'd expected to see Robbie on his hands and knees reaching for the toy, but if he was, he must have crawled under the bed. She took a step closer, and saw that the bedclothes were humped over what looked like a small body.

'Robbie! You *are* hiding, you scamp!' She approached the bed, a giggle bubbling in her throat, and lifted the coverlet, ready to tickle him as she used to do, then froze as realisation dawned. The head on the pillow was not fair, but dark. Not Robbie at all.

All of a rush, she remembered. Hugh had insisted Freddie should sleep in Robbie's room because it wasn't safe for him to be in his own room. Tears sprang to her eyes and her throat tightened with a sob that threatened to choke her. Her hand pressed to her mouth, she dashed out into the passageway, closing the door behind her, and leaned against the wall, where she allowed the wail to escape. Why was Robbie playing these games with her? Where *was* he? It was more than she could bear, to feel him so close and not be able to reach him . . .

'Imogen?'

She looked up so sharply that her neck seemed to snap, and another sob escaped her.

'Oh my dear!' It was Abi. She crossed the passageway, put an arm round Imogen's shaking shoulders and led her to the sanctuary of her own room.

Abi was walking in a shady glade where sunlight filtered through the leafy branches. She could feel the pressure of a man's hand holding hers, and she was happy – so happy! Connor! she thought. But when she looked up, the face that smiled down at her didn't belong to Connor. It was Sir Hugh. Surprised, but with a feeling of utter contentment, she smiled back. A pheasant rose in the undergrowth ahead, startling her, and the dream faded, though the aura of happiness remained . . .

She had woken with a start. For a moment she lay trying to hold on to the aura of the dream, wishing it could have gone on, though at the same time she felt ashamed and guilty. What in the world was happening to her that she should dream such a thing? It must have been her own conscience that had woken her. It had been telling her this foolishness must stop . . .

And then she had heard it. Loud sobbing. It hadn't been her conscience that had woken her at all. Thrusting the last of the dream aside, she had pulled on a wrap and hurried out into the passageway. Imogen was leaning against the wall, her fists pressed against her mouth, tears streaming into them.

'Oh milady, whatever is it?' Abi asked, but Imogen was crying so hard she was unable to speak. Gently Abi led her back to her room, and sat beside her on her bed. She laid a comforting arm around Imogen's shaking shoulders. 'Shh! Don't upset yourself now. It's all over.'

'No!' Imogen looked up at her wild-eyed. 'It was Robbie! I heard him! He was playing with his wind-up toy! I went to find him, and . . . Oh Abi, he was in his bed and hiding under the covers! But when . . . when I turned them back, it wasn't him at all!'

She dissolved into tears again. Abi pressed a clean handkerchief into her hand, feeling totally helpless. It was as if a dam had been breached, and she could do nothing but hold Imogen while she wept.

There was no doubt she truly believed she'd heard Robbie's wind-up toy, and when she had seen a hump under the bedding, she'd thought it was him. Had she still been half asleep? Abi wondered. Or were the delusions getting worse?

Or . . . could what she heard have been Freddie, playing one of his tricks then hurrying back to bed and pretending to be asleep?

At last Imogen's sobs were quietening to soft snuffles. Abi found her another clean handkerchief and sat down again beside her. 'Better?'

Imogen blew her nose and bowed her head. 'Thank you, Abi. I don't know what I'd have done if you hadn't . . . I was so upset . . .' She broke off. 'You understand, don't you?'

'There's no need for thanks,' Abi said. 'And yes, I do understand something of what you are going through.'

Once before, she had come close to telling Imogen of her own secret sadness but had held back, partly because it was too painful, and partly because she had been afraid she might be dismissed as an unsuitable governess for Freddie if the family knew she had borne a child out of wedlock. Now, however, she felt that sharing her story might show Imogen that she really did understand what it was like to lose a child, and decided that it was worth the risk.

'When I was very young, I lost a little boy too,' she began hesitantly

Imogen's puffy red eyes widened. '*You?*'

'It bears no comparison with your loss, of course . . .' Abi swallowed hard, and went on haltingly. 'I never even got the chance to hold him, but I loved him with all my heart, and I always will. That's why I do understand, in some small way.'

'But what happened?' Imogen was engaged now, interested, but not shocked as Abi had feared.

'He was stillborn. That's why I say there's no real comparison.

If he had been the age Robbie was when you lost him, I don't think I could have borne it.'

'Oh Abi . . . I never guessed . . .' Imogen gripped Abi's hand tightly in hers.

'Why would you? But I have thought of him a lot today because of that poor climbing boy. My son would have been much his age if he had lived.'

'I am so sorry. No matter that you never saw him grow, you carried him for nine long months. Of course you still grieve for him. How could you not?'

Abi could feel tears pricking her own eyes and blinked them away. In that moment, she could have wept every bit as hard as Imogen had, but this was not the time.

'If he had lived, I wouldn't be here now,' she said, forcing a smile.

'You would be a wife and mother.'

'Not a wife. Connor, my sweetheart, died before our baby was born. Before he even knew he was to be a father. We would have wed, I'm sure, but it was not to be. My mother and father were shocked, horrified and desperately ashamed of me, of course.' She smiled faintly. 'My father, as you know, was a man of the cloth. But in spite of everything, I was determined to keep my little one and raise him. How could I be parted from my baby – and Connor's?'

'But how would you have survived?'

Abi shrugged slightly. 'I don't know, but I would have found a way. As things turned out, I never had the chance.'

Imogen's eyes were sad, yet warm and sympathetic. 'I am so sorry you lost your baby, my dear Abi, but selfish as I am, I am glad you are here, and I do not feel so alone. We'll help each other, you and I.'

'Of course. Always.'

It had been Abi's intention that when Imogen had been distracted sufficiently to become calmer, she would ask gently if she was quite sure Freddie had been asleep when she had uncovered him. But now she realised she simply could not do it. She couldn't take the risk of upsetting her again.

'Why don't you go back to bed and try to get some rest?' she suggested. 'We can always talk some more tomorrow.'

Imogen bit her lip. 'Will you . . . come with me?'

'Of course.'

Abi accompanied her back to her room, tucked her in, and smoothed a lock of hair from her forehead. 'Go to sleep now, milady.'

'Thank you, Abi.' Imogen sounded drowsy. The sleeping draught must be kicking in once more.

When she was sure she was asleep, Abi crossed to the door to Robbie's room and peeked in. Certainly Freddie appeared to be slumbering soundly. She closed the connecting door quietly; if he was playing tricks, she wanted to ensure Imogen was not disturbed again tonight. Then she returned to her own room, fell into bed, and cried herself to sleep.

Imogen did not appear for breakfast next morning, and Mrs Mears reported that she had asked for a tray to be taken to her room, as she had apparently spent a restless night. There was a gleam of something that might almost have been satisfaction in the housekeeper's eyes as she said it, and Abi wondered if she knew what had happened and was glorying in it. Perhaps the same thing had occurred to Sir Hugh.

'That is only to be expected, given the unfortunate events of yesterday, don't you think?' he said, giving her a look that conveyed disapproval of what she appeared to be implying.

Setting aside his plate, he finished his cup of tea and rose to leave the breakfast room, and as he did so, Abi caught his eye. 'May I speak to you in private, sir?'

Sir Hugh checked his timepiece. 'I have a business meeting to attend shortly, but I can spare you a few minutes if it is important.' This morning he was all formality, and given the dream she had had last night, Abi was grateful for it.

'It is important,' she said.

With a quick word to Freddie to go to the library when he had finished his breakfast and continue with an essay she had set him, she followed Sir Hugh to his study.

'I'm sorry to delay you, but I am very concerned about Lady Hastings,' she began.

Sir Hugh, who had been sorting paperwork into a satchel, looked up, a shadow crossing his face. 'Yesterday's unfortunate events upset her badly, but it's not so unusual for her to request a tray in her room rather than joining me for breakfast when her nerves have been unsettled. And now that it's all over and the boy is safely with the Doels, I'm hoping she will begin to recover.'

'It wasn't just that she didn't sleep well, I'm afraid,' Abi said. 'I was up half the night with her – she was in a terrible way. She thought she'd heard Robbie playing with his wind-up toy and went to look for him. Then she became quite hysterical when she couldn't, of course, find him.'

'Oh Miss Newman – what can I say?' Sir Hugh's tone was distressed, and at the same time apologetic.

'It was no imposition. I'm only glad I was there for her,' Abi said quickly.

'And I can only thank you.'

For a brief moment it was there again, that connection between them, this time in their shared concern for Imogen, before he collected himself.

'These hallucinations do seem to be worsening,' he said grimly. 'Thinking Robert is calling to her is one thing, but to actually imagine he is playing with his toys . . .'

Abi hesitated, uncertain whether she should say what was on her mind. 'I'm probably being ridiculous, but from the way she spoke, it didn't sound like a hallucination. I can't help wondering . . . It couldn't have been Freddie playing one of his tricks on her, I suppose?' she ventured.

Sir Hugh frowned. 'He can be a scamp, it's true, but I find it hard to believe he could do anything so cruel.'

Abi bit her lip. It was only natural that Sir Hugh wouldn't want to believe his son was capable of such a thing, and she wished she hadn't suggested it.

'No, it is undoubtedly all in her tortured mind,' he went on after a moment. 'But Dr Stanley seems no more able to treat her than Mounty, and I fear we are reaching the point where we shall have no option but to seek treatment from experts in the field. Perhaps even have her confined for her own safety.'

'Haven't I been telling you for months that the only place for her is the asylum?'

Abi spun round. Mrs Mears was in the doorway, hands clasped in the folds of her black serge gown and a satisfied smirk twisting her thin lips. She must have been just outside, listening to everything they had been saying.

Sir Hugh's reaction was quick and furious. 'It is not your place to tell me anything, Mrs Mears. And in future you will refrain from eavesdropping if you value your position here.' He turned to Abi. 'I'm sorry, Miss Newman, but I must go now. I am already late for my appointment.'

'Where would we find you in case of emergency, sir?' Abi asked.

'I'm not sure where I will be later in the morning. But I will be home for luncheon.' He picked up his satchel and moved towards the door, forcing the housekeeper to step aside, and as Abi followed, she quite distinctly heard her mutter, 'We all know where you are going, though.'

She bristled. Surely the horrible woman wasn't suggesting he was going to visit a lady friend while his wife was so ill? But Sir Hugh appeared not to have heard her. He left the house, and a few moments later the clatter of hooves on the drive told Abi that his horse must have been saddled up ready and waiting for him. She would have liked to go and spend some time with Imogen, but she really should start on Freddie's lessons. Wondering what mischief he might be getting up to while left unsupervised, and still desperately worried about the lady who had become her friend, she headed for the library.

To her surprise, far from getting up to mischief, Freddie was at his desk, writing furiously.

'Goodness, can this be the young man who professed to dislike studying English?' she asked, summoning a brisk tone.

'I'm writing a play about Robbie,' Freddie said, barely glancing up from his work.

'What a lovely idea! I shall look forward to reading it.' But Abi couldn't help wondering what had made Freddie think of his little lost brother just now. He almost never mentioned him, and had certainly never before written about him.

'Have you almost finished?' she asked, wondering if she would have time to mark his arithmetic book.

'Not really. Can I go on with it?'

Far be it for me to interrupt his literary flow, Abi thought.

'Certainly.' She settled herself in the captain's chair at the big oak desk. But although she opened the arithmetic book, pen in hand, she found it impossible to concentrate, annoyed as she was by Mrs Mears's spite, and worried by the talk of Imogen having to be admitted to an asylum. They were dreadful places, she had heard, and she found it hard to believe that Hugh would actually have her committed to one. But there was no doubt that Imogen was convinced Robbie wanted her to go to him, and that meant she was a danger to herself.

She wondered again if it could be Freddie playing tricks on his stepmother, slipping out of bed and back in again, then pretending to be asleep. Though his father had been quick to defend him, she couldn't help thinking it was just the kind of thing he would find funny, and it would be quite in keeping with the disdain he sometimes showed for the woman who had taken the place of his beloved mother. But what would have put such an idea in his head? Yes, Imogen's fantasies had been talked about in front of him on the day he had been taken ill with measles, but surely he would have been too poorly to take much notice, and in any case, she had begun hearing Robbie calling to her before then. If Freddie was behind it all, Abi thought it was more than likely that someone else had suggested it to him. But who? And why?

The most likely person, in her opinion, was Mrs Mears. She was certainly nasty enough, and she made no secret of her resentment of Imogen. What was more, it was clear that this morning wasn't the first time she had suggested the asylum was where Imogen should be. Could it be that she was trying to get rid of her by making her so ill that there really was no alternative, no matter how little Sir Hugh wanted it? Cunning as she was, perhaps she had suggested it to Freddie as a prank, and he was playing his tricks for the sheer fun of it.

The more Abi thought about it, the more likely it seemed she had hit upon the answer. She tried to dismiss the small seed of doubt that perhaps the whole thing really was in Imogen's imagination. Was she clutching at straws in blaming Freddie and the housekeeper? Anything rather than admit that Imogen really was so ill that there could be no way back for her?

She chewed on her pen, troubled and confused, and wondering what, if anything, she could do. Should she raise the subject with Freddie? But he would simply deny it. As for accusing Mrs Mears outright, she couldn't do that without proof. No, for the moment she couldn't see any solution but to remain silent and vigilant. And if Imogen was being tormented deliberately, she would do everything in her power to put a stop to it.

Chapter Twelve

Sir Hugh kicked Hector to a gallop. The horse responded eagerly, and as it covered the ground with long, easy strides, Hugh began to relax, the tension in his muscles easing and the fog that had been clouding his brain dispersing.

His meeting with Constance Bingham had not gone as he had planned. When she'd sent word asking him to meet her at her father's house, it had felt like a summons. She was already beginning to get her claws into him, and he didn't like it. He remembered all too clearly how she had clung to him when he'd ended their relationship, how difficult it had been to shake her off, and how she had tried to worm her way back into his life after he had married Imogen. He'd never have agreed to her offer to help him if he hadn't been so desperate to get access to the land his father had leased to Percival Symonds, and now he felt trapped between the devil and the deep blue sea. He had decided that when he met her today, he would put an end to it.

But she had wound him in again.

'I expect you would like to know why I asked you to meet me,' she had said when the door of the parlour had closed after them.

Judging by her teasing tone, her carefully rouged lips and – most of all – the daringly low cut of her violet silk gown, Hugh could hazard a guess. But for the moment he bit his tongue.

'You have news for me?'

'Indeed I do. Come and sit beside me, and I will tell you.'

Hugh remained where he was, thrusting his hands into the pockets of his breeches. 'Don't play games with me, Constance.'

She looked at him from under her lashes, pouting flirtatiously. 'You are a hard man, Hugh Hastings. Very well, I'll tell you. I have had documents drawn up that will end the lease.'

Hugh frowned. 'That's an expensive business.'

'Not if you know the right people.' She smiled smugly. 'Anyway, they are done, and you have no need to worry about the cost. As for the signing . . . when Percival is in his cups – which is frequently – I shall have no problem in persuading him to scribble his name in the appropriate place.'

'And witnesses?' Hugh asked.

'Something else you do not need to worry about.'

For a long moment he was lost for words. This had quite taken the wind out of his sails. If she could carry through on her plan – and with her wiles he had no doubt that she could – he would have what he had wanted for so long. If he said what he had intended to say to her today, that would be the end of it.

'Well, Hugh?' Her lips curved, the smile of a cat facing a saucer of cream. 'What do you think of that?'

'I can scarcely believe it, Constance. That you would go to so much trouble on my behalf.'

She shrugged. 'Is that not what friends are for?'

The moment for a decision had arrived. Should he play along for a while longer? Or should he tell her he no longer needed her assistance and walk away from all his plans for his coalfield? No, he couldn't do that. He had wanted his land back for too long. He could handle Constance. He'd done it before, and he could do it again.

'I don't know how to thank you,' he said.

'Oh, I'm sure I can think of a way.' She ran her tongue over her red lips. 'How is your wife? Still tiresome, I imagine.'

Instantly he was regretting his decision. 'Tiresome is a harsh word,' he said. 'She is ill – very ill. Tormented still by the loss of our son.'

Constance tossed her head, annoyed that Hugh was not taking her bait. 'Pathetic!' she said scornfully. 'Really, Hugh, I don't know what possessed you to marry her. You were lonely, I suppose. Men often are when they lose a wife, especially one they were besotted with.'

Hugh stiffened, seething inwardly, at himself as much as at Constance. 'I really must leave you, Constance. I have another appointment to keep. Will you keep me informed with regards to the lease?'

She tipped her head to one side, teasing again. 'Oh, I expect so. And do be sure not to have other appointments arranged when next we meet.'

Now, as he rode hell for leather away from her, Hugh was still cursing himself. If he'd offended her, it was always possible she would abandon the mission she had set herself; though knowing her as he did, he didn't think she would give up so easily. Well, he would just have to deal with the situation when the time came. But he was determined on one score. She would never get what she wanted. He despised her for what she was doing, the sly way she was setting out to cheat Percival Symonds, even if it was what he himself wanted. Despised her for everything she was. How dare she speak so of poor tormented Imogen! Imogen was worth a thousand Constances.

But he had to admit she might have been right in what she had said about him being too hasty in marrying again. He had always known that he could never love Imogen in the way he had loved Marigold, but she was sweet-natured and pretty as a picture, from a well-respected family. Most important of all, he had known she would be a wonderful mother to Frederick. He had vowed to do everything in his power to make her happy, and he still believed that if it were not for the loss of Robbie, it would all have turned out well. But their different ways of dealing with their overwhelming grief had created a dangerous chasm between them. And now an attraction he had no right to be experiencing was threatening to fill the emptiness.

Despite her good looks, at first he'd only thought of Abigail Newman as a solution to the problems with Frederick. But the more he got to know of her, the more her bright mind and her compassion for those around her had drawn him to her. When he dared to think about it, he feared that she was beginning to present a challenge to the high standards he had set himself, and he could not, would not, succumb.

With grim determination, he turned his thoughts to Imogen and the different ways they had been affected by Robert's death. He had been devastated just as she had, but he had found solace in his plans for the expansion of his mining enterprise. Moving forward was the only way, in his opinion. Whereas she . . .

Grief was driving her to madness, and Hugh feared there would be no way back for her.

Constance smiled grimly as she watched Hugh ride away. Oh, he was a hard nut to crack, but she would manage it in the end. She was no longer the girl she had been when he had left her the first time. Now she was a woman who could always find a way to get what she wanted. When he was alone again, as he would be, he would be putty in her hands.

As he disappeared in a cloud of dust, she smoothed her skirts and turned her thoughts to the other part of her plan.

* * *

As he had promised, Sir Hugh was back in time for luncheon, though he seemed preoccupied. Imogen put in an appearance, but she ate little and spoke less.

Abi watched her anxiously, and when the meal was over and Sir Hugh had left for his office, she made a suggestion.

'Why don't we go for a walk in the garden? The fresh air would be good for you, and Freddie could do with some exercise too.'

To her surprise, Imogen agreed, and taking Freddie with them, they went out into the sunshine.

'We've been so lucky with the weather this year,' Abi said as they crossed the lawn.

'If only Robbie were here with us to enjoy it.' Imogen was still in a world of her own.

As they approached the walled garden, they heard voices, and when they turned in through the gateway, they found Rex Doel, who was inspecting the fruit trees, together with his wife Prudie, and Jimmy, the climbing boy, whom they were looking after until he recovered from his ordeal.

Instantly Freddie, who had been lagging behind and beating the long grass beside the path with his butterfly net, overtook them, making a beeline for the boy, though he managed to avoid being in proximity to Prudie. Abi couldn't contain a smile of amusement. Clearly the ticking-off Prudie had given him over the slugs in the laundry had left its mark. As for Jimmy, with his ragged clothes and roughly shorn haircut, Freddie had never before met anyone quite like him. She suspected too that the boy's brush with death only added to the fascination, and she couldn't deny she was curious herself about his history, and how he had come to be in the orphanage.

'Oh milady, I've just brought the lad out for a breath of fresh air. I hope you don't mind,' Prudie greeted them, looking flustered, as if she felt they had no right to be there.

'Of course I don't mind, Prudie. He is so pale, and I'm sure the sun will be good for him.'

'At least you can see 'is face now 'e's 'ad a good wash. 'Tis no wonder 'e's pale, when he's bin spending most of his time up chimberleys and the rest of it covered in soot.'

'Indeed.' Imogen turned to the boy. 'How are you feeling today – Jimmy, isn't it?'

Jimmy nodded, twisting a cap that must belong to Rex between his hands – it was clean, and looked as if it was far too big for him. Abi caught sight of the livid scar on his arm and looked away quickly. He was probably embarrassed by it, but she couldn't help wondering how it had happened.

'Yes, miss. Not so bad, miss.' He answered Imogen's question surprisingly chirpily.

'Not miss – milady,' Prudie chided him.

'It doesn't matter,' Imogen said with a smile, and Abi was pleased to see how much more like herself she seemed talking to the wife of a servant and a child than she ever did with Sir Hugh. 'Well, you certainly gave us all a dreadful fright, Jimmy. And you must have been terrified too.'

'Yes, miss . . . milady.'

'What is it like going up chimneys?' Freddie asked, unable to contain himself any longer. 'Is that how you came to hurt your arm?'

'Freddie! How can you be so rude?' Imogen admonished him, horrified. 'Why don't you take Jimmy to look for butterflies? He'd like that, I expect, and you are so good at finding them.'

'Yes, but Miss Newman won't let me keep them.' Freddie pouted.

'Quite right too.' Imogen exchanged a glance with Abi. 'Off

you go then – but not too far. And do please be nice to Jimmy.'

When the two boys were out of sight, she turned to Prudie. 'So how has he been? He seems to have recovered remarkably well given his dreadful experience.'

'The doctor thinks 'e's on the improve, praise be. 'E's a tough one, I'll give 'im that,' Prudie said. 'But for all that 'e's no more than a step out of the gutter, 'e's well behaved, and sharp, too. 'E can even read a bit, from what I can see of it.'

'That's astonishing!' Imogen shook her head in disbelief. 'Where did he learn, I wonder? I wouldn't think they'd have taught him in the orphanage.'

'Don't ask me, milady. I can't get nothin' outta 'im about where 'e was afore. But 'e wouldna learned there, that's for sure. They'd 'ave 'ad 'im working for 'is keep every hour God sent.'

'Perhaps he'll open up and tell us more when he becomes used to us,' Imogen said.

'You be goin' a keep 'im then?' Prudie asked.

'We wouldn't dream of letting him go back to a life like that,' Imogen said decisively. 'When he is fully recovered, we'll find him a room in the servants' quarters, and Sir Hugh will decide what work he can do. In the meantime, I am most grateful to you for looking after him. I only wish I could do something to help all the poor boys like him. But at least I can take comfort in knowing Jimmy will not be climbing any more chimneys.'

'I 'ardly like t' ask . . .' Prudie hesitated. 'But would 'e be awright wi' Freddie fer a bit? Then I can get on wi' gettin' the dinner.'

Imogen smiled at her. 'Yes, of course. You must have things to do.'

'Thank 'ee, milady.' Prudie bobbed a half-curtsey and hurried off, and Abi and Imogen went in search of Freddie and Jimmy.

As they turned on to the lawn, they spotted the two boys

running about near the flower beds. Jimmy was wielding Freddie's precious butterfly net, and Imogen commented that they must be getting along well if Freddie had been prepared to lend it to him.

'Company of his own age will be good for him,' Abi said.

Imogen nodded. 'I was thinking the same thing. And it seems Jimmy is a clever boy. Fancy being able to read a few words! We should nurture him, and I'm wondering . . . how would you feel about giving him lessons alongside Freddie? Would it be possible? Hugh wouldn't want Freddie's education to suffer, of course, but if you could manage them both, I'd like to think we were able to give the boy a chance in life. Who knows – he might once have had a good home, and ill fate has robbed him of that.'

'It would cause no problem for me.' Abi was touched by Imogen's kindness. 'I was used to classes of many more than two pupils when I was teaching at my mother's dame school. Freddie would be well ahead of him, of course, but I could put in some extra hours to help him catch up.'

Imogen nodded, smiling. 'That's good of you, Abi. I shall speak to Hugh at once and suggest it.'

Abi could scarcely believe the change that had come over her, and she found herself remembering what Imogen had once said – that little boys were very precious. Perhaps in all of them she saw the son she had lost, and tried to do for them what she would have done for him. Certainly she always took Freddie's part, although he often treated her disgracefully, and now she had another chick to take under her wing.

It could be the saving of her, Abi thought.

Anxious to waste no time, Imogen left Abi in the garden watching the two boys play and hurried to the study, where she knew she would find Hugh.

An ancient map was spread out across his desk and Sir Hugh was poring over it.

'Imogen.' He looked up, his finger still marking the spot he was interested in – the boundaries of the land that was leased to Percival Symonds. 'Is something wrong?'

'No . . . It's just that I wanted to speak to you about Jimmy, the climbing boy. He's a clever lad, it seems, and I am wondering if perhaps he could share Freddie's lessons. Abi – Miss Newman – has no objection. She has even offered to give him extra tuition in her own time to make up for all the schooling he has lost.'

Sir Hugh was frowning. 'I'm not sure that is a good idea, Imogen.'

'But it would be so nice to know we had given him the start in life that he has been denied,' Imogen went on enthusiastically. 'And he and Freddie seem to be getting along together very well. I think it would benefit Freddie too, to have a friend of his own age.'

'I hardly think the boy would be a suitable friend for Frederick. He may well lead him astray,' Sir Hugh said flatly. 'And as for them taking lessons together, at the very least he would be a distraction, and Frederick, I'm afraid, is easily distracted. I'm sorry to disappoint you, Imogen, but what you are proposing is a step too far. I have already agreed to find work for him, but that is as far as I am prepared to go.'

Tears welled in Imogen's eyes as she realised further argument was useless. Her chin dropped to her chest in an effort to hide them. 'Thank you for hearing me out,' she managed, then left the study, utterly deflated.

Abi delivered Jimmy back to the Doels' cottage, then, leaving Freddie still on his butterfly hunt in the garden, went into the house just in time to see Imogen emerging, clearly upset, from Sir Hugh's study.

She hurried towards her and saw that her face was wet with tears.

'It's no good,' Imogen said forlornly. 'He won't hear of it. He thinks Jimmy would be a bad influence, lead Freddie astray, distract him from his studies.'

In Abi's opinion, Freddie was the one likely to lead Jimmy astray rather than the other way round, though she could understand Sir Hugh's fear that his lessons might suffer. But she didn't think it was a good idea to discuss this in the hallway, where they could be overheard. She slipped a hand beneath Imogen's elbow, led her to the library and closed the door.

'Don't upset yourself, Imogen. At least you tried,' she said consolingly.

'I did so want to be able to do something for the poor little boy,' Imogen went on. 'I cannot understand why Hugh should be so set against it.'

'Would you like me to speak to him?' Abi offered, thinking it was a dreadful pity Imogen was upset again just when she had seemed to be getting over yesterday's fright and her broken night's sleep. 'If I can convince him that having Jimmy sit in won't be to Freddie's detriment, perhaps he might change his mind.'

'Oh would you, Abi? He's far more likely to listen to you than he ever does to me nowadays. But maybe this would not be the best time. He hates being interrupted when he's working.' Imogen paused, her face brightening. 'That could be the reason he wasn't amenable to my idea, couldn't it? If he was annoyed with me . . .'

'Perhaps that's it,' Abi said. 'Let's sit down, shall we? I'll ring for some tea. That will make you feel better, I'm sure.'

She pulled on the bell rope, then took a seat beside Imogen on the small sofa. A few moments later, Mary appeared in answer to the summons, and was soon back with a tray of tea and a plate of biscuits.

'You see, Jimmy makes me think so much of Robbie,' Imogen said when the maid had left again. 'I cannot help imagining – supposing it were Robbie in that position? I want to do this for him. In his memory.' She took a sip of her tea and set her cup down on the occasional table beside the sofa. 'I truly thought I would find him last night,' she said, after a moment. 'He was playing a game – hide-and-seek – teasing me. But next time might be different.'

Abi sighed silently. As if it were not bad enough that Imogen was convinced her little lost son was with her, hiding behind a veil, worse still was that she had got up in the middle of the night to search for him. Who knew what could have become of her, wandering about in a half-asleep state? She could easily have fallen down the stairs, or toppled over the banister if she thought she saw him in the hallway below and leaned over. And there was always the risk that she might go into Freddie's room, where the wall had been torn down to free Jimmy. The thought of her tumbling down the chimney was a terrifying one.

'I don't think you should go looking for him, Imogen,' she said carefully. 'If he is playing games, it will only encourage him. What you must do is remain in bed and wait for him to come to you.'

Imogen's face clouded again. 'Do you really think so?'

'Yes,' Abi said emphatically. 'He'll tire of the game soon enough.' She might be bolstering Imogen's fancies, but if it was the only way to stop her from wandering in the night, it was a price worth paying.

'Perhaps you are right. He is such a little imp.' Imogen smiled faintly, then returned to the subject of the climbing boy's education. 'You will speak to Hugh about Jimmy sharing Freddie's lessons, won't you?'

'I will. Just as soon as he is free,' Abi promised. 'And I'll do my best to get his agreement.'

The tea was finished now, though the biscuits remained untouched.

'I think I will go for a rest,' Imogen said, standing up and smoothing her skirts. 'With so little sleep last night, I am feeling very tired.'

'And I will find Freddie. He's been playing outside for quite long enough, and there is still time for us to spend an hour with his books before getting ready for dinner.'

The two women left the library. As Abi stood for a moment watching Imogen climb the stairs, she became aware of someone behind her. Hearing the rattle of keys and smelling the musty odour of Mrs Mears's heavy black gown, she spun round. The horrible woman was regarding her with an expression of scorn.

'Oh my, Miss Newman, you have such a high opinion of yourself, don't you?' she hissed. 'But you may not be quite as clever as you think. If you continue championing her ladyship, you may very well find yourself in the same position. And that, I promise you, is not a good place to be.'

Determined as she had been not to be intimidated, the dreadful things the housekeeper had said and her thinly veiled threat had shaken Abi badly. The woman exuded evil from every pore, and Abi wondered once again if she could be behind the night-time happenings that were causing Imogen to sink deeper and deeper into a state of delusion and mental torment. Could it be that she was taking her revenge on Imogen for being the mistress of Bramley Court in the place of her beloved Marigold? And if she was successful in her endeavours to see Imogen incarcerated in a madhouse, would she then turn her attention to Abi? From the very beginning she had made it clear that Abi was not welcome here, and the bonds Abi had formed with both Imogen and Freddie had only made things worse.

If Mrs Mears set out to get rid of her too, Abi had no doubt she would find a way to do it. It would be something quite different, of course – Abi wasn't emotionally frail as Imogen was, and she wasn't given to letting her imagination run away with her. No, most likely the housekeeper would try to discredit her in some way. Perhaps she would accuse her of theft, or something else that would be cause for dismissal, and since she seemed to hold some sway over Sir Hugh, he would no doubt believe that Abi was guilty.

Abi winced at the thought of her employment being terminated, and the prospect of having to return home in disgrace. Yet there seemed something even darker in Mrs Mears's threat, something unimaginable. Far-fetched as it sounded, she couldn't help believing there was nothing the housekeeper was incapable of.

With an effort she thrust the disturbing thoughts aside. She no longer felt like an hour's teaching, but she would go in search of Freddie anyway – she wanted to ensure he released any butterflies he might have caught.

As she neared Sir Hugh's study, she saw that the door was no longer closed, but ajar, and hesitated. Did it mean that he had finished whatever it was he had been working on, and if so, might this be a good time to speak to him about Jimmy, as she had promised Imogen?

She approached cautiously, her slippered feet making no sound on the polished tiles, and peeked inside. Sir Hugh was there, but he wasn't working. Instead, head bent, elbows on his desk, he was massaging the back of his neck with both hands.

Flustered and horrified that she had witnessed such a private moment, she backed away, but too late. Something must have alerted him to the fact that he was no longer alone – perhaps Abi hadn't been as quiet as she had thought – and he called out, 'Miss Newman? Is that you?'

She moved into the doorway, her cheeks reddening with both guilt and embarrassment. 'I'm sorry, Sir Hugh. I didn't mean to disturb you . . .'

'No apology is necessary. Come in.'

Sir Hugh looked tired, and not at all like his usual self, his hair tousled and his cravat askew. She couldn't have chosen a worse moment.

'Don't be shy,' he said, as if sensing her hesitation. 'I have a very good idea as to why you are here. No doubt my wife has asked you to plead the case for allowing the climbing boy to attend Frederick's lessons.'

'Actually, I offered,' Abi said. 'Her heart is set on it, and I think that taking an interest in his welfare would be good for her.'

'Let us hope you are right.'

Abi's eyes widened. 'You mean . . . ?'

He nodded. 'You may tutor the boy if you so wish, providing Frederick's education does not suffer.'

'Thank you. I won't neglect Freddie – Frederick – I promise.'

'That's settled then. I expect you will be anxious to convey the good news to my wife.'

Abi took that for a dismissal, and was turning away when she felt his hand on her arm. 'It is I who should be thanking you. I cannot tell you how grateful I am for all that you do. For Imogen, for Freddie, for . . .' He broke off, looking directly at her with a small twisted smile, as if he had been about to say 'for me', and had thought better of it.

'I'm happy to do what I can,' Abi managed.

A potpourri of unfamiliar emotions swirled within her as she left the study and climbed the stairs. His touch still tingled on her skin. Her pulses raced. Breathless excitement trembled in her stomach, as if she were standing on a cliff edge and the rock was crumbling away beneath her feet, along with something that might almost have been tenderness for the vulnerability she had glimpsed in this usually commanding and self-confident man.

And guilt.

How could she for one moment be feeling these things? Sir Hugh was her employer. More importantly, he was Imogen's husband. It was wrong, so wrong. Somehow she had to rid herself of this madness.

She stood for a long while in the shadows at the bend of the stairs, waiting for her breath to steady before she went to tell Imogen the good news.

Chapter Thirteen

In East Denby, the knock at the vicarage door came in the early evening. Malcolm Rayner was at his desk in the little front room, working on his sermon for Sunday's Matins; it was not going well, and he wasn't sorry to put down his pen and go to answer it. It would most likely be for him. Maisie rarely had visitors in the evening, while many of his parishioners called when their working day was done. It could be someone who wanted to arrange for banns to be called for a wedding, or to ask him to include a sick relative in his prayers; or it might be his churchwarden with some concern relating to the church.

There was a stained-glass panel in the front door of the vicarage, and usually when someone called, Malcolm could see a shadowy silhouette through it. This evening, however, there was only the glow of the setting sun. The visitor must be a child or – heaven forbid – Dolly Green, a woman who stood no more than four feet tall and was, in Maisie's words, 'not all there'. His heart sank at the prospect of having to endure her inexplicable ramblings; even struggling with his sermon was preferable to that.

He grappled with the heavy bolt that he kept meaning to oil but never seemed to get around to, turned the cast-iron knob and opened the door. To his surprise, there was no one there. It must have been the local lads playing knock-out ginger, he surmised, and grinned wryly as he imagined them daring one another to do the deed, then scooting away. About to close the door again, he happened to glance down, and to his surprise saw a carpet bag on the doorstep.

Puzzled, he opened the door wide again. The bag was loosely fastened with what looked like woven curtain ties, so it was impossible to see what was inside – but what on earth was it doing here? And who had left it? He bent and picked it up; it was feather-light, but it was wobbling, almost as if whatever was inside was moving.

Those scamps must have captured a cat or a squirrel and thought they would give him – or Maisie, more likely – a fright. He carried the bag to the low stone wall that bordered the garden, set it down carefully and loosened the ties, then stood clear, half expecting a furry creature to leap out. But that didn't happen, and the scent that was emanating from it was certainly not an animal smell, but slightly sweet and metallic, not something he immediately recognised. Cautiously he opened the bag wide, and gasped in shock.

Lying on a piece of old sheet and wrapped in a crocheted shawl was a tiny baby.

A moment's panic gripped Malcolm. Apart from performing baptisms, he didn't think he had ever held a baby, and then they were placed gently in his arms, where it was easy to cradle them while signing a cross on their little foreheads with holy water. Sometimes they cried and wriggled, but the mother and godmothers were always close at hand to take over. Never, ever had he had to pick one up, and he was afraid that if he tried, he would drop it. But Maisie would know what to do even if it was more than twenty years since she'd fed and bathed her own baby.

Carefully he lifted the bag by its handles and, supporting it with his free hand, carried it up the path and into the house.

'Mrs Newman!' he called as he kicked the door shut behind him. 'Mrs Newman! Come quickly!'

Maisie appeared in the kitchen doorway, wiping her hands on her apron – from the delicious smell emanating from behind her, Malcolm guessed she had been baking.

'What's up? What have you got there?'

'It's a baby.'

'*What?*' Maisie was incredulous, as if she thought he had taken leave of his senses – or had been drinking communion wine. 'A *baby*?'

'A baby,' Malcolm repeated. 'Somebody has left a baby on our doorstep.'

'Lawks-a-mussy!'

''Tis very young, I'd say.' He thrust the bag with its precious contents at Maisie. 'Needs . . . Well, I don't know what it needs. Can you . . . ?'

'Oh, give it here.' After only a brief hesitation, Maisie took the bag from him, carried it into the kitchen and set it down on the table, dispersing little clouds of flour she hadn't yet got around to wiping away. 'Well, you're right about it being young. Newborn, I'd say.' She gesticulated in the direction of a wooden cupboard. 'Fetch me the ironing blanket – you know where it is.'

Malcolm did as he was told, and Maisie lifted the bag to allow him to spread the blanket over the table.

'Let's have a look then.' She took the baby out, clucking her teeth as she did so. 'Newborn all right. Not even cleaned up properly, poor little mite. You didn't see who left it, I suppose?'

'No – there was nobody there when I answered the door,' Malcolm told her.

'Well, you'd best go into the village and fetch Queenie Clegg. She'll see to it.' Queenie Clegg was the one to send for when it came to delivering babies or laying out the dead. 'And you'd better have a word with Dr Carter while you're about it. Somewhere not so far off, there's a woman in need of attention.'

'I'll go now.' Grateful to be able to do something of use, Malcolm put on his jacket and left the house.

On the road linking it to West Denby in the one direction and the small town of Stoneham in the other, the village of East Denby sprawled like the strands of a spider's web into the shallow valley below. Beyond it the hills rose steeply, wooded, then opening out onto flat pastureland, which, it was said, had been the site of a bloody battle in the time of the Civil War. Certainly, where the open ground met the woods, there were long, uneven strips of ground that might once have been dug as trenches.

Queenie Clegg lived in one of a rank of cottages on a lane immediately below the steepest part of the hillside. In winter it was not unknown for rainwater to come rushing down, passing straight through the cottages and turning the lane into a quagmire, but with the recent fine, dry spell, the ruts that remained caused Malcolm no problem, just as long as he watched his step.

Queenie's cottage stood out amongst the others as being by far the best kept. The door and window frames had been freshly painted, the knocker polished to a high sheen and the doorstep freshly scrubbed, the sign of a woman who was a stickler for cleanliness. Malcolm lifted the latch on the little picket gate, walked down the path between a small lawn and neat flower beds and knocked at the door.

For what seemed like an age there was no response. He knocked again, longer and louder. He was beginning to worry that Queenie might be out, attending a confinement, perhaps. He would find her husband, Art, in the local alehouse, no doubt, but discovering Queenie's whereabouts would be no help if she was in the throes of delivering a baby, and he didn't know what he would do then.

He was about to give up when he heard footsteps from within, and the creak of the latch being lifted. The door opened and Queenie was standing there, as neat and clean as her cottage, with a big apron wrapped around her grey cambric dress.

'Vicar!' She seemed surprised to see him. ''Ave you bin 'ere long? I was out the back, so I wouldn't 'ave 'eard you knocking.' *Out the back* probably meant she had been in the privy at the bottom of the garden, Malcolm thought.

'Don't worry about it,' he said. 'I'm just glad to find you at home.'

'So, what can I do for 'ee?'

'We have a . . . situation.' Malcolm ran his finger around the inside of his clerical collar, which felt uncomfortably sticky. 'I'm here because we are in need of your help. With a baby.'

'A baby?' Queenie's astonishment showed in her face.

'A baby,' Malcolm repeated. 'It's a newborn, and it has been left on our doorstep.'

Queenie's hand flew to her throat. 'Oh my Lord! Whatever next!'

'It's an imposition, I know, but it needs attention, and Mrs Newman and I know nothing about such things. Whereas you . . .'

'You want me to come and see what's what, is that it?'

'If you would.'

'Course I will. Just let me get me things an' I'll come with 'ee.'

Leaving Malcolm standing on the doorstep she bustled back indoors.

It wasn't long before she emerged wearing what looked like another clean apron and carrying a bag. Malcolm took it from her, and as they walked along the lane, he asked, 'Who could have done such a thing, do you think?'

Queenie tutted. 'Somebody who couldn't think of any other way, poor soul.'

'Well, yes,' Malcolm agreed. 'A family with more mouths than they can afford to feed, or a young woman in trouble. Can you think of anyone that might apply to?'

'Can't say that I can. The only folk I know who's expecting are those that 'ave booked me for their due dates.'

That made sense. But Malcolm was thinking that whoever had left the baby on the vicarage doorstep would have been trying to cover up their pregnancy. They wouldn't want to advertise the fact that there was an unwelcome baby on the way if they intended to abandon it.

'I 'aven't noticed anybody getting fatter, either, if that's what you're thinking,' Queenie said. 'An' believe you me, I can spot that sort o' thing a mile off.'

'I'm sure you can.' Malcolm lapsed into silence. Queenie either couldn't or wouldn't express an opinion as to who the baby might belong to. She was, he knew, the soul of discretion. But on this occasion, he was inclined to believe her.

That meant that the poor mother didn't live in East Denby. But she couldn't come from far away if she knew where to find the vicarage – the safest place she could think of to leave her child, he supposed.

They were approaching the turning to the lane that led to the doctor's home.

'I think I should have a word with Dr Carter while I'm here,' Malcolm said. 'If you don't mind walking the rest of the way alone, I'll call on him now.'

'Course I don't mind,' Queenie replied briskly. 'I'm used to being out on my own all hours, an' it's not even properly dark yet. I'll go on to the vicarage, an' you go and see the doctor. Let's just hope he can throw some light on it all.' She paused, then added: 'But if you should 'appen to see the constable, I wouldn't mention anything about it to 'im yet, or they'll be whisking the poor babe off to the orphanage afore you know it.'

By the time Malcolm got back to the vicarage, he could see that Queenie had everything under control. The baby – a boy – had been washed, wrapped up tightly in a binder, and dressed in a gown she had brought with her. He was lying quietly on a blanket on the sitting room sofa, and seemed to be asleep.

'Is the doctor comin' to 'ave a look at 'im?' Queenie asked.

'He didn't want to come out tonight.' Malcolm didn't want to be so uncharitable as to relay his impression – that Dr Carter had been drinking. 'He said he'll see him in the morning if we take him to the surgery.'

'Hmm.' Queenie tutted, and Malcolm guessed she had a pretty good idea what state the doctor was in without being told.

'But how will we get him there?' an agitated Maisie asked. 'And what's going to happen to him until then? We can't keep him here! He'll want changing, and feeding. I can't—'

'Don't you worry your head about that. I'll take 'im 'ome wi' me,' Queenie said decisively. 'I'll look after him till we can find out where he belongs or till it's decided what's to be done with him. Dr Carter didn't have any idea who the mother might be, I suppose?'

Malcolm shook his head. 'No. But really, Mrs Clegg, are you sure?'

Queenie shrugged. 'I can't see any other way outta this. My Art won't be best pleased, but 'e'll 'ave to like it or lump it. This little 'un's far too young to be in the orphanage. I don't care for the way they treat the babes there. And we got no way o' getting 'im there tonight anyway.'

Maisie crossed to the fireplace, lifted a china jar from the mantelshelf and tipped some coins out onto the table.

'Let me give you something, Mrs Clegg. I wouldn't want to see you out of pocket.'

'Don't be daft! I've got everything I shall need,' Queenie said impatiently, and Malcolm hoped Maisie hadn't offended her.

'But what about milk?' Maisie persisted. 'Won't you have to pay a wet nurse?'

'Nah. One o' my mothers 'as got plenty more'n she needs – she'll be only too glad to see some of it go where 'tis needed. I'll manage fine wi' me pap bottle. What I could do with, though, is some help gettin' the babby home. Vicar? Would you mind giving me a hand?'

'Of course. I'll take your bag if you can carry the baby.'

'Oh, I'll carry 'im awright. I don't want you droppin' 'im!' She chuckled. 'Let's get 'im wrapped up then and be on our way.'

'Thank you, Mrs Clegg,' Maisie said.

She sounded mightily relieved, Malcolm thought.

'I'll make some enquiries tomorrow to see if I can discover who the baby belongs to,' Malcolm said as he and Queenie walked back to the village. 'I'll go over to West Denby, and Stoneham too. Someone might be able to shed some light on it.'

'Try the village shops,' Queenie suggested. 'There's bound to 'ave bin talk, and the shop's a hive of gossip. That's 'ow I'm sure it can't be anybody 'ere in East Denby, unless they've bin keeping it very quiet. Could be a young girl, o' course. Sometimes they can get away with hiding it until the very last. Or they don't even realise they're in the family way. There was one lass –

Mary Pickering's girl – an' until Dr Carter got called in for what they thought was stomach pains, nobody had any idea of what was goin' on. Poor Mary got the shock of her life when the little 'un put in an appearance. They kept 'er, though, give 'em their due. She's five years old now, an' her mother's married to the lad who was the cause of all the trouble, with another little 'un and a new baby on the way. 'Tis all blown over an' forgotten now. A nine day wonder. To tell the truth, I don't know why folk get so worked up about it. 'Tis only nature, after all.'

They had reached Queenie's cottage by now. 'Don't you worry any more, Vicar,' she said, shifting the baby onto her shoulder. 'I can take it from 'ere.'

'I'll see you safely inside,' Malcolm insisted, unlatching the gate.

'I'm fine, really. I don't want my Art givin' you an earful, an' he might when he sees what I've got 'ere.' Queenie pulled a rueful face.

'Well, let me open the door for you at least.'

He preceded her down the path, unlatched the door and pushed it ajar.

'Right, let's face the music.' Queenie stepped inside.

'I'll be in touch,' Malcolm said. 'Let you know if I find out anything, and see how things are going with you. And really, Mrs Clegg, I can't thank you enough for what you're doing.'

Queenie smirked over the top of the baby's head. 'Truth to tell, Vicar, I'm rather enjoying it.'

When he got back to the vicarage, Malcolm was surprised to find Maisie still up. She was usually one for an early bed.

'What a to-do!' Her voice was thick, and Malcolm thought her eyes looked puffy and red. Either she was very tired, or she had been crying.

'Don't upset yourself, Mrs Newman. The baby will be well looked after now, Mrs Clegg will see to that.' He went to the dresser and reached for a mug. 'I'm going to have a drink of milk. Would you care for one?'

'Thank you, but no.' Maisie got up from her chair, looking a bit sheepish. 'I've had a small port, and now I am going to bed.'

'There's no harm in that,' Malcolm assured her. 'It will help you sleep. It's been quite a night.'

'You're right there. I'll say goodnight, then.'

'Goodnight, Mrs Newman.'

Malcolm went to the kitchen and poured his milk, surprised that Maisie should have been so affected. It was upsetting to think of some poor girl so desperate that she would abandon her newborn baby, and worrying to think that she might be in need of medical attention, but it wasn't like Maisie to become emotional about things that weren't of personal concern to her. He'd only ever seen her cry when Abi had left.

He took the mug of milk to his usual chair in the parlour and sat down, stretching out his aching legs. It would be a while before he was able to sleep, he knew – this whole business would play on his mind and keep him awake. But tomorrow he would try to find whoever had left the baby on his doorstep and do what he could to help the poor soul.

Chapter Fourteen

'You've done well, Jimmy.'

The climbing boy had just spent his first day sharing Freddie's lessons. Now he coloured slightly with pleasure at Abi's praise. 'Thanks, miss.'

The change in the lad was startling. Dressed in some of Freddie's cast-offs, his face clean, and the accumulation of soot, grease and grime washed out of his hair, he looked a completely different boy. He was still pale from lack of exposure to sunlight, and thin – the clothes hung on him even though it was at least a year since Freddie had outgrown them – but that was nothing that fresh air and good food wouldn't take care of.

His whole demeanour was changing too. It would be a while before his diffidence completely disappeared, but already he was standing taller, and Abi had seen the hint of a twinkle in his brown eyes, which were fringed with long lashes any girl would envy. When his confidence was fully restored, he might be something of a scamp, she thought. And certainly he was bright as a button. She'd set him some simple sums while Freddie was working on his fractions and decimals, and he'd managed them with ease. He could read almost as well as Freddie, and write, although his letters were round and painstakingly formed, as if his early education had come to an abrupt end when he was perhaps four or five. But he had certainly had lessons at some time, of that there was no doubt, and she had high hopes that he had a bright future ahead of him.

The hours she had set aside for lessons were coming to an end now, and she would have liked to send the two boys outside for some of the fresh air and exercise Jimmy was so badly in need of, but the spell of fine weather had broken, and today heavy rain was falling from leaden skies, making deep puddles on the paths and pooling on the lawns, which had been baked hard by the long dry spell and hot sunshine.

What could she suggest they do together? she wondered. The two of them seemed to be getting along famously, and she was anxious to encourage that. It would be good for both of them to bond as friends. Should she ask Freddie to show Jimmy some of his toys? Workmen had finished rebuilding the section of wall in his room that had had to be demolished in order to rescue Jimmy, but she wasn't sure that was a good idea, at least until the new brick had been plastered and painted. As it was, bare and new, it would be a stark reminder to Jimmy of his ordeal, and might very well prompt Freddie to ask tactless questions as to what it had been like to be stuck in the chimney.

Freddie might not want Jimmy playing with his toys anyway. He could be very possessive of them. He had loaned Jimmy his butterfly net on that first day, it was true, but then the climbing boy had been something of a novelty to him. Abi didn't want to risk any arguments or shows of pique on Freddie's part that might put a damper on their blossoming friendship. No, much safer to suggest something quite different, well away from the scene of the near-disaster, and something Freddie had no special claim on. Inspiration struck.

'Why don't the two of you have a game of draughts?' she suggested. 'Or dominoes? Have you ever played dominoes, Jimmy?'

'No, miss. I don't think so,' Jimmy said doubtfully.

'You've never played dominoes?' Freddie asked incredulously.

Jimmy shook his head. 'What are they?'

'Here! I'll show you!'

Freddie jumped up and went to a cupboard in the wall, returning with a long, narrow wooden box. He inserted a fingernail into a groove in the sliding lid and pulled it back, exposing the black tiles with their patterns of white dots, then tipped them out on the table and began arranging some end to end. 'They're dominos. Look – the three goes against another three. And then you need a six . . .'

Jimmy looked bewildered. 'I don't understand.'

'It's easy. I'll show you.'

Satisfied, Abi smiled to herself, gathered up her things and left them to it.

She found Imogen in her room, working on a cross-stitch sampler. The sight pleased her enormously; it was the first time she had seen Imogen take an interest in anything that didn't concern Robbie, and she thought it was a very good sign.

She looked over Imogen's shoulder, full of admiration for the fine work in delicate shades of green that was taking shape on the open-weave fabric stretched tight over a wooden frame. 'That is very pretty! You are so clever! I'm all fingers and thumbs when it comes to sewing. All I'm capable of is "a long stitch and a lie flat", as my mother would say.'

Imogen blinked, rubbed her eyes and looked up.

'This is the wood, do you see? The trees on the edge of the lake.' She pointed to a hank of azure thread. 'It will be blue – the lake – not murky. Just as it was on the day Robbie . . .' Her voice wobbled and she broke off for a moment before recovering herself and going on. 'And this . . .' indicating some golden thread, 'this is just the colour of his hair, and the cream is for the blouse he was wearing.'

A feeling of despair engulfed Abi. This wasn't a distraction from Imogen's morbid obsession at all. It was a memorial she was creating to the little boy she had lost so tragically.

'It's beautiful,' she said lamely.

'When it's done, I shall have it framed and hung on the wall. In his room, perhaps. That would be fitting, wouldn't it?'

'Yes.' Abi was at a loss to know what else to say, then her heart sank as Imogen laid the sampler down on the table beside her and went on. 'Freddie is to move back into his own room tonight, so it's Robbie's again, thank goodness. Mary changed all the linen this morning, so the bed is made up the way it should be, and I've been putting all his things back in their places. Would you like to see?' She rose, going to the connecting door, which, as always, had been left ajar.

Abi followed her wordlessly. Robbie's room did once again look exactly as it had when she had first seen it, the stuffed monkey sitting on the pillow, his nightgown draped over the bed rail as if waiting for him.

'I expect Hugh will be cross with me,' Imogen said ruefully. 'He thinks Robbie's things should have been cleared away long ago. But why would he want to remove every trace of our little boy? I don't understand it at all. This is all we have left of him. And how could he even think of suggesting that Freddie should move into Robbie's room? Have him disturb all Robbie's belongings? Sleep in his bed . . .'

She was becoming agitated again, and for the first time, Abi felt utterly unequal to pacifying her, as if she too was drowning under the weight of Imogen's grief. In that moment, she could see why Sir Hugh was losing patience and beginning to despair of Imogen ever putting it behind her and moving on. But at the same time, her heart bled for her poor tortured friend.

She slipped an arm around Imogen's waist. 'Why don't you do some more work on your sampler?' she suggested. 'Just think how satisfied you will feel when it's finished.'

To her relief, Imogen brightened. 'You are right. That's what I will do. Oh, I can't wait to hang it on Robbie's wall! Will he like it, do you think?'

'He will, I'm sure,' Abi said, humouring her. But Imogen's words were yet another sign that her poor mind was still as sick as ever. Where would it end? Abi was beginning to think that much as she despised Mrs Mears, the horrible woman might be right. Robbie's death had left Imogen totally broken, her reason shattered like a crystal ornament, and there might be no way of ever putting the pieces back together.

Thankful to escape, a feeling of which she was deeply ashamed, Abi left Imogen to her needlework and went back downstairs.

Mrs Mears was in an even more sour mood than usual. The bad weather had meant that the sheets that had been washed this morning could not be pegged out in the garden; they were draped over the beam in the laundry room, still wet, and when they were eventually dry, instead of the scent that came from fresh air and sunshine, most likely they would smell faintly mouldy. To add to her ill humour, Cook had managed to burn a pan of stew, and a crystal decanter had slipped through Mary's arthritic hands and smashed on the flagged floor, wasting a pint of good red wine into the bargain.

As she made her way to the dining room to check that the table was correctly laid for dinner, she heard voices coming from the parlour – Frederick, and that climbing boy. Mrs Mears bristled. What could Sir Hugh be thinking of, allowing Frederick to mix with him? Marigold would be turning in her grave.

Really, though, she shouldn't be surprised by anything he did. She'd lost all respect for him a long while ago. It had been totally disgraceful to marry so soon after Marigold's death – he'd wanted a woman in his bed, she supposed. Nothing but carnal lust, just like all men. But still he wasn't satisfied. Not only had he taken up with that strumpet Constance Bingham, she'd seen the way he looked at Frederick's governess – a girl far too pretty for her own good, who most likely had her eye on the main chance. Well, Mrs Mears could deal with her if needs be. She'd already made sure Miss Abigail Newman knew that she was to be reckoned with.

But it wasn't only Sir Hugh's roving eye that enraged her. It was the way he had marginalised Frederick after that woman had given him a second son. Sending him off to boarding school. Forever chastising him for every little thing when he was at home, though she couldn't see any harm in his mischief. Expecting him to behave like a gentleman at only nine years old. Oh, she'd seen the way the wind was blowing. Robert had been the apple of his eye, and no doubt would always be favoured. When her beloved Marigold had died, she might well have left Bramley Court but for Frederick. As it was, she had made up her mind to remain here and protect his interests whatever it took, just as she had always protected Marigold.

I was more of a mother to her than the woman who gave birth to her ever was, Mrs Mears thought bitterly. Cared for her from the day she was born, held her when she was dying. Broke my heart, it did, that I couldn't save her.

But at least she could look out for Marigold's son, and she would. Robert was gone, and soon that pathetic creature Imogen would be gone too, consigned to an asylum, well out of the way, and – most importantly – not in a position to give Sir Hugh any more children who might usurp Frederick.

Or bring ragamuffins into the house to lead him astray.

She looked through the doorway, wondering what the boys were up to – just in time to see Frederick push aside the dominoes that had been laid end to end.

'You're a cheat, Jimmy! A rotten cheat!'

'I'm not!' the climbing boy protested. 'I did everything just like you told me.'

'You must have been cheating to beat me.' Freddie swept at the dominoes again, sending them skittering across the table in all directions, and Mrs Mears strode into the room.

'Stop that at once! You're scratching the table!' she thundered. But of course, it was Jimmy she was addressing, Jimmy she was blaming, not her precious Frederick. 'Why are you here anyway? Lessons are over for the day – you should have gone back to Mrs Doel's. Go on now! Off with you!'

To his credit, Freddie owned up to having been the one who had scattered the dominoes, but spoiled it by adding: 'But I wouldn't have if he hadn't been cheating.'

'I never,' Jimmy muttered, but Mrs Mears was having none of it.

'Didn't you hear me? Off you go. Now, before I tan your skinny backside.'

Freddie relented. 'Don't make him go, please, Mrs Mears. He's my friend. Perhaps he didn't cheat . . .'

'What's going on?' Abi had come downstairs unnoticed.

Mrs Mears folded her arms across her bosom. 'This boy is trouble.'

'Oh, surely not . . .' She broke off as Jimmy jumped up from his chair, scuttled across the parlour and darted for the door, pushing past the housekeeper, but not before Abi had seen his screwed-up face and the tears that he was struggling to hold back. With a shake of her head and a glare at Mrs Mears, she grabbed a shawl and went after him.

'What's happened, Jimmy?' she asked when she caught up with him on the path.

Jimmy said nothing. His head was lowered again, the toes of his boots scuffed on the paving stones.

'Don't take any notice of Mrs Mears,' Abi said gently. 'She can be very unkind.'

'I don't care about *her*,' Jimmy said, so softly she had to bend to make out the words. 'But Freddie . . . he thinks I cheated, and I didn't – honest!'

'Oh Jimmy. He didn't mean it, I'm sure. He just doesn't like losing.'

But Jimmy had relapsed into silence once more.

'I'll walk with you back to Mrs Doel's. And try not to upset yourself. All this will be forgotten by tomorrow.'

When he had finished his house calls for the day, Giles Stanley had made for Bramley Court. Neither Freddie nor the climbing boy was in need of his attention now, but he wanted to find out how Imogen was.

Sir Hugh, however, had not been helpful. He had said his wife was resting and shouldn't be disturbed, and was evasive about her condition. 'Much the same' was as far as he'd gone. Giles had understood that he was busy – Edmund Buchan, his second in command in the management of his mines, was just leaving when Giles had arrived, and there was an untouched mound of paperwork on Sir Hugh's desk that Giles guessed had been left for his attention. But he also had the feeling that Sir Hugh didn't want to discuss his wife. He suspected he was burying his head in the sand and didn't want to be told again that she should be receiving specialised care in the asylum. The time would come when he could avoid the inevitable no longer, but it seemed he hadn't reached it yet.

Simmering with frustration, Giles made for his pony and trap, and had just removed the covers from the driving seat and was leading the pony towards the drive when he caught sight of Abi and the little climbing boy. What luck! He hastily pulled the covers across the seat again and hurried to catch her up.

'Good afternoon, Miss Newman! You are just the tonic I need after a long day with the old and sick. But why are you out in this weather?'

'It's only drizzling now, and I'm seeing Jimmy back to the Doels' cottage. And you?'

'I was hoping to see Lady Hastings. Unfortunately, that wasn't possible. But perhaps you could enlighten me as to her condition?'

'I'm sorry, Doctor,' Abi said, 'but I don't think it's my place.'

Giles frowned. He'd thought he was getting somewhere with Abi, but her words and demeanour were far from encouraging.

'Miss Newman!' he said in a hurt tone. 'I thought we were friends! Have I done something to upset you?'

'No, of course not. But I need to get Jimmy home. And this is not the time nor the place.' She indicated the little boy with a flick of her eyes and an almost imperceptible nod of her head. 'Good day, Doctor.'

She walked on, and puzzled and once more frustrated Giles could do nothing but watch them go.

From the window of his study, Sir Hugh had seen Abi leave the house and follow Jimmy, who was looking as cowed and dejected as when he had first arrived. He had seen her touch his arm reassuringly and walk alongside him, her head bent, saying something to him that no doubt was comforting. Presumably seeing him safely back to the gardener's cottage.

How typical of Abi! he had thought. Kind. Caring. Empathetic. And beautiful. At this distance he couldn't make out her features, but he could picture them in his mind's eye. Small straight nose, big brown eyes, a well-shaped mouth that lifted her cheeks when she smiled. Her hair was covered by her shawl, but he knew exactly how it was – so dark it was almost black, with a hint of curl, sweet-smelling like summer. Her every move was graceful, each step flowing effortlessly into the next, her skirts flowing with them.

He was startled and shamed by the sudden admission of just how strong his feelings for her were. Since losing his beloved Marigold, he'd never felt such desire for any woman. He'd tried to deny it. He had no right to feel this way. He had married Imogen, promised to be there for her in sickness and in health, and now that she needed him more than ever, he was determined to keep that promise.

As he had battled with his growing desire for Abi, he'd considered dismissing her; having her under his roof was both painful and dangerous. If she was no longer here, he would be able to concentrate on Imogen and her welfare, and on his precious mines. Even if he was unable to forget her, the constant temptation would be removed.

On the other hand, though, she had done so much good here. Frederick liked and respected her; he was more amenable to his education than he had ever been, and his behaviour had improved. And there was no doubt that she was able to comfort Imogen when no one else could reach her. Imogen would be dreadfully upset if Abi was sent home.

As he watched her walking with the little climbing boy, Giles Stanley appeared, leading his pony towards the driveway, then suddenly pulling the covers over the driving seat of the trap and hurrying after her. Hugh was suddenly filled with jealousy.

He'd wondered before if they might be attracted to one another, and tried to convince himself that his reaction to such a possibility was simply because he didn't want to lose her as a governess. Now he could fool himself no longer. He wanted her. And seeing her with another man was a knife in his heart.

He turned abruptly away from the window, cursing himself for his seeming inability to control his emotions, and the cruel twist of fate that had brought about the tussle between his desire and his duty and was tearing him apart,

Why did I do that? Abi asked herself as she walked back to the house after leaving Jimmy with Prudie.

Since acknowledging her feelings for Sir Hugh, she had been constantly on her guard, worried that she might somehow give herself away. A friendship with Giles Stanley could provide a smokescreen; if the members of the household thought she was carrying a candle for the young doctor, they would be far less likely to guess the truth. That she had fallen in love with a man who was her employer – and a married man. Her friend's husband no less. Nothing could ever come of it, even if he felt the same way as she did. Which of course he did not.

She pulled her shawl more tightly over her head as if to hide her foolish, treacherous emotions from the rest of the world, and turned her thoughts to how she could ensure that her feelings remained secret.

In his room, Freddie lay on his stomach half-heartedly moving the toy soldiers around in his fort. For once he couldn't summon up any interest in the manoeuvres. Instead, the tiff with Jimmy was playing on his mind.

He shouldn't have accused Jimmy of cheating. He'd known all along he hadn't been, but he hadn't been able to stop himself. Losing – especially to a boy so clearly his inferior – was more than he could bear.

Now he regretted it. Inferior or not, Jimmy was the closest he'd ever come to having a friend of his own age. True, there was George Buchan, but they hadn't met since he had given Freddie the measles, and Freddie had never liked him much in any case. Nor had he got on very well with any of his peers at boarding school, never been accepted into their gangs, as they called them. For some reason he had always been an outsider.

Was it his fault? Was it that he wasn't a very nice person? Sometimes, he felt a little frightened by the pleasure he got from doing things that in his heart of hearts he knew were wrong. Why did he enjoy stamping on caterpillars, or watching trapped butterflies flutter helplessly inside his glass jar? As for the tricks he played, he didn't want to think about them right now. When he did, he felt ashamed, and just at the moment he felt bad enough about his temper tantrum over the dominoes.

As for Robbie . . . he didn't want to think about Robbie either.

His face crumpled and he hurled his precious toy soldier towards the newly bricked-up wall. Oh, if only his mama hadn't died. Perhaps he'd just forgotten, but he didn't think he'd ever had these awful dark feelings when she had been alive, and if he had, she'd have held him until they went away, just as she had when he'd had a bad dream. If he closed his eyes, he could still conjure up the way it had been when she took him into her bed, feel the warmth of her body, smell the lavender scent on her skin, hear her voice singing softly to him. But one day she just wasn't there any more, and nobody would tell him anything. Not where she had gone, or why, or when she was coming back.

But he'd felt the horrible gloomy atmosphere, and for the first time in his life had seen his papa and even Mrs Mears crying. He'd known then that something was terribly wrong. His papa never cried, and nor did Mrs Mears.

Just as he'd feared, Mama had never come back. Instead he had what they'd called 'a new mama', and before long, a little brother. He'd resented them both. It wasn't right that they were there and Mama was not.

But then Robbie had died too, and it was all his fault . . .

A knock at his door; Miss Newman calling his name. Freddie sat up abruptly, scrubbing away the tears that had started to his eyes. Miss Newman was nice, but he couldn't let her catch him crying.

He crossed to the door and opened it a crack.

'I know why you're here,' he said, struggling to keep his voice steady. 'I was horrid to Jimmy and I'm sorry. Please tell him I won't do it again.'

Then he closed the door and hoped she would go away.

Abi could tell from his voice that Freddie had been crying, and she thought he genuinely was regretting the way he'd behaved to Jimmy. No point in saying any more about it. Better to just leave it there; he'd hate her to see him upset. His fierce pride wouldn't stand being thought a baby, even though he was, after all, still just a little boy.

Her heart bled for him. Really, sometimes he was his own worst enemy. But with all the tragedies that had befallen this family, it was no surprise that he had been deeply affected. And all she could do was her best – for the two boys, each lost in their own way, and of course for Imogen.

Chapter Fifteen

'I can't do it.'

The woman who had knocked on the door of the vicarage soon after Maisie had left to spend the evening with Sukie was a stranger to Malcolm. She wasn't one of his parishioners and she didn't look like a villager either, dressed as she was in a revealing gown of cheap taffeta, her hair unkempt and her cheeks stained with the remnants of rouge. But her heartfelt words and her ravaged face left him in no doubt who she was, and why she was here.

He'd tried his best these last few days to discover who the baby who had been left on his doorstep belonged to, without success; now here she was, standing in front of him.

'My dear,' he said. 'Won't you come in?'

She shrank away, tugging her shawl nervously over her décolletage.

'I'm not what you think . . . well, not now, anyways . . .'

Malcolm guessed she was afraid her appearance might give him the impression she was here to ply her trade. 'I know,' he said gently. 'And I can guess why you've come. But we can't talk out here. It's still raining, and besides, if I'm right, I don't imagine you are in any fit state to be on your feet so soon after what you've been through. Come inside, where you can make yourself comfortable.'

He stood aside to allow her to pass. Still the woman hesitated, swaying, and holding on to the door jamb for support. Malcolm reached out and took her arm, and reluctantly she allowed him to help her into the little parlour, where he moved the book he had been reading from the most comfortable chair and indicated that she should take it.

She sat down abruptly then, as if her legs would no longer support her, but her eyes, dark pools in her thin, pale face, skittered around.

'Where is he?'

'Don't worry, he's safe,' Malcolm assured her.

'But where *is* he?'

He was unwilling to divulge the baby's whereabouts until he knew more about this woman. If he told her, she might run off to find him even though she looked to be on the point of collapse; besides, he had the child's safety and well-being to think of. 'He is being well cared for,' he told her.

'Not in the orphanage!' She sounded terrified. No doubt she was thinking that if her baby was in the care of the authorities, she might never get him back, and despite having abandoned him, that was clearly what she was desperate for now.

'Not the orphanage,' he promised her. 'He's with a woman who is well qualified to look after him.'

'I shouldn't have left him,' she said distractedly. 'I just didn't know what else to do.'

'I promise I will do all I can to help you.' Malcolm moved towards the door. 'I'll fetch you something to drink and then we'll talk. Some water, perhaps?'

Though he didn't think the woman would run off without learning the whereabouts of her baby, he was reluctant to leave her alone for the time it would take to boil a pan of water and make tea.

'Water would be good,' she said faintly.

'I'll only be a minute,' he said. 'Just sit quietly and rest.'

In the kitchen, he poured water into a cup and cut a slice from a fruit cake that Maisie had baked that morning. When he returned to the parlour, he saw that the woman was sitting back in the chair, her head resting into the wing, her eyes closed as if she was fighting exhaustion. But the minute she realised he was back, she sat bolt upright, alert again. He handed her the cup of water and set the slice of cake down on the occasional table beside his book. But though she drank thirstily, she showed no interest whatever in the cake.

'So.' Malcolm perched on an upright chair, facing her. 'Shall we introduce ourselves? My name is Malcolm Rayner, and I am the vicar of St Barnabas, though I am guessing you know that. May I know your name?'

The woman bowed her head as if she was ashamed. Malcolm waited. 'Priscilla,' she said at last. 'Prissie Robinson.'

'Do you have family, a husband?'

She looked up, her haunted eyes meeting his. 'I don't 'ave no one, sir.'

'So where are you living?' Malcolm didn't want to press her yet as to who was the father of her child. Judging by her appearance, she might not even know his name.

'I went back to our cottage, in the woods on the other side of the village. But 'tis damp and dark, no place for a baby. I couldn't keep him there with me. 'Twould 'ave bin the death of 'im.'

'Where are you thinking of taking him now? Assuming that you want him back, that is.'

Prissie raised her chin. 'I'll find somewhere. I 'ave to! I do want 'im back. More than anything in the world.'

Malcolm decided not to pursue this line of questioning for

the moment, though he was far from satisfied that Prissie had any kind of plan.

'Tell me how all this came about,' he said instead.

Her lips twisted into a grim smile. 'You've guessed my profession, I'm sure. 'Twas my mother's before me, and it was the death of her. She caught the disease from one of the men who used to knock on the door of our cottage. I was seventeen when she died. I had no way of supporting myself, and truth to tell, I'd never known anything different to what she did to put food on the table and clothes on our backs.' She raised her chin again, defiant and proud. 'I bettered myself, though. There's a club in town what caters for gentlemen's needs. Nate Blackthorne, the owner, took me on, gave me a room of me own, and board and lodging so long as I gave him my earnings, and bought me some fancy gowns so I'd meet my gentlemen's expectations. It wasn't so bad, a sight better than what my poor ma had – though underneath their good clothes, I don't reckon they were much different to them men as used to knock on our door.' Her lip curled. 'Animals!' She spat the word, hatred blazing suddenly in her eyes. 'Bliddy animals!'

'Oh my dear . . .' Malcolm shook his head, shocked and saddened at what this poor girl had had to endure, and ashamed of his gender.

'I s'pose I should a knowed how it would end,' Prissie went on. 'A baby with no bugger to call father. Just like me and me ma. I kept it to meself as long as I could, but when I started showing, Nate guessed. 'E told me I'd have to pay old Fanny Grimes a visit. She'd take care o' me. But I weren't goin' to do that. I weren't goin' t' 'ave 'er poking about inside me with 'er knittin' needle. Me ma warned me about that plenty o' times. She knew girls that was ruined for life, and more'n one what died. Besides, 'twas my baby! Me own flesh and blood, no matter who its father was.'

Tears welled in her eyes suddenly, and she brushed them away impatiently.

'Thought I could keep it, I did. Thought 'ow nice 'twould be t' be a family. But I found out soon enough that our cottage weren't fit fer a baby. 'Twas tumbledown enough when Ma were alive, an' since I'd left an' gone t' live in town, it'd got a lot worse. When it rained, the water came through the roof like 'twere a sieve, an' there were black mould all round the windows and growin' on the ceiling – what were left of it. I put up wi' it till the baby came. But then . . .'

'You gave birth in the cottage?' Malcolm said, shocked. She nodded. 'All alone?' She nodded again. 'Dear God!' He raised his eyes to heaven. 'You had no one to help you?'

She shrugged. 'Animals do it all the time on their own.'

'But you are not an animal!'

She winced, pressing her hands to her stomach, as if suddenly aware of a pain she had been desperately trying to ignore, then sat forward in her chair.

'So there you be. I've shocked you, I 'spect. But I've done my bit. I've told you what you wanted ter know. Now 'tis your turn. Tell me where I can find my baby.'

Malcolm was silent for a few moments, thinking. He couldn't allow Prissie to take her baby when she had nowhere to go but back to her damp, dilapidated cottage. She must be out of her mind with desperation to even consider it. But to refuse her plea would be utterly heartless. Unchristian. And what was a vicarage if not a safe haven for those who needed it most? There was an unoccupied room upstairs – Abi's room. Prissie and the baby could have the use of that until he could make alternative arrangements for them.

There was her medical condition to consider, too. If she'd given birth alone, unaided, she might very well be in need of attention, and certainly in no fit state to be wandering about the countryside. He made up his mind. He didn't know what Maisie would have to say about it, but he couldn't worry about that now. This was his home now, not hers, though she still treated it as such, and the decision to offer sanctuary to this poor girl was up to him and him alone.

'You can have a room here for the time being,' he said decisively. 'I'll go and fetch your baby and bring him to you.'

Her eyes widened and her mouth fell open, as if she simply couldn't believe what she was hearing. Then she struggled to her feet. 'I'll come with you.'

'No. You will stay here and rest. I'll not be gone long. And I'll bring someone back with me who can take a look at you, make sure everything to do with the birth is as it should be.'

'Not . . .' A shadow of fear crossed her face, and Malcolm guessed what she was thinking.

'Not anyone in authority,' he assured her. 'This woman is a midwife with years of experience. She's kind, and she's discreet; you need have no fears on that score. Now, as I say, I won't be long, and I want you to simply rest until I return.' He glanced at his timepiece. He thought it would be the best part of two hours before Maisie was back from Sukie's; it was usually a long evening when the two of them started chatting – and arguing too, if he knew anything about it. The sisters were chalk and cheese, but he rather thought their disagreements were part of a long-established ritual that they actually enjoyed.

'I should warn you that I do not live here alone,' he said. 'The previous vicar's widow has stayed on and acts as my housekeeper. She's out at the moment, and I should be back long before she returns. But if for some reason she is home early, just tell her that you are here with my blessing.'

'Thank you,' Prissie said, just those two words, and he saw she was welling up again.

'I'll go now. And while I am gone – remember, rest. Sleep if you need to.' At the door, he turned back, smiled at her. 'And do eat your cake. It's very good, I assure you.'

'It's no wonder then that nobody could shed any light on who the babe's mother might be,' Queenie Clegg said when Malcolm arrived at her cottage and related the surprising turn of events.

'Quite. But it's clear she bitterly regrets what she did. I must admit, I was doubtful at first of the wisdom of returning her baby to her, but I've told her she can stay at the vicarage with him until we are able to find her suitable accommodation, and she has accepted my offer. It would be the best thing all round, don't you agree?'

'It's always best for a babe to be with its own mother,' Queenie confirmed. 'Provided it's safe, of course. But you and Mrs Newman will make sure of that, I've no doubt. You want to take him straight away?'

'Yes. But I'd be grateful if you would come with us, Mrs Clegg. If the poor woman gave birth alone and unattended, she may well be in need of medical attention. Would you be willing to take a look at her?'

'Course I would. But you'll 'ave to send for the doctor if needs be. I won't be responsible for missin' summat and puttin' 'er life at risk.'

'Understood. I'll happily foot the bill for any expenses,' Malcolm said swiftly.

'Give me a minute to get some things together then.' Queenie peeked at the baby, fast asleep in a Moses basket on her sofa. 'We'll need to take the crib, too. I don't suppose you've got anythin' fer 'im to sleep in.'

'You suppose right.' Malcolm was cross with himself for not having thought of such a basic necessity.

'Well, if you'll carry the basket, I'll take the babe,' Queenie said. 'But we'd best get goin'. I mustn't be gone too long. I've a lady what's close to 'er time, an' I don't want 'er poor 'usband waiting on me doorstep an' wonderin' where the divil I am.'

'I don't want to leave Prissie alone for longer than necessary either.'

While he waited for Queenie to gather the things she would need, Malcolm crossed to the Moses basket and took a look inside. It seemed to him the baby had grown even in the few days since he had last seen him, but perhaps it was just that the little mite was no longer pinched with the cold. Queenie had put a knitted cap on his head, covering the sparse dark down Malcolm remembered, and the little face was rosy beneath it.

She was soon back with a small pile of second-hand clothes, a soft shawl and a pot of ointment. 'In case 'e gets a sore backside,' she said, packing it all into her carpet bag. 'I'll put in a pap boat as well. I don't suppose 'e'll be needin' it, but you never know. If she ain't bin eatin' proper, she might not 'ave enough milk for 'im.'

She lifted the baby out of the basket, cradling him comfortably. 'Right. Let's be on our way.'

By the time they reached the vicarage, Malcolm's arms were aching and the Moses basket was pressing uncomfortably into his chest. But he didn't mind. Knowing that he was doing something practical to help a poor soul in need more than compensated for that, and he couldn't help thinking that this was a good deal more satisfying than preaching sermons that half the congregation were scarcely listening to, or uttering platitudes that sounded mealy mouthed even to him.

And the best was yet to come. When Queenie carried the baby into the parlour, the look on Prissie's face was a joy to behold. She was out of the chair in an instant, rushing towards them, arms outstretched.

'Just hang on!' Queenie cautioned. 'Sit yerself down. You don't want to be fallin' over wi' 'im, do you?'

Malcolm urged Prissie back into the chair and Queenie placed the baby in her arms, where he nestled against her breast. They exchanged satisfied smiles. For the time being, all was right in Prissie's world. But Queenie still needed to examine her.

'I 'ave to 'ave a look at you,' she told her bluntly. 'Make sure that little 'un hasn't done damage an' the afterbirth's all gone. Let's pop 'im in the basket fer a minute.'

Prissie only clutched him tighter, and Queenie spoke sternly. 'If there's problems, it could kill you. D'you want t' leave yer babe motherless?'

Reluctantly Prissie allowed her to take the baby, and Malcolm left the room while Queenie attended to her.

'Right. She'll do,' Queenie pronounced when she called him back in. 'An' now I gotta get goin'. Call me again if there's any trouble, but I don't reckon there will be. That lass'll know what to do wi'out being told, an' when Mrs Newman gets back, she'll be able to advise her if needs be.'

'Yes.' But Malcolm couldn't help feeling uneasy as to what Maisie's reaction would be when she came home to find a woman of easy virtue and her baby in the house.

He need not have worried. Though initially clearly shocked, and not entirely approving of the young woman sitting in her best chair, Maisie quickly took a practical approach.

'Well, seeing as you've told her she can stay, we'll just have to make the best of it. She'll have to have Abigail's room, I suppose. The bed should be well aired, but it will need making up. That's something you can do. There's clean sheets in the cupboard, and she can have the rocking chair from my room for when she needs to feed the baby. Go on, get to it, or we'll none of us see our beds afore midnight.'

Malcolm didn't mind that Maisie was speaking to him as she might have spoken to one of her older pupils. He was just relieved that she seemed to have accepted the situation, even if she was not best pleased.

Maisie turned to Prissie, her lips tightening a shade. 'Right. I'll see about getting you something to eat. You don't look as if you've had a square meal in days.'

She bustled into the kitchen and set some milk to warm on the trivet by the fire, then cut a hunk of bread, spreading it lavishly with butter, and fetched a plate of cold cuts from the pantry. When the milk was warm, she poured two cups, one for Prissie and one for herself, and surreptitiously added a tot of Malcolm's Scotch whisky to her own.

Back in the parlour, she set everything down on the occasional table beside Prissie's chair.

'I'll take him while you have your supper,' she said, and somewhat reluctantly the young woman allowed her to do as she said.

Maisie settled the baby in the crook of her arm, staring down into the little pink face, and took a long pull of her milk and whisky.

'If you don't have a name for him yet, I reckon you should call him Christian, seeing as God brought him to our door,' she said.

The clock in the church tower was striking three. Malcolm counted the chimes, wondering if he would ever manage to get to sleep, and if he did, whether he would be woken by the baby crying. There had been a bout of it earlier, but he'd heard Prissie singing softly and imagined her rocking her child, and eventually the wailing had ceased. Yet still he found it impossible to relax. His mind was too busy: he was wound up from the events of the evening, and there were too many issues yet to be resolved. Prissie and her baby couldn't stay here forever; he needed to find a permanent home for them. But where? Did the Church have a place for such poor souls? He didn't know, but he would speak to the bishop. He'd need to anyway, to explain why he'd felt it necessary to take them in. He closed his eyes, folded his hands and prayed for guidance, then turned onto his stomach and tried once again to relax. To no avail.

It was Maisie he was thinking of now. Picturing her as he had found her when he'd returned from making up the bed. She'd been nursing the baby, her head bent, staring down at him, and the look on her face had taken him by surprise – a tenderness that was quite unlike her, and something else. Something that might almost have been wistful regret.

Later, when she'd shown Prissie to Abi's room and returned downstairs, she'd simply sat staring into space.

'I'm sorry if all this has upset you,' he'd said. 'But what else could I do?'

'No. It was the right thing.' But she sounded distant, as if her thoughts were somewhere else entirely.

Puzzled, and feeling guilty too, Malcolm had poured himself a tot of whisky. 'Would you like a drop of this? It would help you to sleep.'

To his surprise, she nodded. Maisie rarely touched alcohol. Communion wine was all she needed, she always said.

'Thank you, Malcolm. I think I will.' As he handed her the glass, she added, 'Truth to tell, I had some earlier, in my warm milk.' But he'd thought he saw the glimmer of tears in her eyes, and he couldn't help feeling that whatever was upsetting her was deeply personal.

A random thought occurred to him now. Had the baby and the young mother in distress stirred some distant memory? Was it possible she herself had once been in the same position as Prissie? That she had been forced to part with a child? Oh surely not! It was impossible to imagine Maisie in such a situation. But then again, who knew what she had been like in her youth? Events could change a person beyond recognition.

The baby had begun to cry again. Malcolm pulled the covers over his head and tried once more to still his churning thoughts.

Chapter Sixteen

Unlike Malcolm, Imogen was not even trying to sleep. She had left her sleeping draught untouched, and now sat propped up against the pillows, her wrap around her shoulders, listening for some sound from Robbie's room.

The last few days she had done as Abi had told her, and she felt proud of herself for that. She'd heard the rattle of Robbie's wind-up toy, heard his whispers – 'Mama! Mama!' – but had clenched her hands so tightly that her fingernails bit into her palms and simply waited. Once, when she could bear the suspense no longer, she had called out softly, 'Robbie! Don't tease your mama now! Come to me, my darling!' But everything had gone quiet, and he had not come. Abi's advice did not seem to be working.

Tonight would be different, she had decided. Freddie was back in his own room; there would be no deceptive hump under the bedcovers, and she wouldn't disturb him if she searched for Robbie in all the places he might hide. She trembled with excitement and anticipation. If he came tonight – and she felt sure he would – she would find him. She was convinced of it.

Suddenly, in the quiet house, she heard a faint sound. Not the wind-up toy rattling around, but something soft and melodic. Robbie's music box! It was the first time she'd heard it since he died, but the tinkling notes were unmistakable.

Her heart beat faster. She had left a candle burning on the nightstand just in case; now she slipped out of bed and reached for it. Her hands were trembling so much she was afraid she might drop it and start a fire, and she gripped the curled handle of the pewter holder with one hand while steadying its saucer-like base with the other. She crossed to the door that connected her room to Robbie's and nudged it open with her elbow.

'I'm coming to find you, Robbie!' she called playfully.

She thought she heard movement in the darkness beyond the reach of the candlelight, but for once there was no answering murmur.

Undeterred, she went into the room, where the music box was still tinkling out its soothing tune.

Abi was aware of a creeping feeling of unease. She wasn't sure what had disturbed her. Apart from the intermittent screams of a fox calling to its mate somewhere out in the grounds, the silence was complete. Still heavy with sleep, she pulled the covers over her ears in an effort to mute the mournful cries. She was just being silly, she told herself. She'd probably had a bad dream that had slipped away as she woke, leaving nothing but its aura. She really must sleep; if she didn't, she'd be good for nothing in the morning.

Yet still the awful nagging certainty that something was wrong persisted. The fox screamed again. Though she knew better, it sounded to her more like a yowl of pain than a mating call, and she knew she was never going to get back to sleep if she didn't make sure everything was as it should be.

She clambered out of bed, tossed a shawl around her shoulders and opened her bedroom door, sniffing the air for any smell of smoke or burning, and listening for sounds that might mean an intruder was in the house.

Nothing. But the sense of foreboding was stronger than ever.

She would check on Imogen, she decided. If she was in bed and fast asleep, then Abi would have to accept that this unease was nothing but fancy, brought on by being woken suddenly from a deep sleep.

She went softly along the corridor, her anxiety growing sharper as she saw that Imogen's door – always closed at night – was wide open. She stepped stealthily into the room. It felt empty, and she couldn't hear any sound of breathing. It was too dark to see if Imogen was there, so she crossed to the bed, cautiously reaching out to touch the covers, and realised they had been turned back. The bed was empty. But the air was scented with what she recognised as the melting wax of a candle, though the room was in darkness and there was no smell of it having burned out. Wherever she had gone, Imogen must have taken it with her.

Abi crossed to the door that connected to Robbie's room, hoping she would find Imogen sitting beside her son's bed as she so often did. But she wasn't there.

Beginning to panic now, she told herself firmly that Imogen must be somewhere in the house. Surely she'd never have ventured out into the pitch-dark night – would she?

Taking care to avoid the floorboards that she knew creaked, she went down to the kitchen and found a lamp. As she attempted to light it, her hands, slick with perspiration, kept slipping on the tinder box, but at last she managed it and the wick caught and flared. She slipped the glass shade into place and began her search of the house.

Ten minutes or so later, however, she was forced to admit defeat. She had checked the drawing room, the library, the dining and breakfast rooms, and even Sir Hugh's study, the kitchen and the laundry room, and found them all empty. Imogen was nowhere to be found.

She realised she had no choice but to wake Sir Hugh and tell him that his wife was missing.

'Are you quite certain she's nowhere in the house?'

Sir Hugh had fallen asleep, fully clothed, in his chair. It happened that way sometimes. Whereas too often he tossed and turned in the big four-poster bed with its heavy drapes and tester, there was something comfortable about sitting in the soft lamplight, resting his head against the padded wings of the chair, a glass of whisky on a small table beside him. And more often than not, the sleep that eluded him in his bed crept up on him unawares. That was what had happened tonight, and he would likely not have woken until the small hours had Abi not come rapping urgently on his door.

'I've searched everywhere, but I can't find her.' She tightened the shawl around her shoulders; she wasn't cold, but she was shivering. 'Perhaps you might know of somewhere she could be that I don't.'

'I can but search.' Hugh was wide awake now. 'I can't believe she would have gone outside at this time of night. She is rather afraid of the dark.'

Stopping only to pull on his boots, he began to search, and Abi waited on the landing as he checked each of the bedrooms, including Freddie's. Downstairs, she followed as he looked everywhere that she had and more, opening closet doors she hadn't even noticed were there – a larder, a broom cupboard, a boot store. All to no avail.

Growing ever more concerned, he went to the kitchen door and tried it, but the bolts were still shot; Imogen couldn't have left that way. The front door, too, was locked on the inside, the heavy iron key still in place. But when he pulled back the curtain covering one of the tall windows that flanked it he saw that it was wide open.

'She climbed out of the window?' Abi said in disbelief. But an awful suspicion was growing in her mind, and she couldn't stop thinking of the day she'd found Imogen by the lake. Perhaps Imogen hadn't been able to manage the stiff old door locks, but that she should go this far to get outside was proof, if proof were needed, of the disturbed state of her mind.

'I'll go and look for her.' Already Sir Hugh was struggling to turn the key in the lock, with hands that were clumsy with haste.

'Papa?' A small, frightened voice from behind them.

'Not now, Frederick,' Hugh snapped. The door scraped open. Lifting the lamp he had put down on the floor, he stepped out into the fitful moonlight.

'Miss?' The same small voice, plaintive, tearful almost.

Abi, about to follow Sir Hugh, turned. Freddie, tousle-headed, his bare feet peeping out from beneath the hem of his nightshirt, was at the foot of the stairs.

'What's happening?'

'Your mother is missing,' Abi said, too worried about Imogen to mince her words. 'We are going to look for her. And no, you can't come with us – you've got nothing on your feet. Just wait here.'

She herself was wearing only her thin slippers, but she wasn't going to worry about that now. She hurried out, praying that they would find Imogen quickly.

As he crossed the lawn, a nightmarish sense of déjà vu enveloped Hugh. The same sickening dread he had felt that afternoon almost two years ago when they had been unable to find Robert. It had been broad daylight then, but the bright, hot sunshine had somehow had the aura of a nightmare. Now, with the shadows flickering and dancing as clouds skittered across the moon, it felt much the same.

His stomach clenched as the terrible memories crowded in around him. Discovering the small, lifeless body in the lake. The stagnant water dripping from Robert's hair and clothes as he carried him home in his arms. The indescribable horror of it all. The pain. Was history about to repeat itself? Had Imogen gone to the lake to be with their precious son? Would she wade into the water in search of him? Oh, please God, if she had gone there, let him be in time to save her . . .

'Sir!'

Hugh froze, his heart leaping as for a brief crazy moment he thought it was Imogen calling to him. Fool! Imogen didn't call him 'sir'. He turned and saw Abi running across the lawn towards him.

'No!' he shouted, waving his arms in an attempt to stop her. He didn't want her to be there if he found Imogen drowned. Didn't want her to witness something she would never forget.

But Abi was not to be deterred.

'I'm coming with you,' she said, breathless, as she reached him.

'No – search the grounds.'

'I'm coming with you,' she repeated, determined.

There was no time to be wasted arguing. Every minute counted now.

'As you wish,' he said shortly, and set off again, Abi not far behind.

Abi slipped and slithered down the wooded slope, doing her best to keep up with Hugh. Twigs snapped as she clutched at branches to save herself from falling; little avalanches of dead leaves cascaded downwards from under her feet. Through a gap in the trees she could see the surface of the lake below, shimmering darkly in the fitful moonlight. A rustle in the foliage startled her, and a night bird, disturbed, took flight, so close beside her that she felt the rush of air on her face as it skimmed past. As she took a quick, instinctive step away, she lost her footing, and before she could save herself, she had tumbled into what smelled like a bed of wild garlic.

It was as she struggled to get up that she heard it – what sounded like a low moan. For a moment she thought she had imagined it, but then it came again, soft, but unmistakable. Someone was there, just a few feet away from her. Someone in distress. Her heart missed a beat. Could it be . . . ?

'Imogen?' she called.

Silence. She struggled to her feet and pushed her way through a tangle of branches and small saplings, unable to see beyond them. Then, quite suddenly, they thinned into another path, running downwards at a wider angle than the one she had been following.

'Imogen!' she called again. And saw her.

She was lying just off the path, one arm beneath her, her legs bent as if she had been trying to rise and fallen back again.

'Abi.' Her voice was faint.

'Oh, thank God!' Abi had begun to tremble all over as relief rushed through her veins. 'What happened? Are you hurt?'

Two stupid questions. Clearly Imogen was hurt, and Abi knew very well she must have been making for the lake and fallen. But she asked them anyway.

'My ankle . . . I can't get up . . .'

'Lie still then.' Abi was beginning to think clearly again. 'I'll fetch Hugh.'

'Hugh?' Imogen sounded puzzled. It was almost as if she didn't recognise his name.

'We've been looking for you. We were so worried!'

'Don't leave me, Abi!' Imogen wailed.

'I won't be long.'

This path, such as it was, was much narrower and more overgrown than the one she and Hugh had taken. Abi fought her way through the trees and scrambled as fast as she dared to the ledge where the ground fell steeply away to the lake. She could see Hugh making his way along the bank, all the while peering into the dark water.

'Sir!' she called 'Sir Hugh!' Her voice seemed to be muffled by the canopy of branches, and she called again: 'Sir Hugh! I've found her!'

To her relief, this time he heard her. He stopped, looked up.

'I've found her! She's fallen!' Abi's throat felt raw and scratchy.

'I'm coming.'

Abi waited, watching him scramble up the bank then hastily climb the path.

'This way . . .'

Hugh pushed his way through to where Imogen lay, Abi following.

'Imogen! For the love of God! Oh my dear, what were you thinking?' Relief following on desperate anxiety made him sound impatient, and although she could understand, Abi wished he would use a gentler tone.

But it was Imogen's tearful reply that made her heart sink once more.

'I can't find him! I've tried and tried, but I can't find Robbie!'

Somehow, between them, Hugh and Abi got Imogen back up the path. It was far from easy; she could put no weight on her foot, and cried out each time she tried. Hugh had to half carry her, hoisting her up onto his hip, while Abi held back the branches that obstructed their way. Eventually they reached the point where the woods met the lawn, and he lifted her into his arms, holding her across his body as one would carry a small child.

Two figures were silhouetted against the light spilling out from the front door – unmistakably Freddie and Mrs Mears. Abi's heart sank. She'd guessed that Freddie wouldn't go back to bed until they returned, but she wasn't expecting the evil housekeeper, who was certain to say exactly the sort of thing that would only upset Imogen more – though Abi wasn't sure Imogen was aware of anything but her overwhelming compulsion to find Robbie.

As they crossed the lawn, Freddie broke away and came running towards them, then stopped abruptly, taking a step backwards with a strangled gasp.

'It's all right, Freddie,' Abi said, realising that the sight of Imogen in such a state was something of a shock to him. 'Your mother's had a fall and hurt her ankle, that's all.'

But he looked close to tears, and as they went on towards the house, he lagged behind, as if trying to distance himself.

'Well, this is a fine how-d'you-do!' Mrs Mears greeted them, her tone short and disapproving just as Abi had expected. 'What's she been up to now? This can't go on – you must know that.'

'Just help me upstairs with her, please, Mrs Mears,' Hugh said wearily. 'And you, Frederick, should be in bed.'

Abi stepped to one side – Mrs Mears was far stronger than she was, she knew – and put an arm round Freddie's shoulders, urging him towards the stairs. When the little procession reached the landing, she let the others go ahead and followed them to Imogen's room.

'I'll see to her now. A good stiff dose of her sleeping draught and she'll give no more trouble tonight.' Mrs Mears spoke authoritatively, then turned to Abi and added scathingly: 'And you, miss, would do well to put some clothes on.'

Abi felt a flush rising in her cheeks that was as much anger as it was embarrassment. How dare the housekeeper speak to her like that?

For once, Sir Hugh also seemed annoyed by Mrs Mears's unpleasant, bossy manner.

'I'm not leaving my wife just yet,' he said firmly.

As the three of them disappeared into the bedroom, Abi turned to Freddie.

'Come on, Freddie. Let's get you to bed too.' She ushered him into his room and straightened the tumbled bedding. 'Hop in now, and don't worry about your mother. She'll be fine.'

Freddie sat on the edge of the bed, staring down at his feet and making no attempt to get in.

'Freddie?'

Still he made no move; only muttered something that to Abi sounded like 'I'm sorry'.

Instantly all her old suspicions came flooding back. 'What for?' she asked gently.

He said nothing, his head still bent, and Abi dropped to her knees beside him.

'Freddie? Do you know anything about what happened? Have you been playing silly pranks?'

The boy remained silent, chin resting on his chest, and Abi held her breath. Then he shook his head and mumbled a denial. But she was less than convinced. All this seemed very like an attack of conscience: he had been on the point of confessing, but when it came to it, he couldn't bring himself to do so.

'Well, we must hope that whatever it was that upset your mother doesn't happen again,' she said, kindly but firmly. 'It's very sad that she thinks she hears Robbie playing with his toys.

And if anyone was trying to make her think that, it wouldn't be funny at all. Just very cruel.' She paused to let her words sink in, then added gently, 'Into bed now, and I'll tuck you in.'

This time he obeyed.

'Now try to get some sleep.' She smoothed the covers across his plump little body, then crossed to the door. 'Sleep tight, don't let the fleas bite.'

She thought she heard a muffled sob, but she closed the door after her anyway. She'd done her best, and now she'd leave him to think it over.

The door to Imogen's room was still open, and Abi heard voices – Hugh's and Mrs Mears's. She'd make herself a warm drink, she decided. Perhaps it would help her to sleep too. Feeling utterly drained and despondent, she went downstairs.

Freddie buried himself beneath the bedcovers and thrust his fists into the sockets of his closed eyes, but still he couldn't block out the images of a distraught Imogen, couldn't escape the shame that washed over him in hot waves, couldn't forget what Miss Newman had said. *Not funny at all. Very cruel.* She was right; he'd seen that tonight with his own eyes. What had begun as a game had turned into something that had gone so much further than he'd ever expected it to, and now that he'd witnessed the consequences, he knew he couldn't do it any more. But how was he going to tell that to the person who was egging him on?

Tears squeezed out from beneath his fists and ran down his face. Never before in his life had he been so ashamed, or so frightened.

When she had warmed some milk and stirred in a spoonful of honey, Abi carried it through to the parlour, where she sat down on the padded window seat. She took a sip, but her stomach was churning and the milk seemed to curdle in her throat. Giving up, she set the mug down on an occasional table beside her, reliving the nightmare of the past hour – the dread that had consumed her, the panic she'd felt as she fought her way through the tangled undergrowth with the branches of the trees whipping against her face, the struggle it had been to get Imogen safely back to the house.

And pervading it all, the questions and the doubts. Had she got through to Freddie? Should she have taken a sterner approach? Should she speak to Sir Hugh about her suspicions? Well, they were more than mere suspicions now. She felt sure that Freddie was behind the sounds that Imogen heard in the night. But still she was reluctant. When she'd mentioned it before, he had been dismissive; perhaps he would be again. But if he did accept that his son was responsible, she felt sure he would mete out a very severe punishment, and she hated the thought of what that might be, and the effect it would have on Freddie. Yes, what he had been doing was very wrong, and certainly he needed to be made aware of that. But she had a certain sympathy for him too. He was still a little boy, who had lost both his mother and his brother, and she didn't think he had fully understood the consequences of his actions – until tonight. He'd learned his lesson now, she hoped.

But would Imogen improve if she no longer heard Robbie's toys in the night? Somehow Abi doubted it. Her grief ran too deep; it had drowned her as surely as the lake water had drowned Robbie. It was hopeless. Nothing, it seemed, could save her. Tears of exhaustion and hopelessness sprang to Abi's eyes, blurring the room around her, and she bowed her head, covering her eyes with her hands.

So lost was she in a labyrinth of despair, she didn't hear the click of the door handle as Hugh entered the room; was totally unaware that she was no longer alone until he spoke.

'Abi?'

For a moment she dared not look up; she didn't want him to know she was crying. This wasn't her tragedy; it was his, and Imogen's. She was simply the governess.

'I thought you'd like to know – Imogen is sleeping now,' he said.

'Oh, that's good.' She had hoped the dim light here in the parlour would hide her tear-stained face, but her voice was thick, and trembled on the last word, giving her away.

'Oh Abi, you're upset,' Hugh said, concern in his voice.

'I'm fine,' she said defensively.

'You are not fine at all. And hardly surprising. I'm so sorry to have put you through all this.' He moved towards the chiffonier, and Abi heard the clink of a bottle on glass. 'I'm having a brandy and I think you should have one too.'

'Oh, I don't drink brandy,' she protested weakly.

'You're drinking it now.'

He brought the glass to her, and when she didn't take it, he squatted down on his haunches and lifted it to her lips. As the brandy fumes rose, making her nauseous again, she shook her head, and a few drops spilled over and trickled down her chin.

'I don't want it! Really!'

'Come on. It will do you good. More good than that milk, I promise.'

His gentle insistence was persuasive; Abi didn't feel she had the energy to resist. She took a sip. The golden liquid tingled on her tongue and ran a fiery river down her throat, spreading its warmth all the way to her stomach. But the sensation wasn't un-pleasant, she realised, and she took another sip, and then another.

'Good girl. That's better, is it not?'

Abi looked up, still seeing him through a haze of tears. But as their eyes met, that spark was there again, an unmistakable connection that somehow superseded the relationship of employer and employee. A wild elation that seemed to energise every inch of her. Part dizzying pleasure, part indescribable pain, unlike anything she had ever experienced before. She had loved Connor with all her heart, but this . . . this was crazy, so all-consuming it seemed to make her weak and strong both at the same time. Robbed her of all reason, yet spoke a truth she had been unwilling to acknowledge.

'So – no more tears?'

His hand was still on hers; she'd scarcely noticed it before, but now suddenly she was acutely aware of it, spreading a tingling warmth through her veins just as the brandy had, and when he removed it, fumbling in his pocket for a kerchief, she felt a sense of aching loss. She thought he would hand it to her, but instead he used it to wipe her wet cheeks himself, and tears sprang from her eyes again at the tender gesture. All she wanted was to lay her face against his broad chest and forget the horrors of the past hours in the safety of his arms.

'Oh Abi . . . Abi . . .' It was almost a groan.

She looked up at him again, at the strong planes and angles of his face, and they blurred again, not from tears this time, but because he was now so very close. So close that she could feel his breath mingling with hers. And she was moving towards him, her mouth drawn to his as if by some magnetic force . . .

He pulled away abruptly, releasing her, and the spell was broken. Raised himself to his feet with one hand on the padded window seat.

'Are you going to finish this brandy?' His voice was rough.

Overcome with self-conscious shame, Abi shook her head, and he drained the glass himself.

'I think you should get to bed and try to rest,' he said. No warmth now, no hint of intimacy. It was as if the previous minutes had never been. But they had. And Abi's stomach tightened to knots at the wild abandon she had experienced, and the way she had laid bare her feelings for him.

'Yes, I should,' she said, striving to keep her voice level, determined not to reveal any more of the turbulent emotions churning inside her.

She crossed the floor on legs that she wasn't sure she could rely on. In the doorway she paused, looked back. 'I'm sorry,' she said.

And made for the stairs before he could reply.

Sleep eluded her. She could still feel the touch of his hand; shock waves rippled through her veins and prickled on her skin, but there was no magic in them now. It was wrong, so wrong that she should feel this way. Perhaps it was the strong drink that had made her reckless. But her feelings for him had begun long before that. She wanted him. How could it have happened? She loved him. There was no denying it now. And she thought that for those few brief moments, he had wanted her too. But he had put a stop to what might have been, and though her heart ached, she admired him for it. He was strong, and honourable. He had resisted temptation where she had not. Her stomach curled again with the shame of it. That he knew she had been there for the taking. How she would face him tomorrow, she didn't know.

She buried her face in the pillow and wept. For all of them.

Chapter Seventeen

To Abi's enormous relief, Hugh did not appear at breakfast – according to Handley, the butler, he had eaten early and ridden off somewhere – and unsurprisingly, neither did Imogen. Abi had gone to her room before going downstairs, but she had been intercepted by Mrs Mears.

'She's sleeping,' the housekeeper had said shortly, striding across to block the doorway, arms akimbo. 'And for your information, I am here to make sure she doesn't try anything stupid again.'

'Perhaps I can relieve you later?' Abi suggested. But again Mrs Mears thwarted her.

'That won't be necessary. When I am not here, she is to be locked in, on Sir Hugh's instructions.' And she shut the door in Abi's face, slamming it so hard the woodwork rattled.

There was no sign of Freddie either in the breakfast room. The usual array of dishes was set out in lidded salvers on the sideboard, but Abi didn't feel she could face any of them, and she was drinking her second cup of strong coffee when he eventually appeared, somewhat shamefaced.

'Good morning, Miss Newman.' But he couldn't look at her, going straight to the sideboard and helping himself to scrambled egg and sausages.

Though he loaded his plate as usual, it seemed he had no

more appetite than she did, He picked at his food listlessly, and Abi was at a loss to know what to say to him. Every effort she made at small talk was met with a shrug and stony silence. His conscience was pricking him, she felt sure.

When he put down his knife and fork beside an unfinished sausage, Abi felt she should say something.

'You really must eat more than that, Freddie,' she ventured. 'You'll never be able to concentrate on your work on an empty stomach. And isn't Dr Stanley coming today to give you a science lesson?'

But not even that prospect could lift his spirits, it seemed.

'I don't know,' he muttered.

'I'm sure he said he would be,' Abi persisted. 'That should cheer you up. You know how you enjoy his lessons.'

Freddie scowled and pushed his plate away without replying.

'Come on, Freddie – you know what your papa says about wasting good food,' she chastised him gently.

'He's not here, though, is he?' Freddie scraped back his chair and got up. 'Where is he anyway?'

'He's out. I don't know where,' Abi admitted.

'He has gone to see her ladyship's father.' Mrs Mears was in the doorway. For such a large woman, she was able to move surprisingly stealthily if she bunched the keys that hung from her belt and held them tightly so that they didn't jangle.

'Grandpapa?' Freddie had stopped in his tracks. 'But why?'

'To discuss what's to be done about your stepmother.' Mrs Mears turned her sour gaze on Abi. 'They'll decide she has to be committed to the asylum, no doubt. And not before time,' she added with a smug twist of her lips.

Abi's heart sank, but she was determined not to give the housekeeper the satisfaction of knowing how such a prospect distressed her.

'Have you left Imogen alone?' she asked, going on the offensive. 'Surely that's not wise.'

'As I told you, when she's alone, she is to be locked in her room,' Mrs Mears said impatiently. 'In any case, she is still sleeping. And I'll thank you not to disturb her.'

With that, she turned and left, the keys jangling now on her belt.

'Oh miss!' Freddie had turned pale. 'She's not really going to be sent to the asylum, is she?'

'I don't know, Freddie,' Abi said wretchedly. 'But she is very ill. It may be the only way to keep her safe.'

A flush now spread up Freddie's neck and into his cheeks, vivid against the pallor, and he looked to be close to tears. He was feeling guilty, Abi felt sure, and she made up her mind. If pretending to be Robbie was just his own mischief, perhaps there would be no more of it. But ever since the night when Imogen had heard Robbie playing with his pull-along toy she had suspected he was being encouraged by someone else, for reasons of their own. Now she felt it was important to find out if she was right.

'Freddie, you know what we spoke about last night?' she began. 'The things your mother thinks she hears in the night? It's that, you know, that is having such a dreadful effect on her, and I can't help wondering . . .'

She broke off. She was talking to an empty room. Freddie had fled.

Though she had never in her life felt less like teaching, Abi was in the library by the time the grandfather clock in the hall was chiming the hour. There was no sign of Freddie, but Jimmy was already seated at his desk, his pen, pencil and ruler neatly lined up and a book open in front of him.

'Jimmy! Bright and early as usual!' Abi greeted him, thinking what a pleasure it was to have a pupil who was so eager to learn. 'What are you reading?'

'*The Canterbury Tales.*' Jimmy looked up, his finger marking his place. 'There are really hard words, though, and I don't know what they mean.'

'You've chosen something very difficult,' Abi said – even she found the Middle English difficult to interpret, never mind a nine-year-old boy! 'But I'll do my best to help you if your heart's set on it.'

She laid her books down on the table she used as a desk and leaned over Jimmy's shoulder, explaining as best she could. Then she straightened, rubbing at a crick in her back.

'Where did you learn to read, Jimmy?' she asked.

'When I lived in a house,' Jimmy said, once again marking his place with his finger.

'And where was that?' Abi prompted him.

'I don't know, really.' His face screwed up with the effort of trying to remember. 'I was quite little when they took me to the orphanage.'

'Did you have a mama and a papa?' Abi persisted.

'I *think* so. I must have, I suppose. Sometimes when I'm asleep and dreaming, there's a lady, and she cuddles me. She smells nice, like the petals on the rose bushes.' He hesitated. 'And sometimes there's a man.' He stopped abruptly, and Abi waited. 'They're bad dreams, though. Like when I dream about the orphanage. Or going up chimneys.'

'Oh, that's not nice.' Abi would have liked to press him further about the man who haunted his nightmares. It couldn't be the sweep, unpleasant though he had been – if it was, Jimmy would have said so. Was it someone at the orphanage? Or was it someone from longer ago – his father, perhaps, or an uncle? But she was reluctant to be the one to stir up bad memories, although Jimmy didn't actually seem to be distressed; just sad and pensive, as if he was as curious about his past as she was.

It was incredible how accepting he was of all that had happened to him, she thought, and was unable to help but contrast him with Freddie. Jimmy had been through so much in his short life, yet it was almost as if he had been strengthened by his awful experiences, rather than damaged, as she thought Freddie had been.

'You are a very brave boy,' she said.

He looked up at her, his brown eyes clear and honest. 'You just have to get on with it, don't you?' he said.

Abi had to smile. It was such an old-fashioned thing for a little boy to say, and she wondered where he had got it from. Prudie, perhaps? But he'd only been living with her and Rex for a short time, and it had come out so naturally that she felt it must be something he'd heard often enough, and long enough ago, to belong to his past.

At that moment, the library door burst open and Freddie came in. The time for gentle probing was over.

'I'm sorry I'm late, Miss Newman,' he said, taking his place at his desk.

He still looked sombre and somewhat shamefaced, but his hair was neatly brushed and his face well scrubbed, and Abi resolved not to question him any more, for the time being at any rate. 'Open your books, then, boys,' she said briskly. 'Today I thought we would talk about the Cavaliers and the Roundheads. Jimmy may not have heard of them, and I know you are interested in the Civil War, Freddie.'

Freddie immediately brightened. 'Can we do a play about them, miss?' he asked.

'We could, yes,' Abi said, thinking this would relieve her of some of the pressure of teaching a lesson when she really didn't feel up to it. Freddie was very good at inventing plays, and through them he could teach Jimmy as much as she could, if not more.

'Good-oh!' Freddie turned to Jimmy. 'I'll be the Cavalier, because that's what most gentlemen were. And you can be a Roundhead.'

Abi smiled. Trust Freddie. She took a seat at her desk, opened their arithmetic books, which needed marking, and left them to it.

The boys were enjoying their mid-morning break in the sunshine, and Abi was sitting on the terrace steps watching them as they chased one another around the lawns when a carriage turned into the drive. As it pulled up in the turnaround beneath her, she recognised it as Miss Constance Bingham's.

She rose, straightening her skirts and wishing she could go back inside and avoid the woman, but it was too late for that. She must have been seen, and she didn't want to appear either intimidated or rude. Besides, she was curious.

She waited as the coachman climbed down from his seat and helped Miss Bingham out of the carriage. Today she was wearing a gown of cerise silk, with an elaborate matching hat and slippers, and a reticule studded with little stones that glinted in the sunshine dangled from her wrist. She cast a dismissive glance at Abi as she climbed the steps, then halted and inclined her head slightly in her direction, as if she didn't want to lower herself by speaking to her directly.

'Would you kindly inform Sir Hugh I am here to see him.' Her tone was imperious.

'I'm sorry, but Sir Hugh is out,' Abi said, childishly pleased to be able to deliver the news.

Miss Bingham's rouged lips tightened with displeasure. 'When do you expect him to return?'

'I have no idea,' Abi said carelessly. 'I am only the governess, after all. But I imagine he will be some time.'

The lady huffed impatiently. 'In that case, I shall not wait. But perhaps you would tell him Miss Constance Bingham called.'

'Just that? Is there no message?' Abi asked, hoping in spite of herself to glean some information as to the purpose of Miss Bingham's visit.

'Well, yes. You can tell him I expect him to return my call without delay or I shall be seriously displeased.' With that, she turned and went back down the steps, and the coachman helped her back into the carriage.

Abi was fuming as she watched it disappear down the drive. What an arrogant woman Constance Bingham was! How dare she speak to her like that! How dare she demand that Hugh should call on her 'without delay'! What was she to him? A barb of disquiet pierced Abi's annoyance as she remembered what she had overheard Mrs Mears say – that if Imogen were no longer around, Miss Constance Bingham would be quick to take her place.

Oh, surely Hugh couldn't be involved with her in that way? Abi couldn't believe it of him. He wasn't that kind of man – was he? But she was remembering, too, what else Mrs Mears had said, intimating that he was a womaniser, and suddenly she was thinking of the brief moments of intimate exchanges between them that had excited her so. Had she imagined they were sharing something special when in fact it was nothing but a habit of his as a prelude to seduction?

Her face flamed. Had she made an utter fool of herself? Did he simply see her as easy pickings? Well, he'd soon discover she wasn't that. She would no more play his games, if games they were, than she would allow herself to be swept away by love.

She called to the boys, who had given up chasing one another around the lawns to watch the encounter with the grand lady, and went back to the library to resume the morning's lessons.

It was almost midday before Hugh returned. Abi was about to release the boys from their lessons when he appeared in the doorway.

'My apologies for interrupting, Miss Newman, but I need to speak to you.' There was a brisk formality to his tone that contrasted starkly with what had passed between them last night. With a sinking heart, Abi wondered if that was what he wanted to speak to her about. Could it be that he thought it best for everyone if she resigned her position? Or at the very least, would he make it clear that nothing of the sort must ever happen again?

'It's no problem. We were about to break for lunch,' she said, doing her best to conceal the awkwardness and apprehension she was feeling.

'You'll find me in the parlour, and Mrs Mears will be joining us too – I've asked Mary to fetch her.' He turned abruptly and left.

So it wasn't about last night, or at least not the brief intimacy they had shared. More likely it was to discuss Imogen.

Abi dismissed the boys and went to the parlour, where Hugh was pacing restlessly.

He looked tired, as if he had barely slept, and her heart went out to him. Imogen leaving the house last night and trying to find her way down to the lake must have been the last straw, and his desperate anxiety was etched into every line of his face.

The jangle of keys announced the arrival of Mrs Mears, who strode into the room, making clear her annoyance at being summoned.

'I hope this is important. Some of us have work to do, you know.'

'I fear it is,' Hugh assured her.

'And nothing to do with the lady visitor? I saw her talking to Miss Newman, but I presume it was you she came to see.'

Hugh frowned, and Abi spoke up.

'I haven't had a chance to tell you,' she said apologetically. 'It was Miss Bingham. She is anxious to see you, it seems, and would like you to return her call as soon as you are able.'

Hugh grunted impatiently. 'I hope you told her I have other matters on my mind. But knowing Constance, I don't suppose she gave you the opportunity. Now, there is something I need to tell you both. Shall we all sit down?'

Abi took a chair, but Mrs Mears remained standing. 'I'd rather not.'

She loses some of her authority if she's seated, Abi realised, and when it became clear that Hugh would not sit unless the housekeeper did the same, she got up again, feeling more awkward than ever, as if she had committed some faux pas.

'Well?' Mrs Mears demanded.

'Kindly curb your impatience, Mrs Mears.' Hugh had clearly had enough of the woman's impertinence. 'You may have been wondering why I rode out so early this morning. The fact of the matter is, I have been to see Imogen's father and mother. I wanted to discuss her condition with them so as to reach a decision as to what's to be done.'

'So you've finally realised she needs to be committed to the asylum. Isn't that what I've been telling you?' Mrs Mears crowed.

Abi's heart sank. Surely Hugh wouldn't actually send Imogen to the madhouse? And a moment later, her faith in him was restored.

'Not the asylum,' he said with quiet determination. 'I quite agree that something has to be done, but I still hope it won't come to that. I am not prepared to have Imogen locked away unless there is absolutely no alternative.'

'What then?' Mrs Mears demanded aggressively, but Hugh ignored the interruption and continued as if she had not spoken.

'We feel that Imogen might well benefit from being away from everything that reminds her of Robert. Accordingly, we have decided that she should go to stay with her parents, for the time being at least.'

'Ha!' The housekeeper snorted contemptuously.

'I think it's a very good idea,' Abi said.

'Postponing the inevitable,' Mrs Mears snapped.

'Perhaps. But I'm not prepared to take such a drastic step until every other avenue has been explored. I know you disagree with me, but that is my decision,' Hugh said firmly.

'Very convenient, I'm sure. Palming her off – making her somebody else's problem.'

Abi could scarcely believe the housekeeper dared speak to the master of the house so, and she bristled with indignation and a feeling that might almost have been protectiveness. Bad enough that she should be so rude, but couldn't she see how difficult Hugh found all this? It was all Abi could do not to rush in and berate the woman for her insensitivity.

Hugh, however, refused to rise to her bait.

'I shall be accompanying Lady Hastings,' he said evenly, 'and will remain with her until I am satisfied she has settled in. The estate and the mines will do perfectly well without me for a few days – my managers will see to that. And I am sure I can leave the running of the household in your capable hands, Mrs Mears. Now, perhaps you would be so good as to pack a bag with the things she will need. Miss Newman can help you.'

Mrs Mears bridled. 'I don't need her help.'

'Miss Newman will know which gowns are Imogen's

favourites,' Hugh insisted. 'But she is to take nothing of Robert's – is that clear, Miss Newman? A clean break is what is needed.'

Abi nodded, pleased to see the housekeeper put in her place. 'Do you want us to explain to her why we are packing her things?' she asked.

'No, I'll come and speak to her myself.'

'She won't understand.' Mrs Mears could not resist trying to have the last word, but once again Hugh cut her short.

'Let us waste no more time. I intend to leave immediately after luncheon.'

With that, he left the room, his boots clattering up the stairs, and Abi and Mrs Mears followed.

They had left, and the house felt strangely empty. *He* had left, and though there was nothing between them and never could be, Abi felt bereft. She despised herself for her weakness. How could it have come to this? After all the lonely years, how could she have fallen in love with a man she had no right to feel this way about? And not even realise what was happening to her until it was too late? Now, however hard she busied herself with other things, he invaded her thoughts. She couldn't get him out of her head – or her heart. The husband of the poor tormented lady she called her friend. That was the worst of it. She'd die of shame if he – or anyone else – guessed how she felt.

It was good that he had gone away, for a few days at least. She wouldn't have to face him constantly over the breakfast or dinner table. Wouldn't have to pass him in the hallway and feel his nearness like a physical touch. Wouldn't have to look at him and want him.

Somehow she had to stop this all-consuming foolishness. The trouble was, she honestly didn't know how.

Chapter Eighteen

Life at the vicarage had fallen into a pattern; a very different one, but comfortable none the less. To Malcolm's surprise, Maisie seemed in no hurry for Prissie and the baby to leave – in fact, she had said as much when he'd talked of making enquiries with a view to finding them a permanent home.

'Best not to upset the apple cart just yet,' she had advised. 'Prissie is just beginning to get settled, and she can do without the upheaval of having to start all over again somewhere fresh. A baby needs a calm mother. They can tell, you know, and it's not good for them. Besides, they're no trouble.'

It was true enough. The baby – Prissie had called him Christian, as Maisie had suggested – was very good, and rarely cried now, and rather than making more work for Maisie as Malcolm had feared, Prissie was an enormous help. She was always up with the lark and had the range hot and the breakfast cooking before Maisie got up. She dusted and swept, scrubbed the doorstep and polished the brass, washed the dishes and even the bed sheets when she'd heated the copper to launder Christian's things and her own.

'She's not afraid of hard work, I'll give her that,' Maisie had said. 'I only wish I had half her energy.'

Perhaps that was the reason she didn't seem to want Prissie

216

to move on, Malcolm thought. He'd noticed how tired she got after a long day teaching her pupils, and he'd even suggested she might think of retiring – an idea she had fiercely pooh-poohed. But somehow he couldn't help feeling there was more to her reluctance to see the young woman go than simply the convenience of having what almost amounted to a live-in maid-servant.

She was softer, somehow. She doted on Christian, and never once showed Prissie the disapproval he'd expected, treating her more kindly than he'd dared hope. She had even asked Malcolm to church the girl, and had gone with them, sitting in the front pew while Malcolm performed the age-old rite of giving thanks for the safe delivery of Prissie's baby and cleansing her. She'd be arranging a baptism soon, if he was not much mistaken.

As for little Christian, she doted on him. But when she held him, or rocked his cradle, there was a wistfulness about her, and Malcolm found himself remembering how she had seemed on the verge of tears when he'd got back from leaving the baby with Queenie. There had been more to it than just shock, or sympathy for Prissie's plight, he felt sure.

'Brings back memories, does it?' he'd probed ambiguously, so that if he was wrong, and there was nothing to it, she could take it that he was referring to the days when Abi had been a baby.

But Maisie had turned away abruptly, and not before he'd seen her face change. Tight. Shut in. Her chin wobbling.

'You could say that.' As ambiguous a reply as his question had been, and he didn't feel able to press her further. It was none of his business, he told himself. If Maisie was hiding some secret sorrow, he shouldn't pry.

And then one day, Sukie, who was visiting, said something that seemed to confirm his suspicions.

Prissie was in the garden, picking peas and cutting a cabbage to go with the joint of pork that was roasting over the fire; she had left Christian in his Moses basket in the parlour, where they could keep an eye on him, and when he'd begun to whimper, Maisie had picked him up, sniffing at his bottom.

'You need changing, don't you, little man? Don't worry, I'll make you comfortable,' she'd said, and taken him upstairs, leaving Sukie and Malcolm alone.

'Well I never!' Sukie said wonderingly. 'I don't know what's come over her. Regrets, if you ask me. Trying to make amends.'

'Make amends?' Malcolm repeated. 'For what?'

'Well, what they did to Abigail, of course.' Seeing Malcolm's startled expression, she stopped short. 'Oh, me and my big mouth! You didn't know, did you? You'd best forget I said anything.'

'What are you talking about?' Malcolm was utterly confused. He'd thought that if Maisie had a secret, it concerned something that had happened to her. But from what Sukie had said, that wasn't the case.

Sukie shook her head vigorously. 'No. It's not for me to say. I've said too much already. If you want to know, you'll have to ask Maisie. It would be a good thing for her to talk about it, if you ask me. All these years it's been on her mind, I know – and her conscience. You're a vicar. You could take her confession, couldn't you? Absolve her, or whatever it is you call it.'

'I'm not very used to hearing confessions,' Malcolm said helplessly. 'We don't insist on them as the Roman Catholic Church does.'

'More's the pity, if you ask me,' Sukie said. ''Tis supposed to be good for the soul, isn't it?' She paused, then went on: 'I do worry about her. What happened – what she did – it preys on her, that I do know. At one time I thought she was putting it all behind her, but Prissie and that little baby . . . it's brought it all back. They were wrong, her and Obediah. They only meant it for the best, but 'twas the wrong thing to do.'

A sound from the hall. Sukie broke off, putting a finger to her lips. Maisie was back. The time for confidences, however oblique and puzzling, was over.

'Sweeter now, is he?' Sukie said ingenuously.

'He is.' But Maisie sounded strained, and instead of returning Christian to his Moses basket, she sat down, cradling him in her lap and looking down at him with that same wistful expression Malcolm had noticed before.

'I think I'll go and get a breath of air.' He rose. There was no way on earth he could remain there, chatting as if nothing had happened. He needed to be alone, to process what Sukie had said. He had to admit he was shocked. There was more, far more, to this than he had envisaged, and he needed to think it through, decide what, if anything, he should do about it. He was a vicar, for God's sake. A spiritual adviser. And Maisie, it seemed, was a tortured soul, a lost sheep who had somehow strayed from the flock, widow of a vicar or not. And what of Abi? Was she suffering too as a result of whatever it was Sukie had alluded to?

He went into the garden, avoiding the vegetable patch where Prissie was still bending low over the row of peas. He crossed the little lawn and sat down with his back resting against the trunk of a lilac tree. Just a few weeks ago, it had been laden with fragrant purple blossom; now the spikes lay on the grass all around him, faded and withering.

But next spring the tree would bloom again, evidence of rebirth, renewal, new life. The knowledge gave him hope that he would find a way through this dilemma, be able to help Maisie to come to terms with whatever it was that troubled her, and find peace.

He folded his hands in his lap, closed his eyes and prayed.

* * *

His prayer, it seemed, was answered. That evening when Prissie was upstairs with Christian and he and Maisie were alone, she surprised him by raising the subject.

'She told you about Abi and the baby,' she said bluntly. The unexpectedness of it was disconcerting.

'She didn't exactly tell me anything,' he said.

'Oh, really?' Maisie's lips were set in a tight line, but her hands, working in the folds of her skirts, betrayed her agitation. 'From what I overheard, she said more than enough. After the lengths we went to, all this time keeping quiet for the sake of Abigail's good name, and she has to blurt it out.'

So Maisie must have been outside the door for at least part of the conversation he'd had with Sukie. But Malcolm couldn't have her blaming her sister, especially since Sukie had been adamant that whatever the full story was, it should come from Maisie herself.

'All she said was that she thought Prissie and her baby had reminded you of something from the past,' he said.

Maisie snorted. 'You're telling me Abigail's name wasn't mentioned?'

'Well, yes, it was,' Malcolm admitted. 'But Sukie was very clear that it wasn't her place to go into it. That it was your business, not hers.'

'But you've put two and two together, I'm sure,' Maisie said tightly.

'I can only hazard a guess,' Malcolm hedged. 'And if that's the way you would prefer to leave it, then I shall put it out of my mind. But if you think sharing what is troubling you would be of help, then you can be sure it will go no further.'

'The secrets of the confessional,' Maisie said bitterly.

'I'd like to think I am more than just your priest. I consider myself a friend, and I hope you think of me in that way too.'

Maisie's face crumpled suddenly. 'You know I do.' She lowered her head to hide the tears that shone in her eyes, staring down at her restless fingers for long moments, then she raised a hand, wiping it across her mouth, and looked up at him with something of her earlier defensive denial.

'It wasn't Abigail's fault. She was young – so young – when she took up with this lad, and he led her astray. We brought her up to know right from wrong. To be a good girl. And she was, until she met him. She kept it secret – she knew we would have put a stop to it. But we didn't even know she was seeing him until . . . well, until it was too late . . .'

'He didn't stand by her?' Malcolm could see no reason to be explicit about the predicament Abi had found herself in; it was plain enough without having to be put into words.

'Oh, there was no question of that. We'd never have agreed to it. Abigail was far too young. But it didn't arise. The boy was dead – never even knew about the trouble he'd caused.'

'Dead?' Malcolm repeated, shocked.

'Crushed to death by his father's bull. Old Yeates's son, he was. You know, Farmer Yeates, up at South Hill.'

Malcolm nodded. The Yeates family weren't regular church-goers, but after one Matins, a woman he didn't recognise had lit a candle beneath the statue of the Virgin Mary, and Oliver Doughty, the sidesman, had told him she was Farmer Yeates's wife, and the candle would be for her son, who had been killed in an accident on the farm some years ago. She always came to church on the anniversary of his death, Doughty had said.

'At least they never knew how he'd let them down,' Maisie said. 'Nobody in the village got to hear of it – we made sure of that. When Abigail couldn't hide it any longer, we kept her well out of the way. Told folk she was away visiting. Obediah had a cousin over in Claverton who was a midwife, and she was going to come and attend to Abigail when the time came. But then . . .' She broke off, swallowing hard at what Malcolm guessed was a lump in her throat. 'Trouble was,' she went on at last, 'about a month before her due date, the silly girl tumbled down the stairs, top to bottom, and it started her off. She went into labour.'

She stopped again, overwhelmed by her nightmarish memories.

'The baby didn't survive,' Malcolm posited.

For long moments Maisie didn't reply. Her head was bowed now, staring once more at her hands. For some reason, she couldn't meet his eyes. Then . . .

'That's what we told Abigail,' she said. 'But it wasn't the truth. Perfect, he was. Dark hair, like strands of silk. The bluest eyes you ever did see. Broke my heart, it did, to see him go, though I never expected to feel like that. But 'twas all arranged. Obediah had seen to it.'

'You let Abi think her baby was stillborn?' Malcolm was truly shocked. He'd been prepared for almost anything, but not this. Never this.

'It was for the best,' Maisie said defensively. 'She couldn't keep it – a young girl her age. Her life would've been ruined before it had hardly begun. No decent man would have wanted her. And the talk it would have caused! What would folk have thought? The vicar's daughter, nothing but a common whore with a bastard child. No, it was for the best.'

'Perhaps . . . but to let her believe the baby was dead!' Malcolm was still struggling to process it.

''Twould have been worse for her to know he was out there somewhere,' Maisie said, sounding defensive. 'Always wondering about him. Where he was, if he was all right. Picturing him growing up, wondering what he looked like. This way, she could forget. Live her life as if it had never happened.'

'Somehow I doubt it,' Malcolm said.

'No, 'twas for the best,' Maisie repeated stubbornly, a mantra she had no doubt clung to over the years.

'So you had him adopted,' Malcolm said. 'By whom?'

Maisie shook her head. 'That I couldn't tell you. Obediah made all the arrangements. But it would have been a reputable family, that I do know. He would have made sure of it.'

Composed now, she looked directly at Malcolm. 'I hope you won't feel obliged to enlighten Abigail. It would only upset her, and there would be nothing to gain from it. And,' she added, 'I hope you'll remember – this must go no further.'

Maisie's revelations had left Malcolm reeling. As a vicar, he had listened to the details of many sad stories before, offered help where he could, given absolution for any wrongs when it was requested, been touched by some confessions and privately angered by others, though he had always taken care not to allow that to interfere with his role as God's representative. But never had he been affected by what he had heard as he was now. Never before had a tragic tale involved people he cared deeply about, thought of more as family than friends. This was far too close to home for comfort.

He felt sure that Maisie and her late husband had believed that what they were doing was in Abi's best interests. Not to mention their own, though he couldn't find it in himself to blame them for that. They would have been devastated, trapped in a nightmare they'd never dreamed of, not knowing which way to turn, and deeply ashamed. They would have known the village would be scandalised, feared the whispers and the open condemnation that would spread like wildfire, would have done anything to protect their reputation – and Abi's. But even so, it had been wrong, so wrong. To have spirited Abi's child away and allowed her to believe he was dead was unforgivable, no matter how desperate they had been.

And Maisie didn't even know where he had been taken. Where he was now. It must have tormented her over the years. However she might have wished he had never been conceived, he was her grandchild, her own flesh and blood. Small wonder that the arrival of Prissie and her baby had affected her as it had. A young woman in a similar position, with no husband to support her, a baby as young as Abi's must have been when Maisie had last seen him. It must have sparked emotions in her that she had refused to acknowledge, had buried deep rather than face them.

That Christian tugged at her heartstrings was clear, and what Malcolm now knew explained the tenderness she showed towards the little mite. It explained too her acceptance of Prissie, a woman she would have scorned under other circumstances. And perhaps she felt that offering the girl sanctuary went some way to making up for the way she had treated her own daughter. A recompense of sorts.

So – what had become of Abi's child? Malcolm wondered. He would no longer be a baby, but a young boy. The dark hair Maisie had mentioned would have grown, the blue eyes changed colour, perhaps – Malcolm had been told that the eyes of all newborn babies were blue. Did he take after Abi at all; have any family traits? Was he strong and healthy or sickly? What was he good at? Maisie must wonder. It accounted for her wistfulness when she was nursing Christian.

Perhaps he could find out, he thought. It might be of some comfort to her. As for Abi, though it was unlikely she would ever be any the wiser, he felt he somehow owed it to her to ensure that her child was well and happy. And it would set his own mind at rest.

Since Obediah had been a vicar, it was likely the adoption had been arranged through the Church. If he made enquiries, he should be able to gain access to the old records. That was what he would do.

The decision went some way to easing the burden that had fallen on his shoulders with the telling of the story. It might prove difficult, and he'd have to tread carefully. But at least he would try. He poured himself a mug of porter and downed it with the driving need of a thirsty man in a dusty desert.

Chapter Nineteen

The atmosphere at Bramley Court was hostile. With Hugh away, Mrs Mears had taken absolute control, and her domineering ways were becoming unbearable. Abi kept out of her way as much as she could, spending each day with Freddie and Jimmy, and the evenings mostly in her room or, when it was fine and warm, in the garden.

For some reason known only to herself, Mrs Mears had decided that dinner should be served an hour earlier than the usual time of seven, and instead of eating below stairs with the rest of the staff, she had taken to having her meal in the dining room with Abi and inviting Freddie to join them.

Abi hated it. Mrs Mears pointedly ignored her, talking only to Freddie. Though she had no desire to have a conversation with the horrible woman the slight rankled, and added to the awkwardness she couldn't help feeling. To make matters worse, everything Mrs Mears said was pointed, with the intention of hitting a nerve. In particular she was critical of Jimmy, and made continual references to her opinion that he was bound to be a disruptive influence and have a detrimental effect on Freddie's education. On one occasion, Abi had spoken out. Jimmy was an excellent pupil, far more dedicated to learning than Freddie, never rude or disrespectful, and she had said so, though she tactfully refrained from mentioning that he was fast catching up with Freddie in most subjects. Mrs Mears had taken exception to her praise.

'I suppose you're well used to uncouth and less able pupils, Miss Newman,' she had said with a sneer, and turned away as if Abi was beneath contempt.

It was three days now since Hugh and Imogen had left, and that evening, as soon as she had finished her meal, Abi excused herself, anxious to get away from the unpleasant atmosphere. Freddie had jumped up from the table too.

'Where do you think you're going?' Mrs Mears demanded.

'To meet Jimmy. We're going to look for butterflies. We saw a painted lady yesterday.'

'You will sit down until I've had my coffee,' Mrs Mears said sternly. 'Where are your manners? And you see far too much of that ragamuffin.'

'He's my friend!' Freddie protested.

'Friend indeed! It's quite enough that you have to spend your days with him, never mind the evenings too.'

Freddie obeyed reluctantly, but his mulish expression told Abi he was burning with resentment.

She went out into the garden, feeling guilty that she was in no position to back Freddie up. The sun was still warm, drawing the perfume from the roses and honeysuckle, and her depressed mood was just beginning to lift when to her surprise she saw a pony and trap approaching down the drive, and recognised it as Giles Stanley's. Though he still called in regularly to spend time with Freddie, he hadn't been here since Hugh and Imogen had left, and Abi guessed he didn't know that Hugh had taken Imogen home.

'Giles,' she said as the pony and trap reached her, slowing to a halt.

'Miss Newman. What a pleasant surprise! I've been too busy to visit lately – the warm weather seems to have been breeding a multitude of infections. A spate of measles and diphtheria amongst the young, and our older patients . . . well, a summer cold can give rise to most unpleasant respiratory problems. You have all been keeping well, I hope?'

'Physically, yes.' Abi thought he might as well know the truth. 'Lady Hastings has gone downhill, though, I'm afraid. Sir Hugh has taken her to stay with her parents for a while.'

'Without consulting me?' Giles sounded rather put out.

'There seemed little point in that,' Abi said. 'What could you have done that hasn't already been tried? Sir Hugh was of the opinion that she would benefit from a change of scene.'

'It's possible, certainly – but will they be able to manage her? They are elderly, I imagine.'

'Sir Hugh is staying until he's satisfied she's settled,' Abi explained. 'I'm sorry that you've had a wasted journey.'

'No matter,' Giles said breezily. 'It's Freddie I came to see. I've been neglecting him lately, and as I have a free evening . . .'

'He'll be pleased, I'm sure. Shall I tell him you're here?' Abi offered.

'Thank you. I think we should take advantage of this lovely evening, and meet out here in the fresh air.'

Abi left him to take his pony and trap to the side of the house, where he usually left it, and went indoors to find Freddie, expecting to find him in the dining room still with Mrs Mears.

But the housekeeper was alone, with a half-drunk cup of coffee and what looked suspiciously like a glass of Hugh's best cognac on the table in front of her.

'If you are looking for Frederick, he's in his room,' she said shortly – not best pleased to be caught in the act of enjoying her employer's brandy, Abi suspected.

'I thought he was going to play with Jimmy.'

'He spends too much time with that boy,' Mrs Mears repeated. 'I told him he was to play in his room this evening. You'll find him there, no doubt – unless he has chosen to defy me, and if he has, he'll face the consequences.'

Abi went to the foot of the stairs and called Freddie's name, but there was no reply. Either he hadn't heard or, more likely, he was sulking. She was left with no option but to go up and fetch him.

She found him lying flat on his stomach, playing with his fort.

'Freddie – Dr Stanley is here to see you,' she said.

Freddie continued moving his soldiers to strategic positions. 'I know. I saw him.'

He sounded petulant, and Abi thought perhaps he was upset that it was almost a week since Giles had spent time with him.

'He's very sorry he's been neglecting you, but he's had more patients than usual to attend to,' she said. 'Buck up now. You know how much you enjoy your science lessons.'

'I'm busy.'

'Freddie.' Abi spoke more sternly. 'He's come all this way especially. It would be very rude not to go down and see him. And it would serve you right if he decided not to teach you any more.' But Freddie merely shrugged.

What on earth was the matter with him? Abi wondered, exasperated.

'I thought you'd grown out of this childish behaviour. I know you're upset because Mrs Mears refused to allow you to play with Jimmy, but that's no reason to act this way.' She paused, deciding a bribe might do the trick. 'Dr Stanley wants to spend your time together out in the garden, and when you've finished, nobody would be any the wiser if you called for Jimmy. Just as long as you stay out of sight. And I promise I won't breathe a word.'

Freddie sighed heavily. 'Oh, if I must.' He moved one last soldier into position – not wanting to concede defeat too easily, Abi guessed – and got up.

'That's better!' she said encouragingly, though his mulish expression was very different to his usual pleasure at spending time with Giles. 'Now, let's not keep Dr Stanley waiting any longer.'

Constance was far from happy. Following her visit to Bramley Court, when that infuriating trumped-up governess had delighted in telling her Hugh was out, she had waited in anticipation of him returning her call, growing ever more impatient – and anxious. She had been so sure that, given his all-consuming ambitions for the expansion of his coalfield, she had the whip hand, and with Imogen out of the way, she would be able to rekindle their old relationship and step seamlessly into the breach. Now she was beginning to wonder if her optimism had been misplaced. Memories of the unceremonious way he had cut her out of his life when he had met Marigold resurfaced, memories she had pushed to the back of her mind, and doubts began to creep in.

Had she never been more to him than a pleasurable dalliance? A convenience, even? She was honest enough to admit that that was all she had been to the men she had consorted with since. Oh, one or two of them had been infatuated with her briefly, it was true, but for the most part she had been little more than a trophy, a boost to their egos. But she didn't care about them any more than she cared if people thought her a wanton woman, her way of life scandalous. In return for her favours, her gentlemen friends had given her whatever she wanted. Gifts of beautiful jewellery. The wherewithal to fill her closets with fashionable clothes. One had even provided her with an apartment, which he called a love nest and she called home. They had boosted her self-esteem, proved to the world that she was a desirable woman rather than a plaything to be carelessly tossed aside.

But Hugh was different. Her desire for him had become an obsession. He, and only he, had the power to hurt her – and she was hurting now.

Why had he not returned her call? It could be, of course, that the governess had not passed on her message – that, she told herself, was the most likely explanation. If their positions were reversed, she was sure she would have succumbed to the temptation to keep silent. Perhaps she should pay another visit to Bramley Court. But she was reluctant to do that in case her message had been passed on. She didn't want to appear to be pursuing him. Didn't want to reveal a chink in her armour. And the unpalatable fact remained – the whole reason she had gone to Bramley Court was because it was too long for her liking since he had made contact. She'd thought he would be anxious to find out how things were progressing, but it was almost as if he'd lost interest, and it worried her.

But she couldn't – she wouldn't – give up now. Hugh was the only man she had ever wanted. The one who had eluded her and broken her heart. She wouldn't be beaten by a madwoman and a governess. It was time to refine her plan; sugar the carrot. And she knew exactly how she would do it.

Malcolm was sitting in his study, thinking over the day's discoveries. He had been determined to waste no time in discovering what had happened to Abi's baby. But where to begin? When Maisie had told him the tragic story, his first thought had been that Obediah would have wanted the child to go to a Christian family and arranged for his adoption through the Church, but since he had been anxious to keep Abi's condition secret from everyone but the immediate family, Malcolm couldn't imagine that he would have taken anyone who knew him into his confidence. Had he looked further afield, perhaps to an establishment such as the Foundling Hospital in London? It was well known that it was supported by prominent women from aristocratic families, and the governors and guardians included such distinguished persons as dukes, earls, viscounts, privy councillors and aldermen. If Obediah had turned to them for assistance, they might well have been sympathetic to a man of the cloth whose reputation was under threat. It was entirely possible that they would have been able to arrange the adoption; couples desperate for a child would almost certainly approach the hospital, which would be only too happy to find a home for one of their little charges. It was a long shot, though – London was more than a hundred miles away, and it seemed unlikely that Obediah would have travelled so far. Much more likely that he would have looked closer to home. But where? Malcolm had no idea.

It had occurred to him that there must surely have been correspondence of some kind relating to the arrangements – letters, and maybe even documents. Since Obediah had died so unexpectedly, he had been robbed of the chance to put his affairs in order, and over the past weeks, Malcolm had ploughed through reams of paperwork, much of it years old and no longer relevant, filing what he thought he should keep and making a bonfire of the rest. But there was also a locked tin box tucked away in the bottom of one of the cabinets. Guessing it contained things that were personal and private, he had never so much as considered opening it – it was none of his business. But if it could provide a clue as to what had happened to Abi's baby, then that, he thought, was a good enough reason to investigate.

He had fetched the keys he had found when he cleared out the desk drawers, but he could see at a glance that the key to the tin box was not among them. These were all sturdy and sizeable, while the keyhole in the box was minute. He checked all the drawers in case the tiny key was lurking somewhere, but no, it wasn't there. When Maisie was in the schoolroom, occupied with her pupils, he had searched the kitchen and parlour without success, and come to the conclusion that there was nothing for it but to force the lock. He found a screwdriver amongst a collection of hand tools and set to work to prise the box open.

As he had suspected, it was crammed with personal papers and a few sentimental items. There were birth, marriage and death certificates, a couple of black-edged mourning cards, a flyleaf from a book that had clearly been a Sunday School prize awarded to Obediah when he was a boy, and cards marking Abi's baptism and confirmation. All were yellowed with age. But there was also an envelope that was not discoloured, addressed to Obediah in a spidery hand. Malcolm turned it over. The flap, which had been secured with a blob of red sealing wax, had been neatly slit from end to end – Obediah must have used a paper knife, which made Malcolm think it must be something important. He slid out the single sheet of parchment with care.

It wasn't a long letter, but it was exactly what Malcolm had been hoping for. *In reply to your enquiry, we would be happy to discuss the matter with you if you would care to call on Thursday next at noon.* The signature beneath the script was illegible, but that scarcely mattered. The paper was embossed with the words 'St Margaret's Hospital for Needy Children', and from the address, Malcolm judged that it must be on the outskirts of Westbury. His spirits rose. Westbury was less than twenty miles away; he'd be well able to get there and back in a day.

But less than twenty miles or not, there was still the question of how he would make the journey. He had no transport of his own – all the parishioners he had to visit lived within walking distance. The nearest coaching inn was some miles away, in Stoneham, and he had no idea how frequently the coaches passed through. And the only carriage for hire locally was owned by Isaac Wilton, whose wife, Dolly, was known as an inveterate gossip. If he asked Isaac to take him and Dolly got to hear of it, as she almost certainly would, the story would spread through the village like wildfire, arousing far more curiosity and speculation than he was prepared to risk.

Except . . . of course! Malcolm had brightened as it came to him that he had the perfect cover. Most folk knew by now that Prissie and her baby were staying at the vicarage; if it became known he was visiting a home for unwanted and illegitimate children, it would be assumed he was doing it on her behalf. And he could use the same excuse to Maisie, though he suspected she might well be less than happy at the thought of the two of them leaving. But he didn't want to tell her the truth yet, didn't want to raise her hopes – if finding Abi's child was what she wished for – or risk her objecting if she thought it would be best to let sleeping dogs lie. Only if he was successful would he decide on the next step. But for his own peace of mind, he was determined to try.

Now he got up from his desk and went into the schoolroom, where Maisie was tidying away books and slates. Prissie had taken Christian into the garden and was sitting with his Moses basket on the seat beside her, but he still thought it would be safest to talk to Maisie somewhere there was no danger of being interrupted unexpectedly.

'Malcolm!' She sounded surprised – the schoolroom was very much her domain, and Malcolm only ever set foot in it when he came to teach the weekly half-hour of religious education.

'I wanted to talk to you in private,' he said by way of explanation.

'Oh?' Maisie stacked the slates on a shelf. 'What about?'

'I intend to go to Westbury as soon as I can arrange for Isaac Wilton to take me,' he said, plunging straight in. 'I want to pay a visit to the hospital for needy children there.'

She spun round. 'Whatever for?'

'I think it is time to look at Prissie's options. She can't stay here forever.'

'You're not thinking of having Christian taken into care, I hope!' Maisie was every bit as horrified as Malcolm had expected.

'Of course not,' he reassured her. 'What I'm hoping is that they may be able to suggest somewhere she and Christian can be together.'

'They're together here!'

'For the present, yes. But in the long term, it is far from ideal. They need a home of their own. And supposing Abi wanted to come back? While Prissie is occupying her room she would have nowhere to go.'

Maisie sniffed. 'I think that is very unlikely. Abi has made her decision.'

'But you can't know that for certain. Her circumstances might change. Besides, I'm sure the time will come when you will be glad of some peace and quiet. There won't be much of that when Christian starts running around.'

For a long moment Maisie was silent, and Malcolm thought she was beginning to see the sense in his argument. Then: 'I don't want them to go,' she said plaintively.

'Oh Mrs Newman . . .' Malcolm hesitated, wondering if

perhaps he should tell her what he planned after all. But his reservations still stood. He was more certain than ever that Maisie regretted giving away her grandson, and if he failed in his attempts to find him, then any hopes she might have for a reunion would be dashed. Even if he succeeded, it was quite possible the adoptive parents would refuse to allow Maisie to even see the child. No, much better to keep his intentions to himself, for now at least.

'Don't upset yourself, Mrs Newman.' He placed a hand on her arm. 'Nothing is going to change overnight, and perhaps not at all. I'm exploring possibilities, nothing more.'

'Yes, I understand that.' Maisie was making every effort to recover herself. 'I'm sure that is very sensible.'

'I'm glad you agree.' Malcolm turned to leave, but as he reached the doorway, Maisie spoke again in the same small, lost voice.

'I'm sorry. But I think you know what is upsetting me.'

'Yes.' Malcolm's heart went out to her. She had nursed her private regrets for a very long time, he thought. 'God works in mysterious ways,' he said. 'We never know how, or when, our prayers will be answered.'

Maisie nodded. 'I shall put my faith in the Lord,' she said, and he noticed that her hands were clasped in the folds of her skirts as if already making her supplication.

He would add his prayers to hers, he thought, and hope that God would look kindly on them.

Chapter Twenty

Giles Stanley was not happy. He climbed into the driving seat of his trap, flicked the pony with the reins, and shouted at him for good measure to 'Giddy up!' As he rounded the corner of the house, he saw that Freddie was still standing alone where he had left him, on the path that led to the walled garden, head bowed, shoulders hunched, kicking at the low kerb with the toe of his boot.

Giles slowed as he reached him. 'I will see you again soon, Frederick,' he called. Freddie shrugged, still not looking up.

'Friends?' Giles said. The boy nodded, but not very convincingly. 'Good.'

He loosened the reins again and clipped them against the pony's flanks. As he pulled away, he glanced back over his shoulder and saw that Freddie was staring balefully after him.

His heart sank. Somehow, it seemed, he'd alienated the boy whose help he needed if he was to save his career and the new life he'd built here for himself from total destruction. Without it he wasn't sure how he could achieve the result that a certain dangerous lady required – the only way he could buy her silence.

It was, of course, all his own fault that he found himself in this situation. He'd been greedy and that, coupled with his arrogance, had proved disastrous. While working as his father's juior partner, an opportunity he had been unable to resist had presented itself – the promise of an inheritance that would make him rich. Instead, it had been his downfall.

Mrs Cahill was an elderly wealthy widow who was a patient of his father's. Her late husband had made a small fortune as a merchant, shipowner and slave trader in the city of Bristol. They had no children, and when Edward Cahill had decided it was time to retire, he had disposed of his business assets, sold his grand house in Guinea Street, and bought a rambling manor on the outskirts of Pawley, the small town where Giles's father, John, had his practice. Unfortunately for him, he had not lived long to enjoy the country pursuits he craved. He had collapsed during evensong at the parish church he supported with generous donations, and was dead within the hour, despite John Stanley's desperate efforts to save him.

It was generally assumed that his widow would move away, perhaps back to Bristol and the wide group of friends she had left there, but she showed no sign of wanting to do so. Giles had first attended her as a patient when she took a tumble on an icy step outside her front door, cutting her head open on a wrought-iron boot scraper as she fell. Under normal circumstances his father would have taken the call, but he was suffering from a heavy cold and Giles had gone in his place.

Mrs Cahill had taken a fancy to him – unsurprisingly, given the charm he lavished on her – and from that day on she found many excuses to need a call from the doctor, always stipulating that it should be Giles who visited. But it was not only Giles Mrs Cahill had a fancy for. She was also addicted to laudanum and a variety of other drugs. And this was to be the cause of his downfall.

In Giles, Mrs Cahill saw a way of obtaining the substances she craved. In return for promising to leave him the bulk of her fortune in her will, she persuaded him to keep her supplied with drugs on a regular basis and in quantities his father would never have sanctioned. Undeterred, Giles helped himself to whatever she required, safe in the belief that with his failing eyesight and lapses of memory, John was unlikely to notice.

His confidence, however, was misplaced, and when Mrs Cahill was found by her housekeeper, dead of an overdose, John Stanley had confronted his son with the suspicion that had been nagging at him.

Giles had blustered but was eventually forced to confess. John, horrified, had accused him of endangering both his own good name and that of the practice, and Giles had become belligerent.

'If you knew what I was doing, you are as much to blame as I!'

'It was a suspicion only,' John protested. 'I could not truly believe you capable of such a thing. I told myself you were only taking what Mrs Cahill needed in order to ease her rheumatics. But it must have been considerably more than that for her to have accumulated sufficient for this to happen . . .' The colour was rising alarmingly in his face and neck, and Giles feared his father was about to suffer a stroke.

'I'm sorry,' he apologised in an effort to calm things down, but John was not to be placated.

'You do realise the consequences of something like this? If it comes to light, you could face serious charges. My son! In front of the justices for criminal negligence at best – and at worst, manslaughter! The shame of it!'

'It won't come to that,' Giles had said, with more confidence than he was feeling now that he was beginning to realise the seriousness of what he had done.

'We can only pray you are right.' John Stanley had helped

himself to a large brandy, and Giles hoped it wouldn't send his blood pressure soaring and cause that stroke. He hoped too, desperately, that Mrs Cahill had changed her will in his favour as she had promised. A sizeable inheritance was his only hope of salvation.

But he was to be disappointed. When the will was read and made public, it turned out that she had left her entire estate to a charity that provided for the destitute dependents of men lost at sea. Giles was left seething. He had risked his reputation and gained nothing.

And worse was to come.

It wasn't long before the whispers began, originating no doubt from Mrs Cahill's housekeeper and other members of her staff, who had long speculated amongst themselves as to what was going on. Fortunately for Giles, when they reached the ears of the local law enforcement officer, he refused to believe that a charming and well-qualified doctor could be guilty of such a thing, especially since he was the son of the highly respected physician who had attended the births, ailments and deaths of the whole community for more than thirty years.

But such a juicy story couldn't be hushed up, and it was chewed over in the taverns, local shops, and even places of worship. Sidelong glances were cast as the Stanleys passed by, and more than one family removed themselves from their list and took their allegiance to a practice in the next town.

Eventually John Stanley came to the conclusion that the only solution was for Giles to go elsewhere. But in spite of his disappointment in him, and his anger for the trouble he had caused, John still loved his son and didn't want to see his talent and the long years of study go to waste, his life and career in ruins. He set about looking for a suitable position for him well away from all the gossip, and found it when he approached Dr

Mounty, an old friend, who jumped at the chance to be relieved of the pressures of managing his practice alone. John had expected Giles to react to the news with resentment and hurt, but to his relief, when he told him of the arrangement, his son actually seemed quite happy about it. Branching out would give him a fresh start, he had said. John had no idea how frustrated Giles was with his old-fashioned methods, and how he longed to be able to put into practice all the modern techniques he had learned in Edinburgh.

He had left to take up his new post brimming with confidence that his disgrace was well and truly behind him. How wrong he had been! To his dismay the scandal had followed him, a dark shadow like a storm cloud blotting out the sun, and Miss Constance Bingham was taking full advantage of it. Unless he could do what she required, his reputation, his career and the new life he had built for himself were under threat. Giles' mouth tightened to a determined line. No matter what it took, one way or another, he would do whatever was necessary to ensure that did not happen.

Malcolm was eager to begin his quest to find Abi's lost son, and had hired Isaac Wilton to take him to St Margaret's Hospital for Needy Children. It stood in an expanse of parkland on the outskirts of Westbury, a one-time country house built of Bath stone that glowed like honey in the midday sunshine.

'I hope not to keep you waiting too long,' he said as Isaac pulled the carriage to a halt at the foot of a short flight of steps leading to a dark oak door.

'I hope that too,' Isaac grumbled, though in fact he was quite happy to spend as long as it took wandering around the pleasant grounds and enjoying his snap – fresh bread, cheese and pickled onions – away from his wife's constant nagging.

Malcolm climbed the steps and pulled on a rope attached to a brass bell that hung beside the door. It was opened by a young woman in the uniform of a maid, who gawped as if surprised to see a vicar on the doorstep, though the clergy were surely frequent visitors since the hospital was run by the Church authorities.

'Yes? What d'ee want?'

'I wondered if I might speak with your superintendent,' Malcolm said.

'Who?'

'The person in charge here.'

''Ave you got an appointment?' Her eyes were hostile in her pudgy face, and it sounded to Malcolm as if she was cursed with adenoids.

'No, but I have travelled some distance in order to see him.' He treated her to what he hoped was a winning smile. 'I would be most grateful if you could ascertain if he is available.'

'Oh – I don't know about that . . .' She wasn't very bright either, he thought.

'Then perhaps you could ask someone who does?' he suggested.

The maid eyed him up and down suspiciously, then eventually turned and went in without another word, closing the door behind her. Malcolm tapped the toe of his boot impatiently on the iron boot scraper, wondering how long he should wait before ringing the bell again. Then he heard footsteps approaching from within, and the door was opened by a small, rotund man dressed in outdated knee breeches, stockings and buckled shoes and a striped waistcoat.

'Good day. How may I be of assistance?' he asked.

'I am hoping to speak to the superintendent.' Malcolm was unsure how much of what he had said the maid had taken in.

'I am the superintendent – though I am usually referred to as "the Father of the House",' the little man said with a wry smile.

'My apologies. And I am sorry to have turned up on your doorstep without an appointment.'

'No matter. Come inside.' He opened the door wide and stepped aside.

'Thank you, Father.'

The little man chuckled drily. 'You need not call me that. I am only "Father" to the poor unfortunate children in our care. My name is Francis Pascoe. And unlike you . . .' he gesticulated towards Malcolm's clerical collar, 'I am not a member of the clergy, though I have been in the employ of the Church for many years. And you are . . . ?'

'Malcolm Rayner. I am the vicar of the parishes of East and West Denby.'

'So what can I do for you?' Mr Pascoe closed the door, but sunlight still filtered in through a circular stained-glass panel, casting a rainbow of light on the stained board floor.

'I am trying to discover the whereabouts of a baby boy I believe may have been brought to you some nine years ago, pending his adoption,' Malcolm explained. 'It's a long shot, I know, but it is of great importance to a dear friend of mine.'

'I see. In that case we had best retire to my office. Follow me if you please.'

Mr Pascoe led the way along a corridor to a pleasant room that might once have been a small parlour. Now, however, it was furnished with a large oak desk and straight-backed chairs, and the shelves that lined the walls were filled with heavy old registers and boxes that presumably contained files of paperwork.

'Do please take a seat.' He indicated the chair that faced the desk. 'May I offer you some refreshment?'

'Thank you, no. It's good of you to spare me your precious

time, and I don't want to inconvenience you more than I already am.'

'A welcome break from my usual routine, I assure you. I am intrigued by your request.' He sat behind the desk, moving a ledger, quill pen and inkpot to one side, then leant forward, resting his chin on his steepled hands. 'Please, furnish me with the details.'

Malcolm hesitated. 'It's a delicate matter. I can count on your discretion, I presume?'

Mr Pascoe looked slightly offended, and Malcolm went on quickly. 'As I am sure you have surmised, it concerns a young lady who found herself in an unenviable position. As it happens, she is the daughter of a Church of England clergyman – my predecessor, to be precise. The whole sorry business was kept secret, and the young lady's father arranged for the baby to go to adotive parents. This is the child whose whereabouts I am trying to ascertain. You do facilitate such arrangements, I imagine?'

'Where it is possible, yes. It is always gratifying to be able to place some poor unwanted child with a suitable family.' Mr Pascoe paused, his eyes narrowing as if searching his memory, and Malcolm waited, his hopes rising. 'There have been several such cases, as I recall,' he said at last, adding with a wry smile, 'The daughters of clergymen can be led into temptation as can any young woman, you know. They are as human as the rest of us.'

'And as vulnerable,' Malcolm said, thinking of good, sweet and caring Abi, who must have suffered dreadfully and was in all probability suffering still.

'What is the family name?' Mr Pascoe rose from his chair and went to the shelving to the left of his desk.

'It's Newman,' Malcolm said, realising that he was now beyond the point of no return.

'Newman.' Mr Pascoe pulled out one of the fat leather-bound volumes and peered at the inscription on the spine, then replaced it and took out its neighbour.

'My eyesight is not what it was. An N and an M look much the same to me,' he muttered, and Malcolm was not sure whether the man was talking to him or to himself.

He placed the book on the desk, retook his seat and opened the heavy cover.

'What was the date of this unfortunate event, did you say?'

'About nine years ago.'

Mr Pascoe made a quick calculation. 'The entries are in date order, beginning when St Margaret's was founded, you understand,' he said, squinting at the closely written pages and flicking through the first ones. 'This may take some time, I fear.'

'Would you like me to take a look?' Malcolm offered.

'No, no. If what we are searching for is here, I will find it.' Mr Pascoe's finger moved slowly down the list of entries. 'Norman . . . Not known . . . Oh dearie me, again . . . and again . . . New . . . no, Newcombe . . .'

Malcolm waited, seething with impatience, until eventually Mr Pascoe exclaimed in triumph. 'Newman! And the baby's name was . . . ?'

'I don't know,' Malcolm confessed. 'His grandfather, who made the arrangements, was called Obediah, I believe.'

'Obediah. Mm. This must be what we are looking for, then.'

'May I see?' Malcolm asked.

Somewhat reluctantly, Mr Pascoe turned the book around so that it was facing his visitor.

It was a short entry. Baby Newman had been handed over to a Mr Sharpe a week after his arrival at St Margaret's. But to Malcolm's intense relief, there was an address.

'Corsham,' he said aloud.

'I remember the case now.' But Mr Pascoe was frowning. 'A most suitable placement it appeared to be at the time. Mr Sharpe, yes, a banker with a very pretty young wife, as I recall. They had recently lost a child – or was it two? Mrs Sharpe was most anxious to be a mother again, but nature was not obliging.'

This sounded like excellent news, but for Mr Pascoe's opening remark: *A most suitable placement it appeared to be at the time* . . . And why, Malcolm wondered, was there a thick black asterisk squeezed between the end of the entry and the beginning of the next?

'What does the asterisk denote?' he asked.

'That there is more. We had further contact with Baby Newman – or Baby Sharpe, as he became. Pass me the book, if you please.'

Malcolm swung it round, and Mr Pascoe turned to a separate section at the back. Malcolm could see another asterisk, followed by a paragraph or two. It was impossible for him to read it upside down, but an uneasiness was beginning to replace his previous optimism.

'What does it say?' he asked.

Mr Pascoe took his time, reading every word of the entry, though Malcolm was uncomfortably sure he remembered very well what was written there.

At last he looked up, rubbing his chin and avoiding Malcolm's eyes.

'I am sorry to say it is a very sad story. What seemed to be a perfect placement in the first instance turned out to be nothing of the kind. In the end, there was nothing for it but for the child to be sent to a public orphanage.'

Chapter Twenty-One

'You, my dear, are an inspiration.'

'And you spoil me, Percy.'

'The pleasure is all mine.'

Percival Symonds' face was flushed. He reached for his glass of brandy, which Constance had just refilled, and came close to overturning it, missing the stem so that his fingers collided with the balloon.

Constance smiled to herself. One thing at least that she could count on was Percy in a drunken state by the end of an evening in her company. With Imogen away from Bramley Court, there was nothing Giles Stanley could do at present to hasten her permanent departure from the scene, but Constance still held the trump card in getting what she had desired for so long.

The hook she had baited to snare Hugh wasn't quite what he thought. She had told him that when Percy was drunk enough, it would be child's play to persuade him to terminate his lease on Hugh's land, but that wasn't the whole truth. In fact, the legal document she had had drawn up was quite different. When Percy signed it, he would actually be transferring the lease to her name. She would then be the one with the whip hand. To her mind it was a certain path to becoming the next Lady Hastings. And she rather thought that tonight could be the night when a drunken Percy would sign the document without questioning what it was.

'Percy, dearest, I have a favour to ask you,' she said silkily.

'Constance, my love.' He sighed, and treated her to a look that was both lascivious and regretful. 'I don't believe I am in a fit state to satisfy you. Twice in one evening at my age, and after so much imbibing . . .'

She smiled back. 'Oh Percy, you disappoint me! But that isn't the only favour I have to ask.'

'Really? What then?' His words were slurred.

'Nothing exciting, I fear. It is really a favour for my father. He has made a new will, leaving everything to my youngest brother, Thomas. Charles and Richard, his other two sons, have displeased him – don't ask me how, but there it is. But Papa is anxious they should not know he is disinheriting them. The solicitor who drew up his new will has witnessed his signature, but there is no one he can ask to be a second witness who would not be only too ready to enlighten Charles and Richard. So he has asked me to prevail on you to add your signature beneath the solicitor's.'

'Pff! Is that all?'

'Percy, you are so kind! My father will be so grateful! And it will only take a moment. See – I have it here . . .'

She reached for her reticule, tucked beneath the cushion beside her, and drew out the document, which she had folded carefully so that only the bottom third was visible. 'Don't trouble to get up, my dear. I will fetch pen and ink and bring it all to you.'

'But Constance . . .' Percy was frowning now. 'Am I not right in thinking both parties need to be present at the same time when witnessing a signature?'

Constance's heart sank. Was Percy not as drunk as she had

thought? Had she misjudged things and ruined her chances by her own impatience? But she had gone too far to stop now. The die was cast. She forced a laugh.

'Oh Percy, you are such a stickler for detail! Who is to know you were not both there when my father signed?'

For a few moments Percival was silent, and Constance waited, scarcely daring to breathe. Then he chuckled. 'You are a wicked woman, Constance. You lead an old man into bad ways.'

'I know . . . I know. But I think you rather enjoy it.'

She fetched a book and rested the document on it, placing a hand over the folded portion for good measure and holding out the quill.

As he took it, his other hand juddered and some brandy slopped out of the glass he was still holding and spilled onto the creamy parchment, blurring part of the solicitor's signature and wetting the place where Percy was to sign. Cursing silently, Constance found a blotter and pressed it to the document.

'Best wait for it to dry properly,' she said, hiding her annoyance at the delay.

'Yes, that would be best.'

After a few moments, the parchment had dried, leaving only a brownish stain. Percy signed, and Constance wanted to laugh aloud. It was done!

'There we are, my dear.' He looked up at her with a bleary smile. 'Now, let us continue to enjoy our evening.'

'Oh yes, Percy! Do let's!'

As she returned the signed document to her reticule, she was thinking that she most certainly would.

Sleep was eluding Malcolm. The grandmother clock in the hallway was striking two when he eventually gave up the unequal struggle and went downstairs to make himself a drink of warm milk. He tipped a measure of whisky into it and took it into the garden, where he sat on the wooden bench, which was flooded with moonlight and scented by the honeysuckle that grew up a trellis at the side of the rectory. But still his thoughts churned as they had done ever since his visit to St Margaret's Hospital for Needy Children.

What he had learned had shocked and distressed him badly. Orphanages generally were dreadful places, and the thought of what might have become of the child made him shudder.

He was only glad he hadn't told Maisie the true reason for his visit. She would have questioned him as to the outcome and he would have had no option but to share what the registers had revealed, which would have caused her great distress.

More than ever he was determined to at least attempt to find Abi's lost son. But he was at a loss to know where to begin. There must be a number of orphanages in this part of the world where the child could have been taken; it would be like looking for the proverbial needle in a haystack, and he was concerned that his search would encroach on the time he should be devoting to his parishioners. But he knew too that he would never be able to give his full attention to his ministry while so many questions remained unanswered. Whether Abi's son was alive or dead. Happy or wretched. Healthy, or sick with one of the dreadful diseases that afflicted children, especially those who were deprived of proper food and care.

No, whatever the cost, he must continue searching. The final answer might be one he could never share with Maisie or with Abi, but that was a burden he would have to shoulder if his prayers were not answered.

He looked up and saw a single star winking in the dark sky. Was it a sign? Was Abi's son shining somewhere like the star, just waiting to be found and brought home?

He finished his milk, unsure whether it was the tot of whisky he'd poured into it or some heavenly intervention that was making him feel suddenly optimistic.

As he went upstairs, he heard small sounds coming from Abi's old room – Christian gurgling, and Prissie's sweet voice crooning a lullaby. Another mother, another baby. These, at least, he had been able to help.

In his own room, he climbed back into bed, and was asleep almost as soon as his head touched the pillow.

Constance, too, was awake, too elated to sleep. Though she had looked at the deed and read it over and over again since she'd arrived home after her evening with Percy, she was unable to resist one last peek.

There on the table in front of her was the document that would bring her everything she desired. Hugh would be unable to resist her now. Excitement bubbled inside her, and she laughed triumphantly. Surely he must be back by now, with or without Imogen? He wouldn't want to neglect his beloved coal mines for long. She would pay him a visit, tell him that she'd kept her part of the bargain. Though she wouldn't reveal just yet that the deed was not rescinded at all, but transferred to her. It was always good to keep something in reserve.

She would go tomorrow, she decided. Now it was time to get some beauty sleep so as to be looking her very best for him.

Smiling to herself, she climbed the stairs and went to bed.

'Hugh.' Imogen's voice was piteous. 'Hugh, please take me home.'

'But Imogen, this *is* your home.'

She looked up at him, her eyes full of tears. 'No! It used to be. But now I should be with Robbie. I can't bear to think of him calling to me in the night when I'm not there.'

Hugh stifled a sigh. He had hoped that here, far away from the constant reminders of Robbie's life and death, she would begin to recover her senses. But it hadn't happened. If anything, she was worse. She wasn't sleeping, nor eating enough to keep a fly alive. And it would be the same – or worse – if she were in an asylum. Yes, she would be safe, but she would fret constantly, and descend further and further into the madness that was destroying her.

He had never felt more helpless, more despairing. But come what may, he would never abandon her to such a fate. He might have lost his heart to another, but Imogen was his wife. He had promised before God to love her and to keep her, in sickness and in health, and he would never break that sacred vow.

'Very well, Imogen,' he said resignedly. 'If that is what you want, I will take you home.'

The next day, storm clouds gathered, dark and ominous, and the air felt heavy and close. The fine spell was going to break, Abi thought, and she suggested to the boys that they should get some exercise in the fresh air before the rain came – and possibly thunder and lightning too.

Naturally, they jumped at the offer. It was stuffy and overly hot in the library, and concentration wasn't easy. But it wasn't solely for their benefit. Abi didn't feel like teaching today – truth to tell, hadn't felt like it for the last week. She surmised that Imogen couldn't have settled or Hugh would have been back by now, and her heart ached for her friend. But although she missed both of them dreadfully, at the same time she couldn't help but be grateful that Hugh was not here. After what had passed between them, she didn't know how she could face him, let alone live under the same roof.

Trying to ignore her churning thoughts and emotions, she turned to marking some of the work she had set Freddie and Jimmy earlier, and marvelled at how quick Jimmy was to grasp whatever he was taught. Perhaps she would suggest he could be included in Giles's science lessons. She was still puzzled as to why Freddie should have taken against Giles, and wondered if it might be that the doctor was going too far and too fast, and Freddie was struggling but didn't want to admit it. If Jimmy joined the lessons, Giles would be forced to go back to basics, and Freddie might feel more comfortable. He would even be able to explain things to Jimmy, and that would boost his confidence. In any case, the two boys had become such good friends that simply having Jimmy along would make the time spent with Giles more agreeable to him. She'd suggest it, she decided. Just as long as Jimmy didn't overtake Freddie in this too . . .

Tucked away in the library, Abi was quite unaware of a carriage approaching up the drive. The first she knew of it was when the boys came bursting in.

'There's a lady here asking for Papa,' Freddie announced.

'She looks like those fine ladies who used to visit us in the home and bring us nice things to eat,' Jimmy added, sounding hopeful.

Abi was surprised – Jimmy almost never mentioned the orphanage. For the moment, though, her attention was focused on what Freddie had said. A lady asking for Hugh could only be one person. The haughty Miss Constance Bingham.

'Did you tell her Papa is away?' she asked.

Freddie pulled a face. 'I didn't tell her anything. She talked to me as if I was a baby. You can tell her if you want to. But if you don't, I expect she'll just go away again.'

'It would be very rude to simply ignore her,' Abi said, though to be truthful, that was exactly what she felt like doing. 'Find Mrs Mears and ask her to deal with it.'

'We already looked for her,' Jimmy supplied. 'The maid said she's in her room, resting.'

Abi sighed. It seemed she had no option but to speak to Miss Bingham herself. Drat Mrs Mears! When did she ever take a rest in the afternoon? And why today of all days?

She found Constance Bingham waiting beside the front steps, sheltering beneath a parasol though the sun was hidden behind a bank of cloud.

'I understand you wish to see Sir Hugh,' Abi said shortly.

'I do. Is he not here?'

'He is not. I fear you have had a wasted journey.'

Constance's rouged lips tightened with annoyance. 'Did you give him the message I left with you when I was last here?'

'I did.'

'He has failed to return my call.' Her tone was accusatory.

'I dare say he has been otherwise occupied,' Abi said, refusing to rise to the bait. 'He was at home only briefly before leaving with Lady Hastings for her parents' home, where he has been ever since.'

'Then perhaps when he does return, you will tell him I am in possession of something that will be of considerable benefit to him—'

She broke off as the clip-clop of horses' hooves could be heard rapidly approaching down the drive.

Abi's heart jolted. It was Hugh's carriage, she was certain of it.

And so too, it seemed, was Miss Constance Bingham.

'Well, well! How timely! Sir Hugh, if I am not mistaken,' she exclaimed triumphantly, then frowned as it became apparent he was not alone.

Abi's eyes widened. Imogen! He was bringing Imogen home! Did that mean her condition had improved? Oh dear God, she hoped so!

As Hugh brought the matched pair to a halt, Abi hurried forward eagerly. 'My lady! How good it is to see you!' But to her dismay, Imogen seemed to be looking right through her as if she wasn't there, and she took no notice either of Freddie and Jimmy, who came racing across the lawn.

'Imogen!' Abi said, reverting to the familiarity she used when they were alone. 'It's me – Abi . . .'

Once again there was no response. Imogen might be home, but she was clearly no better. Her eyes were darting around now, and at last she spoke.

'Robbie? Where is Robbie?'

Hugh glanced at Abi and gave a small despairing shake of his head.

'Hugh.' Constance spoke imperiously, demanding his attention.

'Constance. I did not expect to find you here.' His tone implied that he wasn't best pleased.

'We need to talk, Hugh,' she continued unabashed. 'I have in my possession something of great interest – and value – to you.'

'This is not a good time,' he said brusquely. 'Can you not see I am attending to my wife? Whatever it is will have to wait.'

'Really!' Constance's eyes flashed. 'Am I to assume you are no longer interested in what I have been at pains to do on your behalf? But be warned, if the opportunity is lost, as it most certainly will be, you will have no one but yourself to blame.'

She turned for her carriage, fully expecting him to stop her. He did not.

'That would be unfortunate, but just now I have more pressing matters on my mind, as you can see. I will call on you when I can once again give you my full attention.'

Furious, Constance signalled for her coachman to hand her up into the carriage.

'Don't trouble yourself, Hugh. I think you will come to regret treating me so.'

Hugh turned his back on her, ignoring the threat, and gave Imogen his hand. 'Come along, my love. You're home now, as you wanted. When you have had a cup of tea and a good rest, you will feel much better.'

As he helped her down and Constance's carriage pulled away, the two boys, who had been watching from a distance, approached cautiously, aware that something was very wrong.

'Papa . . . ?' Freddie ventured.

'Not now, Frederick. I have to get your mother inside.'

For once, Freddie didn't point out that Imogen was not his mother, but simply stood watching as Hugh took Imogen's arm and led her towards the house.

Abi, too, watched them go, puzzled by the scene she had just witnessed and horribly concerned for Imogen. She wished she could have gone with them so as to try once again to establish a connection with her friend and be of some comfort, but she didn't feel it was her place. Hugh could have suggested it, but he had not. In fact, he hadn't so much as spoken to her. This, she supposed, was the way things must be.

Thunder rumbled in the distance, and she pulled herself together. 'Come along, boys, let's go in. I think the storm is heading this way.'

Still subdued, they did as she said.

'Take me into town,' a furious Constance instructed her coach-man.

'Yes, miss.' He gave her a curious look, but Constance was in no mood to explain. She would give him explicit instructions later, and then he would be curious all over again as to the reason she wanted to see a doctor. But it was none of his business, and he knew better than to ask questions, though he might well gossip about it with her father's other servants later. But gossip had never concerned Constance. She didn't care what people said about her; in fact, she rather enjoyed it.

Giles was at the surgery, as she had expected at this time of day. There were patients in the waiting room: an old man hawking into a kerchief, and a woman with a little girl who was snuffling into her mother's shoulder. Constance glanced at them with distaste. She didn't know if they were waiting to see Giles or Dr Mounty, but she had no intention of taking her place in the queue.

She marched straight up to the door that led to Giles's consulting room and opened it. Giles looked up, startled, from examining a girl who lay on the treatment table, her skirts rucked up to her waist, revealing a swollen belly.

'Constance! I am with a patient!' he protested.

'This will not take long.' She addressed the girl. 'Cover yourself and wait outside.'

Shocked and embarrassed, the girl did as she was told, scarcely hearing the doctor's profuse apologies. But for all his annoyance, Giles knew better than to cross Constance, given what she knew about his past, and what she threatened to do with her knowledge.

He did, however, risk a gentle rebuke. 'Really, Constance, you shouldn't treat my patients so! And why are you here?'

'Imogen is home. It seems she has been staying with her parents, but I expect you knew that and chose not to share it with me.' Her tone was scathing, and a faint colour rose around the ruffled neck of Giles's shirt.

'I never meant to keep it from you, Constance. But I have been busy, and I didn't think—'

'That I would want to know?' she interrupted him. 'I thought I had made it clear – I want to be kept informed of everything that concerns Lady Hastings.'

'My apologies.'

'No matter now.' She brushed the apology aside. 'The fact is that she is back, and in a worse state than ever if appearances are to be believed. It is time now to press home our advantage

'In what way?' Giles was becoming more flustered by the minute.

Constance snorted. 'You caused the death of one woman. It would surely not be so hard to kill another by the same means? I am growing impatient, Giles. If Imogen Hastings is not disposed of, and soon, you will pay the price. Your reputation, your prospects, your whole life depend on you succeeding in this. You will deliver the required result without delay, or by God, it will be the ruination of you.'

Without further ado, she turned and marched out of the consulting room, leaving Giles horribly shaken.

'You may go back to the doctor now,' she said haughtily to the girl whose examination she had so rudely disrupted. Then she left the surgery and instructed her coachman to take her home.

Chapter Twenty-Two

'May I be excused and go to see Jimmy?' a subdued Freddie asked.

He had been allowed to eat in the dining room, as he had done during Hugh's absence, and had now finished his evening meal. The storm that had threatened earlier had moved on elsewhere, and Abi, who was almost done herself, nodded. Hugh had not yet put in an appearance. But if and when he did, she wanted to be able to talk to him about Imogen without little ears flapping. Besides this, she was feeling very apprehensive as to how awkward their meeting would be, and would prefer it if Freddie wasn't present. She was very afraid she might give herself away.

At least she hadn't had to endure Mrs Mears's company; Hugh being back had put a stop to the liberties she had been taking in his absence.

She poured herself another cup of coffee and nibbled on a grape, trying to stem the nervousness that was prickling in her veins at the prospect of being face to face with Hugh. Perhaps she should make her escape while she had the chance. But she couldn't avoid him forever, and she really did want to ask him exactly how Imogen had been, why he had brought her home, and what he planned to do about the situation now.

She was still drinking her coffee, still undecided, when she heard his footsteps in the hallway. Too late for escape! She took a deep breath and prepared herself. Concentrate on Imogen and her welfare. Behave normally. As if she hadn't fancied something special had passed between them. As if she didn't think about him every minute of every day. Couldn't get him out of her head, or her heart.

'Abigail!' He sounded surprised to find her there. 'I thought you would have finished your meal by now.'

Was he trying to avoid her? It hadn't occurred to her before that that could be the reason he was late for dinner. Now it seemed the most obvious explanation, especially as he had practically ignored her when he had arrived home with Imogen.

'I was lingering over my coffee.' To her own ears her voice sounded brittle, false. 'Freddie has finished, though, and gone to play with Jimmy.'

'They are still friends, then?'

'You can never tell with children. Inseparable one day, at one another's throats the next.'

It was almost as if he was making small talk with a stranger. Avoiding anything that could be misconstrued. But at least he wasn't dismissing her as he had dismissed the horrible Constance Bingham. Abi couldn't help a small spike of satisfaction. Time, she thought, to take the bull by the horns.

'How is Imogen now?' she asked.

'Sleeping, thank the good Lord. As you saw, she was in a bad way when we first arrived. I am so sorry she didn't seem to recognise you. The fact is, she was totally fixated on Robert. She seemed to think he would be here, waiting for her.'

'I understand,' Abi said.

'I should have realised what would happen as soon as she was back. Everything here is a reminder of him, and it is as if she has forgotten that he is no longer with us. As if she thinks he is simply hiding, playing games. She couldn't settle at her parents' house; she knew he wasn't there and begged me to bring her home. But I am truly beginning to think there is no help for her anywhere. I am at my wits' end, Abi. The one option I absolutely refuse to consider is to have her committed to an asylum. At least here she is in familiar surroundings, with those who love her caring for her. Do you agree?'

'Absolutely.' Abi was taken aback that he should ask her opinion, but pleased and flattered. 'Just as long as we can keep her safe.'

'I shall make sure of that.' He broke off as Mary entered the dining room with a fillet of fish resting on a bed of spinach, and set it in front of him. 'Thank you, Mary.'

'Sir . . .' The maid hesitated. 'Can I just say how good it is to see Lady Hastings back here where she belongs.'

'That is kind, Mary. But I fear she is still very sick, and cannot be trusted not to harm herself. Unless one of us is with her, she will be confined to her rooms, with the doors secured. Please ensure they are locked behind you whenever you have cause to be there.'

Mary's face crumpled, all the little lines and creases deepening so that she resembled a walnut. 'Oh, I'm so sorry, sir. And I'll make sure the doors are locked, of course.' She bobbed a curtsey and left.

'I expect the servants think it harsh, but we can't have her wandering about alone.' Hugh picked up his knife and fork and cut into his fish. 'You understand, I know, Abi.'

'Only too well,' Abi agreed sadly.

'And I want you to know how much I appreciate the kindness you have shown her,' he went on.

'It's nothing. I'm very fond of her.' As a rush of emotion overcame her, tears pricked Abi's eyes. She bowed her head, swallowed hard and made to rise from the table. The last thing she wanted was for Hugh to see her in tears again. Her pride wouldn't stand it. Besides, wasn't that how things had become rather too intimate on that last evening when they had been together?

'I'll leave you—' *To enjoy your meal*, she had been about to say, but Hugh interrupted her.

'Don't go just yet. There's something I wanted to say to you.'

Breath caught in Abi's throat. Hugh sounded almost embarrassed. It wasn't something she'd ever heard in his voice before. She sank back into her seat, her heart pounding so hard in her chest she thought he must hear it.

'You are wondering, I expect, about my visitor this afternoon.'

'Oh – no, really . . .' It wasn't what she had expected, and she didn't know whether to be disappointed or relieved.

'Come now, I am sure you must be. Especially since it's the second time you have found yourself on the wrong side of her ill temper. You must think her unforgivably rude.'

'I can't say I care for her,' Abi agreed.

'Constance is her own worst enemy, I fear. I have known her for many years – long before I met Imogen, or Marigold, even, and she can behave quite preposterously when things do not go as she thinks they should.'

He was making excuses for the horrible woman! Abi thought. What was it that made him ready to accept such unpleasantness and shrug it off? First Mrs Mears, now Miss Constance Bingham. Well, at least it wasn't because of some kind of romantic entanglement where Mrs Mears was concerned – at least she sincerely hoped not!

'Really, your friends are no concern of mine, sir,' she said swiftly.

'Oh Abi! It's not what you are thinking.' It was as if he had read her mind. 'I can hardly blame you, I suppose. But let me assure you, my relationship with Constance nowadays is strictly a business one. She has been endeavouring to help me with a problem I have regarding a lease on my land. I don't like the woman any more than you do. I don't like her insinuation that you didn't pass on her earlier message. I don't like that she chose to throw a tantrum in front of you, Freddie and most of all Imogen, though I doubt Imogen was even aware of it. Constance assumes far too much. But after this afternoon, I don't think we shall be bothered by her again, at least until I make my peace with her, which I suppose I shall have to do if I am to resolve the matter of the lease.'

'As I said, sir, it's none of my business,' Abi repeated, flustered. 'But thank you for explaining.'

'Less of the "sir", Abi. I thought we were beyond that.'

Her heart jolted, colour rising to her cheeks. Once again she had the dizzying feeling of standing on a cliff edge with an exciting but dangerous drop below. Panic overcame her.

'I must go and find Freddie,' she blurted.

There was a brief awkward silence, then Hugh said, 'Then perhaps on your way, you would tell Mary I am ready for my main course.'

The moment had passed. But still Abi couldn't wait to escape. Without another word, she turned and left.

'Business, he says it is! Business – huh! Funny sort of business if you ask me.'

Abi froze, her hand on the kitchen door handle. There was no mistaking Mrs Mears's scathing tone, and no mistaking what she was talking about. She must have been listening outside the dining-room door and heard their conversation, Abi thought furiously.

'That's twice in a week she's been here. There's something going on, mark my words. It wouldn't surprise me if he isn't behind what milady fancies she hears, and goodness knows what he was up to while they were away. He's trying to drive her crazy so he can be with that one.'

Outraged, Abi pushed open the door and marched into the room. It wasn't like her to be confrontational, but at that moment she was too angry to think twice.

'How dare you say such things about Sir Hugh!' she flared.

Mary's gnarled hands flew to her face, the very picture of shock and shame, but Mrs Mears was unabashed.

'Well, well! Look who's flying to the master's defence! The one with designs on him herself,' she sneered. 'You want to watch yourself, my girl. You don't stand a chance, not when you're up against the likes of Miss Bingham.'

'I have no designs on Sir Hugh,' Abi countered fiercely. 'And neither, for that matter, does he have designs on Miss Bingham. Sir Hugh is devoted to Lady Hastings and is doing all he can to improve her health. What you are suggesting is not just untrue – it's slander, and he could have you up before the magistrates for it.'

Mrs Mears snorted. 'I'd like to see him try! As for you, you're as green as the peas on that dinner plate. He's got you wound around his little finger good and proper, but you'll end up disappointed, I can tell you that, you silly little madam.'

Though she was shaking, Abi stood her ground. 'This isn't about me, Mrs Mears. It's about Sir Hugh. He is a good and honourable man, and you should be dismissed for saying otherwise.'

Mrs Mears laughed scornfully. 'Oh, he'll never dismiss me, Miss Hoity-Toity. He made a promise to my Marigold on her deathbed, and he won't go back on that. She meant the world to him – the only woman he ever loved, or ever will. The rest of you are just his playthings to use and discard when he tires of you. So put that in your pipe and smoke it.'

This wasn't a battle Abi was going to win.

'You are the nastiest woman I have ever met,' she said, and turned for the door, only to remember Hugh's request for his main course. 'And Sir Hugh is ready for his dinner,' she shot at Mary. 'If you can face him, that is.'

As she left the room, she felt her knees crumpling beneath her and grasped at the door jamb for support. She was shaking from head to foot, but somehow she pulled herself together and managed to make it to her room, where she collapsed on the bed, wrapping her arms around herself.

That awful, awful woman! She was evil itself. But as her temper cooled and Mrs Mears's words echoed in her head, a sliver of doubt crept in. From what the housekeeper had said, it was clear she wasn't the one encouraging Freddie to pretend to be Robbie. Was it possible there was some truth in her suggestion that it was Hugh who was behind it? Could it be that he had used and discarded other women since he had lost his first wife? *Did* he want Imogen out of the way to leave a vacancy for a new lover?

No! She couldn't believe it. But the thought, coming on top of the dreadful row with Mrs Mears, destroyed the last of her defences. Abi covered her face with her hands and wept as if her heart would break.

'What's wrong with you, Freddie?' an exasperated Jimmy asked. Freddie didn't seem to be interested in any of the activities he suggested, and was moping about with a face like a fiddle, as Mrs Doel would say.

Freddie shrugged without answering.

'It's your ma, ain't it?'

Another shrug. 'Maybe. Sort of.'

'What d'you mean? Sort of?'

For a long moment Freddie was silent, staring down at his boots and kicking bits of gravel from the path onto the lawn. Jimmy was shocked to see his eyes filling with tears.

'She'll be all right. You'll see,' he said. 'Mrs Shipham at the orphanage got real sick one time and everybody said she was going to die. But she didn't. Worse luck,' he added ruefully.

'Worse luck?' Freddie looked up, hastily brushing away the tears. 'You shouldn't say that.'

'Why not? She was horrid. Everybody hated her. But she's not horrid, your ma, is she? You wouldn't want her to die.'

His words, meant to be of comfort, were anything but to Freddie. The tears were starting again. He thrust his fists into his eyes in an attempt to stop them, but still they trickled through and ran down his cheeks.

'Freddie!' Jimmy said, overcome with embarrassment.

'It's all my fault,' Freddie muttered.

'What? Your ma being took bad?' Jimmy was puzzled and a bit frightened. 'Why is it your fault?'

'I've done something terrible.'

'*You* have?' Jimmy repeated, incredulous.

'It was only a joke,' Freddie wept. 'And I wanted to stop. But he wouldn't let me.'

'Who wouldn't? What are you talking about?'

And Freddie told him what he knew.

The last thing Giles had expected was that anyone here would have known Mrs Cahill, or heard of her suspicious death. But the countryside, he was to discover, could be a very small world.

Percival Symonds had heard the story from a cousin;

Constance Bingham had heard it from Percy. And it had given her an idea as to how she could snare the only man she had ever truly wanted. If the new doctor had supplied a patient with drugs that had caused her death, it gave her the ammunition to coerce him into doing something similar. Emotionally disturbed as Imogen was, there must be drugs that would push her over the edge into madness. She might well attempt to take her own life. If she succeeded, it would suit Constance very well; her way would be clear to become the next Lady Hastings. If not, Imogen would almost certainly be sent to an asylum for her own safety.

Constance had wasted no time in approaching Giles with her proposition. At first she had used her considerable charms in her efforts to persuade him, but Giles was adamant that he had never intended Mrs Cahill any harm. He had only supplied her with drugs so as to worm his way into her favour. This was something else entirely. And in any case, Lady Hastings was Dr Mounty's patient.

Thwarted, Constance resorted to blackmail. He had better find a way to get to her or face the consequences, she told him coldly.

Giles was frantic. Surely the woman must be insane? But mad or not, she was undoubtedly dangerous, and he was terrified of the truth becoming public knowledge; it would be the end of him. But he was at a loss to know how he could do what Constance wanted.

And then, when he was called to treat Frederick's measles, it seemed he had been presented with a solution.

Lady Hastings, it seemed, was suffering from delusions concerning her dead son, and had even put her life at risk in her efforts to find him. Furthermore, Sir Hugh had said – jokingly – that when she thought she heard Robert calling to her, it was in fact Frederick, who was known for his pranks, playing a trick on her. Supposing that really was the case, perhaps he could goad the boy into going even further, so that she became more and more convinced that her lost son was seeking her? Eventually the time would come when Sir Hugh would be forced to agree that the only answer was to have her committed to an asylum. Surely that would satisfy Constance? And there was always the possibility that she would take her own life. That could well have happened already if Miss Newman hadn't found her when she had been wading into the lake where Robert had drowned.

In order for the plan to work, of course, he needed to be able to talk to Frederick alone, but again fortune had seemed to smile on him. The boy was fascinated by the sciences, and had been thrilled when Giles had offered to give him lessons, while Miss Newman was only too ready to agree to the arrangement.

To begin with, Frederick had played along enthusiastically, thoroughly enjoying finding new ways to give Imogen the impression that Robert was there in his old room, and sharing them with Giles, his hero. But for some reason, something had changed. And Giles was seriously worried.

If Lady Hastings had improved during her time away from Bramley, they would have to begin all over again. But Frederick said he no longer wanted to continue playing his tricks. Was it just a childish mood? Would Giles be able to persuade him otherwise when the time came – if it was necessary? And how would Constance react to the inevitable delay? It was vital she should be satisfied. She had him over a barrel, and if she carried out her threat, his career – his whole life – would be destroyed.

Tired and dispirited, Malcolm left the orphanage and climbed into Isaac Wilton's carriage. It was the third he had visited in as many days, and he had still not been able to learn any more regarding the whereabouts of Abi's son. The only help the superintendent here had been able to offer was to suggest yet another, much larger establishment he might try, and Malcolm thought that since it was only a few miles away, he would check it out while they in the area.

'No good?' Isaac asked as Malcolm settled himself.

'No. A dreadful place.'

Isaac didn't know the real purpose of his visits, of course. He believed Malcolm was checking possible homes for Prissie's Christian, and he must be wondering why it was necessary to look at so many. But as long as he was paid, he didn't grumble too much, and didn't ask too many questions.

'Just one more call to make, and then we will go home,' Malcolm said. 'We need to go into the city.' He gave Isaac the address and settled back, once more thinking about the tragic story he had learned at St Margaret's Hospital for Needy Children.

At the time of the adoption, the home Abi's baby had gone to had seemed ideal. Mr Sharpe, the adoptive father, was a banker, and his wife, Elizabeth, was well thought of in the locality, a charitable woman who held musical soirées in the extensive gardens of their home, the proceeds of which she donated to worthy causes. Abi's son would have wanted for nothing in those early years.

Things had begun to go badly wrong when Edwin Sharpe became addicted to gambling, with disastrous results. His losses had mounted, but desperate to recoup what he had lost, he had continued even more recklessly. When he had exhausted every penny he had to his name, he had resorted to embezzling money from the accounts of the well-to-do who entrusted their money to his bank.

How long he had got away with this was unclear, but inevitably his fraud came to light eventually. Faced with disgrace, claims for reparation that he had no hope of paying, and the prospect of a lengthy jail sentence, he had taken his own life –

and that of his wife. Possibly he intended to do away with their adopted son too, but as his father rampaged with a blunderbuss, the little boy had hidden in a cupboard, where he was found next day after the discovery of the bodies of his parents.

In the first instance, he was taken in by Elizabeth's sister, but she had a brood of her own and was not inclined to make the arrangement permanent. Money was tight, she was worn out from too many pregnancies and caring for the children that had resulted, and the little boy was not, after all, her own flesh and blood. She had approached St Margaret's to ask them to take him back, but according to Mr Pascoe, who had been Assistant Father of the House at the time, that wasn't possible.

'It was clear the sister had no intention of keeping the child, and there would have been little hope of arranging another adoption,' he had explained. 'Prospective parents are looking for babies, not four-year-old children. We would have been responsible for the boy's care for many years, and in such cases we have to ask for some payment towards the not inconsiderable expense incurred. Unfortunately, Mrs Sharpe's sister had no means of fulfilling that requirement. We could suggest no alternative other than placing the boy in a publicly funded orphanage.'

The very thought of it made Malcolm shudder, especially now that he had seen for himself just how dreadful these places were.

'I reckon we'm there, Vicar.' Isaac interrupted his reverie.

They had drawn up outside an old building hemmed in by iron railings and with bars on the ground-floor windows. It looked to Malcolm more like a prison than a home for orphaned or abandoned children. With a sinking heart, he climbed down from the carriage.

A gate in the railings was secured by a heavy bolt, placed too high for children to reach. It was rusted, but when he pulled on it, it slid back surprisingly easily. He approached the door and rang the bell that hung beside it. A few moments later, it was opened by a short, squat man, and again Malcolm was struck by the similarity to a prison – the man looked more like a guard than a carer. But when he saw Malcolm's clerical attire, he let him inside without hesitation, and showed him along a dark and musty corridor that smelled of stale food and urine, and into a surprisingly spacious office.

There he was greeted by a buxom woman in matron's uniform, and began the explanation for his visit, which by now slipped easily off his tongue. At least the sad story of how Abi's son had come to be taken to an orphanage was one that would identify the boy he was looking for – it couldn't be often that a respectable banker's son arrived at the institution in such horrendous circumstances. And so it proved.

'Yes, I know the boy,' the matron said, and Malcolm's hopes rose.

'He's here?'

She snorted. 'He were. And nothing but trouble. Hadn't been here five minutes before he scalded his arm with boiling water when he was supposed to be scrubbing the step – on purpose, it wouldn't surprise me. Had to have the doctor out to him. And that was just the start of it. I can't say I'm sorry he's gone.'

'Gone?' Malcolm echoed.

'A few months since.'

'So where is he now?'

But Malcolm's relief at having picked up the trail at long last was short-lived.

The matron shrugged. 'Couldn't tell 'ee that. He runned away, an' we haven't seen hide nor hair of him since.'

Chapter Twenty-Three

It was as if a cloud had descended over the house. Even without her laudanum, which was running low, Imogen was sleeping for much of the time, there was an almost tangible awkwardness between Abi and Hugh, and neither of the boys was his usual rumbustious self. Mary, Handley and the rest of the servants went about their duties in sombre silence. Only Mrs Mears seemed untouched by the situation. If anything, what she conveyed was grim satisfaction that it had come to this.

It was not long after ten next morning when Giles Stanley's pony and trap came trotting down the drive. The doctor went straight to the study, where Hugh was attempting to deal with some of the business matters that had accumulated during his absence.

'I heard you and Lady Hastings had returned,' he said. 'Did the visit to her parents benefit her?'

Hugh was puzzled as to how Giles had come by this information, but assumed he had heard it from one of the tradesmen who had called earlier with deliveries.

'I'm afraid not,' he said. 'The change of scene didn't have the result I had hoped for.'

'I am sorry to hear that,' Giles sympathised. 'Like you, I would have thought that without the constant reminders of

Robert that surround her here, she would make at least some improvement. I'll take a look at her, assess her condition.'

'I'm not having her committed to an asylum, if that's what you are going to suggest,' Hugh said forcefully.

'That is your decision, of course, but . . .' Giles shook his head. 'Caring for her will be difficult, and will cause you a great deal of worry.'

'As you say, it is my decision. But perhaps you could prescribe her some more laudanum. It calms her if she becomes distressed.'

'Is someone with her?' Giles asked.

'At the moment, no. But she was resting peacefully enough when I looked in on her just now, and the doors to her rooms are locked on the outside, so she cannot go wandering again should she become unsettled.'

'And there is nothing sharp with which she could do herself harm?'

'Absolutely not. Her medicines are locked away too. You'll find the key to the cabinet on the shelf beside it, well out of her reach.'

'Then with your permission, I will spend a few minutes with her. And if necessary, I will leave her enough laudanum to last until I call again.'

'Thank you. You'll forgive me if I don't accompany you? As you can see, I have a great deal of work that needs my attention.' Hugh indicated the paperwork piled on his desk.

Giles rose. 'I'll take up no more of your time.'

'I believe Dr Stanley is here,' Abi said to Freddie. 'Perhaps he will give you a science lesson when he has seen your mama.'

At the mention of the doctor's name, Freddie's face became the very picture of alarm. 'I don't want—'

'I was going to ask if he would teach Jimmy too.' Abi smiled at him encouragingly.

The two boys exchanged glances.

'He won't do that,' Freddie said.

'Why not?' Abi was puzzled. 'And why don't you want to have lessons with Dr Stanley any more? You know I can't teach you the things he can – I don't know much about science.'

'I just don't want to,' Freddie said mulishly.

Abi shook her head, thoroughly confused. She would have to dig deeper into this when she and Freddie were alone. But for now, there was no point in further discussion.

'Fractions,' she said. 'Turn to page thirteen of your books.'

Both boys bent their heads in concentration, and Abi put the conundrum out of her head and resumed the lesson.

On the first floor, Giles stopped outside the door that led to Robbie's room. He turned the key, went inside and closed the door behind him. Through the connecting door to Imogen's sitting room he could see her in a chair beside the window, staring into space and seemingly quite unaware of his presence. He picked up Robbie's wind-up toy from where it had run out of momentum against the dresser, intending to set it off, then thought better of it and put it down again. Robbie was only supposed to play with it in the night, and in any case, he didn't want Imogen coming to investigate just yet. Instead he opened his medical bag and took something out, placing it partly under the pillow and partly beneath Robbie's monkey. Then he went out again, leaving the door slightly ajar, and let himself into Imogen's room.

'Milady.'

For a moment Imogen remained motionless, then she turned to look at him without appearing to recognise him.

'Milady! It's Dr Stanley. How are you feeling today?'

'Dr Stanley?' she repeated vaguely.

'You must remember me. I attended you before you went away to visit your parents. You will be pleased to be home, I'll wager. Back with your little son.'

Her face clouded. 'But he's not here.'

'Really? I thought you often heard him calling to you in the night, and playing with his toys.'

'I do. But he didn't come last night.'

'Are you sure you didn't miss him because you were asleep?'

'I wasn't asleep. There isn't much of my medicine left, and what they gave me I spat into my kerchief. I had to stay awake, you see. To listen for Robbie.'

'But he didn't come?'

'No. And I fear . . .' She broke off, tears filling her eyes.

'What?'

'That he thinks I've abandoned him. I've been away for a very long time, and he must have thought I was never coming back. So he has gone away too, back to where he hides in the daytime. Oh my poor Robbie! He wants me to go to him so much, and now he must think I don't love him any more. But I do love him – so, so much. All I want is to be with him.'

'I feel sure he thinks no such thing,' Giles assured her. 'And he will likely have left you a sign as to where you can find him.'

'Do you really think so?' she asked wonderingly.

'I do indeed. Now, I will leave you more of your medicine, but you are not to take it just yet.' He removed a small bottle from his medical bag, put it in the cabinet and replaced the key on top, well out of Imogen's reach. 'I think you should take a rest now, since you had little sleep last night. Why don't you lie down on Robbie's bed? You feel close to him there, don't you? And he will feel close to you.'

She nodded. 'Yes, I think that is what I will do. Mary will be bringing me a warm drink very soon, and when I've finished it, I'll rest. In Robbie's bed.'

'Good.'

Giles left the house and took his pony and trap down the drive to the lane, where he found a suitable spot to wait. He needed to know if his scheme had worked, and he needed to make sure there was no way he could be implicated.

'Here we be, milady.' Mary set a mug of warm milk on the occasional table where Imogen could easily reach it. 'It's not too hot. It won't burn your mouth.'

'Thank you, Mary.' At least Imogen was able to recognise the maid this morning. 'You may go.'

Mary hovered. 'It's all right, milady. I'm in no hurry.'

'Really, I would rather be alone, and I am sure you have duties to attend to.'

'Very good, milady.'

Mary left reluctantly, locking the door behind her. She had been told to stay and see that Imogen finished her drink, just as Cook had been instructed to ensure the milk wasn't so hot that she could scald herself. Every care was being taken to keep milady safe. But as she passed the door to Robbie's room, she didn't notice it was slightly ajar. Her eyes weren't as good as they used to be, and in any case, it would never have occurred to her that anyone would have used it and left it unlocked. Robbie's room was a shrine that was kept clean and tidy by her ladyship herself.

Alone once more, Imogen sipped her warm milk, looking out of the window. Storm clouds were gathering again, and the sun was playing hide-and-seek among them. Imogen imagined she could see Robbie riding his hobby horse in the shadows, not daring to expose himself to the patches of sunlight. A small, sad smile played about the corners of her mouth. Shades and the dark of night were his friends now. He couldn't allow anyone but her to know he was there, for fear they would send him away.

'I'm here, my darling,' she said softly. 'I couldn't bear to be parted from you, so I have come home. I am going to take a rest now on your bed. If you come to me, I can cuddle you just as I used to.'

She set down the mug, got up and went into Robbie's room, almost tripping over his wind-up toy. She smiled again faintly. He had been here while she had been away.

She went to the bed and turned back the coverlet so as not to crease it when she lay down, then sat on the edge of the bed looking around at Robbie's things – his toys, his nightshirt, his music box. Yes, everything was in its place and ready for him. She swung her legs up and swivelled, reaching for his monkey. Then, cradling it against her chest, she let her head fall back onto the pillow.

As she made herself comfortable, something cold and wet pressed into the nape of her neck. She gasped, startled, and jerked upright, twisting round to see what it could be.

Then froze.

Dark green leaves glistening with moisture protruded from beneath the pillow, and as she eased it out, she saw it in all its glory.

A water lily.

It couldn't be! But it was! A water lily, right here beneath Robbie's pillow. He *had* been here! He had! She touched it wonderingly, then picked it up and found herself remembering what Dr Stanley had said. Robbie would likely leave a sign to

277

tell her where to find him. That was what this was. A sign so that she would know where he was hiding.

She stood up and noticed the door to the corridor was slightly ajar. He'd even left it open for her! He wanted her to come to him now! Cautiously she went out into the passage, stopping and listening. All was quiet. No one was about to see her and prevent her leaving. They must all be busy elsewhere. What luck!

She went quickly and quietly down the stairs and into the parlour, where the French windows were open as they always were when it was fine, so as to air the room. As she slipped out onto the lawn, she heard a rumble of thunder. The storm must be coming back. For a brief moment she hesitated. She didn't like thunderstorms. They frightened her. But she couldn't let her fear keep her from Robbie. It was only someone upstairs moving the furniture about, her nanny used to say to calm her when she was a child.

Gathering her courage, she hurried across the lawn towards the woods that led to the lake. She felt sure Robbie was waiting for her there.

'She's gone! Dear Lord, she's not in her room!'

Mary, who had gone upstairs to fetch Imogen's milk cup, hurried down the stairs as fast as her rheumatic legs would carry her. She made straight for Hugh's study, but on discovering he wasn't there, burst into the library where Abi and the boys were working.

'Gone?' Abi repeated, shocked. 'What do you mean, gone?'

'Milady! She ain't in her room! An' I can't find Sir Hugh neither.'

'Perhaps he's taken her for a walk in the garden,' Abi suggested hopefully.

'No, he's gone over to the pit.' Mrs Mears, alerted by Mary's frantic rush down the stairs, appeared in the doorway.

Abi's mind was racing. No time now to wonder how Imogen had been able to escape. She had to be found – and quickly.

'Get Jem to ride for him post haste. He will know to go to the lake. I'm going there too. And have everyone you can muster search the grounds.'

For once, Mrs Mears didn't argue. She scurried out and Abi turned to the boys.

'You two can help. But under no circumstances are you to go to the lake. Do you understand?'

Freddie, who had turned white with shock, nodded wordlessly, while Jimmy, who didn't know the significance of the lake, looked puzzled as well as alarmed.

Without another word, Abi left them and set out at a run across the lawn and into the woods. How long had Imogen been gone? She didn't know. She could only pray that she would find her before it was too late.

Imogen stood on the bank of the lake, cupping the lily between her hands and staring down at the murky water and the lily pad floating on it. This was the spot where Robbie had gathered the flower. Now he was waiting for her.

She took a tentative step forward. The water chilled her feet as it rippled over them. She barely noticed, just as she no longer heard the rumbles of thunder, louder now as the storm approached, or saw the lightning flashes reflected in the lake, or felt the deep scratches made on her hands and arms by sharp branches as she'd slipped and slithered down the path through the woods. Her mind, her whole being was concentrated only on Robbie.

Another step, and another. The water soaked the hem of her

gown, and the pebbles beneath her feet were rough through the sodden soles of her slippers. An especially sharp one jabbed into the soft arch of her foot, and she stumbled and almost fell, but somehow regained her balance and kept moving forward until the water reached her knees.

'Robbie!' she called. 'Robbie, where are you?'

She didn't realise she had reached the point where the lake bed shelved steeply until it was too late. She plunged into water so deep it filled her mouth and nose, stung her eyes. Her ballooning skirts lifted her to the surface – once, twice. She gasped for air. Floundered as she sank again. And still her only thought was that soon she would be with Robbie.

Abi emerged from the woods, breathless and frantic, to see Imogen's long fair hair floating on the surface of the lake.

Dear God! She was in the water! Her heart pounded like a drum, an accompaniment to the rumbles of thunder. Why, oh why, had Hugh gone to his mine just when he was needed most? Jem was fetching him, but he would be too late. Imogen would have drowned, if she hadn't already.

Without a thought for her own safety, Abi waded into the water, knowing she must not tumble over the shelf where the lake deepened suddenly or they were both done for. She inched forward as fast as she dared, testing the ground in front of her before taking a step, and when she could go no further, she dropped to her hands and knees, reaching out towards Imogen. It was no use. She was not close enough. She wriggled forward until her arms were straining in their sockets, her shoulders aching, skin tight over her ribs and her spine extended to its limits. Somehow her fingers closed over a hank of Imogen's hair. She grasped it tightly and tugged, and Imogen's head broke water.

Her face was white as the water lilies, but Abi was not going to give up. Pulling her by her hair, she managed to get her close enough to grab her arm and drag her towards the bank. Imogen was making no attempt to help herself, but to Abi's enormous relief, she coughed, a gurgling splutter, retched and vomited.

She was alive! But no matter how hard she tried, Abi was unable to hoist her up the steep shelf and into the shallows. Her waterlogged clothes were dragging her down, and Abi, exhausted by her exertions, did not possess the strength. All she could do was keep Imogen's head above water and pray that help would come soon.

How long it took for Hugh to arrive, Abi would never know. Time had lost all meaning. Everything had become a hazy blur. Only her determination to keep Imogen from drowning remained crystal clear. The rest was a half-remembered dream. The rush of relief as he raced towards them, took Imogen's weight and dragged her out of the water. Her own efforts to worm her way back to dry land and get to her feet; the dizziness that overcame her when she did so. Hugh steadying her, helping her to sit on a grassy mound, asking if she could manage to make her own way back to the house while he followed with Imogen. His progress would be slow, and Abi should go ahead and seek help.

Then there was the endless struggle through the woods on legs that seemed not to belong to her. The sharp prickling pain as feeling returned to her numb hands, the searing ache in her shoulders and back. Discovering Jem waiting anxiously with Hugh's horse and his own. Offering to hold them both while Jem went to assist Hugh. Drifting away, her head resting against the bay's steaming flank . . .

It was only when Hugh and Jem emerged from the trees supporting Imogen between them that she regained her senses.

'Is she . . . ?'

'She's alive – thanks to you.' But Hugh's grim tone and the anxiety etched into his face told her that Imogen was in a bad way, and his next words to Jem confirmed it.

'Ride for Dr Stanley and tell him this is a matter of life and death.'

The stable lad wasted no time, kicking his horse to a canter even before he reached the drive. Hugh hoisted Imogen up into the saddle and steadied her while Abi took the reins and led the horse across the lawns to the house.

From the shelter of the trees further along the edge of the woods, Giles watched them go, furious at having his plan thwarted. Had it succeeded to some extent at least? Certainly Imogen looked to be in a serious state, and might yet succumb to the effects of the trauma inflicted on her frail body. But whatever the outcome, he wasn't finished yet. It was vital he took care of the one person here at Bramley who knew of the part he had played in this. He couldn't afford to be implicated.

When the procession had vanished into the house, he allowed what he considered to be enough time for Imogen to be settled somewhere she could be attended to in private, and followed surreptitiously. He was confident Hugh wouldn't want Freddie to see his stepmother in this state, nor witness whatever was to come. The boy would almost certainly be in his room. Alone. And Giles would deal with the threat Freddie posed him by whatever means necessary.

Chapter Twenty-Four

Abi sat in the kitchen beside the glowing range, nursing a cup of hot milk laced with brandy. She had changed into dry clothes, and a blanket was wrapped around her, but still she was shivering.

''Tis the shock,' Cook said. 'That's what it be. Drink up. That drop o' brandy will do you the world of good.'

Abi's jaw was clenched tight to keep her teeth from chattering, and she said nothing.

'Oh dearie dearie me!' Mary was sitting in another chair, arms wrapped around herself and rocking to and fro. 'I shall never forgive meself for this. How I came to leave her door open I'll never know. Her ladyship will be all right, won't she?'

'Who knows?' Cook was chopping vegetables for a dinner no one would have any appetite for. 'We done all we could for 'er an' nobody could do more. But rest assured the doctor'll be 'ere soon, if he ain't already. An' the master's wi' her, takin' good care o' her.'

Hugh had decided that rather than try to get Imogen upstairs, she should be settled in the parlour. Mrs Mears had fetched dry clothes and blankets and a hot drink and set a warming pan on the coals, and Hugh had pulled up a chair so that he could sit by her side as she lay on the chaise.

'Miss.' A small voice from the doorway.

Cook spun round, still brandishing her knife. 'What be you doin' 'ere?'

'I'm sorry. I wanted . . .'

Abi turned to see Jimmy standing tentatively in the doorway. Somehow she dragged herself out of the nether world she had retreated to.

'Jimmy? What is it?'

'Where's Freddie?'

'He's in his room. Why don't you go up? I'm sure he would be pleased to see you.'

'Thanks, miss.' He scampered off, almost colliding with Mrs Mears, who was crossing the hall.

'Slow down!' the housekeeper ordered sharply. 'You should know better than to charge about the house, especially at a time like this.'

Chastened, Jimmy slowed his pace to a walk as he headed for the stairs.

'That boy! He's no business here,' Mrs Mears said, coming into the kitchen.

'How is her ladyship?' Cook asked.

'How do you expect? In a bad way. But some of us have work to do.' Mrs Mears swept past her and into the larder, intent on making her regular inventory of supplies and noting what needed to be replenished, in spite of the crisis that had enveloped the household.

It was only moments later, however, that the peace was destroyed again as Jimmy came charging back into the kitchen.

'Miss! Miss!'

'What now?' Cook snapped.

'I need Miss Newman! Miss . . . can you come? Please!'

Though she was still shaky, Abi got up. Jimmy had sounded really panicked, and that wasn't like him at all. Still clutching the blanket around her, she followed him into the hall.

'What's wrong, Jimmy?'

'Oh miss, you've got to do something! The doctor's frightening Freddie!'

'The doctor?' Abi repeated, puzzled. 'What doctor?'

'Dr Stanley. Please, come quick!'

'Very well. Wait here and I'll investigate,' Abi instructed him, more confused than ever.

Had Imogen been taken to her room after all? Why else would Giles Stanley be upstairs? Had her condition deteriorated, and that was what had frightened the boys? She climbed the stairs and headed for Imogen's room, but as she reached Freddie's, she saw that the door was open. And what she saw through it shocked her to the core.

Giles Stanley was there, and she could be in no doubt that Jimmy had been right to be alarmed. The young doctor was looming threateningly over a terrified Freddie.

Giles had achieved his objective of getting into the house without being seen and gone straight to Freddie's room, where the boy was lying on his bed, balled fists covering his eyes.

'Good day, Frederick.'

Freddie had shot upright, and Giles had smiled unpleasantly at the sight of his anguished face stained with tears.

'I hope you're pleased with yourself,' he had said cuttingly.

Freddie's lip trembled. 'I didn't do anything today! I told you I wasn't going to do it any more and I haven't!'

Giles laughed unpleasantly. 'Do you really think anyone will believe you? You've been playing wicked tricks on your stepmother for a very long time and today you've surpassed yourself. You put a water lily under her pillow and left her door unlocked so that she could escape and go to him.'

285

'I didn't!' Freddie's voice was muffled; tears rolled down his cheeks and his whole body shook with sobs. 'I only ever did what you told me to!'

Giles caught Freddie by the shoulders, glaring threateningly into the frightened boy's eyes. 'You are mistaken, Frederick. But be in no doubt of this – if ever you breathe a word about anything that has passed between us, I shall be forced to tell your father what I know. That you were trying to rid yourself of the woman who took your real mama's place. That you wanted her dead, and saw a way to be rid of her.' He lowered his voice to a conspiratorial whisper, but it was no less menacing. 'You killed her, Frederick, and if it becomes known, you will face the full force of the law.' He paused to let his words sink in, then continued, 'But I am your friend, remember that. I don't want to see you charged with murder. I will keep silent, just as long as you do the same. Are we agreed?'

Freddie tried to wriggle free, but Giles thrust him back so that he was pinned to the bed.

'Are we agreed?' Giles repeated through gritted teeth.

It was at that moment that Jimmy had reached the door to Freddie's room and seen Giles towering over his friend, who was cowering on the bed. He realised in an instant that this was connected to what Freddie had told him about the things the doctor wanted him to do, and the threats he had made if he refused.

For just a moment he had stood frozen, unsure of what to do. Then he had turned and run back downstairs to fetch the help of the one person he trusted.

Abi hesitated for only a moment before entering the room.

'Giles? Freddie?' Her voice was sharp with incredulity and horror.

Giles had been unaware of anything but what was happening between him and Freddie, and now, shocked, he jerked upright, guilt written all over his face. The moment he was released, Freddie rolled off the bed and on to his feet, backing away from the doctor.

'What is going on here?' Abi demanded.

Giles shot a warning look at Freddie. 'Horseplay,' he said. 'We were having a game, isn't that right, Frederick?'

Too terrified to contradict him, Freddie nodded like a marionette when the puppet master pulls the strings. 'Yes. May I go now?'

Without waiting for an answer, he rushed to the door, pushed past Abi and was gone, pelting down the stairs.

Giles seemed to have recovered himself somewhat. 'Dear me, what is wrong with the boy?' he said smoothly and almost nonchalantly.

'Why are you with him and not attending to Lady Hastings?' Abi demanded.

Giles shrugged. 'I have been. But Sir Hugh asked me to take a look at Freddie, since he knew he had been badly upset by the day's events. I endeavoured to take his mind off what had happened with a little rough-and-tumble, but . . .' He spread his hands helplessly. 'I very much fear he is as unstable as his mama.'

'Imogen is not his mama. And Freddie is not unstable,' Abi said coldly. 'Mischievous, yes, but otherwise a perfectly normal little boy. And I have to say that you have a strange way of taking his mind off things.'

'Oh, come now. You know as well as I do how Frederick likes to play games.'

His words stirred something in Abi – a revelation almost too outrageous to contemplate. Freddie and his games. She had long suspected that he was behind the sounds Imogen heard in the night, and that someone was encouraging him, using him for their own ends. She had wondered if that someone was Mrs Mears, or even Hugh. Now, however, the pieces of the puzzle were jangling like falling coins as they slotted into place.

On the day Giles had first attended Freddie to treat his measles, Hugh had mentioned Imogen's hallucinations, and suggested jokingly that Freddie might be to blame. Could it be that when Giles had offered to teach Freddie the basics of science, it had been a ploy to spend time alone with him? She couldn't imagine why the doctor would want to encourage him in the tricks he was playing on Imogen, but she had a horrible feeling she was right. It would explain too why Freddie had turned against the doctor immediately after the episode when Imogen had gone missing in the night. Remembering how upset and worried he had been, it made sense that he had realised for the first time the disastrous effect his pranks were having on her, but had been afraid of telling Giles he wouldn't play along any more.

If what she had just witnessed was anything to go by, it seemed he had been right to be frightened.

'What games do you mean?' she asked, playing for time while she tried to make sense of it all.

Giles smiled, an unpleasant, condescending smile. 'I think you and I both know very well. I have done my best to dissuade him, and to protect him from exposure, but perhaps it is time for the truth. As I say, Freddie is a very disturbed young man. We should not blame him too much.'

'Protect him? Not blame him?' Fury ran white hot through Abi's veins. 'I don't believe that's what you are doing at all, Doctor. Quite the opposite.'

His eyes narrowed. He was no longer smiling. 'What has he told you?'

She was right. He had just confirmed it. 'He has told me nothing. He is far too frightened of you. But you encouraged him, didn't you? And when he realised the harm he was doing and wanted to stop, you threatened him. Just as you were threatening him now with your so-called horseplay. I don't know what you thought you had to gain from all this, but I can assure you I'll make sure you don't get away with it.'

She turned, ready to storm out, but before she could take so much as a step, Giles had grabbed her by the arm.

'Not so fast, Miss Newman.'

Abi swung round, the fury still blazing in her eyes. 'Unhand me!'

'I think not. Do you really imagine I am going to allow a silly girl like you to ruin everything?'

As he spoke, he began to drag her across the room, and the first sharp pangs of alarm spread through Abi's veins like icicles. What was he doing!

'Let me go!' She struggled and dug her slippered feet into the rug, but it was useless. Exhausted as she was by her exertions in saving Imogen, she was no match for him, and he continued to pull her towards the window, which had been opened to let in some fresh air. The gusting wind that had accompanied the storm had blown in the rain. The floorboards were wet beneath Abi's feet, and the drapes hung heavy with damp.

'Well, well! A Juliet balcony! How convenient! And how fitting!' Giles sneered. 'That is another story that had no happy ending, one that I'm sure you are familiar with.'

What was he talking about? Had he gone mad? Then he pushed her forward, and as realisation dawned, Abi was almost paralysed with blind terror.

He stopped, looking into her face as if he was storing away this moment to gloat over, then went on. 'Given all she has been through, who will question that the governess took her own life? Such an experience is quite enough to unhinge the mind. And who knows? Maybe Frederick had been playing games with her too.' He pushed aside the drapes with one hand while still holding her securely with the other. 'Come along, Miss Newman. Onto the balcony.'

'No!' Abi screamed. Giles was quite capable of hoisting her up on to the waist-high rail, she knew, and crazy enough to do it. Besides, this balcony was identical to the one in her own room, which she had been warned was rotten and unsafe. He wouldn't need to force her over the rail. It was all too likely that it would give way beneath her weight and she would go crashing down to the paved area below.

She screamed again, 'No!' and with every bit of her remaining strength grasped the door surround, hanging on, fighting for her life. But her fingers were slipping on the wet wood and she was losing her grip. This was a battle she couldn't win. In desperation, she swivelled round, lashing out at Giles's face, catching his cheek with her fingernails and startling him into relinquishing his hold on her.

But her relief was short-lived. Furious, Giles changed tactics. His hands went around her throat, squeezing, so that the world spun and stars exploded before her eyes. She was going to die. The roaring in her ears drowned out any other sound, and she was as unaware as Giles that someone had entered the room. Darkness was closing in, claiming her; her knees buckled beneath her and she knew no more.

Mrs Mears had been crossing the hallway on her way back to the parlour when she heard the scream. She stopped, her lips pursed tight in disapproval. Those boys! What was wrong with them? Couldn't they play nicely? Didn't they know her ladyship needed peace and quiet? Well, she would soon put a stop to their antics!

Angrily she ascended the stairs, pushed open the door of Freddie's room – and stopped short, scarcely able to believe her eyes.

At first she didn't realise that the man struggling with Abi at the open window was Dr Stanley. His back was towards her and her first thought was that it was an intruder. But whoever it was, whatever he was doing was clear enough – forcing Miss Newman out onto the balcony, which everyone in the house knew was unsafe. If she didn't do something, and quickly, the governess could well go crashing down to the paving below.

For all that she was a big woman, Mrs Mears was capable of moving very quietly when she so wished, and she moved quietly now. A large ornamental Chinese vase stood on top of the tallboy to the left of the door; she picked it up, holding it against her chest with one hand while clutching her keys in the other to keep them from jangling and announcing her presence. Then, when she was close enough to the intruder, she raised the vase, using both hands now, and with all her considerable strength brought it down on his head. The china smashed as it connected with his skull, and as he jerked round, she realised with a sense of shock that it was Dr Stanley.

She hadn't killed him, then. But she had stunned him. Giles staggered drunkenly, clutching at the frame of the window, which swung closed, trapping his hand. He batted at it drunkenly, and as it flew open, he staggered again, forwards this time, out onto the balcony, and collided with the waist-high rail. For just a moment he teetered there, then, with a loud splintering sound, it gave way under his weight.

He flailed as the rotten wood crumbled, then both he and the remnants of the rail were gone. And in the stillness that had followed the storm, the thud as his body hit the paving stones below was as chilling as another clap of thunder.

A reluctant Dr Mounty had been forced to take the call, since his junior partner was nowhere to be found. He had examined Imogen and now he and Hugh were in the hallway.

'Will she pull through?' Hugh asked anxiously.

'Lady Hastings has had a most fortunate escape,' the doctor said somewhat testily. 'The greatest danger now is from the lake water she ingested and inhaled. There are many unpleasant diseases that she could contract from it. We must hope for the best but be prepared for the worst.'

He turned to leave, anxious to get the journey home over and done with. His gout was troubling him, and all he wanted to do was take off his boots and rest his foot on his favourite ottoman, with a glass of whisky to ease the pain.

Hugh, however, was not ready to let him go.

'I'd be grateful if you would take a look at Miss Newman before you go,' he said. 'It's thanks to her that Imogen is alive, and she was in a poor state herself.'

'She's young and healthy . . .'

Dr Mounty broke off as Mrs Mears suddenly appeared at the head of the stairs.

'Sir, you must come at once!' She sounded unusually flustered. 'And you too, Doctor. Something terrible has happened.'

Once again the house was plunged into uproar, with everyone running in different directions. It was plain even to a layman that nothing could be done for Giles Stanley, and a shocked Dr Mounty took less than a minute to pronounce him dead. Hugh covered his broken body with his coat, and the two men returned to the house, where Hugh instructed Freddie and Jimmy to go to the Doels' cottage and remain there until they were told differently.

'How could this have occurred?' he asked Mrs Mears, who had been waiting for them in the hallway. She seemed to have recovered her usual composure.

'For some unknown reason, he appeared to be attacking Miss Newman. I went to her assistance. Dr Stanley retreated onto the balcony and fell against the rail, which gave way.' The housekeeper saw no reason to mention striking him with the Chinese vase unless she was forced to. She'd sweep up the broken pieces and hope it wasn't missed.

'He was attacking Miss Newman? Is she harmed?' Hugh sounded frantic.

'She swooned. More than that, I couldn't say. I helped her onto the bed and came directly to tell you of the accident.'

'Go and sit with Lady Hastings, if you please.' Hugh was already making for the stairs. 'Dr Mounty, come with me.'

Consumed by anxiety, Hugh took the stairs two at a time. In that moment, nothing mattered but Abi. Not Dr Stanley's body lying on the patio, not even poor tormented Imogen, and certainly not his coalfield and his plans for it.

'Abi?'

She was lying on Freddie's bed, propped up against the pillows. As Hugh entered the room, she tried to speak, but managed nothing but a croak, and her hand went to her throat, but not before he had seen the weals encircling it.

'Oh my dear!' He went down on his knees beside the bed, taking her free hand, which lay limply on the coverlet. As Dr Mounty appeared in the doorway, breathless and flushed, Hugh turned to him.

'Mounty – attend to Miss Newman, if you please.'

The old doctor approached the bed. 'A swoon, your

housekeeper said . . .' He broke off, shocked to see the livid marks on her throat. Marks that could only have been made by a man's hands. 'Dear God!' he muttered. 'Did Stanley do this to you?'

Abi swallowed with an effort, tried again in vain to speak.

'Don't try to talk,' he said hastily. 'Sir Hugh – water.'

Hugh did as he was bid, pouring some from the carafe on the washstand into a tumbler and putting it to Abi's lips. Though most of it trickled down her chin, she managed a few sips, and it seemed to revive her.

Hugh wiped the dribble of water from her chin with his kerchief and smoothed her hair away from her forehead. It was still damp from the rain, and splashes of lake water, and his emotions ran riot. Fury at the man who had done this to her for no explicable reason. Horror at what she had gone through today. Awed admiration for the courage and determination she had shown in saving Imogen's life, as well as her remarkable selflessness, and her concern now, not for herself, but for her friend. And love. Deep and all-consuming. A love he had fought against. A love he had thought he would never again feel for any woman after he had lost Marigold. He loved Abi with his whole heart, and he could no longer deny it.

But it could not be. He had made vows before God to love, honour and keep Imogen, and she needed him now more than ever she had.

With a heavy heart, and oblivious to the doctor's presence, he leaned forward and kissed Abi's cheek. 'I have to leave you for a while. I have things to attend to. But Dr Mounty will look after you, and Mary will come and sit with you when he is done. And rest assured, I will be back soon.'

He locked eyes with the doctor, who nodded his under-standing, and left the room to deal with the aftermath of what had happened.

* * *

When the doctor had gone, Abi closed her eyes, floating on clouds of muzziness as the sleeping potion he had given her worked its magic. The horrors of the day drifted away, along with the pain in her throat and the ache in her limbs. All she was aware of now was the touch of Hugh's hand on her forehead and his lips on her cheek, and the blissful awareness of the connection that had been there between them once more. Contentment suffused her as reality faded away.

She loved him. And he loved her. She felt it in every beat of her heart, with every shallow breath she took. For the moment, it was more than enough.

Chapter Twenty-Five

Prudie Doel was worried about Freddie. He'd eaten next to nothing of the mutton stew she'd put in front of him, excused himself from the table as soon as she and Jimmy had finished their meal, and gone upstairs to Jimmy's room, where he was to share a bed with his friend tonight. It was understandable that he should be upset after all that had happened today, and she had tried to talk to him about it, thinking that might help him come to terms with it, but she couldn't reach him. He had closed in on himself, tight as a clam.

Prudie was a perceptive soul, and it seemed to her almost as if he was blaming himself for what had happened, but that made no sense at all. He looked wary and frightened too, and she supposed it could be that he was in shock. But somehow she couldn't help feeling there was more to it than that. Well, whatever it was, if anyone could throw light on it, it was Jimmy. The two boys had become very close friends.

Prudie went into the garden, where Jimmy was bouncing a ball against the cottage wall.

'What's up wi' Freddie?' she asked, going straight to the point.

Jimmy shrugged, not meeting her eyes, and bounced the ball again with unnecessary force, so that it shot off into the lavender bush. Prudie knew she was right. The two boys were hiding something. She tried again.

'Stop that, Jimmy, and pay attention do. I asked 'ee a question.'

Unusually for him, Jimmy ignored her, bending over the lavender bush, looking for the ball.

'Hey, me lad! I be talking to you.' This time she spoke sharply, and reluctantly Jimmy straightened up, the lost ball in his hand.

'There's some'ut up wi' Freddie, and I'd'a want to know what it is.' She gave him a straight look.

'Sorry, missus.' But he couldn't look her in the eye. 'It's not for me to say. Freddie made me promise not to tell.'

Prudie tried another tactic. 'Very well, I'll just 'ave t' ask 'im meself.' She half turned, as if to go into the house in search of Freddie, and just as she took hold of the doorknob, Jimmy spoke, his voice small but urgent.

'Don't do that, missus.'

She turned back. 'Be 'ee goin' t' tell me then?'

Jimmy's lip wobbled. He looked utterly wretched. 'I don't want to get him into trouble.'

'Fer pity's sake!' Prudie exploded. 'The boy's in an awful state. 'E needs to come clean. Whatever trouble you think 'e might be in, it can't be any worse for 'im than this. Now – be 'ee goinna t' tell me or not?'

There was a long silence while Jimmy stared miserably at his boots.

'I be waitin', Jimmy.'

'It was the doctor's fault,' he said at last. 'He was making Freddie do it.'

'The doctor? You mean 'im as fell through the balcony?'

Jimmy nodded.

'You b'ain't makin' sense. What did 'e make Freddie do?'

'Play tricks on her ladyship,' Jimmy said, his voice little more than a whisper. 'But when Freddie didn't want to do it any more, the doctor said that if he breathed a word about it, he'd tell Sir Hugh what he'd done. Nobody would believe Freddie, and he'd be in awful hot water. Then today, after they had to pull her ladyship out of the lake, the doctor went crazy. Trapped Freddie on his bed, threatening him with all sorts.' The words were tumbling out now. 'Freddie thought he was going to do for him, but Miss Newman came in and Freddie managed to get away. An' that's all I know really.' He raised anxious eyes to Prudie's. 'You won't tell, will you? Freddie thinks it's all his fault, like when his little brother fell in the lake and got drowned.'

'Oh my life.' That terrible day was as clear to Prudie now as if it had been just yesterday, and her heart went out to Freddie. What she couldn't understand, though, was why that young doctor should have encouraged him to play such cruel tricks on Lady Hastings. But one thing was clear. Sir Hugh must be told what had been going on.

'I won't say nothing, Jimmy, but Freddie must, and the sooner the better,' she said firmly. 'Why don't you fetch 'im down now? I'll 'ave a word with 'im, tell 'im it's the doctor Sir Hugh will blame, not 'im. I reckon 'twould be best to find Sir Hugh right now and get it over with. And there'll be biscuits in the oven when 'e gets back. 'E's fond of my biscuits, is Freddie.'

Jimmy found Freddie in his room, curled in a ball on the bed.

'Freddie?' he said nervously. 'I got something to tell you, and you're going to kill me, I expect.'

It was the wrong choice of words.

Freddie rolled over, his face crumpling. 'I never wanted to kill anyone!'

'I know. I'm sorry. But I don't suppose you'll be my friend any more when I tell you.'

'Why not? What have you done?'

Jimmy took a deep breath. 'I told Mrs Doel about the doctor. I had to, Freddie. She made me.'

Freddie sat bolt upright. 'You told?'

'I made sure she knew it was all his fault.'

'Did she believe you?'

'I think so. Yes, she did. And she said you've got to tell your pa.'

A look of sheer horror crossed Freddie's face. 'I can't!'

'Yes, you can. It won't be so bad. I saw the doctor attacking you, and so did Miss Newman. That's proof enough that he's the one to blame – he wanted to hush you up, to stop you telling on him. Well, he's dead now. He can't frighten you any more. And you'll feel a lot better when you've got it off your chest.'

Freddie chewed his lip. 'Do you really think so?'

'Yes. Come on. Do it now and get it over with.'

'Will you come with me?'

'Course I will.'

Resigned, Freddie got up. Perhaps Jimmy was right.

Sir Hugh was in his study, attempting to process all that had happened and come to a decision as to his best course of action. His head was telling him that Abi could no longer remain at Bramley Court. He simply could not trust himself to keep his marriage vows to Imogen while he and Abi were under the same roof, and his high moral standards insisted that he must. His heart, however, told a different story. Sending her away would be the most painful thing he had ever done, and she was going to be dreadfully hurt too, which in turn would only add to his pain. But it had to be done. The alternative was unfair to both women.

As he wrestled with the problem, there was a tap at the door.

'Come,' he called tersely.

The door opened, and to his surprise, it was Frederick and Jimmy who entered, somewhat hesitantly. They stopped midway between him and the door, looking decidedly nervous.

'What is it?' he asked, half expecting to be told of some new catastrophe.

It was Jimmy who took the initiative. 'Freddie's got something to tell you.'

For once Hugh did not correct the use of Frederick's pet name. Under the circumstances, it simply wasn't of any importance.

'Speak up then, my boy,' he said, not unkindly.

Freddie raised his eyes to meet his father's, then dropped them again. 'It was me,' he said in a whisper.

'What was you?' Hugh asked, puzzled.

'Playing tricks.' Freddie looked up again. Tears were trickling down his cheeks. 'But it wasn't me today. I didn't do anything today, honestly I didn't. I told him I wasn't going to do it any more. It must have been him?'

'Oh Frederick.' Hugh was beginning to see where this was leading. 'By "him", I take it you are talking about Dr Stanley?' Freddie nodded miserably, and Hugh pulled a chair close to his. 'Come and sit down, my boy, and let's begin again, shall we?'

Freddie gulped, crossed to the chair and sat down. Jimmy followed, and stood behind him, offering moral support, and slowly, haltingly, Freddie told his father the whole story.

Though shocked, Hugh listened without uttering a single word of reproach. By the time it was done, Freddie was weeping again. 'I'm sorry, Papa. I'm so, so sorry . . .'

Hugh laid a hand on his son's arm, patting it comfortingly. He was at a loss to understand why Frederick should ever have thought of doing something so cruel, but this was no time to pursue that. He was clearly dreadfully upset and guilt-ridden.

'It was very brave of you to admit all this,' he said.

'You're not angry?' There was something like disbelief in Freddie's tear-filled eyes, and Hugh felt a stab of guilt of his own as he wondered if sometimes he had been too hard on the boy, who was, after all, still a child.

'It was wrong of you, but you know that now, don't you?' he said. Freddie nodded. 'And you'll never do anything like it again?' He shook his head. 'Then for the moment let's say no more about it.'

After the relieved boys had left the study, Hugh leaned his elbows on the desk and lowered his head so as to massage the taut muscles at the nape of his neck. Frederick might have been able to unburden himself, but a weight still lay heavy on Hugh's shoulders.

Before the day was out, he would have to do the right thing with regards to Abi and Imogen, even though he knew it would break his heart.

Malcolm was feeling inordinately pleased with himself. So far all his efforts to discover the whereabouts of Abi's son had come to nothing, so it was good to have succeeded in the other mission he had set himself – to find suitable accommodation for Prissie and her baby.

His enquiries had led him to an almshouse, one of a row of five in the neighbouring village of Stoneham. It had become vacant when its elderly occupant had recently died, and after pleading Prissie's case, he had managed to persuade the Church authorities to allow her to occupy it. In exchange, she would be expected to keep both the church and the vicarage clean, for which she would receive a small wage.

He broke the news to Maisie first, as tactfully as he could, and to his immense relief, she was far less upset than he had expected.

'Well, at least it's not far away,' she'd said. 'I shall be able to visit, and Prissie knows she is always welcome here.'

Perhaps the shine of having a baby in the house had worn off, Malcolm thought. Christian did seem to cry a lot, especially at night, and he couldn't help thinking it would be good to have peace and quiet restored to the vicarage.

He raised the subject with Prissie when she joined him and Maisie for their evening meal, and she was understandably delighted and profusely grateful.

'Oh Vicar, I don't 'ow I can ever thank 'ee,' she said, happy tears welling in her eyes. 'I never thought I'd have a proper home of me own.' Then, anxious that she might have offended Maisie, she added quickly, 'It's not that I've not been happy here – I have. An' you've been so good to me. But to 'ave a place with a roof that don't leak, and a bit of a garden where Christian can play an' be no trouble to anybody – oh, you don't know 'ow good that do feel.'

'You've been no trouble at all,' Maisie assured her. 'It's been a pleasure. I shall miss you and Christian.'

'An' we'll miss you.'

'Just as long as you think you will be able to manage on your own,' Maisie said.

'We shall be all right, don't you worry.' Prissie smiled happily.

'You will have good neighbours, I'm sure,' Malcolm said. 'Several of the occupants of the almshouses attend church regularly. I shall have a word with them when next I see them.

But if ever you are in need of help in any way, you know we are here for you.'

They had finished their main meal – a meat and potato pie Maisie had made the evening before – and she was just ladling freshly stewed rhubarb into bowls when there was a knock at the front door. Malcolm rose from the table and went to answer it, expecting the caller to be one of his parishioners, or perhaps his churchwarden – the man was a terrible fusspot, forever fretting over unimportant details regarding his duties. But as he passed the little hall window that overlooked the front entrance, he saw a roan that he recognised as Hugh's horse tied up at the gatepost, and when he opened the door, it was his old friend himself who stood on the doorstep.

'Hugh!' A frisson of alarm prickled under Malcolm's skin. 'What are you doing here?'

Hugh's reply did nothing to quell his anxiety.

'I need to talk with you, Malcolm. In private.'

'We can go to my study.' Malcolm opened the door more widely.

'I would prefer to be outside, where I can keep a watch on Hector. He may become restless, and your gatepost might not be strong enough to restrain him.'

'Very well. Give me a moment and I'll join you.'

Malcolm went into the dining room, where Maisie and Prissie were waiting for him to rejoin them.

'Carry on with your meal,' he said. 'I may be some time.'

Maisie gave him a questioning look, but Malcolm did not enlighten her.

Outside, Hugh had returned to Hector and stood rubbing his nose somewhat distractedly.

'What is it?' Malcolm asked. 'Is it Abi?'

'Not entirely.' Hugh turned his attention to Malcolm, though

303

his gentling hand continued to stroke Hector's strong neck. 'I regret to say we are in turmoil at Bramley. It has been a terrible day, culminating in a shocking tragedy – I'll tell you about it later. But yes, Abi is the reason I am here. I have come to ask if you would be willing for her to come home.'

'Come home?' Malcolm repeated, bewildered. 'Why do you want to send her home?'

'I don't want to send her anywhere,' Hugh snapped, then quickly apologised. 'Forgive me. I'm not myself. The reason I am suggesting it is because I believe it would be in her best interests.'

'I think,' Malcolm said evenly, 'that you really need to tell me what all this is about.'

Hugh ran a hand through his hair. 'It's a long story, my friend, and not a pretty one.'

'Go on,' Malcolm said grimly, bracing himself for what was to come, and Hugh began.

When Hugh had left, galloping away, Malcolm remained in the garden for some time. He was stunned by the terrible story Hugh had told him, saddened at what had become of Imogen and full of sympathy for his friend. But most of all, he was shocked to the core that the family doctor should have attacked Abi and then fallen to his death from the balcony. That, coming on top of her heroic efforts to save Imogen from drowning, must have left her in a dreadful state, both emotionally and physically. He was in no doubt but that Hugh was right: the best place for her, at the moment at least, was here at home, where she could be cared for by people who loved her, well away from the setting of the traumatic events. Thank the Lord that he had arranged for Prissie to move into the almshouse! It would have to happen much sooner than he'd anticipated, but at least the little house was fully furnished with the previous occupant's belongings, and there was nothing to stop her taking up residence right away. But he would have to work fast. Hugh had said he would bring Abi home tomorrow.

He returned to the dining room and ate the dish of stewed rhubarb that had been left for him on the table, still deep in thought, then went in search of Maisie and Prissie to update them on the revised timeline for Prissie's move to her new home.

The sun was dipping low over the western horizon as Hugh rode home. Jem was in the stables awaiting his return; Hugh dismounted, handed him the reins and went into the house. He checked on Imogen, who was still in the parlour, Mrs Mears at her side; then, satisfied that she seemed somewhat better and was resting quietly, went upstairs.

Abi was in her own room now, and alone. At first he thought she was asleep, but when he pulled up a chair and sat down, taking her hand, her eyes opened and she smiled; just a small curve of her lips, but it warmed his heart.

'Hugh.' Her voice was still husky and slurred, and the deep red mark around her throat was livid against the pallor of the surrounding skin. The sight of it aroused his anger once more, blood boiling in his veins. If Giles Stanley were not already dead, he would have killed him with his bare hands.

'How are you feeling?' he asked. 'Don't answer if it hurts you too much. Just squeeze my hand.'

A shadow of a smile lifted the corners of her mouth and her fingers tightened around his. 'Better,' she managed.

'That is good. Giles Stanley will never hurt you or anyone else ever again.' He saw the question in her eyes and went on. 'He fell from the balcony. Thank God Mrs Mears arrived when she did. But what you have been through today is indescribable.

As if what you endured in order to save Imogen's life was not enough. I am totally in awe of your bravery and determination. If it were not for you, she would have drowned, not a doubt of it. But I'm happy to say she is recovering now, thanks to you.'

Abi's eyes clouded. 'Poor Imogen . . .'

'Freddie has told me everything,' Hugh went on. 'He was indeed playing his foolish tricks on Imogen, just as you suggested, but it was Dr Stanley who was encouraging him for some inexplicable reason. When Freddie realised the serious consequences of what he was doing and wanted to stop, Stanley threatened him. But why he should attack you so savagely is beyond me . . .'

'Because I had guessed the truth, and he knew it, I imagine, though I have no idea why he would do such a thing.' Abi's hand went to her sore throat; she swallowed with an effort and went on. 'When Freddie confessed . . . you weren't cross with him?'

Once again she was thinking of everyone but herself. Hugh's heart swelled with love and admiration.

'Only a bit,' he said with a wry smile. 'He should never have started it at all, of course, but I don't believe he meant Imogen any harm. He didn't realise how cruel such a thing was – he never does when the imp of mischief tempts him. And then Dr Stanley took advantage of him and his mischievous ways and began manipulating him.'

'He was so upset when he realised she was actually searching for Robbie. And I do so hope that now it's all over, Imogen will begin to improve . . .' Abi's croaky voice faded, and with a sinking heart Hugh knew he could no longer delay what he had to do. The hardest thing he had ever done in his life.

He strengthened his resolve. 'You need to rest now, Abi. And tomorrow I am taking you home.'

'Home?' she whispered, puzzled.

'It's for the best. You need to be taken care of by those who love you, and you will recover much more quickly if you are away from the constant reminders of your ordeal.'

'But . . . I don't want to go! I don't want to leave you.'

'My sweetheart.' The endearment slipped out before he could stop it, and his voice was as gentle as his hand on hers. 'I don't want you to go either. But you must see . . .'

He didn't want to say it. That if she stayed here, he could not trust himself to remain true to Imogen. His wife. Who needed him now more than ever.

But she understood. He saw it in her eyes. And only loved her the more for it.

Chapter Twenty-Six

Abi sat in the stubbly grass at the top of the rise that overlooked the spot where she and Connor had made love.

Home. The place where she had grown from a child to a woman. Fallen in love. Had her heart broken twice over. Where she knew everyone and everyone knew her. Where the paths and byways, the woods and fields were as familiar to her as the fate lines on the palms of her hands. But now it felt strange and alien. The dimensions had changed, the open ground seemed wider and the rooms in the vicarage smaller and darker.

Emptiness yawned inside her. The ache of love and longing, the knowing it could never be. She missed Hugh so. His commanding presence, his voice, the touch of his hand, however rare and brief. If she closed her eyes, she could see his face in every detail, just as she had been able to see Connor's when she lost him . . .

It was the reason she had come here, because she had felt the need to remember Connor. To forget him because she had a new love would be a betrayal of all they had shared. And she wanted too to remember the girl she had been, so young and naïve, so full of optimism and passion.

It had seemed to her that if she could recapture something of the past, she could perhaps come to terms with being back in a place where she seemed no longer to belong, a place she had no hope of ever leaving again. Even if the opportunity arose, what would be the point? Wherever she went would be empty and meaningless without Hugh.

'Abi?'

Lost in her thoughts, she had not heard Malcolm's approach. She turned, forcing a smile, and he sat down beside her.

'You're missing Bramley,' he said, plucking a blade of grass and twiddling it between his fingers.

'Yes,' she admitted. It wasn't just Hugh, it was Imogen too, and Freddie and Jimmy. The purposeful bustle. The lessons to be prepared and taught. 'My life was so full there. Here . . . well, there's nothing really to occupy my days. Mother doesn't need my help with her school now she has her new assistant, and I feel quite lost.'

'She'd find a place for you if you asked her, I'm sure,' Malcolm said.

'Something, yes,' Abi agreed. 'But it wouldn't be the same. I've become used to doing things my own way. With only two pupils rather than a dozen, I've been able to give them my full attention, and I liked that. It was especially rewarding to teach Jimmy, like starting with a clean sheet, and he was so eager to learn.'

'Jimmy – the little boy who got stuck in the chimney?'

'Yes. He's a very clever child, much brighter than Freddie, truth be told. He could already read and write, which is something of a mystery, since apparently he was in an orphanage before the chimney sweep took him on as his apprentice. It seems unlikely he learned there.'

'No, quite.' Malcolm thought of the dreadful places he had visited recently in search of Abi's lost baby.

'I hate to leave him, actually,' Abi said. 'Apart from his education, he's making such good progress in every way. He's gaining in confidence, putting on weight and getting some colour in his cheeks. You have no idea of the state he was in when I first set eyes on him – skinny as a rake, filthy . . .' She paused, remembering the poor little wretch with the blanket wrapped around his skinny shoulders, covered from head to foot in soot and the plaster that had been dislodged to free him from the chimney, coughing, spluttering, scarcely able to breathe. 'He'd been ill-treated, too,' she went on. 'His back was covered in ridges, scars from beatings, and he'd been burned at some time, or scalded. Perhaps he fell into a tub of hot water at bath time, or perhaps it was spilled on him deliberately. That wouldn't surprise me. But he would never talk about it.'

'Dear God!' Malcolm raised his eyes heavenward. How could a loving Father allow such terrible things to happen to innocent children?

'The poor little chap must have been in agony,' Abi went on. 'Even now the skin on his arm is red and bubbly.'

'His arm, did you say?' Her words jolted Malcolm out of his reverie.

'Yes. From his elbow almost down to his wrist. It will never heal completely.'

Malcolm's head was reeling. 'He'd been in an orphanage, you say? Where?'

'I don't know. He wouldn't talk about it. But I think the sweep found him living on the streets, so I suppose he must have run away.'

Malcolm was silent as his chaotic thoughts chased one another. Surely it couldn't be the case that while he had been haring about from one orphanage to another in his search for Abi's lost son, the boy had been there all the time, sitting in her classroom? It was unbelievable.

'Have you noticed any other scars?' he asked.

She shook her head. 'No. Just a birthmark like a dollop of strawberry jam on the back of his neck, above the hairline,' she said.

Malcolm got to his feet. He needed to be alone to think about all this.

'I'm going to have to leave you. I have a sermon to prepare,' he said.

'Oh, don't let me keep you,' Abi said hastily. 'I think I shall stay here for a bit longer.'

Alone again, Abi leaned back on her elbows, idly picking at the grass and the daisies and clover that were regrowing now that the cows had been moved to another field, just as they had been on the day she and Connor . . .

Her fingers closed around a thin stalk and she broke it off, enclosing it in the palm of her hand, then opening her fingers and looking at it.

A four-leaf clover. She'd never found one before, however hard she had looked. Weren't they supposed to be lucky? Her spirits lifted a touch. It was just a silly superstition, of course, but perhaps it was an omen. A promise of better times to come.

How that could be, she couldn't imagine, but she was happy she had found it all the same.

Malcolm had to know if the idea that had occurred to him was the solution he had been seeking. But how? He couldn't go to Bramley to question the boy himself; Hugh would think he had taken leave of his senses, and presumably he had no idea that Abi had given birth to a child. Even she herself didn't even know that her baby had lived and been given away. He needed to be sure this wasn't all nothing but wishful thinking before he said a word to either of them.

It came to him in a flash. It was from the unpleasant matron at the last orphanage he had visited that he had learned that Abi's son had scalded himself while he was there. That alone wasn't enough to positively identify the boy, but if he could find out if the lad had also had a birthmark . . . Surely the matron would have noticed it when she was supervising bath time or washing his hair?

He made up his mind. He would hire Isaac Wilton to take him there again and ask her. Looking up at the sky, he murmured a prayer that it would prove to be so.

Malcolm stepped out of the door of the foul-smelling orphanage and gratefully breathed in sweet fresh air. The place was truly appalling. No wonder so many of the poor children incarcerated there did not survive. But nothing could dampen his elation. Against impossible odds, he had found Abi's lost son.

He hadn't prompted the matron beyond asking her if the boy who had run away had had a birthmark of any kind.

'The mark of the devil, you mean? He did that. A bloomin' great red blotch on 'is neck. Oh, the devil was in him awright.' Her mouth had curled unpleasantly in what might almost have been satisfaction. 'Found 'im dead in some back alley, 'ave you? The devil come back to claim 'is own?'

Malcolm, disgusted, did not enlighten her. He had what he wanted – confirmation that the little climbing boy was one and the same as the child who had hidden, terrified, in a cupboard while his father rampaged around the house before taking his own life and his adoptive mother lay dead. The very same child who had passed through St Margaret's Hospital for Needy Children after being taken there by Obediah for adoption. It almost defied belief that he should have ended up in the house where Abi was employed as governess. Just as it did that Prissie should have chosen his vicarage as a safe place to leave her baby, which had stirred up memories and guilt in Maisie and led to her sharing her story with Malcolm.

It was, he thought, as if the hand of God had orchestrated it all along the way, and he hoped that the Lord would guide him now. Maisie was unaware of what he had been doing; Abi didn't even know that her baby was alive, let alone living at Bramley House.

He had already decided that if his quest was successful, he would confess to Maisie first. It was her place to tell Abi that she and Obediah had lied about the stillbirth. He would tell her too that the child had been found, but he hoped to be there when she gave Abi the glad tidings. He very much wanted to witness her amazement and joy.

Isaac Wilton was waiting for him outside the orphanage. Malcolm climbed into the carriage and instructed him to take him home.

Constance, who was now more or less residing at Pridcombe House, had been stunned to learn of Giles's death. How in heaven's name had it happened? What had he been doing on a balcony at Bramley Court? All manner of rumours were flying about, but it seemed the household had closed ranks, and how Giles had come to meet his end remained a mystery. Even the coroner had learned nothing beyond that a balcony rail had given way when he had leaned on it, and he had not pressed the matter further. He suspected that the doctor had been dallying with one of the servants, or perhaps even Lady Hastings, and didn't want to embarrass his lordship with what could be the makings of a scandal.

Constance had also heard from Percy that there was talk that Lady Hastings had almost drowned in the lake on the same day, and her hopes had risen briefly, only to be dashed when it transpired she had been saved. She didn't know if the two events were connected, but either way, that part of her plan was in ruins.

But she still held the trump card, she consoled herself. When the dust had settled, she would go to Bramley and tell Hugh the lease was now in her name, and that if he wanted access to his land, he would have to dance to her tune. She wouldn't be able to become Lady Hastings just yet, but when she had Hugh in her pocket, she was sure she would be able to find a way

As soon as he had her to himself, Malcolm confessed to Maisie the true reason he had been visiting orphanages. As he had expected, her initial reaction was shock and outrage.

'You've done all that without telling me?' she flared. 'How dare you! What business is it of yours?'

'None, I grant you, beyond that I care very much for the people whose concern it is. I feel sure you very much regret what you did, and I didn't want to raise your hopes of being able to put things right only to dash them if I was unable to discover the boy's whereabouts. Which, I have to say, seemed the most likely outcome. In fact, though, I have been able to do so, which is why I am telling you now.'

He saw Maisie's face change, her anger replaced by a look of disbelief. 'You've found him? But how? Where is he? Is he well . . . ?' She broke off, covering her mouth with a trembling hand.

'I'll tell you everything in good time.' Malcolm guided her to a chair and urged her to sit down. 'I'm sorry all this has come as a shock to you. But given the way you are with Prissie's baby, I hope it is a happy one.'

Maisie said nothing, but tears were filling her eyes. He had been right, he thought. She did regret what she had done, and probably had done ever since she had given the child away. But a sudden thought must have occurred to her, because her head jerked up and her expression now was one of panic.

'Does Abigail know about this?'

'Not yet,' Malcolm said. 'And it will be even more of a shock to her, since she believes her baby died at birth.'

'You can't tell her! She'd never forgive me!' Maisie wailed, and Malcolm's heart went out to her. What she had done was terribly wrong, but he had no doubt it had been with the best of intentions. Now, any relief in knowing her grandson had been found was outweighed by her terror that she was going to lose her daughter.

'I shall tell her nothing,' he said firmly but gently. 'It's for you to do that. But tell her you must. It will ease your feelings of guilt to know that she can be reunited with her son, and I think it will make you happy too.'

For a long moment Maisie was silent as the tears streamed down her cheeks. Then she took a deep breath and nodded. 'I'll tell her when she's regained her strength.'

'In my opinion, there could be no better tonic.'

'I don't think she's up to such a shock. Besides, I need time to digest all this myself.'

Malcolm managed a sympathetic smile. 'I expect you do. But please – don't take too long about it.'

Three days had gone by and Maisie still had not plucked up the courage to tell Abi the truth about her baby. Countless times she rehearsed what she would say, but just thinking about it brought her out in a cold sweat. For all the excuses she had made to herself over the years, she knew that what she and Obediah had done was very wrong, and she was rightly ashamed and fearful of Abi's reaction.

Eventually Malcolm decided enough was enough. It was a Saturday. There was no school today, and he thought there would be no better opportunity.

He found Maisie in the kitchen, boiling the kettle to make a pot of tea.

'It's high time you spoke to Abigail,' he said without preamble. 'This has gone on long enough.'

'Fiddlesticks! There's no hurry,' Maisie protested.

'There you and I must disagree. The longer you leave it, the harder it will become, and if you won't tell her, I will,' he said bluntly.

Maisie's lips tightened. 'I've said I'll talk to her, and I will.'

'When?'

'This evening.'

'You will only delay again, Mrs Newman. Best get it over with. Abi is in the parlour – go and speak to her now. This minute. I'll prepare her.'

Maisie could see that he was leaving her no choice. Quaking, she followed him to the parlour, where she waited outside the door while he went in.

Abi was writing a letter to Freddie. She looked up questioningly when Malcolm came in. At this time on a Saturday he was usually closeted in his study, putting the finishing touches to the next day's sermon.

'Your mother wants to talk to you about something very important,' he said. 'But she is going to find it difficult, and you, I am afraid, will be shocked by what she has to say. Please try to understand, and not blame her too much. She has only ever had your welfare at heart.'

He turned and left the room, gesturing to Maisie to take his place.

Abi, perturbed and puzzled, set aside the letter.

'What is Malcolm talking about?' she asked as Maisie took the chair opposite hers, sitting bolt upright, hands clasped in the folds of her skirts to keep them from shaking.

'There's something we should have told you a long time ago, but your dear father wouldn't hear of it,' Maisie began, defensive already. 'About your baby.'

'My baby?' Abi repeated. 'What about my baby?'

'We told you he was dead. It was for the best.' Maisie's tone was defiant.

'What?' Abi was bewildered. 'What was for the best?'

'That you thought he had died. We couldn't let you ruin your life. Your good name would have been trampled in the mire. No decent man would ever have wanted you. You must see we couldn't allow that.'

Light was beginning to dawn, but Abi couldn't believe it.

'What are you saying? That my baby . . . ?'

'Didn't die.' There, it was said. 'We told you he had so you wouldn't do anything else silly. We were only thinking of you, Abigail. Of your future.'

Abi's jaw dropped. She gazed at her mother, stunned.

'He was alive? My baby was born alive? But . . . you said you'd buried him while I was still too ill to leave my bed. That isn't true?'

'No.'

'Then . . . what happened to him? Where is he?'

'He was adopted. Your father arranged it all. He went to a good home. A loving family. A mother and father who could give him a good life . . .'

'No . . . Oh!' Abi's wail was that of a wounded animal. 'No! No! No!'

'Stop that, Abigail!' Maisie ordered sharply, and repeated her mantra. 'It was for the best.'

'How can you say that?' Abi's voice was thick with tears. 'You stole my baby! How could you? How could you do that? I want him back!'

Malcolm, listening outside the door, had heard enough. He stepped into the room and dropped to his knees beside Abi, taking her clenched hands in his. 'Hush, Abi. There's more.'

She raised her head, her agonised eyes meeting his. 'You knew about this? You knew, and I didn't?'

'I found out a few weeks ago, and—'

'That I have a son I'll never know!'

'Shh. Listen to me. You do know him, Abi. I have found your son. That's why your mama is telling you now. Because I have found him. And you already know him.'

She shook her head, uncomprehending.

'You know him. You've been teaching him.'

'Freddie?'

'No, not Freddie. The little boy Hugh took in after he got stuck in the chimney.'

Still overwhelmed, she couldn't take in what he was saying.

'Jimmy? No, that can't be. Jimmy wasn't adopted. He was in an orphanage . . .' She turned to Maisie. 'You said my baby was adopted. By a good family . . .'

'He was.' It was Malcolm who answered her. 'But sadly his adoptive parents died, and there was no one to take care of him. It's a long story, Abi, and I will tell you all of it when you have had a chance to recover from the shock this has caused you. For now, all you need to know is that your son has been found, and you and he can be together at last.'

Malcolm had ushered Maisie out of the parlour, urging her to give Abi time and space to process all she had learned. Abi could hear her mother weeping, and Malcolm's soothing voice as he did his best to comfort her, but everything was hazy and unreal, as if she was dreaming.

Her baby – not dead after all, but alive! That in itself was almost unbelievable. But that she actually knew him – loved him . . . Joy surged through her veins, so intense that she was heady with it, and she was laughing and crying both at the same time.

Jimmy . . . Jimmy! That darling boy! But what a terrible time he'd had! The dreadful things he'd endured . . .

As more waves of emotion overwhelmed her, a picture rose before her eyes. Jimmy as he was when she'd first set eyes on him. Black with soot, dressed in rags. Frightened. Scarcely able to breathe . . . She gasped, and her pain was a physical one, cramping her stomach, constricting her lungs as his had been.

All she wanted to do was take him in her arms and never let him go. Tell him he was safe now. Give him the love he'd never had. She wrapped her arms around herself and rocked in her chair, lost in the wonder of it.

It was only as her euphoria gave way to practicalities that Abi realised that if she was ever to see her son again, Hugh would have to be told the whole story. It was a prospect that made her heart sink. He was a man of such high principles, she couldn't believe he would feel the same way about her when he knew of her past. But she could see no alternative.

She would write to him, she decided, tell him everything, and hope that he would allow Jimmy to remain at Bramley Court, at least for the time being – he was settling in so well after all the trauma he'd endured, and she didn't think it would be good for him to be uprooted yet again so soon. Perhaps Hugh would even allow her to return to her position as governess if what he had learned of her didn't fill him with disgust. There would no longer be any danger of their feelings for one another leading to a betrayal of Imogen. But it would be best to leave it for a day or so. Just now, her emotions were running riot, and she needed to have a clear head so as to be sure the way the account was worded was exactly right.

She would speak to Malcolm, though, talk it over with him and ask if he would deliver the letter to Hugh, given the unreliability of the post boys. Besides, he would put her side of things to his friend, she felt sure. And given what a shock the contents of her letter would be to Hugh, that could only be a good thing.

It was done. The letter was finished, and after reading and rereading it several times, Abi had sealed the envelope with a blob of red wax. Malcolm had hired Isaac and his carriage, refusing to allow Maisie to cover the cost as she had wanted to.

'You shouldn't be out of pocket,' she had said, tight-lipped and self-righteous as she had been ever since Abi's outburst. But Malcolm had been adamant.

'I began all this, and I need to see it through.'

Now, with the carriage drawn up outside, Abi walked with him to the vicarage gate.

'You will wait while he reads it, won't you?' she begged him. 'I have to know what he decides to do.'

'He may not be able to come to a decision so soon,' Malcolm warned her. 'This is going to take the wind out of his sails, and I would think he'll need time to absorb it and think things over.'

'I suppose.' Abi bit her lip. 'But please, *please* be sure to emphasise that he mustn't tell Jimmy I am his mother. I've told him that in my letter, but I want to be sure he understands that it's much too soon. Jimmy has only just found stability, for the first time since he was a small boy and I don't want him upset all over again. He knows me as the governess, and that's the way it should stay until I've had the chance to gain his trust and forge the beginnings of a relationship.'

'Very well,' Malcolm agreed, somewhat reluctantly.

Abi caught at his arm. 'Malcolm, I am so, so grateful for everything, and I haven't thanked you properly. I haven't been thinking straight . . .'

He smiled. 'There's no need for thanks. I'm just happy that things have turned out as they have.'

'But the lengths you went to! You are the best friend I could ever wish for.'

He reached out and squeezed her hand, too overcome by emotion to be able to say all he would have wished to.

'Bless you, Abi,' was all he could manage, and even on those few words his voice choked up.

He climbed into the carriage, Isaac clipped the pony's flanks, and they moved away.

Tears filled Abi's eyes as she watched them go. What she would give to be in the carriage with them! Returning to Bramley. To Hugh. And to her son.

Impatiently she brushed the tears away. Hugh could never be hers, but one day soon, she and her baby would be reunited. It was the most unexpected, the most precious of prizes. More than she could ever have dreamed of. She was even beginning to find it in her heart to forgive Maisie for what she had done. It wouldn't be easy, but she couldn't think of anything better than sharing her joy with her mother.

Hugh and Malcolm sat together in Hugh's study, each nursing a glass of malt whisky. Malcolm watched nervously as Hugh read Abi's letter, his brow furrowed. From time to time he uttered an expletive and took a gulp of his drink.

When he had reread it, this time in silence, he looked up, shaking his head. 'Dear God.'

'It must have come as a terrible shock to you that Abi bore a child out of wedlock, and that he should have turned up here as apprentice to a chimney sweep,' Malcolm ventured.

'It is beyond belief. What my dear Abi has been through! If only I had known . . .'

'You don't think too badly of her?' Malcolm ventured.

A startled look came over Hugh's face, as if such a thing had never crossed his mind.

'Think badly of her? How could I? I only wish she'd felt able to tell me her story. Though she had no idea, of course, that her baby was alive. Let alone that Jimmy . . .' He broke off, refilling his glass from the crystal decanter.

'She is most anxious to see him, naturally. Is there no possibility of her resuming her position here?' Malcolm asked tentatively.

Hugh shook his head sadly. 'I can't trust myself to be under the same roof as her, and that's the truth. I'll find a way for her to spend time with Jimmy, of course, until such time as she decides to take him to live with her. But whatever my feelings for Abi, my allegiance is to Imogen. I vowed before God to love and care for her in sickness and in health, so long as we both shall live, and that is what I will do.'

'How is Imogen?' Malcolm felt bound to ask.

'Surprisingly, a good deal better. Thankfully she has showed no sign of having caught an infection from the lake water, as Dr Mounty feared. And it is as if almost losing her life has brought her to her senses somewhat. The improvement in that regard is quite remarkable.'

'That's good to hear.'

'It is. Now, can I pour you another drink, Malcolm? Your glass is empty, I see.'

'Thank you, but I shouldn't keep my driver waiting any longer.' Malcolm rose, then turned to Hugh once more. 'You will be sure not to tell Jimmy any of this? Abi is most insistent he shouldn't learn about it just yet; I rather think she will want to tell him herself.'

'I understand. Now, I'll walk with you to your carriage. And I thank you most sincerely for everything you have done.'

'I only did what I thought was right,' Malcolm insisted.

As they moved towards the door, neither of them was aware that someone had been standing just outside and had heard everything they had said.

Imogen, who had decided to come down and join them, turned and glided silently away.

Chapter Twenty-Seven

When Malcolm had left, Hugh sat for a while in his study, refilling his whisky glass more often than he should and attempting to process what his friend had told him. There had been so much he hadn't known about Abi. Yet far from feeling any judgement, what he had learned only made him love her more. All that sadness in her life, but somehow she had risen above it. All the pain, but still her first concern was not for herself, but for others. He could imagine her joy at discovering that the baby she had believed dead was not only alive, but living here at Bramley Court. He could only be grateful that he had not turned his back on the climbing boy, but had given him a home. He would move him into the house at the earliest opportunity; perhaps, if Imogen recovered sufficiently, she would agree to him having Robert's room. It was too early to suggest it yet, but the improvement in her emotional state made him feel optimistic. If – when – she was better, she would surely see how unhealthy it was to keep it as a shrine. And she had already taken to Jimmy, pleading his case for him to be educated alongside Frederick. It would be good for her to have another fledgling to take under her wing.

He found her in her sitting room.

'You had a visitor,' she greeted him.

'Yes. My old friend Malcolm Rayner. It was he who recommended Miss Newman as governess – do you remember?'

She nodded. 'But where is Abi?'

'She had to go back to East Denby – you knew that. I shall have to find someone to replace her.'

'It is a terrible shame. Freddie and Jimmy are very fond of her.'

'Yes.' Hugh didn't want to talk about Abi. It was too painful. 'How are you feeling?'

'Quite well, thank you.' For a long moment Imogen was silent, then she met his gaze directly. 'Hugh, I want you to take me home.'

'I'm not sure that's a good idea, Imogen,' Hugh said. 'When you were there before, all you wanted was to come back. Have you forgotten?'

'That was because I thought Robbie was here,' Imogen said simply. 'I know now that he's not.'

'No, he's not. Robert is with the angels. And you also know that the things you heard was just Frederick playing tricks,' he said patiently.

'Yes. Freddie can be very mischievous. But that's not how I know for certain that Robbie's not here.'

'How then?' Hugh asked, humouring her.

'Because I thought he was waiting for me in the lake, do you see, but he wasn't. There was nothing but weed and horrible murky water. It tasted . . .' She screwed up her face at the memory. 'And I couldn't breathe. I was so frightened.'

'Don't think about it now,' Hugh urged. 'It's over.'

'No, listen to me. All of a sudden, it wasn't dark any more. I could see the sky. There was light spilling out from behind the clouds. A rainbow. And then I saw him! I saw his face, there in the rainbow. And I heard his voice so clearly, as if he was speaking right inside my head. "Mama!" he said. "You must go back. It's not time."' She paused, an expression of wonder lighting her face. 'One day, Hugh, I will be with him in the rainbow. But not yet. Robbie said it's not time. And now I want to go home.'

All this was beyond Hugh. 'Imogen, I can't leave Bramley.'

'I know that. I'm not asking you to. I shall be with my family, and you . . .' She reached for his hand. 'I want you to be happy, Hugh.'

'I am happy, Imogen. Happy that you are recovering at last.'

She smiled sadly. 'I'm sure you are. Because you are a good man. But you don't love me, not as you loved Marigold. You never have.'

He couldn't deny it. But: 'I do love you, Imogen,' he said.

She shook her head. 'Not in that special way. But there is someone. Someone you care deeply for – and who loves you so much. Someone who deserves to be happy, just as you do. I don't want the two of you to be parted because of me. I don't want all that love to be wasted.' She took his hand. 'Take me home, Hugh. And then you must find once more what you shared with Marigold and tragically lost. With Abi.'

'I'm beginning to tire of being a mine owner, with all it entails. At my age, it's something I could well do without. The meetings are tiresome, the paperwork tries my eyes, and I would much prefer to spend what time I have left in pursuits that give me pleasure.' Sir Percival, reasonably sober for once, regarded Constance narrowly over the rim of his brandy glass.

'That would be a terrible shame, and you do yourself an injustice,' she said silkily. 'You have the constitution of a man half your age.'

'That may be so. But my mind is made up. And I intend to

326

begin by building bridges with Sir Hugh.' He paused, watching her closely. 'I intend to tell him he can have the access he wants over the land his father leased me. In fact, I think I shall relinquish the lease altogether.'

'I don't believe that is a good idea at all,' Constance said.

'Really? I rather think that is my decision, my dear, not yours.'

Constance smirked. 'And I think differently. Perhaps it is time to confess to a trick I played on you.'

'Ah! The document you had me witness.' It was Percy's turn to smirk. 'Do you really think me such a fool that I would put my signature to a legal document without knowing what it contained? Especially since it was you who was so desperate for me to sign it. I know you and your little ways only too well.'

'But you did sign it,' she said smugly.

'Not without taking precautions. Do you remember, my dear, that I happened to spill some of my cognac on your precious document? Not only did it stain the signature of your tame solicitor, whoever he may be, but we had to wait for the parchment to dry before I could add my name.'

'So?' Her eyes were blazing.

'If you try to make use of that deed of transfer, I shall contest it. And I shall win. The stain runs over the solicitor's name, whilst the opposite is true of my signature. Clearly the other witness had signed before I did so.'

For a moment, Constance was speechless with rage.

'Oh dear me, you see all your assets slipping away, do you not? The benefits of being my . . . close companion, shall we say?'

She controlled her seething anger with an effort. 'I think it would be fair to say our companionship has benefited you too.'

Percy smiled. 'Indeed. Which is why I am about to suggest a

solution. One that I think would suit us both very well. If you were my wife, you would benefit from everything that is mine. And I would be able to continue enjoying your favours without fear of you plotting against me for your own ends. What do you say?'

Again – and most unusually – Constance was lost for words. She didn't care for the idea of being tied to this old duffer, or indeed any man but Hugh. But he, it seemed, was out of her reach once more, and as Percy had pointed out, there would be considerable benefits to being Lady Symonds.

'I will certainly give it my earnest consideration,' she said. 'Now, would you like me to pour you another drink?'

Prissie had come to East Denby to visit, bringing Christian with her.

'My, how he's grown!' Maisie said, settling the baby on her knee when Prissie handed him to her. 'And just look – those eyes are still blue! I reckon now they'll stay that way.'

It was the first time Abi had met Prissie, though she had heard a great deal about her, and was grateful that it had been because of her that Malcolm had begun his search for her missing child. Now, however, she couldn't help feeling envy for the young woman, who was able to cuddle and feed her baby, watch his development and feel a mother's pride when strangers cooed over him. Why, she even had a house of her own that she could turn into a home for them both. If only Abi had been so lucky!

'How are you managing?' Maisie asked Prissie.

''Ee still gives me some sleepless nights, but we're doing fine, aren't we, Christy?' Prissie leaned over and chucked the baby under his chin, making him laugh.

'Christy?' Maisie repeated disapprovingly. 'His name is Christian!'

'But that be such a mouthful! You call 'im Christian if you like, but when 'e starts to walk and runs away from me, it's "Christy!" I'll be shouting after 'im.'

Abi was startled to see that Prissie didn't seem at all in awe of her mother, and Maisie not in the least put out by Prissie's response. Perhaps she should have stood up to her mother more, rather than always striving to please, she thought.

'Let's go outside,' Prissie suggested. ''Tis a lovely morning, and 'tis a shame t' waste it. We had rain in the night, and I reckon there's more t' come.'

Abi knew her mother always preferred to be inside, whatever the weather, but she didn't object.

'You'd better have Christian, then. My knee's a bit shaky this morning.'

Maisie handed the baby back to his mother and got up, gingerly testing her leg as she held onto the arm of her chair, and once again Abi was surprised at the rapport that existed between the two very different women. In the past, her mother would have had nothing but contempt for what she would have termed a fallen woman. Now it was almost as if Prissie was her daughter, not Abi, and a favourite one at that.

It was pleasantly peaceful in the garden. A blackbird hopped across the lawn, head cocked as it listened for worms beneath the neatly kept grass, and the air was sweet with the fragrance that follows rain on parched earth and everything growing in it. Maisie and Prissy sat together chatting on the wooden bench, breaking off frequently to coo over Christian and talk baby talk to him. Abi perched on an old garden chair, lost in a world of her own as she once again thought over everything Malcolm had told her of his visit to Bramley Court.

It was good to know Hugh didn't think badly of her, but she was bitterly disappointed that he was still adamant she couldn't return. He was right, of course, but she had so hoped to be able to see Jimmy each and every day, and not just when a visit could be arranged. And though she knew it was wrong of her, she longed to see Hugh too, even if there could never be anything between them. She missed him so much . . .

The sound of a horse's hooves in the lane disturbed the quiet. It wasn't unusual, but this wasn't the steady clip-clop that heralded the approach of a delivery cart, or the plodding tread of a carthorse, but rather a fast rhythmic trot. For an instant Abi glimpsed the rider above the clipped hedge to the right of the house, before he disappeared behind a stand of yews that Malcolm had said were badly in need of trimming.

Her heart missed a beat. Hugh! For all the world the rider had looked like Hugh. But that couldn't be. Thinking about him had made her imagine things.

The trot slowed to a walk as horse and rider neared the vicarage gate and came into view once more. Breath caught in Abi's throat and her heart pounded against her ribs. She hadn't been mistaken. It was Hugh! He was dismounting, fastening Hector's reins to the gatepost. And the world was spinning around her.

As if in a dream, she saw him open the gate and enter the garden. Maisie was staring in bewilderment, Prissie with open curiosity. Through the pounding of her blood in her ears, Abi heard Hugh apologising for the intrusion, introducing himself, before he turned to her.

'Abi.' His tone was warm, but his expression was serious, and a shiver of apprehension made her stomach turn over. Had something bad happened to Imogen? Was that the reason he was here?

'Hugh?' she said anxiously.

'Can we talk?'

Her apprehension ratcheted up a notch. 'What's wrong?' she asked sharply.

'Nothing is wrong. But can we speak in private?' He turned to Maisie. 'Will you excuse us?'

'Yes . . . of course.' Maisie was flustered and trying to disguise it.

'There's another lawn at the back of the house,' Abi suggested, but Hugh didn't want to leave Hector unattended, so instead they went out into the lane, hidden from Maisie and Prissie's view by the bushy fronds of the yew.

'You have me puzzled,' Abi said with a shaky laugh, and to her surprise, he took her hand.

'Will you come back to Bramley?'

'But . . .' She faltered. 'I thought . . .'

'I'm sorry – I should have explained before asking you the all-important question. Imogen is much improved. She has come to realise Robert is not at Bramley, and never will be again, and she has chosen to return to her old home, to reside with her mother and father. Please don't think for a moment that it was my idea, or that I put pressure on her. Quite the contrary. But she is adamant. She wants to start afresh, away from the constant reminders of what she has lost. So let me ask you again – will you come back to Bramley?'

Abi was lost for words, unable to believe what was happening; afraid she would wake at any moment and find this was all a dream.

'I think you know how I feel, Abi,' Hugh said, his eyes meeting hers. 'The question is, do you feel the same way?'

'Oh Hugh,' she said softly but with feeling. 'Of course I do.'

He lifted her hand to his lips, all the while holding her eyes with his, and it was there again, that connection between them that needed no words, making her catch her breath, running an arrow of warmth through her veins, tugging at cords in the deepest part of her.

'I could send the coach for you,' he said. 'Or . . . will you ride with me?'

'Now? Today?'

He smiled. 'I am not known for my patience.'

Her happiness bubbled over.

'Of course I'll ride with you,' she said.

It was dreamlike, unreal. Packing a few things into Hugh's saddlebag. Explaining to Maisie, who was surprised but understanding – she would be fine, she assured Abi. She had Prissie and Christian and Malcolm, and of course Abigail wanted to be with her son. Saying her goodbyes. Hugh hoisting her onto Hector's broad back and climbing up himself. Riding behind him, her arms around his waist, her face pressed against his shoulder, breathing in the warm, masculine smell of him. Catching her first glimpse of Bramley as they rode down the drive. It merged, all of it, into a haze of joyous wonder.

And then they were outside the stables, Hugh was lifting her down, and Freddie and Jimmy were running towards them, their faces a picture of surprise and excitement.

'Miss! You're back!' Freddie cried.

'Yes, and I'm afraid lessons will begin again tomorrow,' she said, laughing.

She was answering Freddie, but she had eyes only for Jimmy. His dark curls, so like Connor's, his brown eyes sparkling in his cheeky little face. Her son. The baby she had thought she would never know. She felt she would burst with happiness.

Hugh slipped an arm around her waist. 'Let us go inside.'

Not even the sight of Mrs Mears waiting for them by the

door could dent her joy. But to her surprise, instead of glowering and making some unpleasant comment, the housekeeper nodded quite civilly.

'You're back, then. You'd like a cold drink, I expect. I've had Cook make some fresh lemonade.'

She bustled away and Abi cast a puzzled look at Hugh.

'She's grateful that you intervened when Giles was threatening Frederick,' he said. 'But I'm afraid that is the best you'll get by way of an apology for the way she treated you.'

Abi smiled. 'It's quite enough. Besides, she saved my life, remember.'

'For that,' Hugh said, 'I would forgive her anything.'

Abi and Hugh sat together in the parlour, Abi sipping a glass of Cook's cool, freshly made lemonade, Hugh cradling a tumbler of whisky. The excitement and euphoria were settling now, though the feeling of unreality remained. Abi could scarcely believe she was back at Bramley. With Hugh. And with her lost son. One day she would tell him the truth – that she was his mother – but for the moment it was enough that she would be with him every day, helping him learn, watching him play, seeing him grow from a boy into a man. But at the same time, her thoughts were with Imogen, casting a shadow of doubt, concern and guilt over her happiness.

'How was Imogen when she left?' she asked Hugh now. 'Was she in a fit state to make such a momentous decision?'

'She was calm and determined, thinking more clearly than she has for a very long time,' he assured her.

'Will she come back when she is fully recovered?'

'I think not. Her parents will take good care of her, and hopefully she will find peace once she is no longer surrounded by the constant reminders of all that has happened here.'

'But . . . she is still your wife.' It was a fact Abi could no longer ignore.

Hugh swirled the whisky in his glass. 'I fear I wasn't the husband to her I should have been, and with Robert gone . . .'

'You were a good husband, Hugh!' Abi protested swiftly. 'No man could have been more caring, more concerned for her welfare.'

'But she knew I didn't love her as I loved Marigold,' he said soberly. 'And truth to tell, I don't think in her heart of hearts she loved me as she had loved her first husband. He died in a foreign land, fighting to thwart the Yanks in their bid for independence. To her, he will be forever young, and just as he was when she wed him.' He looked up, meeting Abi's eyes squarely. 'But she knew me well enough to realise the deep feelings I have for you. No matter how I tried to conceal it – deny it, even – she could see it. And . . .' a wry smile twisted his lips, 'she could see that you had feelings for me too. I think it was that that clinched her decision. She didn't want to stand in the way of our happiness.'

'Oh Imogen!' Abi bowed her head as tears pricked her eyes and her heart filled with pity, admiration and warm affection for her poor tormented friend.

'She is the sweetest of women,' Hugh said. 'She deserves far more than I could ever give her, and I hope with all my heart that one day she may find it. But for the moment, it seems that offering us this chance is something that has given her immense satisfaction, and a modicum of peace.' He hesitated, then took Abi's hands in his and looked deep into her eyes.

'I love you, Abi. More than anything in the world I want us to be together as completely as a man and a woman can be. But you must know marriage is out of the question. I could never inflict the shame of divorce on Imogen. If we are discreet, though, perhaps we could live together, not as master of the house and hired governess, but as man and wife. What do you say?'

For a moment, Abi was unable to speak. In all the excitement of her return to Bramley, she hadn't thought beyond the ecstasy of simply being here with Hugh and Jimmy, and now she was overwhelmed by his proposal. She had not the slightest doubt that it was what she wanted, but at the same time she had to be sure he truly did not harbour any negative feelings concerning her past. That knowing he had not been her first lover would not upset him. That he wouldn't come to blame her when the first heady flush of love faded a little, as it surely must. That he wouldn't look at Jimmy and be reminded that she had borne another man's child.

'Hugh . . .' she faltered.

'I understand,' he said, taking her hesitation for reluctance to accept his conditional offer. 'I realise such an arrangement flies in the face of convention, and the last thing I want is for you to be seen as a loose woman, ostracised perhaps . . .'

'No!' Abi said quickly. 'It's not that! Well – perhaps in a way it is. Given my past, I'm afraid you might come to think of me as a woman with no morals. Giving myself to one man, living with another outside of wedlock . . . and all with the evidence of my immorality – Jimmy – right in front of your eyes.'

'Stop.' His hands closed more tightly over hers. 'I would never think of you in that way, Abi. Every one of us makes mistakes, and yours was only because of your capacity for love. I was shocked, yes, when I read your letter, but because of what you have suffered, not because of any impropriety. I swear I love you for who you are, just as you are. And as for Jimmy, I promise to treat him as my own son. Why, already Freddie and he are like brothers. I shall see to it that neither of you suffers any more. I will take care of you both, you have my word for it.'

'Oh, thank you . . . thank you . . .'

Hugh wiped away the tracks of her tears with his fingers. 'So, with that little matter taken care of, do you think you might consider the arrangement I suggested?'

'Oh yes – yes please!'

He took her in his arms and his lips found hers, setting the seal on a union that had seemed impossible, but which, they both knew, had from the very first been meant to be.

Chapter Twenty-Eight

Ten years later

The western sky was stained red in the gathering dusk, and a light covering of snow lay over the grounds surrounding Bramley Court. But inside the house, fires blazing in every grate had driven out the chill, and hot mulled wine, served in pewter goblets, was warming those gathered in the drawing room.

A white Christmas, but not so heavy a snowfall as to disrupt Hugh's plans for a festive celebration. As he surveyed the scene, he found himself remembering Christmases past. In his father's day, the season had been one of merriment and hospitality, stretching from the parties in mid December, when the house was thrown open to the tenants and workers of the estate, through the family celebrations of feasting, the exchange of gifts and the burning of the Yule log and candles, to Twelfth Night, when the entire household was treated to a night of jollity. There were games – apple bobbing had been a great favourite – an enormous wassail bowl filled to the brim with hot toddy, and the Twelfth cake – a fruit cake from which everyone was given a slice. A bean and a pea had been baked into it along with the fruit, and whoever found them in their portion was crowned king or queen for the night. Whatever they decreed was the law and must be obeyed, and Hugh recalled one hilarious occasion when a tipsy footman had ordered his father to go down on all fours and beg like a dog.

In the years that had ensued, many of the old traditions had been abandoned and made way for less extravagant family Christmases, but since Abi had come into his life, Hugh had resurrected some of them – such as decking the rooms with holly and greenery – and also adopted some new ones. This year, a small potted tree on a round table was hung with wax candles in tiny holders and sugar ornaments, and surrounded by gifts – but then this year was a very special one. This was why he had invited Malcolm, Maisie, Prissie and Christian to join them to share the traditional feast of roast goose and plum pudding, sending a carriage to collect them as soon as Malcolm had closed the doors of the church when Matins was done.

He was, Hugh thought, the luckiest man in the world. It was three years now since Imogen's health had failed. Her parents had cared for her until the last, and Hugh and Abi had visited regularly. They had been at her side, holding her hands and speaking softly to her, when she passed away. A year later, they had wed, and had been able at last to abandon all pretence of a platonic friendship.

They had long ago told Jimmy the truth about his parentage, and he would never forget the moment when Jimmy had rushed into Abi's arms and she had held him close, tears streaming down her cheeks. Hugh had kept his promise to treat the boy as his own son, and to do so had been a source of endless pleasure. Both Jimmy and Freddie had now, of course, grown into young men, and although they were at different colleges – Freddie studying medicine at St Bartholomew's in London, and Jimmy at the Royal Military College in High Wycombe – they had remained firm friends. At present they were at the billiards table in the adjoining room, amusing Christian, who was now a strapping ten year old and proving a promising pupil under Maisie's practised instruction, whilst Maisie, Malcolm and Prissie chatted together like the old friends they now were.

But Hugh knew they were all eagerly anticipating the reason they were here today. To make the acquaintance of the latest addition to the Hastings family.

Philip Charles Newman Hastings. Born three weeks ago today.

In the bedroom she could now share openly with Hugh, Abi tested her legs gingerly and crossed to the crib where her new son lay. It was the first day she had been allowed to get out of bed, and she was apprehensive about picking Philip up for fear she would wobble and either fall or drop him.

'It's all right, milady. I'm here.'

Annie, the new parlourmaid, who had already helped her get dressed, touched her arm reassuringly, and taking her courage in both hands, Abi reached into the crib and lifted the sleeping baby into her arms.

'See? I told you you could do it, didn't I? Now, why don't you just sit down for a minute and get your bearings, and then I'll fetch Sir Hugh so he can help you downstairs.'

'You're a treasure, Annie.' Abi smiled at the girl, of whom she was already very fond.

When she had become Lady Hastings, Hugh had wanted to engage a lady's maid to attend her. 'We can well afford it now that the coalfield is prospering so,' he had said. But Abi had declined the offer just as Imogen had before her. She didn't need a lady's maid; she was perfectly capable of looking after herself, and the domestic staff could take care of her laundry and anything else that needed to be done.

Similarly, when she had discovered that a baby was on the way, she had been adamant that she didn't want a nursemaid or a nanny looking after him. She'd missed out on all that with Jimmy, and she had no intention of doing so again. Besides, she couldn't help remembering that it was Robert's nursemaid who was to blame for him wandering off and finding his way to the lake. She was determined not to take any chances with her baby's safety, though at the same time she reminded herself that she mustn't be tempted to mollycoddle him either.

For a few minutes she remained quite still, gazing down at her sleeping child in wonder. Long lashes lay against softly rounded cheeks, dark down covered his head, and tiny pink nails tipped the little fingers of a hand that had freed itself from his swaddling. She breathed in the scent of him – sweet and milky from the feed she had given him before Annie had helped her to dress – and could hardly believe that this wasn't some wonderful dream from which she would soon awake. Her baby – hers and Hugh's – who would grow into a child and then a young man as Jimmy had done, except that this time she would be here to see it. A rush of love filled her heart and soul, bringing tears of joy and contentment to her eyes.

She blinked them away and looked up at Annie.

'Will you fetch Hugh then, please? Really we should get Philip down to meet his family before he wakes and wants feeding again.'

It was Annie who was entrusted to carry baby Philip down the stairs, whilst Abi clung to the banister and Hugh supported her.

'How was that?' he asked her anxiously when they reached the hall below.

Abi nodded. 'I'm fine.'

'Not giddy?'

'Just a bit.'

'Then let's get you sitting down. I'll take the baby, Annie, if you will just ensure Lady Hastings gets to a chair safely.'

All eyes turned towards the doorway as the little procession entered the parlour, and Malcolm hastened to Abi's side, taking her other arm and guiding her to an armchair. Meanwhile, Maisie approached Hugh, eager for a first sight of her grandson but still somewhat in awe of her son-in-law and his place in the gentry. Freddie, Jimmy and Christian abandoned their game of billiards and, somewhat self-consciously, stood in a group in the archway that divided the two rooms. Prissie squeezed herself back into the deep cushions of her chair, anxious not to intrude on what was essentially a family occasion.

'Well, he's got his grandfather's nose and no mistake,' Maisie declared, her usual outspokenness overcoming her reserve.

'Mother! It's much too early to know that,' protested Abi, who was hoping Philip would take after Hugh.

Maisie nodded sagely. 'We'll see. And if I was a betting woman, I'd wager you'll discover I'm right.'

'Would you like to hold him?' Hugh suggested.

'I don't know about that . . .' Maisie had taken a nervous step backwards.

Hugh smiled. 'He is your grandson after all.'

'Sit down, Mother, and Hugh will put him on your lap,' Abi suggested.

Maisie's cheeks burned red. 'Oh . . . very well.'

'I could have him,' offered Freddie, incorrigible as ever. 'If I'm going to be a doctor, it will be good practice for me.'

'You will have plenty of opportunity to practise, Freddie,' Hugh said, and Abi was pleased to hear him use the diminutive form of his name that Freddie preferred. In the beginning, he had wanted Jimmy to be addressed as James, but she had put her foot down – the name he was known by was one of the few things he possessed. Now, he was always Jimmy, and somewhere along the line Hugh had begun calling his son Freddie, as she did. Well, at least there could be no argument about Philip, she thought, smiling. Unless he wanted to be called 'Pip' . . .

Freddie pulled a wry face. 'It was a joke. Babies leak at both ends, and I'd rather he didn't leak on me.' He turned to Jimmy and Christian. 'Shall we finish our game? I was winning, I seem to recall.'

'Only if you moved the balls when we weren't looking,' Jimmy said good-temperedly. 'And to be truthful, that wouldn't surprise me in the least.'

Elbowing one another playfully, the two young men headed back towards the billiard room, followed by Christian. Jimmy had Freddie's measure all right, Abi thought, and there was no doubt they had been good for one another.

Philip was beginning to stir, opening his eyes and looking up at his grandmother with an expression that might almost have been surprise.

'Oh look! And his eyes are blue, just like . . .' Maisie broke off. *Just like Jimmy's*, she had been about to say.

'All new babies' eyes are blue, Mother,' Abi said, shaking her head. 'It'll be a while before we know what colour they're going to be.'

'I know, I know . . . But he's going to be very handsome whatever,'

'Of course he is. I only hope he'll let us have our meal in peace before he needs feeding again.'

'Perhaps Prissie would like to hold him for a bit,' Maisie suggested. 'Would that be all right, Abigail?'

'Oh no . . . I couldn't . . .'

Abi could see that Prissie was overwhelmed by the company she found herself in, but at that moment the door opened, letting in a delicious smell of roasting goose, and Mrs Mears, whose hair was now streaked with grey, appeared.

'Dinner is served.' Her voice was as commanding as ever, but somehow it had lost its bitterness, and the lines in her face seemed to have softened. 'Would you all like to follow me?'

The guests trooped out, Maisie returning Philip to Abi as she passed.

'I'll call Annie to take him while we eat,' Hugh said.

'Could we wait for a minute?' Abi rose, still holding Philip, and Hugh gave her a questioning look.

'You're not becoming overtired, are you?'

'No. It's just that . . .' Her eyes found her husband's. 'It's lovely having all the family together, but there's someone missing. I wanted a moment for us to remember her.'

Hugh's face clouded. 'Imogen.'

'Yes, Imogen. And of course, Robbie too.'

Wordlessly Hugh put his arms around her, encircling her and his new son. He bent his head and closed his eyes, and Abi did the same.

A warmth that didn't seem to come from the Yule log in the hearth filled her, along with a sense of peace and happiness. Over Hugh's shoulder she saw what looked like the last rays of the setting sun arcing in through the window.

Imogen was here. She was with them. Abi felt sure of it. Perhaps she had brought Robbie with her.

It was as if she was giving Abi, Hugh and their new baby her blessing.

The Christmas gathering was now complete, and the future stretched ahead, bright with promise and filled with love.

Author photograph © Will Nicol

Jennie Felton grew up in Somerset, and now lives in Bristol.
She has written numerous short stories for magazines as
well as a number of novels under a pseudonym. As well as the
standalones *The Stolen Child*, *A Mother's Sacrifice*, and *The Smuggler's
Girl*, she is also the author of the Families of Fairley Terrace Sagas
series, about the lives and loves of the residents of a Somerset
village in the late nineteenth century, which started with
All The Dark Secrets.

Stay in touch with Jennie!

Visit her on Facebook at
www.facebook.com/JennieFeltonAuthor
for her latest news.

Or follow her on Twitter @**Jennie_Felton**